Midnight Whispers

V. C. Andrews™ Books

Flowers in the Attic
Petals on the Wind
If There Be Thorns
My Sweet Audrina
Seeds of Yesterday
Heaven
Dark Angel
Garden of Shadows
Fallen Hearts
Gates of Paradise
Web of Dreams
Dawn
Secrets of the Morning
Twilight's Child
Midnight Whispers

Published by POCKET BOOKS

Midnight Whispers

V.C. ANDREWS™

POCKET BOOKS
New York London Toronto Sydney Tokyo Singapore

This book is a work of fiction. Names, characters, places and incidents are either products of the author's imagination or are used fictitiously. Any resemblance to actual events or locales or persons, living or dead, is entirely coincidental.

An *Original* Publication of POCKET BOOKS

POCKET BOOKS, a division of Simon & Schuster Inc.
1230 Avenue of the Americas, New York, NY 10020

ISBN: 0-671-69516-9

Cover design by Myles Sprinzen

Printed in the U.S.A.

Dear Virginia Andrews Readers,

Those of us who knew and loved Virginia Andrews know that the most important things in her life were her novels. Her proudest moment came when she held in her hand the first printed copy of *Flowers in the Attic.* Virginia was a unique and gifted storyteller who wrote feverishly each and every day. She was constantly developing ideas for new stories that would eventually become novels. Second only to the pride she took in her writing was the joy she took in reading the letters from readers who were so touched by her books.

Since her death many of you have written to us wondering whether there would continue to be new V.C. Andrews novels. Just before she died we promised ourselves that we would find a way of creating additional stories based on her vision.

Beginning with the final books in the Casteel series, we have been working closely with a carefully selected writer to expand upon her genius by creating new novels, like *Dawn, Secrets of the Morning, Twilight's Child,* and now *Midnight Whispers,* inspired by her wonderful storytelling talent.

Midnight Whispers is the fourth book in a new series. We believe it would have given V.C. Andrews great joy to know that it will be entertaining so many of you. Other novels, including some based on stories Virginia was able to complete before her death, will be published in the coming years and we hope they continue to mean as much to you as ever.

Sincerely,
THE ANDREWS FAMILY

Prologue

Dear Aunt Trisha,

I'm so happy you will be able to attend my Sweet Sixteen party. Mommy told me you would try, but I didn't think you would be able to break away from rehearsals, especially rehearsals for a new Broadway show!

Although Mommy always tells me she is not envious, I know she is, for I have often found her sighing and gazing longingly at a program from one of your Broadway productions. Daddy knows she's envious too, and he feels sorry for her. Singing at the hotel from time to time is not enough, especially for someone with Mommy's talent. I think it hurts more when someone comes up to her afterward and says, "You were wonderful; you should be on Broadway."

We have this wonderful hotel, which has grown more and more successful, and Mommy is highly respected as a business woman, but I think to Mommy the hotel is like a ball and chain. I have already told both Mommy and Daddy that I don't want to become a hotel executive. My brother Jefferson can be the one who steps into their shoes, not me. I want to be a pianist and attend the Bernhardt school in New York just like you and Mommy did.

I know I should be very happy. Mommy and Daddy are making my Sweet Sixteen the grandest party ever at the hotel. Everyone is coming, even Granddaddy Longchamp and Gavin. I'm so looking forward to seeing Gavin; it's been months and months since we've seen each other although we write to each other practically every week.

I bet Mommy wishes that Aunt Fern couldn't leave college and come, although she wouldn't tell Daddy that. Last time Aunt Fern was home, Mommy and she had a terrible row over her grades and a behavior report the dean sent.

Bronson will bring Grandmother Laura, but I doubt she will know where she is or whose party she's at. Sometimes when I see her, she calls me Clara. Yesterday, she called me Dawn. Mommy says I should just smile and pretend to be whoever she thinks I am.

In a few days, I will be sixteen and get mountains of wonderful presents. In so many ways, I really am a very lucky girl. My classmates tease me and call me Princess because I live high on the hill in a beautiful house and my family owns one of the most luxurious resorts on the East Coast. My mother is a beautiful and talented woman, and Daddy is more wonderful to me than my mysterious real father could ever have been, and, even though he's a brat, Jefferson is a cute little nine-year-old brother. Don't tell him I said so.

But, sometimes I can't drive away those sad feelings that sneak into my heart. It's as if there is always a dark cloud hovering, even though the rest of the sky is blue. I wish I could be more like you and always see the cheerful side of things. Mommy says you have bubbles in your blood.

Maybe I'm just being silly. Daddy says it's nonsense to believe in curses, but I can't help wondering if one wasn't put on our family. Look at the terrible thing Grandfather Cutler did to Grandmother Laura, and look at what Grandmother Cutler did to Mommy when she was just born. No wonder Aunt Clara Sue was so wild and died so young. I feel sorry for Grandmother Laura because she lives in a world of confusion as a result of all this.

People say all great families have tragedies and there's no reason to believe ours has been chosen for anything special. Yet, I can't help feeling there's something terrible waiting for me, too, a dark shadow just waiting to cast itself over me. Not all the music, all the lights, all the laughter and smiles can drive it away. It waits there, watching like some ugly, hunchbacked monster hatched in a nightmare.

I'm about to be sixteen and I still sleep with a small light on. I know I'm being ridiculous, but I can't help it. Only Gavin never laughs. He seems to know exactly what I mean. I see it in his dark eyes.

And you don't laugh at me, although you're always bawling me out for not smiling enough.

I promise, I'll try. I can't wait to see you. I can't wait to see everyone. It's going to be the greatest weekend of my life!

See, I bounce from one mood to another. No wonder Daddy calls me a ping-pong ball.

Aunt Trish, if you have a program from your new show, please bring it along. I'm so proud of you and I hope and pray that some day you will be just as proud of me.

Love,
Christie

Sweet Sixteen

THE THICK LAYERS OF CLOUDS THAT HAD BLOWN IN FROM the ocean overnight still hung in the sky when I woke early in the morning. I couldn't sleep late, not today, not the most special day of my life. I threw off my pink and white down comforter and practically leaped out of my pink polka-dotted canopy bed to rush to the window and gaze out over the grounds between our house and the hotel. Most of the grounds staff were already out there trimming hedges, cutting grass and washing down walkways. Here and there, I saw a guest taking an early morning walk. Many of our guests had been coming to Cutler's Cove for years and years and were elderly.

Off to my right, the ocean looked as silver as coins and the seagulls could be seen hungrily swooping down to the beaches in search of breakfast. In the distance an ocean liner was nearly lost against the gray background. I had so wanted to wake up to a morning filled with sunshine. I wanted the sea to sparkle as it had never sparkled before, and I wanted the sunlight to stream through the petals of the roses, the daffodils, the tulips and turn the leaves of the trees into a rich spring green.

When I was very little, I used to dream that the hotel, the grounds, the beaches and ocean were my own private Wonderland into which I had fallen like Alice. I gave everything silly names and even pretended people I knew were animals dressed like people. Nussbaum the chef was an old lion and his nephew Leon, his assistant with the long neck, was a giraffe. The bellhops that scurried about were rabbits, and Mr. Dorfman who prowled about the hotel at all hours with his eyes wide looking for mistakes and inefficiency was a snooty owl. I would look up at the painting of Grandmother Cutler in the lobby and think of her as the wicked witch. Even Uncle Philip and Aunt Bet's twins, Richard and Melanie, who really did look alike, were afraid of Grandmother Cutler's picture and would try to scare each other, or me and Jefferson, by saying, "Grandmother Cutler will get you!"

Although Mommy had really never told me all the gruesome details, I knew she was treated horribly when she was brought back to Cutler's Cove. It seems impossible to me that anyone could have despised my beautiful, loving Mother. When I was little sometimes I would stare up at Grandmother Cutler's portrait, trying to see in that lean, hard face the clues to her cruelty. When I walked past that portrait, her cold gray eyes always followed me and I had many a nightmare with her in it.

The picture of her husband, Grandfather Cutler, was different. He wore a sly smile, but one that made me look away just as quickly and make sure all my buttons were closed. I knew vaguely that he had done a very bad thing to Grandmother Laura Sue and as a result, Mommy had been born; but again, what exactly had happened had not yet been told to me. It was all part of the mysterious past, the somber and unhappy history of the Cutlers. So much of my heritage was kept under lock and key, buried in old documents stuffed away in iron boxes or sealed in photograph albums kept in dusty cartons somewhere in the attic of the hotel.

And there were fewer and fewer people working here who remembered Grandmother and Grandfather Cutler. Those who did remember never wanted to answer my questions and always said, "You should ask your mother, Christie. That's family business," as if family business were the code words for *top secret.* Our housekeeper Mrs. Boston had a stock reply whenever I asked her any questions. She had been Grandmother Cutler's housekeeper, but she always replied with, "It's better you don't know."

Why was it better? How bad could it have been? When was I going to be old enough to know? Daddy said it was too painful for Mommy to talk about any of it in great detail and would only bring back bad memories and make her cry.

"You don't want her to cry, do you?" he would ask me and I would shake my head and try to forget.

But it was impossible to forget a past that still lingered about in shadows and in between sentences, a past that suddenly could turn smiles into looks of sadness or fear, a past that called to me from the old paintings or from the tombstones on Randolph's and Aunt Clara Sue's graves in the old cemetery. Sometimes, it made me feel as if I were only half a person, as if I had yet to meet the other half of myself which would emerge someday from those dark shadows to introduce herself as the real Christie Longchamp.

Nothing made me feel this way more than knowing only scant details about my real father. I knew his name, Michael Sutton, and I knew from looking him up in the reference books in the school library that he was once a popular opera star who also sang in London and Broadway theater. His career had taken a very bad turn and he had disappeared from sight. Mommy wouldn't talk about him. She wouldn't tell me how they had fallen in love enough to have had me or why I never saw him. Whenever I asked, she would say, "Someday, I'll tell you all of it, Christie, when you're old enough to understand."

Oh, how I have always hated it when people said that to me. When would I ever be old enough to understand why grown-ups fell in and out of love, why they hated and hurt each other, why someone like Grandmother Laura Sue who was once young and beautiful, was now twisted and crippled and shrunken up inside? I knew early on that it wasn't my age that was the problem, it was that Mommy found the past too painful to talk about. I felt sorry for her but I had grown to feel sorry for myself, too. I had a right to know . . . to know who I was.

As I gazed out my window, I shivered and buttoned the top button of my pajama top because the June morning was as grey and chilly as my thoughts. Even the sparrows that usually pranced and paraded on the telephone wires outside my room seemed strangely quiet today. It was as if they knew it was my sixteenth birthday and wanted to see just how I would react to the dark skies. They fluttered their wings nervously, but remained squatting down, staring.

I frowned at them and folded my arms under my breasts, slouching my shoulders just the way Mommy hated. I couldn't help the way I felt. Daddy called me a weather vane.

"One look at your face," he said, "and I can tell whether it will be a nice day or not."

He was right. I was like a window pane, so easy to see through and read what was written inside. The weather always affected my moods. When it rained and rained, I wouldn't even look out the window. I would pretend it was nice outside and just ignore the pitter-patter of drops on the roof. But when the sunshine came pouring through my lace curtains and kissed my face, my eyes would pop open and I would spring out of bed as if sleep had been a prison and daylight was the key opening the heavy, iron door.

Mr. Wittleman, my piano teacher, said the same things about me. He deliberately chose a heavy piece, a Brahms or Beethoven, to practice on dark, cloudy days, and something light or sweet, a Tchaikovsky or Liszt, on sunny days. He said my fingers must weigh ten pounds more whenever it rains.

"You should have been born a flower," he said, his heavy, dark brown eyebrows tilting inward. They were as thick as caterpillars. "The way you blossom and frown."

I knew he was teasing me, even though he didn't smile. He was a firm but tolerant man who tutored a number of young people in Cutler's Cove. He let me know in little ways that I was his most promising pupil. He told me he would tell Mommy that I should definitely audition for Juilliard in New York City.

I turned away from the window when I heard my little brother Jefferson come out of his room and down the corridor to mine. I watched expectantly for my door handle to turn slowly. He loved sneaking in while I was still asleep and then screaming and jumping on my bed, no matter how many times I bawled him out for it. I told Mommy that the cartoonist who made Dennis the Menace must have known Jefferson first.

This morning, since I was already up, I would surprise him. I saw the handle turn and the door opening little by little until Jefferson could tiptoe in. The moment his foot came through I grabbed the door and thrust it open.

"JEFFERSON!" I cried and he screamed and then laughed and charged to my bed, burying himself in my comforter. He was still in his pajamas, too. I slapped him firmly on the rump. "I told you to stop doing that. You have to learn to knock."

He poked his head out from under the comforter. Jefferson was so different from me. He was never depressed, never upset about the weather unless it prevented him from doing something he had planned to do. He could just as well play outside in a warm, light rain as he could play in sunshine. Once he was enveloped in his world of make-believe, nothing mattered. It took Mrs. Boston four or five times to get him to hear her calling, and when he was interrupted, he would narrow those sapphire eyes of his into dark slits and scowl angrily. He had Daddy's temper and Daddy's eyes and build, but Mommy's mouth and nose. His hair was dark brown most of the year, but in the summer, maybe because he spent all his waking hours in the sun, his hair would lighten until it was almost the color of almonds.

"Today's your birthday," he declared, ignoring my complaints. "I'm supposed to give you sixteen pats on your backside and one for good luck."

"You are not. Who told you that?"

"Raymond Sanders."

"Well you just tell him to slap himself sixteen times. Get out of my bed and go back to your room so I can get dressed," I ordered. He sat up, folding the blanket over his lap, and peered at me with those dark, inquisitive eyes.

"What kind of presents do you think you will get? You will get hundreds and hundreds of presents. So many people are coming to your party," he added, his hands out, palms up.

"Jefferson, it's not polite to think about your presents. It's nice enough that all these people are coming, some from very far away. Now get out of here before I call Daddy," I said, pointing toward the door.

"Will you get a lot of toys?" he asked anxiously, his eyes filled with expectation.

"I hardly think so. I'm sixteen, Jefferson, not six."

He smirked. He always hated it when he got gifts of clothing on his birthdays instead of toys. He would tear open the boxes, gaze at the garments for an instant, and then go on to the next hopefully.

"Why is sixteen so important?" he demanded.

I brushed back my hair so it fell over my shoulders and sat at the foot of the bed.

"Because when a girl gets to be sixteen, people are supposed to treat her differently," I explained.

"How?" Jefferson was always full of questions, driving everyone crazy with his "Whys" and "Hows" and "Whats."

"They just do. They treat you more like an adult and not a child, or a baby like you."

"I'm not a baby," he protested. "I'm nine."

"You act like one, sneaking in on me every morning and screaming. Now go on, get dressed for breakfast," I said and stood up. "I've got to take a shower and pick out something to wear."

"When's Aunt Trisha coming?" he asked, instead of leaving. He would ask a thousand questions first.

"This afternoon, early."

"And Gavin?"

"About three or four o'clock. All right, Jefferson? Can I get dressed now?"

"Get dressed," he said shrugging.

"I don't get dressed in front of boys," I said. He twisted his mouth from one side to the other as if he were chewing on this thought.

"Why not?" he finally asked.

"Jefferson! You should know enough by now not to ask such a question."

"I get dressed in front of Mommy and Mrs. Boston," he said.

"That's because you're still a child. Now out!" I said pointing to the door again. Slowly, he slipped off the bed, but he paused, still considering what I had said.

"Richard and Melanie get dressed and undressed in front of each other," he said. "And they're twelve."

"How do you know they do?" I asked. What went on at Uncle Philip's and Aunt Bet's always interested me. They still lived in the old section of the hotel, Uncle Philip and Aunt Bet now sleeping where Grandmother Laura and Randolph once slept. The twins had their own rooms now, but up until this year they had shared a room. I didn't go up there much, but whenever I did, I would pause by the locked door to what had once been Grandmother Cutler's suite. I had never even had the opportunity to glance inside.

"I saw them," Jefferson said.

"You saw Melanie getting dressed?"

"Uh huh. I was in Richard's room and she came in to get a pair of his blue socks," he explained.

"They share socks?" I asked incredulously.

"Uh huh," Jefferson said, nodding. "And she was only in her underwear with nothing over here," he said, indicating his bosom. My mouth dropped open. Melanie had begun to develop breasts.

"That's terrible," I said. Jefferson shrugged.

"We were getting ready to play badminton."

"I don't care. A girl that age shouldn't be parading around half-naked in front of her brother and cousin."

Jefferson shrugged again and then had a new thought.

"If you get any toys, can I play with them tonight? Can I?"

"Jefferson, I told you. I don't expect to get toys."

"If you do," he insisted.

"Yes, you can. If you get out of here right now," I added.

"Great," he cried and charged to the door just as Mommy knocked and opened it. He nearly ran into her.

"What's going on?" she asked.

"Jefferson was just leaving so I could get dressed," I said, fixing my eyes on him furiously.

"Go on, Jefferson. Leave your sister alone. She has a lot to do today," Mommy advised.

"She said I could play with her toys tonight," he declared.

"Toys?"

"He thinks I'm getting tons of toys for presents," I said.

"Oh." Mommy smiled. "Go on, Jefferson. Get dressed for breakfast."

"I'm a pirate," he announced, raising his arm as if he held a sword. "Yo ho ho, and a bottle of rum," he cried and charged out. Mommy laughed and then turned to me and smiled.

"Happy birthday, honey," she said and came over to give me a kiss and a hug. "This is going to be a wonderful day." I could see the brightness and happiness in her eyes. The flood of color in her face made her look as beautiful as the models who stared out of the pages of fashion magazines.

"Thank you, Mommy."

"Daddy's showering and getting dressed. He wants us to give you your first gift at breakfast. I think he's even more excited about your birthday than you are," she added, stroking my hair.

"I can't wait until everyone comes," I said. "Aunt Trisha's still coming, right?"

"Oh yes, she called last night. And she said she's bringing you play programs and a lot of other theatrical souvenirs."

"I can't wait." I went to the closet and picked out a light blue skirt and button-down collar blouse with short sleeves.

"You'd better wear a sweater this morning. It's still a bit nippy," Mommy said. She joined me at the closet to look at my party dress again. "You're going to look so beautiful in this," she said, holding it out.

It was a pink silk strapless dress with a sweetheart neckline and billowing skirt to be worn over layers of crinolines. I had had shoes dyed to match and would wear gloves, too. When I had first tried the dress on, I thought I looked foolish in it because of my small bosom, but Mommy surprised me by buying me an uplift bra. Even I was shocked by the effect. It took my breath away to see my breasts swell up to create a cleavage. My face reddened along with my chest and neck. Could I wear this? Would I dare?

"You're going to look so grown up," Mommy said and sighed. She turned to me. "My little girl now a little lady. Sooner than we think, you will graduate from high school and be off to college," she added, but she sounded melancholy.

"I want to do what Mr. Wittleman says, Mommy. I want to audition for Juilliard or maybe Sarah Bernhardt," I said and her smile faded. For some reason Mommy was afraid of my going to New York and didn't encourage me about it very much.

"There are a number of good performing arts schools outside of New York—several right here in Virginia, in fact."

"But Mommy, why shouldn't I want to go to New York?"

"New York is too big. You can get lost there."

"New York is where there is the most opportunity," I replied. "Mr. Wittleman says so, too."

She didn't argue. Instead, she took on this sad look, lowering her soft blue eyes and drooping her head. She was usually so bright and alive that whenever something made her mood grow dark, I felt a terrible foreboding and emptiness in my heart.

"Besides, Mommy," I reminded her, "that's where you went to performing arts school, and that's where Aunt Trish went, and look at where she is now!"

"I know," she said, reluctantly admitting what I said was true. "I just can't help being afraid for you."

"I won't be much younger than you were when you took over all this responsibility at the hotel," I reminded her.

"Yes, honey, that's true, but responsibility was thrust on me. It wasn't something I wanted. I had no choice," she complained.

"Will you tell me all of it, Mommy? Why you left the Sarah Bernhardt School? Will you?"

"Soon," she promised.

"And will you finally tell me the truth about my

real father? Will you?" I pursued. "I'm old enough to know it all now, Mommy."

She gazed at me as if she were seeing me for the first time. Then, that angelic smile came over her lips and she reached out to wipe some strands of my golden hair away from my forehead.

"Yes, Christie. Tonight, I will come to you in your room and tell you the truth," she promised.

"All of it?" I asked, nearly gasping. She took a deep breath and nodded.

"All of it," she said.

Daddy, as handsome as ever, was already at the table reading the newspaper when I came down to breakfast. Mommy had to go into Jefferson's room to help him hurry along. He would diddle-dawdle forever if he suddenly got interested in one of his toy trucks or trains while he brushed his teeth or combed his hair.

"Happy birthday, honey," Daddy said and leaned over to kiss me on the cheek when I sat down.

He still looked more like my older brother than my stepfather. Both my parents were so young-looking that all my friends were jealous, especially my best friend, Pauline Bradly who was Mrs. Bradly's granddaughter. Mrs. Bradly was in charge of our front desk at the hotel.

"Your dad has such dreamy eyes," Pauline often said. In the summer his skin would turn a deep bronze color from so much outdoor work. Against his tan his dark eyes became as bright and shiny as polished onyx, and he had beautiful white teeth that gave him an ivory smile. He was muscular and tall, and lately he had let his hair grow longer and he brushed it up in a soft wave in front. I had no trouble understanding why Mommy had been in love with him ever since they were children.

"So how does it feel to be the ripe old age of sixteen?" he asked, his smile warming me.

"I don't know. I'm too excited to feel anything, I think," I said and he smiled even wider.

"From the way your mother's behaving, you would think it's her Sweet Sixteen," he quipped.

"What was that you said, James Gary Longchamp?" Mommy cried, coming through the door with Jefferson right behind her.

"Uh oh." Daddy snapped his paper and pretended to go back to his reading.

"Meanwhile," Mommy said, sitting down, "Your father here has been the one worrying about the food, the decorations, the music. He's the one driving everyone around the hotel crazy, insisting that every hedge be cut just right and every flower stem be perfectly straight. You would think we're giving a party for the Queen of England!"

Daddy shifted the paper so he could see me and he winked.

"Daddy, Daddy, can I ride on the rider mower with you today?" Jefferson begged. "Can I? Please."

"We'll see," Daddy said. "It depends on how well you eat your breakfast and how many people you drive crazy an hour."

Mommy and I laughed.

"Happy birthday, Christie," Mrs. Boston said, coming into the dining room with our platter of eggs and grits. After she put it down, she gave me a hug and a kiss.

"Thank you, Mrs. Boston."

"You're going to make one fine birthday girl."

"You're coming to the party, aren't you?" I asked her.

"Oh sure. I went and bought me a new dress, a modern one." She eyed Daddy quickly. "And don't you say nothing about it, Mr. Longchamp."

Daddy chuckled and folded his paper. Then he reached down beside his chair and came up with a small package.

"This is the only opportunity the family will have today to be alone and together, so your mother and I decided to give you this now," he declared. "We thought it might come in handy today, considering how important every minute is."

"Wow!" Jefferson said, impressed with the gift wrapping, which was silver with a deep blue ribbon around it.

Nervously, I started to unwrap it, taking care not to rip the pretty paper. I wanted to save every memento, every memory from this day. I opened the long box and looked down at a stunning gold watch.

"Oh, it's beautiful," I cried. "Thank you, Daddy." I hugged him. "Thank you, Mommy," I said and kissed her.

"Let me help you put it on," Daddy said and took the watch out.

"Does it have an alarm? Does something pop up? Is it waterproof?" Jefferson demanded.

"It's just a lady's watch," Daddy said, holding my arm gently as he fastened the watch. "Look at that," he added when I held my wrist out.

"It looks beautiful on you, Christie," Mommy said.

"Is it the right time?" Jefferson asked. "It's so small, how can you tell?"

"I can tell. Yes." I smiled at everyone, so happy that we were together, that we all cared so much about each other. For a few moments, I even forgot it was cloudy outside. There was so much warm sunshine inside. "It's the best time of all!" Mommy and Daddy laughed and we proceeded to eat our breakfasts, everyone chattering away.

On weekends, besides looking after Jefferson, I usually helped out in the hotel, relieving people at the front desk. Sometimes Pauline came over and worked with me. At various times she had crushes on different bellhops, as did I, and it was fun flirting with them in the lobby, as well as answering the phones and speaking to people who called from as far away as Los Angeles, California or Montreal, Canada.

But today, my special day, I didn't have to do anything. As soon as breakfast was over, I wanted to go to the ballroom to see how the decorations were coming along. Naturally, Jefferson begged to go with me.

"You should leave your sister alone today," Mommy warned him.

"It's all right, Mommy, as long as he's good," I said, glaring at him sternly. I might as well have tried to melt ice with my look. No one but Daddy and Mrs. Boston could get Jefferson to behave if he didn't want to.

"I'll be good," he promised.

"If you are, you can come out and help me with the lawns this afternoon," Daddy said. That was enough to make him sit up straight, finish his breakfast and drink his milk. Afterward, he took my hand obediently, and we hurried out the door, down the steps and across the grounds, even beating Mommy to the hotel.

The grand ballroom was all lit up because the staff was putting up the decorations. Mommy had decided my party should have a musical theme, so there were huge pink and white styrofoam cut-outs of tubas, trumpets, drums and trombones, as well as violins, oboes and cellos along the walls. On both ends there were enormous cut-outs of pianos. From the ceiling the staff had hung multicolored styrofoam notes and on both ends of the ballroom there were to be huge clumps of balloons, all with the words: *Happy Birthday Christie, Sweet Sixteen* on them. Mommy said that after everyone sang "Happy Birthday" to me, the balloons were to be released.

When we arrived, the dining room staff was already there setting up the tables, putting on pink and blue paper cloths that picked up the musical theme with notes and bars. Each table would have a basket of party favors that included combs and mirrors, the mirrors with my picture on the back.

At the front of the room was the dais at which Daddy, Mommy, Grandmother Laura and Bronson, Aunt Trisha, Aunt Fern, Granddaddy Longchamp, his wife Edwina, and Gavin would sit with me and some of my best friends from school. Jefferson was excited because he had his own table for his school friends, as well as Richard and Melanie.

Just for this party, the lighting on the dance floor had been changed to include colorful revolving balls and pulsating spotlights. We had the hotel band and Mommy promised to sing a song or two with them.

Everyone was saying that this would be the best party ever held at the hotel. All the members of the hotel staff were either invited or working at the party, and most were as excited about it as we were.

Jefferson and I just stood in the doorway drinking in everyone and everything. They were all so busy, no one noticed us. Suddenly though, we heard someone say, "This is going to be a very expensive party."

We turned around to face Richard and Melanie,

who stood so closely to each other it was as if they were attached. As usual, they wore matching outfits: Melanie in a navy blue skirt with a white blouse with blue polka dots, and Richard wearing navy blue pants and an identical shirt. Aunt Bet spent a good deal of her time finding them identical clothes. She was so proud of having twins and never missed an opportunity to show them off. They both had similar thick-lensed glasses, both having the same eyesight problems.

Richard and Melanie had straw blonde hair and Uncle Philip's clear blue eyes. They had identical pinched faces with Aunt Bet's sharp nose and thin mouth. Richard was slightly heavier and an inch or so taller, but Melanie had straighter teeth and smaller ears. Richard had more of a Cutler's shape —wide shoulders and narrow waist, and held his head more arrogantly, speaking with Aunt Bet's nasality. Of the two, Melanie was more withdrawn, and, I thought, more intelligent, despite Richard's air of superiority.

"Hi," I said. "It does look fabulous, doesn't it?"

"Fabulous," Richard mimicked dryly. He turned to Jefferson. "Father says we're going to sit at your table, so please don't embarrass us and Christie by spitting food or throwing spitballs."

"Jefferson isn't going to do anything like that tonight, are you?" I asked pointedly.

"Nope," he said, driving his hands deeply into his pockets. "I'm going to cut grass with Daddy this afternoon."

"Great," Richard said out of the corner of his mouth. "There is nothing I would like to do more than bounce around on a machine belching gas in the hot sun."

"What are you going to do now?" Jefferson asked, unaffected by Richard's sarcasm. I always enjoyed Jefferson's indifference to Richard's nastiness. He acted like Richard had some strange illness and it was best not to bring any more attention to it than necessary.

"We were on our way to the game room," Melanie said. "We're going to play Parcheesi with some guest children."

"Can I watch?" Jefferson asked.

"I doubt that you can just watch," Richard said caustically. "But . . ."

"You can come along," Melanie finished. "Do you want to come, too, Christie?" she asked.

"No, I'm going to see Mr. Nussbaum. He told me to stop by this morning."

"The kitchen . . . ugh," Richard said.

"You shouldn't despise the hotel so much, Richard," I chastised. "You're a Cutler."

"He didn't say anything bad," Melanie snapped, coming to his defense quickly. It was as if I had said it to her.

"It's bad to look down on our staff and give them the impression you feel superior."

"We own the hotel," Richard reminded me.

"But it wouldn't be any good to us if staff members didn't want to work here and do a good job," I said pointedly. The two of them gaped at me through their thick lenses, which magnified their eyes so they looked more like frogs than kids. Richard finally shrugged.

"Let's go," he said to Melanie.

"Oh," Melanie said, turning. "Happy birthday, Christie."

"Yes," Richard cried like a parrot. "Happy birthday."

Jefferson followed them away and I headed for the kitchen. Mr. Nussbaum's face brightened the moment he set his eyes on me. Mommy said he had been with the hotel forever and probably lied about his age. She estimated him to be in his early eighties. During the last few years, he had agreed to take on an assistant, his nephew Leon, a tall, lanky, brown-haired man with sleepy chestnut eyes. Although he always looked half-awake, he was a wonderful chef and practically the only person Nussbaum would tolerate interfering in his kitchen.

"Ah, the birthday girl," Nussbaum said. "Come . . . see," he beckoned and I approached one of the counters on which he had trays and trays of hors d'oeuvres prepared. "There will be three different kinds of shrimp, each baked in a special dough, fried won-tons, fried zucchini and a cheese selection, some with ham and some with bacon. That one Leon made," he added and pointed. "Come," he said and took my hand to show me the fine cuts of prime rib.

"I have a chicken in wine sauce for those who don't want the beef. See what my baker has made," he added, showing me the small rolls and breads. The breads were shaped into musical notes.

"You can't see the cake yet. That's a big surprise," Mr. Nussbaum said.

"It all looks so wonderful."

"So, why shouldn't it be wonderful? It's for a wonderful young lady. Right, Leon?"

"Oh, yes, yes," he said, cracking a smile quickly.

"My nephew," Mr. Nussbaum said, shaking his head. "That's why I can never retire." He beamed his smile at me. "But you don't worry about anything. Just enjoy."

"Thank you, Mr. Nussbaum," I said. I left the kitchen and headed for the lobby, but when I rounded the corner, I met Uncle Philip, who was coming from the old section of the hotel.

"Christie," he cried. "How wonderful—a chance to congratulate my favorite niece privately. Happy birthday." He embraced me and pulled me to him and then pressed his lips to my forehead, softly at first and then, surprising me by continuing his kiss down the side of my head to my cheek.

Uncle Philip was handsome, a debonair man who always dressed elegantly in tailored sports jackets and slacks with creases so sharp they looked like they could cut your fingers, gold and diamond cufflinks, gold rings, and gold watches. His hair was always well trimmed and brushed, not a strand out of place. I never saw him with shoes not polished into mirrors. His idea of being sloppy was wearing a jacket without a tie.

Aunt Bet was just as prim and prissy, not wearing anything that wasn't in style or created by some designer. She never came down unless her hair was perfect and her make-up was applied to bring out what she believed were her best features: her long eyelashes, thin mouth and small chin.

Uncle Philip did not release me after he lifted his lips from my cheek. He held me out at arms' length and looked down at me, nodding.

"You have become a very, very lovely young lady, even lovelier than your mother was at your age," he said softly, so softly it was practically a whisper.

"Oh no, I'm not, Uncle Philip. I'm not prettier than Mommy."

He laughed, but still kept me in his arms. I was beginning to feel uncomfortable. I knew that Uncle Philip loved me, but sometimes I felt I was too old for his affectionate hugs and caresses and they embarrassed me. I tried to shrug out of his arms without being rude, but his hold grew a little tighter.

"I like the way you're wearing your hair these days," he said. "Your bangs make you look very grown-up, very sophisticated." He ran his forefinger along my forehead gently.

"Thank you, Uncle Philip. I'd better get out front. Aunt Trisha is arriving any moment."

"Oh yes, Trisha," he said, smirking. "That woman drives me mad sometimes. She can't sit still. She's always spinning and turning and rushing here and there, and those hands . . . they're like two birds attached to her wrists always trying to break free."

"She's like that because she's a performer, Uncle Philip."

"Right. The theater," he said, his voice light but his look serious as he looked down, still holding me.

"I've got to go," I repeated.

"Me too. Happy birthday again," he said, kissing my cheek once more before he released me.

"Thank you," I said and hurried away, something wistful in his look making my heart skip a beat.

Just as I entered the lobby, I saw Mommy greeting Aunt Trisha. They hugged as I ran across the lobby. Aunt Trisha was wearing a dark red dress with a long skirt that came nearly down to her ankles. When she spun around, the skirt flew about like the skirt of a flamenco dancer. She had sandals with straps up her calves and wore a white shawl loosely around her shoulders. Her dark brown hair was drawn back from her face and pinned up in a chignon that I thought looked very glamorous. Long earrings made of sea shells dangled from her lobes.

"Darling Christie!" she cried and held out her arms for me. "Look at you," she said, holding me out at the shoulders. "You grow more beautiful every time I visit. This one's headed for the stage, Dawn," she said, nodding.

"Perhaps," Mommy said, gazing at me proudly. "Are you hungry, Trish?"

"Ravenously. Oh, I can't wait for your party," she said to me.

"I'll tell Julius to bring your things to the house," Mommy said. "You'll be staying there . . . in Fern's room," she added.

"Isn't she coming home from college for this?" Aunt Trisha asked, her eyes wide with surprise.

"Yes, but she agreed to stay at the hotel," Mommy said. The look between Aunt Trisha and Mommy explained it all—how glad Mommy was that Aunt Fern was staying at the hotel instead of the house, how there had been new problems, problems my parents tried to discuss privately. But the walls have ears and both Jefferson and I knew Aunt Fern had gotten into some serious trouble at college again recently.

"Come," Mommy said. "I'll take you to the kitchen for something special. You know how Nussbaum likes to fuss over you. And we'll catch up."

"Okay. Christie, I have the show programs in my suitcase."

"Oh thank you, Aunt Trisha." I kissed her again and she and Mommy went off to the kitchen, the two of them talking a mile a minute, neither waiting for the other to finish a sentence.

The rest of the day moved far too slowly for me. Of course, I was anticipating Gavin's arrival and hovered about the front of the hotel as much as I could. Finally, late in the afternoon, a taxicab from the airport arrived. I rushed out and down the steps hoping it was Granddaddy Longchamp,

Edwina and Gavin, but Aunt Fern stepped out instead.

She wore a pair of old jeans and a faded sweatshirt. Since I had seen her last, she had chopped her hair off, her beautiful, long silky black hair that Daddy said reminded him so much of his mother's hair. My heart sank, knowing how disappointed he was going to be.

Aunt Fern was tall, almost as tall as Daddy, and had a model's figure—long legs and slim torso. Despite the terrible things she did to herself: smoking everything from cigarettes to tiny cigars, drinking and carousing into the early morning hours, she had a remarkably clear and soft complexion. She had Daddy's dark eyes, only hers were smaller, narrower, and at times, downright sneaky. I hated the way she pulled her upper lip up in the corner when something annoyed her.

"Take the bag inside," she commanded the driver when he lifted it from the trunk. Then she saw me.

"Well, if it isn't the princess herself. Happy sweet sixteen," she said and took a pack of cigarettes from her back pocket. Her pants were so tight fitting, I couldn't imagine any room for anything in the pockets. She stuck a cigarette in her mouth quickly and lit it as she looked at the hotel. "Every time I come back here, my body tightens into knots," she muttered.

"Hi Aunt Fern," I finally said. She flashed a quick smile.

"Where the hell's everybody? In their offices?" she added sarcastically.

"Mommy's with Aunt Trisha at the house and Daddy's in the back working on the grounds."

"Aunt Trisha," she said disdainfully. "Has she taken a breath yet?"

"I like Aunt Trisha very much," I said.

"First off, she's not really your aunt so I don't know why you insist on calling her that, and second, good for you." She paused, took a puff, blew the smoke straight up, and then gazed at me. "Guess what I got for you for your birthday," she said, smiling coyly.

"I can't imagine," I said.

"I'll give it to you later, but you can't show it to your mother or tell her I gave it to you. Promise?"

"What is it?" I asked, intrigued.

"A copy of *Lady Chatterley's Lover.* It's about time you found out what it's all about," she added. "Well, here I go. Home again," she said and marched up the stairs and into the hotel.

A ripple of apprehension shot down my spine. I hadn't spoken to her for more than a few minutes, but already my heart was pounding in anticipation of what was yet to come. Aunt Fern was like unexpected lightning and thunder shaking the very foundations of any happiness. I looked out toward the ocean. The clouds were still thick, still rolling in with fervor, determined to hold back the sunshine. I bowed my head and started up the stairs when I heard the sound of a horn and turned to see another taxi approaching.

A hand was waving from the rear window, and then I saw a face.

It was Gavin, his wonderful smile driving the emptiness out of the pit of my stomach and bringing the hope of sunshine back as quickly as it had been driven away.

And Never Been . . .

GAVIN STEPPED OUT OF THE TAXI QUICKLY, BUT paused. I wanted to run to him and hug him, but I knew that would turn his face bright crimson and send him stuttering with embarrassment if I did any such thing, especially in front of his mother and father. I called his father Granddaddy Longchamp because he was Daddy's father. He was a tall, lean man with deeply cut lines in his face. His dark brown hair had thinned considerably, but he still wore it brushed back on the sides and flat on top. More and more gray had snuck in since I had last seen him, especially along his temples. His lanky frame, long arms and hands, and often sad eyes made me think of Abraham Lincoln.

Gavin's mother, Edwina, was a very sweet and warm woman who spoke softly and seemed always terribly in awe of the hotel and the family. Aunt Fern never hesitated to remind her in whatever ways she could that she was only her stepmother, this despite the friendliness and love Edwina tried to show her. In his letters and whenever we were together, Gavin often told me about the mean things Aunt Fern had said or done to his mother.

"She's my half-sister," he told me, "but I'd much rather she wasn't."

"Well now," Granddaddy Longchamp exclaimed when he stepped out of the taxi, "the birthday girl!"

"Happy birthday, honey," Edwina cried, as Granddaddy Longchamp kissed me on the cheek and then looked around, his hands on his hips, standing just the way Daddy stood sometimes.

"Hi Gavin," I said, anxiously turning to him.

"Hi." His eyes quickly turned soft, meeting and locking with mine.

"Where's Jimmy?" Granddaddy Longchamp asked, but before I could reply, Daddy appeared in the doorway.

"Hey, Pop, welcome," he cried, coming down to them. He hugged and kissed Edwina and helped them with their bags. Gavin and I followed behind then as we all entered the hotel.

"How was your trip?" I asked Gavin. I tried not to stare at him, but I could see he had grown taller and his face had filled out, so he looked more mature.

"It was long and boring," Gavin replied and then added, "I wish I lived a lot closer to you."

"So do I," I confessed. He flicked a quick smile at me and looked around the hotel lobby. "Anything different?"

"Wait until you see the grand ballroom," I told him.

"You coming up to our suite, Gavin?" Granddaddy Longchamp asked him.

"It's all right. I'll see to your things," his mother said, seeing his reluctance. "He wants to visit with Christie. They haven't seen each other for quite a while," she said and Gavin turned red with embarrassment. I didn't know any boy as shy.

"Thanks, Mom," he muttered and gazed at something on the other side of the lobby.

As soon as Daddy walked off with Granddaddy Longchamp and Edwina, I turned to Gavin.

"Do you want to take a walk through the gardens and to the pool?" I asked. "They're doing a lot of work out there."

"Fine. I bet you have a lot of your school friends coming tonight," he said as we started away.

"Everyone in my class. I didn't have the heart to leave anyone out."

"Oh? Any new friends since your last letter?" he asked tentatively. I knew what he meant: did I have a new boyfriend?

"No," I said. His smile widened and his shoulders rose as he brushed back his long black hair, hair as ebony as Daddy's. He had the longest eyelashes, too, so long and thick they appeared false. "What about you?" I asked.

"Nope," he said. "I'm still hanging around with Tony and Doug and Jerry. I didn't tell you, but Doug's sister got engaged and married all in a month," he added as he passed through the rear exit and out to the walkways.

"A month!"

"Well," he said, pausing, "she had to."

"Oh. Is everybody upset?" I asked.

"I guess so. Doug doesn't talk about it much. Every family has its black sheep, I guess. Which reminds me," he said, "is Fern here yet?"

"Uh huh. She cut her hair down to nothing. I don't think Daddy's seen her. She'll be sleeping at the hotel and Aunt Trisha is staying at the house and will be sleeping in her room. Mommy wanted it that way."

"I can't blame her. How's Pauline Bradly? Does

she still twirl her hair with her forefinger when she talks to people?" he asked. I laughed.

"She just gets nervous, Gavin. She's really a very shy girl," I explained.

He nodded. When I looked back toward the ocean, I saw that the clouds were beginning to break up. Patches of blue could be seen. That and Gavin's arrival warmed my heart. Gavin knew what I was gazing at; he always teased me about the way the weather affected my moods.

"Sorry for the clouds," he said. "I tried to blow them off, but . . ."

"At least it won't rain," I said. "It looks like it's clearing."

"It wouldn't dare rain. Are you very excited about your party?" he asked.

"Yes. I'm so glad you could come," I added.

"Me too," he said, pausing to look at me. "You look very . . . nice."

"Do I look older? I don't feel older," I said quickly. "Even though everyone is treating me as if I am."

He studied me with those soft dark eyes for a moment.

"I think you look older," he said. "And prettier," he added. He turned away as soon as he uttered the words, but for me they lingered like the scent of blooming roses. "Hey, isn't that Jefferson on the lawn mower out there?" He waved and Jefferson saw us and urged Buster, the grounds worker, to stop so he could get off and run to us.

"GAVIN!" Jefferson cried. Gavin scooped him up and swung him about.

"How you doing, little nephew?"

"I'm working, Gavin, cutting the grass. Later, I'm going to help repair the steps on the pool. They're chipped."

"Oh, sounds important," Gavin said, winking at me. I was still quivering from the way he had looked at me and had said, "prettier."

"You wanna see? Come on, I'll show you the steps," Jefferson said, clamping his hand around Gavin's. Gavin shrugged helplessly. I followed behind, my head down, my heart in a happy pitter-patter.

How confusing our lives were in so many ways. Gavin and Daddy were half-brothers, and Gavin was therefore my brother Jefferson's uncle, but he was no blood relation to me. He used to tease me, however, and tell me I had to call him Uncle Gavin, because he was technically my step-uncle. Even though we joked about our relationships, the strange union of families made us reluctant to talk about how we really felt about each other. I wondered if we would ever get past that and if we did, wouldn't it just complicate everyone's lives even more?

After Jefferson had shown Gavin the work that had to be done on the pool, he ran back to Buster to complete the cutting of the lawns and Gavin and I were alone again. The wind was blowing the clouds apart faster and faster. Sunlight was beaming down on parts of the hotel and grounds. Gavin and I continued our walk through the gardens, talking about our school work and things we had done since we had last seen each other. We both repeated a great many things we had written in our letters, but it seemed as if he had to keep talking just as much as I had to. The silences that fell between us made us both feel funny. When our eyes met, we would shift our gazes to something else and both try to think of something else to say.

"I guess we better get back," Gavin finally said.

"It's getting late and I'm sure you want to start getting ready."

"I'm suddenly very nervous," I said. "Not for myself as much as I am for Mommy," I added. "She wants this to be a great party."

"It will be. Don't be nervous," he said, smiling and squeezing my hand quickly. My fingers moved toward his when he released them. "Will you save me a dance?"

"Of course I will, Gavin. In fact, you will be the first person I dance with, okay?"

"First?" The idea seemed to frighten him. He knew it would make us the object of everyone's attention.

"Why not?"

"Maybe you should dance with Jimmy first," he suggested.

"I'll see," I said coquettishly. It made him blush. "Don't go hiding in a corner with Ricky Smith and Warren Steine. I'll just come looking for you," I threatened playfully.

"I won't hide," he said. "Not tonight; it's too special a night for you."

"I hope it will be for you, too," I said and he brightened.

Across the grounds, I saw Mommy waving and calling to me from the front of our house.

"I have to get going," I said. "See you soon."

I reached out and he did, too. Our fingers touched for an instant, the feeling sending a warm, electric sensation up my arm and through my bosom until it reached my heart and sent it fluttering. I turned to run off and stopped.

"I'm glad you're here," I cried back.

"Me too," he said.

I ran on, crossing from the gloom of clouds into the sunshine that had broken through and promised me the most exciting night of my life. The ocean breeze kissed my face and lifted my hair. I was fleeing from childhood, rushing headlong onto the threshold of womanhood, both excited and terrified by the new and deeper feelings that lay in waiting.

After my shower Mommy came in to do her hair and make-up beside me at my vanity table. Now that we were side by side, giggling excitedly about the upcoming extravaganza, I could see why most people thought we looked more like sisters than mother and daughter. Of course, Mommy had been so young when she had had me. She was only in her early thirties now, and she had the sort of face and complexion that would take centuries to show her age. I hoped I would look just like her forever and ever, but at this moment, with our faces next to each other in the glass, I could vividly see the differences, differences that had to be attributed to my father. I paused in brushing down my bangs.

"What did he look like, Mommy?" I suddenly blurted.

"He?"

"My real father?" I said. Somehow, gazing at each other through the mirror made it seem as if we were speaking to each other from a distance and that distance made the questions and the answers easier to ask and to answer. I was hoping Mommy would seize the opportunity to tell me now the things she had promised she would tell me tonight.

"Oh," she said and continued to brush her hair for a few moments. I thought she wasn't going to answer. Then she stopped. "He was very handsome, movie-star handsome, with broad shoulders and dark, silky hair," she said, her voice quiet and sounding far-away. "He always looked elegant and he had these dark blue eyes that sparkled with an impish glint." She smiled at her memories. "All the girls at the school were totally in love with him, of course. And he knew it!" she added, brushing her hair harder. "You will never meet a more arrogant . . ."

I held my breath, afraid that if I moved or spoke, she would stop.

"I was just another one of those wide-eyed, foolish teenage girls he took advantage of easily. I'm sure to him I was a sitting duck, swooning, believing everything he told me, walking around with my head in the clouds."

"Do I have his eyes then?" I asked cautiously.

"Yours are the same color, but his were usually oily slick and full of false promises."

"I must have his mouth," I offered. She studied me a moment.

"Yes, I suppose, and your chin is shaped like his. Sometimes, when you smile . . ." She stopped as if coming to her senses.

"Was he always terrible, even in the beginning?" I asked quickly, hoping that she would keep talking about him.

"Oh no. In the beginning he was beguiling, charming and loving. I believed everything he told me, swallowed a feast of his lies eagerly. But," she added, tilting her head, her eyes suddenly growing sad, "you have to remember, I was a young girl without any real family to call my own. Grandmother Cutler had agreed to send me to New York, mostly as a way to get rid of me, and my mother was incapable of helping herself, much less me. I was truly an orphan.

"Then along came this devastatingly handsome, world-famous music star showering his attention on me, promising me I would someday sing alongside him on the world's greatest stages. Why wouldn't I fall head over heels and believe every promise? Like a vulture of love, he sensed that," she added bitterly.

"And no one knew?" I asked intrigued with the mystery. Despite Mommy's hardships afterward, the adventure of such a romance fascinated me.

"We had to keep everything a secret. He was a teacher and I was his student. Grandmother Cutler had her spies, just hoping to find some reason to hurt me. I even lied to Aunt Trisha until I could lie no longer," she said. "I was pregnant with you."

"What did he do when you told him?"

"Oh," she said, brushing her hair again, "he made new promises. We would get married and have a mother's helper and travel. I would still be a musical star." She paused and smirked. "As long as I continued to keep everything a secret so he could safely finish his tenure at the school.

"Then," she added, gazing into the mirror with her eyes so narrow and cold, it was as if she could see him there, "he simply sneaked off. Trisha came home one afternoon, full of excitement because Michael Sutton had abruptly ended his teaching career, supposedly because he was called off to London to star in a new production.

"All lies," she added, shaking her head. "He had deserted me."

"How horrible," I said, my heart pounding. I wondered what I would have done in such a predicament.

"I couldn't confide in my mother and I knew Grandmother Cutler would gloat at my disaster. I went mad, wandered the city streets in the midst of a snowstorm and was hit by a car. Luckily, it wasn't a serious injury, but it ended all the lies; only afterward, I was left even more vulnerable than before and completely at the mercy of Grandmother Cutler, who moved swiftly to have me transferred into the hands of her witch sister Emily back at their family plantation, The Meadows.

"The rest of it is too awful to tell," she concluded.

"I was born there?" I asked.

"Yes, and stolen away from me. But Jimmy arrived and thank God, we were able to get you back," she said, her eyes so filled with warmth and love that I felt that finding me was the best thing that had ever happened to her. "There now," she added, kissing me on the cheek. "You've made me tell you all of our sad history on your special birthday."

"But you haven't told me all of it, Mommy. And you promised," I cried.

"Oh Christie, what else must I tell you?" she asked, the corners of her mouth drooping.

"Once my father came here, right?"

"Not here," she said. "He called from Virginia Beach. He begged me to bring you to see him, claiming that was all he wanted—to set eyes on his daughter. What he really wanted was to blackmail me and get some money, but my attorney frightened him off.

"To tell you the truth, I felt sorry for him. He was a shadow of the man he had been. Alcohol and wild living had taken its toll both on him and his career."

"Mommy," I said, bursting with a memory, "that old locket I have buried in my box of jewelry . . ." I opened the box and sifted through until I found it and took it out. She nodded. "It was my father who gave this to me, then?" She nodded again.

"Yes, that's all he ever gave you," she said.

"I can't remember him . . . there's just a picture of some sad face . . . dark, melancholy eyes . . ."

"It was just an act to get my sympathy," she said coldly.

"You hate him then?" I asked.

She turned and gazed at herself in the mirror for a long moment before replying.

"Not anymore, I suppose. In my mind he is some sort of ghost, the spirit of deceit, perhaps, but also, the ghost of a young girl's fancy, the ghost of her dream lover, the impossible dream lover. It's what happens when we make our frogs into princes," she said. She turned to me abruptly. "Be careful of that, Christie. Now that you have become a beautiful young lady, you will find yourself very popular. I never had a mother to warn me, but I fear that even if I had, I would still have fallen prey to the charm and the smiles and the promises.

"Be smarter than I was. Don't be afraid to love someone with all your heart, but don't give your heart freely. A little skepticism is a good thing, a necessary thing, and if a man really loves you, truly loves you, he will understand your fears and your hesitation and never try to move too quickly. Do you know what I mean?" she asked.

"Yes, Mommy," I said. Even though Mommy and I had never really had a heart-to-heart about sex, I knew she was talking about going too far with sex as she had.

She kissed me again and squeezed my arm gently.

"Now let's see, where were we?" she said, smiling in the mirror. "Too bad Grandmother Laura isn't well enough to be here with us. She would be parading up and down behind us like a coach, telling us what shades of lipstick and makeup to wear, what earrings, how to wear our hair."

"I want to look like you, Mommy," I said. "Natural, simple, myself. I don't want to put on tons and tons of makeup and impress people with pounds of jewelry."

She laughed.

"Nevertheless," she said, "there are a few things we can do with our looks—fix our eyebrows, a little rouge, the most complimentary shade of lipstick, and perfume." She squirted a drop of her favorite scent down my cleavage and under the towel I had wrapped around me. We both laughed loudly, loudly enough to bring Daddy to our doorway.

"I thought I had wandered into the dorm at some college," he declared, smiling.

"Never mind, James Gary Longchamp, just be sure you put on your tuxedo like you promised. You should be flattered, Christie," Mommy added, "he's doing it only because it's for you. I can't get him to wear a tie otherwise."

"Why a woman can be as comfortable as she wants and a man has to wear a monkey suit is beyond me," Daddy complained. "But," he said quickly when Mommy scowled, "I'm doing it, gladly doing it." He backed out, his hands up.

When he was gone, Mommy's face softened, her glowing eyes and radiant complexion betraying a love that still loomed larger than life.

"Men are babies," she said. "Remember that. Even the strongest and toughest are more sensitive than they care to admit."

"I know. Gavin's like that," I said.

She stared at me a moment, that angelic smile on her lips.

"You like Gavin very much, don't you?" she asked.

"Yes," I said tentatively. She nodded as if confirming a suspicion.

"Don't you like him, too, Mommy?"

"Oh yes. He's a very sensitive and polite young man, but you have a long time to go before you fall in love with anyone," she said. "You will have dozens of boyfriends."

"You didn't," I said quickly. "Are you sorry you didn't?"

She thought a moment.

"Sometimes," she confessed. "I wouldn't trade Jimmy for anyone, but I wish I'd had a normal childhood and gone to lots of dances and on dates and . . ."

"You had no boyfriend when you went to high school and didn't go on dates?" I asked. Her dreamy look instantly faded.

"Not really," she said quickly. "Oh Christie," she added, "let's stop talking about depressing subjects and just think about your wonderful party. Back to work," she commanded and we returned to our hair and makeup.

But why, I wondered, was talk about high school boyfriends so upsetting? Every time I learned something new about my mother, it brought a lot of mysterious baggage along with it. One puzzle was no sooner solved when another was just as quickly born. Questions fell like rain around me.

After we completed our hair and makeup, Mommy went to her room to dress and I put on my gown. I had just slipped on my shoes and gone back to the mirror when Aunt Trisha knocked on my door.

"Can I have a peek?" she asked, poking her head in.

"Yes, of course."

"Oh honey, you look so beautiful. I hope they take dozens and dozens of pictures," she exclaimed.

"Thank you, so do you, Aunt Trisha." She still had her hair up but now she wore a dress of shimmering periwinkle blue. Around her neck was the most beautiful pearl necklace I had ever seen and on her ears were matching pearl earrings. Her green eyes sparkled when she smiled at me.

"Well," Daddy said, coming up beside her. "How foolish do I look?"

"Oh Daddy!" I cried. In his black tux and tie with his dark hair neatly brushed and his deep tan, he looked more handsome than anyone I had ever seen. "You look like . . . like a movie star," I said, blushing as I recalled the way Mommy had described my real father. Aunt Trisha laughed.

"I don't feel like a movie star; I feel like a store front mannequin," he replied, pretending to be in pain.

"You're nothing of the kind," Mommy said, coming up behind them. She wore a luminous gown of white satin that was very low-cut and was held up at her shoulders by spaghetti straps. The bodice of her dress fit snugly; then at her waist the skirt flared out like a fairy princess's all the way to her ankles. With her diamond and ruby necklace and her diamond earrings, she looked like royalty.

"Mommy, you look beautiful!" I exclaimed.

"I have reason to be," she replied. The three of them gazed in at me. "Isn't she gorgeous, Trisha?"

"Absolutely. Agnes Morris would cast her as Juliet or Cleopatra immediately," she said and they both laughed.

"Who's Agnes Morris?" I asked.

"Our house mother when we were at Sarah Bernhardt," Trisha explained.

"I'm ready," we heard Jefferson cry. He came running out of his room where Mrs. Boston had helped him dress. In his little blue suit and tie with his hair neatly brushed, he looked adorable.

"What a handsome young man," Aunt Trisha said. "Would you be my date tonight?"

"Uh huh," Jefferson said, looking up at her with wide eyes. Everyone laughed and we started for the hotel. My heart was pounding so, I thought I might faint on the stairway. Mommy saw the tension in my face and put her arm around me quickly and kissed me.

"Everything is going to be wonderful," she promised. "Just enjoy."

"Thank you, Mommy. I have the best parents a girl could have. Thank you for loving me so much," I said. She smiled, but her eyes were filled with tears.

At night, with the band playing, the lights flashing on the dance floor and the decorations sparkling, the ballroom looked spectacular. At the last minute, so it would be a surprise for me, the staff had hung up an enormous banner that read, HAPPY SWEET SIXTEEN CHRISTIE, WE LOVE YOU in bright pink letters.

People began flooding in, literally arriving in droves, so many so fast, I barely greeted one set of guests before I was approached by another and another. The waiters dressed in starched white shirts with bow ties, dark blue vests and slacks, and the waitresses in cute pink blouses and skirts began circulating with trays of the hot and cold hors d'oeuvres that Mr. Nussbaum and his nephew Leon had concocted. On the left two enormous glass punch bowls had been set up for the young people. Down right in a far corner was a bar for the adults.

Uncle Philip, Aunt Bet and the twins arrived soon after we did. Richard wore a dark blue suit and tie and Melanie wore a dress the same shade of dark blue with sleeves that reached to her elbows. After they greeted us, Uncle Philip lingered by Mommy and me. He raked his eyes over me, nodding with approval.

"I don't know who's more beautiful tonight," he said, swinging his eyes from me to Mommy and then back to me, "you or your mother. "Actually," he added quickly, before either of us could claim the other was prettier, "Christie is like a small flawless diamond and you, Dawn, are the royal jewel."

"Thank you, Philip," Mommy said quickly and turned her attention to the arrival of Bronson and Grandmother Laura. "Oh, Mother's arrived."

"You greet her first," Philip said, a wry smile cocking his lips. "I hate it when she calls me Randolph and Bronson's standing right beside her." Mommy nodded and took my hand so I would follow. I glanced at Uncle Philip who continued to linger and gape at us, and then I hurried alongside Mommy to the door. Grandmother Laura had had her hair washed and styled. Lately, because of terrible arthritis in her hips, she had taken to a wheelchair. She looked like the dowager queen, bedecked in her sable fur stole. She wore one of her prettiest gowns and her thick diamond necklace and matching earrings with a diamond tiara. Although she appeared to enjoy being brought here, in her eyes was a look of confusion.

Caring for Grandmother Laura had taken its toll on Bronson Alcott. Although he was still a tall, sleek-figured man, his shoulders slumped a little more each time I saw him. His Clark Gable mustache had filled with gray, as had his chestnut brown hair. However, he was still quite handsome and distinguished looking. I liked his soft-spoken, kindly manner. No one reminded me of what a rich Southern aristocrat should be like more than Bronson did. I couldn't help admiring him for the patience and love he bestowed on Grandmother Laura, who, according to Mommy, was still quite spoiled, despite her periodic losses of memory.

"Mother, you look lovely," Mommy said as she leaned over to hug and kiss her. Grandmother Laura looked pleased and then lifted her eyes toward me.

"Happy birthday, dear," she said. How wonderful, I thought. She remembered and knows. "Bronson, give Clara her present," she said and my heart did flip-flops. Mommy flashed me a conspiratorial look and Bronson winked. I nodded.

"Thank you, Grandmother," I said and hugged and kissed her, too. My nose filled with the scent of her heavy perfume. It seemed like she had taken a bath in it.

"Wheel me, wheel me," Grandmother Laura commanded, waving her hand. "There are people to greet."

"Happy birthday, Christie," Bronson said and slipped a gift into my hands and kissed me on the cheek as he wheeled Grandmother farther into the ballroom.

"I'll take that for you," Mommy said. "Go circulate among your friends."

"Thank you, Mommy." I looked around for Gavin, but neither he nor his parents had yet arrived. Moments later, Pauline Bradly came bursting in with some of my other school friends and we clumped up in a corner and giggled and hugged, the girls all searching the party for signs of the boys they liked.

"This is the best party I've ever seen!" Pauline exclaimed excitedly. "Is that Gavin?" she cried. I turned to look where she pointed and my heart fluttered a little as I saw that he and his parents had finally arrived.

In his light blue sports jacket, slacks and tie, Gavin drew many a female eye. Even from this distance, I could see his dark eyes smiling warmly at me. I waved and he started toward us. Granddaddy Longchamp and Edwina went off to greet Mommy.

"Hi," he said, ignoring everyone else. "You look great."

"And so do you," I said, my voice barely above a whisper despite the music and chatter around us.

"Thanks. I bought this jacket especially for your party," he said.

I quickly became aware of the way my girlfriends were staring at us. "You remember Pauline," I said, turning.

"Oh sure. Hi."

Pauline stood there with a dumb smile on her face and started to twirl her hair in her fingers. Out of the corner of my eye, I saw Mommy calling for me to come and meet someone.

"Pauline, why don't you introduce Gavin to everyone while I go see what my mother wants," I said.

"Sure," Pauline replied, her eyes twinkling happily. Gavin looked sad about my deserting him so quickly and was obviously very uncomfortable as the center of attention, but for the moment, there was nothing I could do. Mommy had dozens of people for me to greet: prominent business people from Cutler's Cove and Virginia Beach, hotel guests who were almost members of the family by now because of the frequency with which they came to our hotel, and of course, members of the hotel's administrative staff, like Mr. and Mrs. Dorfman.

"It's almost time for everyone to sit down," Mommy said.

"I haven't seen Fern come in, have you?" Daddy asked as he gazed around.

"It would be just like her not to show up," Mommy muttered. Daddy looked very nervous about it, and it was right for him to be so, for a few minutes later, just before the band leader asked everyone to take their seats, Aunt Fern made her grand entrance. It was apparent that Daddy had not seen her until this very moment, for the first words he uttered were: "She's gone and cut her hair to shreds!"

But that was the least of it. She had chosen to wear an outfit that was so outrageous, even Aunt Trisha, who was the most sophisticated of all of us, was shocked. Her flimsy skirt was slit up the side, the cut reaching the very top of her thighs. The skirt was so sheer that in the light, anyone could see that under it she wore only the bikini bottom of an exercise outfit. She wore a sheer black blouse of the sort meant to be worn over a special bra. But to my embarrassed amazement she wore no bra at all and her shapely breasts were so visible through the delicate fabric she could have just as well walked in topless. Needless to say, her entrance drew a great deal of attention. The room fell absolutely silent for a long moment, then there was whispering and finally loud chatter as the people who didn't know her were told who she was.

"What the hell are you wearing? And what did you do to your hair?" Daddy demanded when she reached us.

"Hello to you, too, brother," she said and

smirked. "Happy birthday, princess," she said, handing me the wrapped copy of what I knew was *Lady Chatterley's Lover.* "To be opened in a dark place," she added, winking. "Hi Dawn. You look . . . well . . . thy," she said and laughed. "And Trisha, how nice to see you again," she said, reaching for Aunt Trisha's hand and smiling like a Cheshire cat.

"Hello, Fern," Aunt Trisha replied, shifting her eyes to my mother who was fuming.

"Fern," Daddy said and took her roughly by the arm. He led her away and spoke to her harshly.

"She's like an albatross around his neck these days," Mommy said, shaking her head, "doing everything she can to try his patience and make us miserable. Frankly, I'm ready to give up on her. It's horrible to say, I know, but I rue the day we found her."

"Oh, she's just feeling her oats, Dawn," Aunt Trisha said. "A typical college girl."

"Hardly. She's this close to flunking out," Mommy said, squeezing her thumb and forefinger.

The band leader stepped up to the microphone and asked everyone to take his or her seat. We hurried to the dais, Daddy still crimson with anger as he came up behind Fern. I had it arranged so that Gavin would sit on my right and Mommy on my left.

The staff began serving the dinner. As we ate, the band played and people were able to dance between courses. I expected Daddy to be the one to ask me to dance, but Uncle Philip surprised me.

"May I be the first?" he asked with a twinkle in his eye. He glanced at Mommy, who didn't look very happy about it. For a moment I didn't know what to do. "Unless you've saved that honor for someone special," Uncle Philip added, looking pointedly at Gavin. Gavin turned bright red and I moved quickly to save him any embarrassment.

"Oh no, Uncle Philip. I'd be happy to dance with you first," I said. He led me to the dance floor and we began. As he held me closer and tighter, I looked toward the dais and saw Mommy watching with a very sad, even a frightened look on her face. When Uncle Philip turned me, I caught a glimpse of Melanie sitting at Jefferson's table. Despite her thick glasses, her eyes looked small and her face tight, not so much filled with envy as with anger. I did feel sorry for her. None of the boys her age or a little older would probably ask her to dance. I was sure she wished her father had, but Uncle Philip never took much interest in Melanie. He didn't spend much time with his own children, but what time he did allot to them he usually spent with Richard.

"You know you really have become a most beautiful young lady," Uncle Philip whispered, his breath tickling my ear a little. "How I wish I were eighteen again so I could chase after you."

"But even if you were eighteen, you would still be my uncle, wouldn't you?" I said surprised at how sincere he sounded.

"Oh, I wouldn't let a small thing like that stand in my way," he said. "I'm really only your half-uncle," he added.

When he held me now, he had his face so close to mine that his lips grazed my hair. The intimacy of his arms around me and his breath on my face made me squirm a little. I thought everyone must be looking at us and wondering why a man Uncle Philip's age would dance with his niece so closely. Suddenly I wanted this dance to be over and I was relieved when the music ended and I could return to the table. He held my hand as I turned away.

"Thank you," he said softly. I nodded and hurried back to the dais. The main course was being served.

Afterward, I danced with Daddy. How different it was being swirled around and around so smoothly while he talked about the party and made funny remarks. While we danced, I saw Pauline go to Gavin and get him to dance with her. He looked terribly uncomfortable. I made up my mind I would dance with him as soon as Daddy and I were finished. Every once in a while, Daddy paused to look at Aunt Fern who was off with the waiters and busboys now, smoking and laughing.

"She's up to no good," he muttered, flicking his worried gaze Fern's way. "I just know it."

"She'll be all right, Daddy," I said, but he didn't look happy.

Before I could dance with Gavin, the band leader announced that my mother would sing the next song. Everyone returned to their seats as Mommy walked to the microphone. She thanked everyone for coming and hoped they were all having a good time. Then she nodded to the band leader and they played "High Hopes." The applause was deafening. Instead of coming back to the dais, however, she asked me to come forward to accompany her next song on the piano. I was so taken by surprise, I didn't know what to do. The guests cheered and cheered until I stood up and went to the piano.

"Mommy, this is very tricky of you," I said.

"It was Aunt Trisha's idea. Blame her. Let's do 'Somewhere Over the Rainbow.' We've done it before."

I began to play and Mommy sang like she never sang before. As soon as we finished, we were surrounded by guests congratulating us. The band started playing again, and before I knew it, I was being swept onto the dance floor, dancing first with some of the bellhops and then with some of the boys in my class. One no sooner asked me to dance, when another tapped him on the shoulder. I grew dizzy from being spun around so much and finally begged to rest.

Laughing and sipping punch, I gazed around for Gavin, but I didn't see him at the dais or anywhere on the dance floor. I did see Pauline come walking in from the patio. I waved and she came rushing over.

"Have you seen Gavin?" I asked.

"Yes. He went outside. I followed him, but he wanted to be alone," she added.

"Outside?" I thanked her and hurried to see what was wrong. I almost didn't see him standing off in the shadows in the corner. He was standing quietly, gazing out toward the ocean. The sky had cleared considerably, so that there were stars twinkling, some so close to the horizon they looked like they were on the water.

"Gavin?"

He spun around.

"I didn't mean to frighten you," I said.

"I wasn't frightened," he replied quickly. I went to him.

"Are you all right?"

"Sure. I just wanted to get some air. Fern's smoking up the place all by herself, I think," he added disdainfully.

"Is that all that's wrong?" I pursued. I didn't like the way he avoided my eyes.

"Sure," he said quickly, too quickly.

"I'm sorry I didn't get to dance with you yet. I was just . . ."

"That's all right," he said. "It's your party; you're the center of attention. Anyway, I don't blame all those guys for wanting to dance with you." He looked at me finally. "You played great. You're going to be a famous pianist and tour all over the world. You'll meet a lot of wealthy, famous people and probably even play for queens and kings. You probably won't even remember me!" he said, firing all this at me as he narrowed his beautiful eyes.

"Gavin! What a terrible thing to say! Is that how little you think of me?" I demanded, my hands on my hips.

"Huh?"

He set me on a tirade; my face flushed and I felt as if I were rolling head over heels down a steep hill and couldn't stop.

"You think I would be so egotistical and selfish that I would forget the people I care about the most? When did I treat you like that? Why should you make such a horrible prediction? I wouldn't want any success if it would turn me into such a monster, and no matter what you think, I wouldn't forget you for a day. Why, you're in my thoughts almost all the time," I added before I could stop myself.

"I am?" he said. I swallowed and nodded. "Why?"

"You just are," I said. "Not a day passes when I don't think something about you or something I'm going to write to you."

"You're not just saying this to make me feel better, are you?" he asked suspiciously.

"Oh Gavin, it's just like a man to think that. Men are more afraid to believe in someone. They steal hearts so often, they're terrified of giving their own sincerely."

"I'm not," he declared. "Not to you, anyway," he added.

"Well then . . . have a little more faith in me," I said.

"Sure."

We stared at each other.

"You didn't even kiss me happy birthday yet," I said, my heart pounding.

"Happy birthday," he whispered and leaned toward me, his eyes closing first. I closed mine and felt his lips touch my lips so softly it was as if a gentle breeze had caressed my face. I couldn't help feeling disappointed. He must have seen it immediately, for just as I started to open my eyes, his lips touched mine again, only this time harder, and with it his hands came to my shoulders so he could gather me to him. It was the first real kiss of my life.

We separated, neither of us able to speak for a moment. And then we heard the shouting. My perfect night was about to be ruined after all.

Two Hearts Entwined

GAVIN AND I WENT TO THE END OF THE PATIO TO LOOK out and see who was shouting. Daddy had pulled Aunt Fern roughly out of the ballroom through the French doors to another patio at the rear.

"Jimmy, you're hurting my wrist!" she cried and spun out of his grasp, nearly losing her balance and falling. Straightening up, she stood there rubbing her wrist and glaring at him, but even from where we were standing, Aunt Fern looked like she was wobbling.

"How could you do that?" Daddy demanded. "How could you try to sabotage this wonderful affair? Is there no decency in you?"

"I didn't do it," Aunt Fern insisted.

"You didn't do it? You stink from it," he said, waving his hand wildly.

"I drank some, but I didn't put the whiskey in the punch bowl," she claimed. Gavin and I looked at each other. Small children were drinking that punch, too, as well as all my school friends. Their parents would be angry and annoyed. How horrible.

"One of the bellhops saw you do it, Fern, and I

believe him. He's a very reliable young man," Daddy said. Aunt Fern stepped farther away from him, but had to take hold of a railing to steady herself.

"Sure, you take the word of one of the hired help over your own sister," she moaned and turned away.

"He doesn't have a reputation for lying; my sister does, I'm sorry to say. And besides," Daddy stressed, "this isn't the first time you've done something like this, Fern."

"He's lying!" she wailed into the night. "I wouldn't dance with him, so he's trying to get even."

"Stop it, Fern. This isn't all the bad we've heard about you this weekend. I wasn't going to bring this up until tomorrow because I didn't want to cast any shadows over the evening, but Dawn received a phone call from your dorm mother complaining about your bringing whiskey into your room," Daddy revealed. Fern spun on him.

"More lies. She hates me because she caught me making fun of her one day. It wasn't me who brought the whiskey into the dormitory. It was . . ."

"It was you. Don't deny it. Don't even try," Daddy said. "According to you, everyone who's ever come to us to complain about you has had another reason. You're always the one being picked on."

"I am!" she bawled. "Dawn can't wait to hear bad things about me and bring them to you. She can't!"

"That's ridiculous. Dawn has tried to be a mother and a sister to you, but you are ungrateful for every generous and loving thing she does for you and now you've gone and embarrassed all of us," Daddy said, ignoring her histrionics. "Not just Dawn and me, but Daddy, too and . . ."

"Embarrassed my father?" She threw her head back and bellowed as if he had said the funniest thing ever.

"Stop that," Daddy commanded.

"Embarrassed my father," she said, now with a smirk in her voice. "How can I embarrass an ex-convict?" she retorted, throwing her words back at him as if she were tossing a glass of that spiked punch in his face.

Beside me, Gavin sucked in his breath.

"I hate her," he muttered, his lips close to my ear. "I just hate her."

I pressed my fingers around his arm. When he looked at me, I saw tears of anger and pain in his eyes. Then we both turned back to Daddy and Aunt Fern quickly. Daddy had raised his hand, intending to strike Fern. She screamed and cowered in anticipation. I had never seen him strike her or anyone before. Usually a reprimanding look or a sharp word from him was enough, even for Jefferson. He didn't do it though; he lowered his arm slowly and regained his composure.

"Don't you ever say such a thing. You know very well why Daddy went to jail and how it wasn't his fault. Grandmother Cutler got him and Momma to kidnap Dawn, lying about the reasons."

"He still went to jail and everyone knows it. I don't embarrass him," she insisted. "He embarrasses me. I tell everyone at college my father, as well as my mother, is dead," she said. "I don't want to think of him as my father." Her words fell like freezing raindrops on both my and Gavin's ears.

For a moment that stretched like eternity no one said anything. Daddy simply stared at her. Aunt

Fern crossed her arms under her bosom and looked down at the ground.

"That was a terrible, terrible thing to say, Fern," Daddy began slowly. "If you can't think of Daddy as your father, you can't think of me as your brother."

Aunt Fern lifted her head slowly. In the glow of the outside lights, I could see her mouth twisted ugly.

"I don't care," she spat. "You're not my brother. You're Dawn's slave, believing everything she says about me, doing everything she wants. All she has to do is snap her fingers and you jump like a puppet on a string."

"THAT'S ENOUGH!" Daddy screamed. "Now go to your room and sleep off all that whiskey you consumed. Go on!" he ordered, his arm out, finger pointing.

"I'm going," she said. "Maybe I won't stop. Maybe I'll run away." She wobbled again and then turned and stumbled away. Daddy stood there watching her.

"I hope she does. I hope she runs far away," Gavin said. "He should have slapped her. All those horrible things she said about my father and about Dawn."

"She's drunk, Gavin."

"It doesn't matter. She would have said them even if she hadn't been," he replied.

Before we could say another word about it, we heard a drum roll inside.

"WHERE'S THE BIRTHDAY GIRL?" the band leader cried into the microphone.

I wasn't in the mood to return to the party just yet, but there wasn't anything I could do. Daddy hurried back inside.

"You better go inside," Gavin said.

"Are you coming? I won't go back unless you do, too," I threatened.

"All right." He finally smiled, seeing the determination in my face.

When we re-entered, the band leader announced it was time for the birthday cake to be wheeled in. He asked everyone to return to his or her seat. The drum roll began again and then Leon rolled the cake down the center aisle. He and Mr. Nussbaum had baked an enormous white cake in the shape of a piano. All the keys were pink and there were sixteen candles on top.

Mommy stepped up proudly beside the cake and smiled at me. Then the crowd of guests grew silent as Leon helped her light the candles.

"Dawn," she called. I stepped up to the cake. The drummer began another long roll. I closed my eyes and fervently made my wish and then I blew with all my strength, putting out all sixteen candles.

As soon as the candles were blown out, the band started to play "Happy Birthday to You," and Mommy began singing, all the guests and staff joining in with her. There were tears running down my cheeks, but even after the scene outside they were tears of great happiness. Everyone applauded. The balloons were released and the younger children, led by Jefferson, laughed and squealed as they rushed about trying to grab the dangling strings.

"Happy birthday, honey," Mommy said, drawing me to her and kissing me.

Before I could say thank you, Daddy was hugging me, too. Then came Aunt Trisha, Granddaddy Longchamp, Edwina, Aunt Bet, and finally Uncle Philip, who held on the longest and kissed me twice. I looked for Gavin, but he was well toward the rear, standing and smiling. I nodded at him, giving him a look that said, "You didn't get away with it, Gavin Longchamp." He understood and laughed.

Pauline and my other school friends came up to congratulate me and then the waiters began to serve the cake. The tempo of the party slowed down as people had their dessert. Shortly after, our guests began to leave, all of them coming to the dais to say personal goodbyes and wish me a happy birthday one more time. No one but Gavin and I had witnessed the ugly scene between Daddy and Aunt Fern, so as far as everyone else was concerned, it had been a perfect evening.

Even Grandmother Laura had enjoyed herself immensely and remained longer than I had anticipated she would. When Bronson had danced with me earlier, I had looked over and had seen Grandmother Laura smiling so softly, I could understand why she had been considered one of the prettiest women in Cutler's Cove. Beneath her heavy makeup lay the smile of a woman who thought herself a young girl again. Her eyes twinkled and her lips curved gently, lovingly.

"She looks good," Bronson had said, when he caught the object of my gaze. "She's reliving her own Sweet Sixteen," he added with a note of melancholy.

Now, he wheeled her off with the others after Mommy and I had kissed her good night. Mommy and I stood together and watched them go. She squeezed my hand and I saw her eyes well up with tears. Before either of us could utter a sad thought, however, we were inundated with well-wishers, including Aunt Bet, Richard and Melanie. Jefferson had, after all, behaved rather well and Richard had to tell us so. Of course, he took credit.

"He knew he had to be a gentleman at my table," Richard bragged. With his stiff demeanor, his hoisted shoulders and habitually serious expression, he looked more like a little old man than a twelve-year-old boy. Melanie wasn't much different. She kissed me good night, but when she stepped back, I saw that her eyes shifted quickly to her father. Uncle Philip's gaze was locked on me instead of her.

"Good night and once more Happy Birthday to the new princess of Cutler's Cove," he said, moving forward to embrace me and kiss me on the cheek.

"I'm not a princess, Uncle Philip," I said. Some of my school friends who lingered behind were sure to tease me after hearing him pronounce my title.

"Sure you are," he said. "Who else could be?" he added. I saw Melanie's eyes darken.

"What about all the presents?" Jefferson asked. He had been circling the pile of gifts on the table all night, anxious to tear off the wrapping paper and discover something he could play with.

"They will be brought to the house later," Mommy declared. "Go get your jacket."

Disappointed, he rushed off. I searched the straggling crowd and found Gavin hovering near the doorway, talking to Ricky Smith and Warren Steine.

"I'll be home in a little while, Mommy," I said. Perceptively, she looked toward Gavin.

"Don't be too late, honey. You're a lot more tired than you think," she cautioned.

"I won't." I hugged her tightly. "Thank you for a wonderful party."

"You're welcome, honey," she said.

Gavin's eyes locked with mine as I approached him. He excused himself and stepped toward me.

"I'm too excited yet to go to sleep," I said. "Do you want to go for a little walk?"

"Sure."

We slipped away from the lingering guests and I led Gavin through the rear of the lobby and outside to the rear of the hotel. The sky had almost completely cleared and the stars themselves looked like the twinkling tips of so many birthday cake candles. I took Gavin's hand in mine and turned down the walkway toward the gazebo, but a shrill peal of laughter coming from the pool cabana caught our attention. We stopped walking and looked. A second cry of laughter confirmed our suspicions.

"It's Fern," Gavin whispered. We heard a male voice. He sounded and looked like one of our newest bellhops. Unable to put a lid on our curiosity, we walked toward the pool and saw Aunt Fern on a lounge, the bellhop lying beside her. Her all too sheer blouse was unbuttoned most of the way. Gavin and I paused, neither of us speaking, both hardly breathing. The bellhop was kissing her shoulders and lowering his face to her breasts. But Aunt Fern suddenly lifted a small bottle and brought it to her lips.

"You've had enough," the bellhop said.

"I never have enough," she replied and laughed again, only this time, her laugh turned into a cough, the cough into the sound of choking.

"Hey," her lover cried as she began to heave. He spun himself off the lounge just in time. Aunt Fern began to vomit hard and loudly, the grotesque sound carrying through the night. When it was over, she moaned and clutched her stomach.

"Oh, I feel like I'm dying," she wailed. "And it's all over me."

"You had better get to a bathroom," the bellhop declared. All she could do was moan a reply. He helped her up and led her away, keeping her at arm's length as they stumbled down the pathway toward the hotel. Gavin and I remained in the shadows until they were gone.

"I'm glad," Gavin said angrily. "She got what she deserved."

"It's not the first time I've caught her out here with someone," I said. "The first time I ever saw her out here, I got so frightened at what she was doing, I ran all the way home and up into my room."

"And the next time?" Gavin asked.

"I watched for a while," I confessed.

"You never put that in any of your letters."

"I was too ashamed," I said. We headed for the gazebo again.

"Despite her, you had the greatest party," Gavin said when we sat down.

"I know. I can never thank my parents enough." A cool ocean breeze made me shiver.

"You're cold," Gavin declared.

"No, it's all right," I replied, afraid he would say we should go back in; but he had his jacket off and quickly put it over my shoulders.

"Now you'll be cold," I said.

"I'm all right," he replied bravely. "You danced with a lot of guys tonight," he remarked, trying to sound casual about it.

"Not with you though, and I wanted to very much, Gavin," I declared. He nodded sadly. Then, he smiled.

"Well, it's not too late," he suddenly decided. Although the music still coming from the hotel was very subdued, we could hear it. Gavin stood up and held out his hand. "May I have this dance, madame? Or is your dance card full?"

"No, I have a spot for one more," I said, laughing, and stood up. He put his arm around my waist and slowly drew me to him. We giggled at first, but as we danced on the gazebo, looking into each other's eyes, we moved closer and closer together until my cheek was touching his. I was sure he could feel my heart pounding.

Suddenly, as if we both had sensed the need at the same time, I lifted my head and my lips met his, the kiss starting very softly, tentatively, full of uncertainty, and then, as the warmth and excitement grew, turning harder, firmer, both of us surrendering to the warmth. I laid my head on his shoulder and we continued to dance, both of us afraid to speak.

"I wish I didn't have to go right home tomorrow," he finally said. "But Daddy's got to get back to work."

"I know. I wish you could stay longer, too. Did you talk to your father and mother about working here this summer?"

"Yes. It's all right with them."

"Oh Gavin, even though it's only a few more weeks, I can't wait. We'll have such a good time. We'll go boating and swimming and . . ."

"Hey, I'm supposed to be working, not playing here," he chastised softly.

"Everyone has time off, and I have some pull with the boss," I said, but Gavin didn't smile.

"I don't want to take a job and not do it right," he said firmly.

"Don't worry, you won't." He was just like Daddy, full of pride and ready to hoist up his flag of self-respect at a moment's notice; yet just like Daddy, Gavin could be soft and tender, sensitive and loving.

From where we stood, I could see Mommy, Jefferson, Mrs. Boston, Aunt Trisha and Daddy returning to the house.

"I better start for home," I said. "It's late."

"I'll walk you."

He held my hand and I kept his jacket on my shoulders until we reached the house.

"Thanks for the use of your jacket," I said, slipping it off.

"Didn't you feel anything in the pocket?" he asked as I returned it.

"Pocket?" I noticed that he wore a coy grin. "Gavin Steven Longchamp, what do you have in there?" I demanded. He laughed and plucked out a slim gift-wrapped box.

"Daddy and Momma gave you a gift from all of us, but this one is just from me. I wanted to give this to you privately," he said, handing it to me. "Happy birthday, Christie."

"Gavin!"

My heart pounding in anticipation, I tore open the gift and opened the box. Lying on a bed of soft paper was a beautiful gold identification bracelet. Above and below my name were two hearts entwined.

"Turn it over," he said softly and when I did so I read: With Love, Forever, Gavin. It took my breath away.

"Oh Gavin, it's beautiful. It's my best gift," I declared. "But it must be so expensive."

"There's no one I would rather spend my money on. When I have any, that is," he said, laughing. "Here, let me help you put it on."

I held out my wrist and he carefully snapped the chain lock into place. As he did so, I gazed at his face and saw how soft and loving his eyes became as his fingers held mine. He finished and then looked at me in that special way that kept me thinking about him often.

"Thank you." I kissed him quickly on the lips

and he stared at me, suddenly looking so much older.

"You had better go in," he said, "before you get cold again."

"I'll never sleep tonight!" I cried. "I'll see you at breakfast bright and early."

"I'll be there early, but I won't be bright," he called as I scurried up the steps. He stood there watching me and smiling as I opened the door and walked slowly into the house, reluctant to put an end to the most wonderful night of my life.

It was nearly impossible to fall asleep, but when I did, I dreamt about my party. Only in my dream, there was an additional guest, a surprise guest who showed up at the very last moment. Mommy was singing "Happy Birthday" and the party crowd was joining in chorus when suddenly, a tall, dark-haired, good-looking man appeared. He walked slowly down the aisle from the main entrance, smiling as he drew closer and closer. Mommy stopped singing.

"Hello Christie," he said, "Happy birthday." He had the whitest teeth, teeth almost as white as piano keys, and his ebony eyes were glowing softly.

"Who are you?" I asked while people were still singing "Happy Birthday" around us.

"I'm your real father," he said and he leaned toward me to kiss me, only when he drew near, his face became Uncle Philip's face, a leering, smiling face with wet lips. I tried to back away, but he seized my shoulders and drew me closer to him, closer and closer until . . .

I sat up in my bed, sweating and breathing hard. For a moment I didn't know where I was or what had happened. My heart was thumping against my chest. I took a deep breath and hugged myself. Then I felt the identification bracelet that Gavin had given me on my wrist. It comforted me; I could almost hear Gavin saying, "Don't be afraid." I lay awake for a while, wondering about my dream. Finally, my eyelids became heavy and I could keep them open no longer.

Although it was a bright, sunny morning, I didn't wake up before Jefferson, who I imagine had gone to sleep dreaming of ripping open my gifts. He burst in upon me shouting and I groaned.

"Can I start opening them? Can I? Can I?" he chanted.

"Jefferson!" He was patting me vigorously on the leg. "Okay, go ahead," I cried.

"YAY!" he yelled and went charging out of my room and down the corridor and stairs.

I moaned again and sat up. When I saw the time, I hurried out of bed. I knew Granddaddy Longchamp would want to get his usual early start to the airport and I was afraid of missing Gavin. Mommy knocked on my door and came in. She was already dressed.

"I overslept, Mommy," I said.

"It's all right, honey. Daddy's already over at the hotel. I'll meet you in the dining room. Mrs. Boston will make breakfast for Jefferson here. He won't leave while there's one gift of yours left to inspect, anyway," she said.

"Tell everyone I'll be right there," I called and hurried into the bathroom to shower. By the time I got over to the hotel and into the dining room, everyone was at the big table. Aunt Trisha looked fresh and happy in her colorful print skirt and blouse. She was telling stories that had everyone smiling and laughing. The moment I entered the dining room, Gavin looked up from his plate and beamed. He had kept the seat beside him empty. I hurried to it.

"Here she is, a day older, a day brighter," Aunt Trisha declared. Everyone said good morning, and I apologized for being late.

"You have a right to, honey. You had a big night. It was a wonderful party, the best one I was ever at," Edwina declared. Everyone agreed.

"What time are you leaving?" I asked Gavin.

"As soon as we finish eating. You know my father. He should have been a train station manager. We'll get there too early and the plane will leave late, and he'll be complaining to everyone and anyone who will listen," Gavin said gazing at Granddaddy Longchamp. He complained about him, but there was no doubt in my mind that Gavin loved his father dearly.

A few moments later, Aunt Fern sauntered in. She looked pale and tired, her short hair scraggly, and she wore a pair of dark sunglasses. I didn't think she had taken a brush to it even for a few seconds. She wore a faded college sweatshirt and a pair of tight jeans, dirty sneakers and no socks. She shot an angry glance at Daddy, whose face had turned ashen as soon as she had appeared looking so disheveled and unkempt. Mommy grimaced and everyone stared as Aunt Fern plopped herself down in a seat.

"Just coffee," she moaned to the waiter.

"What time are you leaving for college, Fern?" Aunt Trisha asked her.

"As soon as I can get myself together," she replied. She sipped her black coffee and slumped back in her seat, not listening or talking to anyone.

After breakfast, Gavin and I were able to visit a while longer in the hotel lobby while his parents went up to finish packing. Aunt Trisha was the first to leave. Daddy, Mommy and I hugged her, and Mommy promised we would all come to New York to see her in her new show. She hugged and kissed me one more time before getting into the taxicab.

"It was a beautiful party, honey. I was so happy to be here." She glanced at Gavin who stood a few feet behind me. "You're growing up fast and you've become very beautiful."

"Thank you, Aunt Trisha."

We watched her go off and then returned to the lobby. I hated good-byes, especially when I said good-bye to people I really loved. It gave me an empty feeling that started in my stomach, and then spread all over until I felt like a shadow of myself. Each good-bye diminishes me a little, I thought. Some part of me leaves along with the person I love, too. And there's always that horrid feeling that I might have said good-bye forever without realizing it.

I dreaded saying good-bye to Gavin, but the time finally came. Daddy had Julius bring up the hotel limo for them. We all hugged and kissed and promised to call and write each other. Gavin waited until the last minute to get in. We eyed each other and the people around us, neither daring to attempt a kiss.

"I'll call you tonight," Gavin whispered in my ear.

"Promise? No matter how late?" I asked, cheered by the thought.

"I promise." He turned to Mommy and Daddy. "Goodbye Dawn." She hugged him. "Well, big brother," Gavin said to Daddy. They shook hands like men and then Daddy smiled and hugged him.

"Keep out of trouble, little brother," he said,

running his hand through Gavin's beautiful, thick dark hair. "Watch out for those wild Texas women."

Gavin shot a glance at me and reddened.

"He's got no time for that," Granddaddy Longchamp bellowed.

"Whatever you say, Daddy," Jimmy replied, smiling. He, Mommy and I stood on the steps and waved as the limo took them off. When it disappeared around the bend, my heart sunk so low, I nearly burst into tears. Mommy saw the look on my face and embraced me quickly as we all turned to go back into the hotel.

"There's always a letdown after something as big as this, honey. But there will be other good times, many, many other good times."

"I know, Mommy."

It was Sunday, and Sundays always meant a big check-out at the hotel. Rather than sit around and brood, I made myself useful at the front desk. Mrs. Bradly and the others couldn't stop talking about the party. They were very complimentary about my piano playing and, of course, Mommy's singing. Sometime early in the afternoon, Aunt Fern appeared in the lobby with her suitcase. She was still wearing her dark glasses. She stopped at the front desk and lit a cigarette.

"Why do you smoke so much, Aunt Fern?" I asked her.

"It calms my nerves and around here, I need something to do that," she replied. Then she lowered her glasses on the bridge of her nose and peered at me over the frame. "Did you sneak a peek at *Lady Chatterley's Lover* last night?"

"No," I said. "And anyway, I don't like keeping things from Mommy."

"Oh pull . . . leeze," she moaned. "You're sixteen. What do you think she was doing when she was your age?"

"She wasn't doing anything wrong," I retorted.

"Oh no." She stared at me a moment and then leaned against the counter. "I bet you don't know what went on between her and Philip at the private school, do you?" she said.

It was as if someone had pressed a hot palm over my heart. I felt the heat rise into my neck.

"I don't know what you're talking about," I said quickly.

"I figured that," she replied, nodding. "Just remember this, Princess, everyone around here is not as lily-white pure as they make out to be. You ought to ask your mother to tell you what happened when she and Jimmy went to Emerson Peabody, a ritzy private school in Richmond."

"I know they went there. Granddaddy Longchamp was a maintenance supervisor and . . ."

"Yeah, yeah, I'm not talking about why or how." She leaned closer to me. "Your Uncle Philip went there, too, you know. That's where your mother and he first met." She smiled slyly. "You're old enough to know all the nitty-gritty details now," she added.

Julius appeared in the doorway.

"Thank God, I'm out of here," Aunt Fern said. She started away and then stopped and leaned toward me again. "Chapter ten," she said, smiling. "That's a good one. There's my suitcase," she shouted at Julius and pointed. He picked it up and hurried out before her. In a moment she was gone, but she had left me standing there staring after her with my heart thumping. What did she mean by those shifty smiles and innuendos about my mother and Uncle Philip? Why did she say everyone wasn't as lily-pure as I thought? Was she just trying to hurt us? Or was she referring to one of those dark passages in our strange family history that were still kept secret?

With my heart going pitter-patter, I left the front desk and hurried down the corridor to Mommy's office. She was just finishing up a meeting with Mr. Dorfman when I knocked and entered.

"It was a wonderful party," he told me as he left. I thanked him and sat down.

"Mrs. Boston called to tell me your brother started a fire in the garbage can using the make-up mirror the Hammersteins gave you and the magnifying glass from the stationery set the Malamuds gave you," she said, shaking her head.

"What? How?"

"He directed the sunlight into the can and used the magnifying glass to burn a hole in some of the gift wrap paper. I think I had better give Mrs. Boston a raise," she added and sighed.

"Aunt Fern just left," I said.

"Oh. That's good, although I think her days at this particular college are numbered," Mommy said.

"I don't know why she's so mean and unhappy, Mommy. You and Daddy are always nice to her and have done so much for her."

Mommy sat back a moment and thought. Then a smile of wisdom flashed in her eyes.

"Momma Longchamp used to say some cows are just born to give sour milk, no matter how sweet the grass they feed on."

"It must have been so strange for you, Mommy, having two mothers," I said. She nodded. "You first met Uncle Philip when you and Daddy went to Emerson Peabody, right?" I asked. Her eyes grew small.

"Yes," she said. "And Clara."

"And for a long time, you didn't know he was really your brother?"

She stared at me for a moment.

"Yes, Christie. Why do you ask? Did Fern say something to you about it?" she demanded quickly.

I nodded. I couldn't keep anything secret from her.

"She would do that." She paused and then after a deep breath, she said, "It's true, I met Philip there and for a short time, we became boyfriend and girlfriend, but nothing ugly happened, no matter what Fern told you," she added quickly.

"She didn't really tell me anything. She just made it seem as if . . ."

"Fern hates herself so much, she just wants to make life miserable for everyone else too," she said.

"I wouldn't believe anything she said anyway," I said. She smiled and nodded.

"You really are growing up fast, honey, and you should be told everything about the family. I want you to know something, Christie," she declared, her eyes fixed on me so intently, my heart began to race. "Uncle Philip . . . well, Uncle Philip never quite got over everything, especially the discovery about who he and I really were to each other. Do you understand what I'm trying to tell you, honey?"

I swallowed over the lump that had risen in my throat. What she was trying to tell me, I had felt and seen in so many different ways, but as a much younger girl I had not understood. Time rolled backward and memories of Uncle Philip's intense gaze at Mommy, a gaze that appeared hypnotic at times, returned. I recalled the way he always seemed to be hovering close to her, searching for and seizing upon opportunities to touch her or kiss her.

"But he loves Aunt Bet, doesn't he?" I asked. I couldn't help but be seized by fear because of these revelations.

"Yes," Mommy said reassuringly.

"But not the way you and Daddy love each other," I declared.

"No," she said, then smiled a little. "But few people do." She stood up and came around her desk to me. "Let's not dwell on these sad and troubled thoughts, honey. Aunt Fern was cruel to bring them up." We walked to the door together. "You're going to graduate from high school and go on to be a wonderful pianist. And your brother is going to become tame," she added with wide, hopeful eyes. We laughed.

"I love you, Mommy, and I never would believe anything ugly about you, no matter what Aunt Fern or anyone else says."

Mommy's face grew serious, her eyes smaller, darker.

"I'm not perfect, Christie. No one is, but I won't ever lie to you or betray you, not the way people who were supposed to love me lied to me and betrayed me. I promise." She kissed me on the cheek. "Now go check up on Jefferson for me, and enjoy the beautiful sunshine.

"I just dread receiving Jefferson's report card tomorrow," she added. "His behavior report is sure to be all in red."

"Maybe we'll all be pleasantly surprised tomorrow, Mommy," I said.

"Maybe, but I doubt it," she said, but neither Mommy nor I could ever realize how prophetic her statement was.

* * *

It took me most of the remainder of the afternoon and much of the evening to make a dent in the pile of gifts I had received. I wanted to get my thank-you cards out as quickly as I could. Jefferson was rather cute, sitting beside me on the floor in the living room announcing each gift and who had given it. I had received some very expensive gifts which included clothing, jewelry, perfume and other toiletries, as well as things for my room.

When Mommy insisted Jefferson get ready for bed, I stopped but promised him I wouldn't continue until he could help me tomorrow after school. I was quite tired myself and retired to my room, mainly to await anxiously Gavin's promised phone call. My eyes fell on Aunt Fern's tightly wrapped gift. It was one I didn't want to open in front of Jefferson or anyone else for that matter, especially Daddy. But I couldn't help but be curious.

I opened it slowly and then casually turned the pages. Why was Aunt Fern so determined I read this story? I wondered, and recalled her final coy comment about chapter ten. I scanned the pages and discovered why. Of course, I had read and seen things more revealing, but somehow, maybe because it had come from Aunt Fern whom I had witnessed doing these sexual things, it all seemed that much more forbidden, and what they said about forbidden fruit would always be true. I couldn't take my eyes from the words describing the lovemaking. As I read on, I began to imagine myself and Gavin. I was so deeply involved in the chapter, I didn't hear the phone's first ring. When it rang a second time, I scooped it up quickly and slammed the book closed.

"Hi," Gavin said. Hearing his voice after imagining ourselves together made me blush with guilt.

"Hi. How was your trip?" I asked quickly.

"Just as long. No, longer since I was going away from Cutler's Cove."

"Just Cutler's Cove?"

"And you," he said. "Things quiet down?"

"Yes. Jefferson and I went through some of the pile of gifts. I got so many nice things."

"I bet."

"Tomorrow's our last day of school. Mommy's afraid of what Jefferson's report card will look like."

"Mine wasn't too good at his age either," Gavin said. "Anyway, I wanted to tell you how much I enjoyed your party and, especially, our private dance."

"Me too," I said. "Thanks again for the wonderful gift."

We were both silent for a moment.

"I'll write you every day this week," I promised. He laughed. "I will."

"Great. Well, I'd better hang up. I can't wait to see you again," he said. "Sleep tight and don't let the bedbugs bite."

"Good night, Gavin." I held the phone in my hand for a long moment after he had cradled his receiver. It was as though mine still contained his voice, still promised the warmth it had brought. "Good night," I whispered into it again and then hung it up.

I looked down at the copy of *Lady Chatterley's Lover* and thought about Aunt Fern giving it to me. She didn't do it because she wanted me to learn about love and how it could be warm and wonderful; she wanted to tease me. She probably hoped I would become like her.

Well I would never become like her, I vowed. I took her present and shoved it into the rear of my closet. Someday I might read it again, I thought, but not as forbidden fruit, not as something evil from Aunt Fern.

I crawled into bed and closed my eyes and fell asleep dreaming of the upcoming summer and Gavin's return.

Jefferson wasn't as eager to get up the next morning, knowing we were going to school to get our end-of-the-year report cards. Mommy had to shake him out of bed and he tried to take forever to eat his breakfast. From the look on his face, I assumed his teacher had already indicated some of the bad things that would be put on his report card.

Unless there was some conflict with guests arriving or going, Julius took all of us to school in the hotel limousine. He always picked us up and brought us home.

As usual Richard and Melanie wore the same color, he in a jacket, slacks and tie and she in a dress. He was the only seventh grader who went to public school dressed so formally, but I couldn't imagine him dressing any other way. Today, the last day of class, he looked even more prim and proper with his hair brushed and slicked down neatly, his tie knotted even tighter, his shoes polished perfectly, and the handkerchief in his top pocket creased so sharply into a point, it looked like it could be used as a knife.

Today, Jefferson was unusually subdued when he finally crawled into the back seat with me and sat across from Richard and Melanie.

"Couldn't you be ready even on the last day?" Richard asked dryly.

"We've never been late for school, Richard," I replied just as dryly.

"Only because Julius drives faster. The school

bus children always get there before we do," he added as if that were something terrible.

"And I never have enough time to talk to my friends before homeroom," Melanie added to bolster Richard's complaint.

"Well, today's the last day of the school year, so you won't have to put up with it again until next fall," I told her.

"Jefferson probably will still be in the same class." Richard said, a cruel smile on his face.

Jefferson looked up sharply.

"No, I won't," he snapped.

Melanie's smile widened.

Jefferson frowned and looked up at me. I closed my eyes and opened them to signal he shouldn't argue, and he sat back and pouted the rest of the way.

All the chatter at school was about my party. My classmates had really enjoyed themselves. Pauline couldn't wait to ask me about Gavin and tell me how good-looking she and most of the other girls thought he was.

We had an abbreviated school day, the purpose of which was to conduct the end-of-the-year activities: returning books and locker keys, straightening and cleaning out desks and lockers, returning overdue library books and settling other school debts, as well as getting some preliminary information about the beginning of the next school year.

Naturally, there was a great deal of excitement in the air as everyone talked about the coming of summer, the places some of them would go to and the things they would do. The school corridors were filled with laughter and chatter, even the teachers happy and less severe about the rules.

Finally, the last bell rang and we all charged out

into the warm, late spring sunshine. There were cheers and screams and shouts of good-bye as friends who wouldn't see each other for a few months parted. I spotted Jefferson walking slowly from the elementary school, his head down. He had his report card tucked under his arm.

"How bad is it?" I asked him when he reached me. I held my breath, afraid of the answer. He just looked up at me and started toward the limousine, in which Richard and Melanie were already waiting. "Let me see it, Jefferson," I demanded. He paused and reluctantly, he passed the envelope to me. I took out his card.

It wasn't only that he received Unsatisfactory marks for every behavior category; he received two U's in his school subjects as well. Actually, it was his worst report card ever.

"Oh Jefferson," I cried. "Mommy and Daddy will be so upset with you."

"I know," he replied and began bawling in anticipation.

"Get into the car," I said sternly.

"Well?" Richard asked, a crooked smile of self-satisfaction already on his face. "How bad is it?"

"I don't want to talk about it, Richard. It isn't funny," I said sharply. Jefferson turned into the corner of the seat and began to cry. When he was like that, all I could do was comfort him, even though I knew he didn't deserve it.

"You can't cry over spilled milk," Melanie said. "You just have to do better."

Jefferson wiped his eyes and turned around.

"Melanie's right about that, Jefferson," I said. "You're going to have to make a thousand promises," I advised him, "and not get into a single bit of trouble this summer, not even a teeny-weeny bit," I said. He nodded.

"I'll be good," he promised. "I'll clean up my room and pick up my clothes and never leave the front door open."

"Believe that and you can believe there really is a tooth fairy," Richard said.

"There is a tooth fairy," Jefferson spat back. "She left me a quarter under my pillow."

"I told you," Richard replied, shaking his head, "your mother or your father put it there."

"Or maybe they had Mrs. Boston do it," Melanie suggested.

"They did not!"

"Stop teasing him," I cried. The twins looked at each other and then out the window.

"Hey!" Richard suddenly said. "What's that?"

We all leaned forward and that was when we first saw the tower of ugly black smoke rising above the roof of the main building of our hotel.

Burning Curse

"JULIUS, WHAT IS THAT?" I CRIED. I WAS SEIZED WITH fear.

"I don't know, Christie," he replied, but sped up. It took us almost ten more minutes to get there because of all the other people hurrying to the scene, and when we arrived, we found policemen and firemen on the street blocking traffic around the front of the hotel. People were out of their cars and gathering in clumps along the road to watch the flames spit out of the roof and the windows of the top floor of the great Cutler's Cove resort. Their eyes were wide, their faces lit up with the reflection coming from the fire and from their own excitement. I saw guests and members of the staff huddled together on the front lawn far back from the ropes put up to keep people away from the activity.

"There's Mother," Melanie said, pointing to where Aunt Bet stood with some people, but I didn't see Mommy or Daddy beside her, nor did I see Unclc Philip. I imagined they were with the fire chief. My heart sank, realizing how terrible they all must be feeling. What a horrible thing to have happen just before our summer season.

"Wow!" Jefferson whispered, his face filled both with awe and fear.

"What happened?" Julius asked the policeman who was directing traffic to the side.

"A boiler blew up in the basement and the fire spread quickly. That part of the hotel is quite old and had no sprinkler system," he added, smirking. "By the time the fire department could get up here, the fire had a good hold on the place."

"Where are my parents?" I wondered aloud now. No matter where I looked, I didn't see them. "Julius, take us closer."

"Yes," Richard commanded, sounding years older than he was. "Quickly."

"I have the owner's children with me," Julius explained to the patrolman.

"You can't drive any closer. You will have to park here," the policeman ordered, "and stay behind the lines."

Julius pulled over but almost before he came to a stop, I grabbed Jefferson's hand in mine and thrust open the car door. I pulled my little brother out behind me and shot across the road.

"Christie, wait!" Julius cried, but I couldn't listen to him or anyone. I was aware that Jefferson was gripping my hand tightly, but other than that, I could think of or see nothing but the fire.

I found Mrs. Bradly off to the side with other members of the staff, but not my parents. She was embracing herself and sobbing, her face streaked with tears and soot. I gazed around frantically, and still I didn't see Mommy or Daddy. Where were they? My heart began to pound harder and faster and my stomach felt like dozens of moths were loose inside and flapping their paper-thin wings.

"Where's my mother?" I screamed. "Where's my daddy?"

Some people heard me, but no one spoke. Mrs. Bradly simply began crying harder.

"Hey! Stop!" a fireman cried as we ducked under the first set of security lines to charge up the lawn. Ashes danced in the air and the flames were so intense, we could feel the heat. Firemen were screaming to each other and pulling hoses this way and that, but the flow of water coming out of them seemed to have no effect. Defiantly, arrogantly, the flames snapped and spread, greedily eating through curtains and furniture. I could practically see it rushing down the corridors, licking and biting into every possible corner, a hot, burning, ravaging animal of hell consuming all that was once beautiful and historic, tearing down pictures and walls, sending chandeliers crashing into floors. Nothing could stand in the way of this fire or slow its relentless onslaught.

Impatient, I pulled Jefferson along and went around to the far corner where I finally saw Uncle Philip standing by himself. His normally neat hair was wild. He had taken off his sports jacket and tie and his eyes looked so ablaze, it was as if the fire had gotten into him as well. Either he was mumbling to himself or he thought someone stood beside him.

"UNCLE PHILIP!" I cried, running toward him.

He looked at me, but he didn't speak. He seemed not to recognize me. His mouth moved spasmodically, but he didn't say anything. He looked up at the fire again and then at me, shaking his head.

"Where's Mommy, Uncle Philip? Where's Daddy?" I desperately demanded.

"Where's my Mommy?" Jefferson chorused, his tears flowing harder. He pulled himself closer to me and looked up at Uncle Philip.

"Uncle Philip!" I screamed when he simply continued to stare at the fire, hypnotized by the flames and activity. He turned slowly this time and gazed at me for a long moment. Then, he smiled.

"Dawn," he said, "you're all right. Thank God."

"Uncle Philip, it's me, Christie. I'm not my mother," I replied, astounded. He blinked quickly and then his smile faded like smoke.

"Oh," he uttered, bringing his hand to his cheek. He looked toward the fire again. "Oh."

"Where are they, Uncle Philip?" I asked, much more desperately. Tears were streaming down my cheeks now and my throat ached from the smoke. The horrid odor from the burning hotel turned my stomach, and the heat from the towering flames fell over us so intensely it was as if we had fallen into the hottest summer day ever.

"Where are they?" he repeated. I nodded. He shook his head in bewildered fashion.

"Where?" I screamed and tugged hard on his arm. It drew him out of his daze.

"Jimmy . . . was in the basement when the boiler exploded," he said. "The fire shot up the stairways and through the heat and air ducts. It popped out of every grate and the floor in the card room collapsed," he recited.

"Where's Mommy?" I asked in a whisper.

"I ran around getting everyone out, shouting, pulling, helping the older people. I think everyone's out."

"Mommy and Daddy are all right?" I asked, smiling hopefully through my tears.

"What?" He looked at the hotel again, but he didn't speak. He was lost in a trance once more.

"Where's Mommy?" Jefferson cried. "Christie, where's Mommy?" He ground his small fists against his eyes and clung to me.

"Uncle Philip?" I pulled on his arm again. "Where's my mother?"

He simply shook his head.

"Christie?" Jefferson moaned. "I want Mommy."

"I know, I know. Let's go talk to someone else, Jefferson," I said, seeing there was no sense in talking to Uncle Philip. He was too confused to make any sense. I lifted Jefferson into my arms and carried him toward some firemen who were standing back and giving orders to the others. One wore a hat that read Chief.

"Excuse me," I said.

"Hey, you shouldn't be here, honey. Billy, get these kids behind the lines," he shouted to a young fireman off to the left.

"Wait. I'm Christie Longchamp. My parents are owners of the hotel. I have to find out what happened."

"Huh? Oh," he said. "Look honey, I don't know enough details yet. Apparently, a boiler blew and started this."

"But where's my mother? Where's my father? Have you seen them?" I asked quickly.

"I haven't time to talk to you, miss. Now you had better take your little brother and get back. Those walls look like they could fall any moment and they could fall in this direction. Go on," he ordered. "Billy, get them out of here," he repeated and the young fireman took my elbow to turn me away.

"But . . . my mother . . ."

"You better listen to the chief. He doesn't have time to waste," the young fireman said.

Jefferson started to cry harder and louder, burying his face in my shoulder.

"This can't be happening," I said. "It can't." I let

him lead us to the ropes. I spotted Aunt Bet, Richard and Melanie off to the right and hurried to their side.

"Oh Christie, honey," Aunt Bet said, holding her arms out. "And Jefferson. It's so horrible, so horrible."

"Where's my mother, Aunt Bet? And where's Daddy? Uncle Philip doesn't make any sense when I ask him."

She shook her head.

"They're still inside, dear," she said. "They never came out. We've all been standing here, waiting and hoping."

"Never came out?"

I turned and looked at the hotel. Flames were shooting out of the front entrance. There was smoke flowing out of almost every window.

"Maybe they got out the back," I said. "Or maybe they're safe in the basement, waiting until the firemen reach them. Yes, that's it," I said nodding.

"Oh Christie, poor Christie," Aunt Bet muttered.

"They're okay, Aunt Bet." I smiled through my tears and tightened my grip on Jefferson. "Sure. They're fine. You'll see. They're probably standing somewhere in the rear of the hotel," I added and started away.

"Christie!" Aunt Bet cried.

"I've got to go to them. They're probably worrying about Jefferson and me," I said and hurried around the ropes and the firemen and all the people until we were able to go behind the hotel. Even though Jefferson was quite heavy, I didn't realize I had been carrying him until we were at the rear of the hotel.

There were firemen around there, too, spraying

this part of the roof and the walls with water they were drawing from the pool. I searched frantically for signs of Mommy and Daddy, but all I saw were some staff members and firemen.

"Where's Mommy and Daddy?" Jefferson asked, his eyes wide and hopeful. "I want Mommy."

"I'm looking for them, Jefferson." I put him down, took his hand and approached the closest fireman.

"Hey," he said when he saw us, "you children better get back."

"We're looking for my parents," I said. "Did they come out back here?"

"No one's come out back here. Now take that little boy and get back," he ordered firmly.

With my heart pounding, I retreated with Jefferson slowly. We went to the gazebo and sat on the steps, watching the firemen work. Jefferson's eyes swelled from crying, as did mine. Finally, we both sat silently, dry-eyed, simply staring ahead, waiting. Jefferson laid his head against my shoulder and I held him tightly. The flames began to grow smaller, even though the smoke grew darker and thicker. It drifted off in a sooty cloud and the ocean breezes carried it into the distance. I don't know how long we were sitting there, stunned and afraid, but finally I heard Richard scream, "THERE THEY ARE!"

With relief bursting through me I turned in his direction. I saw Richard, Melanie, Mrs. Boston, Julius and Aunt Bet. They hurried in our direction. Jefferson sat up, his eyes widening, the sight of Mrs. Boston bringing him the most comfort.

"Where's Mommy?" he demanded.

"Oh honey child, oh baby," Mrs. Boston said.

"My mother?" I asked her. "Daddy?"

She shook her head.

Jefferson started to wail again, loudly this time, and his cry, shrill and sharp, got caught up in the same breeze that carried the ugly smoke away. Mrs. Boston scooped him into her arms and rained kisses of comfort over his face.

I stood up, my legs feeling like rubber, but my head so light I thought it was like a balloon and might snap off and be carried away with the smoke and Jefferson's screams.

"Christie," Aunt Bet said.

"Where are they?" I asked and held my breath. "Didn't they come out?"

She shook her head.

"WHERE ARE THEY!" I demanded.

"They found them together . . . in the basement," Aunt Bet said and bit down on her lower lip. Her eyes were red and swollen with tears. "Oh, Christie," she added and began to sob.

Then, my feet turned into air and so did my legs and my stomach and my chest and my neck until my head had nothing to hold it up.

I folded and fell softly, just like the balloons on my birthday, floating down, down, down. The world around me which had once been as colorful and as magical and wonderful as a soap bubble popped and everything went dark.

"She will be all right," I heard someone say. I thought I had my eyes open, but it was pitch dark. "Just give her some light, sweet tea and a little toast. An emotional trauma like this can be as devastating to the body as something physical. But she's young, she's strong. She'll recuperate."

"Mommy?"

"She's waking up," I heard Aunt Bet say.

"Yes. Keep the cold compress on her forehead a while longer."

"Mommy?" The darkness began to retreat. It fell back like the tide, and in its place, I saw the ceiling of my room and then the walls as my eyes moved slowly, hopefully downward, anticipating Mommy's concerned and loving face near me. But all I saw were Aunt Bet and Doctor Stanley, our family physician. He smiled and nodded, strands of his light brown hair down over his forehead and nearly over his eyes. As usual, he needed a haircut desperately. I once told Mommy that Doctor Stanley reminded me of a poodle. She laughed and confessed she thought so too.

"He's a very good doctor and a very nice man, but he doesn't take much care with his personal appearance," she admitted. I could hear her voice so clearly in my memory, I was sure she was somewhere in the room.

"Where's Mommy?" I asked, turning to look everywhere. I could barely utter words, my throat ached so; and my chest felt as if something heavy had been on it for hours and hours. When I didn't see her, I lifted my head from the pillow and instantly, the room spun. I groaned and closed my eyes.

"You have to take it easy, Christie," Doctor Stanley advised. "You've had quite an emotional shock and your equilibrium has been sent into orbit."

"I feel so tired," I said, or at least I thought I said it. I couldn't be sure anyone heard my words. But I felt Aunt Bet take my left hand into hers and I opened my eyes and saw her beside me. She smiled weakly, her eyes swollen from crying. She looked so much thinner to me, her nose sharper, her cheekbones and jawbone so much more pronounced. Her normally obedient hair was in revolt everywhere, strands falling every which way.

"Aunt Bet," I said. She bit down on her lower lip, her eyes filling with tears. "My mother and father . . . they never got out?" She shook her head.

I felt as if someone had punched me in the stomach. My body shook with new sobs.

"Now, now, Christie," Doctor Stanley said. "You've got to get a hold on yourself, dear. You don't want to get yourself so sick you can't be of help to your little brother, do you?"

"Where is he?" I asked quickly. "Where's Jefferson?"

"He's in his room, dear," Aunt Bet said. "Sleeping."

"But he'll be waking up soon and he will need you," Doctor Stanley said. "He'll need his big sister. Now you just get yourself some rest, try to take a little tea and some toast and jelly. You have a very difficult and trying few days ahead of you, Christie. A great deal has fallen on your young shoulders. Do you understand?" Doctor Stanley asked. I nodded. "Good. I'm terribly sorry for your sorrow and for this tragedy and I will be here to help you as much as you need it," he added.

I looked at him again. Mommy had liked him and had believed in him enough to trust him with our family's health. Mommy would want me to listen to him, I thought.

"Thank you, Doctor Stanley," I said. He smiled again and then he left.

"Tell me what happened, Aunt Bet," I said as soon as we were alone.

"We don't know every detail yet," she said. "Something exploded in the basement while Jimmy was down there. It caused an immediate fire. The smoke flew up into the rest of the hotel and set off alarms. Guests were ushered out. Philip was everywhere, charging down corridors, knocking on doors, screaming and helping people. Your mother and I helped clear the lobby and then we left together when we felt sure everyone had been evacuated. The fire was building so quickly, we could already see the flames toward the rear of the lobby.

"When we got outside, Dawn cried out for Jimmy and realized he hadn't emerged. She was frantic. The firemen hadn't yet arrived, but the police were there. One policeman tried to stop her from rushing back in, but she broke out of his grip and charged through the front entrance, screaming she had to get Jimmy. That was the last I saw of her," she added and began to sob silently.

"And afterward?" I said, determined to know it all.

"Afterward, when they were able to get into the basement, the firemen found them together. Your mother had reached Jimmy, but they had been trapped in a storage room. They died clinging to each other," she concluded and took a deep breath.

"Philip's devastated," she continued, now speaking like one in a trance. "He's wandering about the wreckage in disbelief. He's so angry, no one dares go near him."

I closed my eyes. Maybe, if I closed them hard and tight enough and squeezed my body until it hurt, I could drive away this nightmare. I would open my eyes in a moment and it would be morning, a bright, sunny late spring morning. Jefferson will be charging through my door any moment, I thought, and Mommy will come in after him, telling him to leave me alone and get dressed. Yes . . . yes.

"How's she doin'?" Mrs. Boston asked from the doorway and my dream-prayer died.

"The doctor said to give her sweet tea and some toast and jelly," Aunt Bet said sharply. "Get it immediately." She was never as nice to the staff as Mommy was and frequently spoke harshly to the servants. Mommy said it was because of the way Aunt Bet had been brought up. Her parents were so rich, she had always lived like royalty.

"Yes ma'am," Mrs. Boston replied.

"I don't want anything," I said defiantly.

"Now come on, Christie. You heard what the doctor said. You're going to need your strength," Aunt Bet advised. Reluctantly, I nodded. They were right; I couldn't bury myself in make-believe and refuse to face the truth. Jefferson needed me to be strong. But I felt like a small lost child myself, scared of tomorrow. How could I be strong enough for someone else when inside I was shaking so hard I could barely breathe?

"Do Granddaddy Longchamp and Gavin know what's happened yet?" I asked. "And Aunt Fern?"

Aunt Bet nodded. "I have Mr. Dorfman calling everyone who should be informed," she said.

"And Bronson and Grandmother Laura?"

"Yes. Bronson is beside himself. Thankfully, I think, your grandmother is too confused to understand."

"I'd better go see Jefferson," I said, sitting up again, this time more slowly. My body ached as if I had been running for hours and hours.

"He's still sleeping, Christie," Aunt Bet said. "I promise I'll let you know as soon as he awakens. Just lie here and rest," she ordered. "I'm going to see about Richard and Melanie. My poor dears: they are so upset." She sighed deeply, patted me on the hand and got up. "Rest," she said and shook her head. Her eyes shone with unshed tears. Then she turned and left me.

I closed my eyes and fought the urge to sob and sob and sob until my throat ached badly. A short time later, I heard someone enter my room and opened my eyes to see Uncle Philip carrying a tray with my cup of tea and toast on it. Although his face was ashen with grief and mourning, he had brushed his hair, straightened his clothing, buttoned his shirt and retied his tie, the knot as perfect as ever. He set the tray down on my night table and smiled. His eyes were no longer glazed with confusion.

"How's my poor princess doing?" he asked.

"I can't believe my parents are gone, Uncle Philip. I won't believe it," I said, shaking my head.

He fixed his eyes on me and I watched them grow small and dark. His lips trembled and then he turned back to the tray. "You need something hot in your stomach."

"Where's Mrs. Boston?" I asked.

"She's busy trying to settle everyone down and get some meals together, so I offered to bring your tray up to you," he said. "Try to sit up and drink some of this and maybe eat a bite or two."

"I want to do what the doctor says, but I don't think I can swallow anything right now, Uncle Philip."

"I know," he said, nodding sympathetically, "but you have to keep up your strength."

I sat up and he brought the tray to my lap and sat down on the bed.

"Oh Christie, Christie," he moaned and took my hand into his. "A terrible, terrible thing has happened," he began. His fingers moved over mine as he spoke. "And we are all suffering because of it, but I promised myself, I promised your mother I would take care of you."

"You promised? When?"

"When she ran back inside," he replied. "She cried out to me and said, 'If anything happens to me, take care of my Christie.' "

"Mommy said that?" He nodded. "What about Jefferson?"

"Oh, Jefferson too, of course. Anyway, I will. From now on," he said, the blue in his eyes softening, "you will be no different from my own. I will love and cherish you no less," he added, holding my hand tightly.

"We're going to be all right," he continued, his fingers traveling up my forearm and then down as if he were searching for an invisible line. "We're still a family and we'll rebuild the hotel quickly."

He looked up, his eyes small and determined. "We've got insurance and we'll put it right to work. Oh, we won't be able to open the hotel this summer, but we'll restore it to just the way it was before this horrible thing happened. Of course, we'll modernize so that it won't ever happen again."

I looked toward the doorway because I heard a lot of noise. Richard and Melanie were speaking loudly, too. They sounded excited, but not like people in mourning.

"What's going on?" I asked.

"Some of the staff are helping to move our things in," Uncle Philip said.

"Move in?" It never occurred to me that that was what would happen next.

"We're moving in whatever we can," he said. "Most of our things have been ruined by the fire. There was so much smoke. I wanted to get the other things out as quickly as I could." He smiled. "We're your family now," he said. "I would give everything not to have had this happen, but it has and we must do all the right things. After all, I'm a Cutler; I've inherited my grandmother's backbone," he added and straightened up as if to illustrate that literally. "She had a strength, a power to overcome any inconvenience."

"Inconvenience? This is more than an inconvenience, Uncle Philip," I snapped. No matter how great a woman Grandmother Cutler was thought to be and no matter what were her accomplishments, she would always remain the wicked witch in my mind because of the way she had treated Mommy.

"Of course. You're right. I didn't mean to make it sound small. What I do mean is to reassure you that I will always be here for you and we will build ourselves back and return to being the great family we were."

"Not without Mommy," I moaned, shaking my head. "Not without Daddy. We'll never be what we were."

"Of course not, but we've got to try. Your mother would have wanted us to try, wouldn't she? She wasn't the type to give up and crawl under the bed. She was too strong for that and I'm sure you will be, too. Am I right?" He brushed the hair from my forehead just the way Mommy often did.

"Yes," I said, looking down. "I suppose."

"Good. You have inherited very strong genes, Christie. Just think of the terrible things your mother endured and look how beautiful and successful she became. And she didn't even have a family behind her the way you will," he added. "I'll be right beside you, every step of the way. Every crisis you have will be my crisis, too; every obstacle, my obstacle." He smiled. "I hope you will accept my help. I'll always be right here, as well as Aunt Betty and your cousins."

"Where will you all sleep?" I asked, looking up quickly.

"For the time being, Richard and Melanie will share the guest room Fern uses whenever she's here. There are twin beds in it. Whenever Fern comes, she can sleep on the couch in the den or in one of the guest bungalows untouched by the fire."

"And you and Aunt Bet?" I anticipated the answer and it made me sick inside.

"We're going to have to use your parents' room, of course. In a day or so, when you're up to it, you can go in with Aunt Bet and tell her what things of your mother's you want to keep and what we should pack and put up in the attic. I wouldn't want to see everything stuffed away, of course. Your mother had some very pretty things, some of which might fit Betty."

The tears began streaming down my cheeks.

"Now, now, Christie, don't make me tell you all these details. It's too soon. Look at what it's doing to you," he said and leaned forward to kiss the tears away from my cheeks. But I pulled back.

"I'm all right," I said. "I've got to look in on Jefferson," I added.

"Of course. I'm in the process of making the funeral arrangements," he said, standing. I looked up quickly.

"When will it be?"

"In two days. We'll bury them in the old cemetery, of course."

"My mother wouldn't want to be too close to your grandmother," I fired back with heat in my face. He stared at me a moment and then smiled coldly.

"Don't worry. She can't be too close. The closest spot that's left is mine. There's plenty of room in the rear. I'm sorry about all this, terribly sorry. I wouldn't bother you with any of it, but I think you're old enough now to accept responsibility and understand some adult things."

"I want to know everything," I retorted, "every detail of what happens and what's to be done."

He nodded.

"Now that's the spirit I knew you had, the spirit she had. You've inherited more than just her beauty," he added, his eyes full of satisfaction. "You'll be just like her . . . you're just the way she was when I first met her—full of fire and spirit.

"Someday when our sorrow is not as thick, I'll sit down and tell you about those days." He sighed. "Well, I better see about the moving. Call me if you want anything. I will always and forever be here for you, Christie." He shook his head. "My little princess," he added and formed a small smile before he turned and left me trembling in my bed.

The phone began ringing and didn't stop for the rest of the day and night. Before I could go in to see Jefferson, he awoke and came to me. He stood in my doorway, his small fists grinding at his eyes.

"I want Mommy," he moaned and I looked up.

"Oh Jefferson." I held my arms out to him and he came running. Now it was I who was comforting him the way a mother would. I had suddenly been thrust into both roles: sister and mother forever.

"Where's Mommy and Daddy?" he asked. "Why didn't they come out of the hotel?"

"They couldn't, Jefferson. The fire was all around them and there was too much smoke."

"But why didn't Daddy try? Why?" Jefferson demanded, his sorrow beginning to change to anger.

"I'm sure he did try, but you saw how big the fire was."

"I want to go find them," he decided. "Now. Come on, Christie." He got off the bed and tugged on my hand. "Come on."

"The firemen found them, Jefferson."

"They did? Then where are they?" he asked, lifting his small shoulders.

I knew Jefferson understood what death was. We had had a cat: Fluffy, who had been hit by a car the previous year. Jefferson had been devastated. Daddy buried her behind the house and we had a little ceremony. There was still a marker out there. Jefferson knew what had happened to Mommy and Daddy. He just didn't want to face it.

"They're gone, Jefferson. They've gone to Heaven together."

"Why? Why did they leave us?"

"They had to," I said. "They didn't want to, but they had to."

"Why?" he demanded.

"Oh Jefferson." I started to cry. I knew I shouldn't; I knew the moment I did, he would cry, too. The sight of me bawling frightened him. I sucked in my breath quickly and bit down on my lower lip. "You've got to be a big boy now. We have to help each other. You're going to have to do many of the things Daddy used to do," I told him. That idea stopped his tears, but he embraced me again and buried his face against my bosom. I lay there, rocking him until Mrs. Boston appeared.

"Oh, he's here. I went to see how he was. How's he doing?"

"He'll be all right," I said quietly. My voice was bland, lifeless, my eyes staring ahead, vacant. I felt like a mannequin, a skeleton of myself. Mrs. Boston nodded. Her eyes were bloodshot from hours of crying, too.

"Gavin said to tell you he and his parents are on their way," Mrs. Boston said.

"Gavin called? When? Why didn't anyone tell me?" I asked quickly. Mrs. Boston scrunched up her face and shook her head.

"Miss Betty answers the phone every time it rings. She told him he couldn't talk to you just now, but she gave me the message," Mrs. Boston replied.

"I would have spoken to Gavin," I moaned. "She had no right . . ."

"Well, he will be here tomorrow, honey. No sense in making more trouble, everyone's plenty upset as it is," she added wisely. She came forward and put her arm around Jefferson. He turned and buried his face in the nook between her shoulder and neck. She winked at me and then picked him up.

"Jefferson needs something to drink and something to eat," she said. "Maybe some chocolate milk, okay?" Jefferson nodded, but kept his face buried.

I tried to smile at Mrs. Boston but failed. Thank God she was with us, I thought.

People began arriving to offer their condolences all the next day and into the evening. Aunt Bet made herself prim and proper and took over the house, greeting people and making arrangements. She made sure Richard and Melanie were dressed in their formal clothes: Richard wearing a dark blue suit and tie and Melanie wearing a dark blue dress with matching shoes. Both had their hair brushed and styled, not a lock out of place. They sat as still as statues on the sofa.

Aunt Bet came into my room to see what I would

be wearing and then went to see Jefferson. I followed her because I knew he wouldn't like her telling him what to wear. As I expected, when she went to his closet and began picking things out for him, he glared defiantly.

"My mommy says I can wear that only on special occasions," he snapped at her.

"This is a special occasion, Jefferson. You can't greet people looking like a ruffian, can you? You want to look nice."

"I don't care," Jefferson retorted. His face flamed red.

"Of course you care, dear. Now you will wear this and then, let's see . . ."

"I'll pick out the proper things for him to wear, Aunt Bet," I said, coming in behind her quickly.

"Oh." She stared a moment and then smiled. "Of course. I'm sure you'll choose the right things. Call me if you need anything, dear," she said and pivoted to leave.

"I'm not wearing what she wants me to wear," Jefferson repeated, his cheeks still crimson with anger.

"You don't have to," I said. "You can wear this outfit instead," I suggested. "If you want," I added. He glared a moment and then softened.

"Okay," he said. "But I'm not taking a bath."

"Suit yourself," I said, shrugging.

"Are you taking a bath?"

"I have to shower before I put on clothes," I said. "Mommy always liked you to be clean," I added pointedly. He thought a moment and then nodded.

"I'll take a shower too."

"Do you need any help?"

"I can do it by myself," he said sharply. I watched him begin to organize his clothes. He resembled a little old man. Tragedy and great sorrow, I thought, make us grow older very quickly.

Gavin, Edwina and Granddaddy Longchamp arrived late in the evening. Uncle Philip had them put up in one of the guest houses we used when the hotel became overbooked. One look at Granddaddy Longchamp's face was enough to tell me how much the tragedy had crushed and overwhelmed him. In one fell swoop, he had lost his son and the young woman he had always considered his daughter. He looked years older, the lines in his face sharply deeper, his eyes darker and his skin paler. He moved slowly and spoke very little. Edwina and I hugged and cried, and then Gavin and I had a chance to be alone.

"Where's Fern?" Gavin asked.

"No one seems to know," I said.

"She should have been the first one here to help you with Jefferson," Gavin said angrily.

"Maybe it's better she's not. She's never been much help to anyone but herself," I said. "Maybe she's feeling bad that she and Daddy had such a terrible argument the last time she saw him."

"Not Fern," Gavin concluded. We stared at each other. We had just naturally wandered away from everyone and found ourselves in the den. Mommy and Daddy often used it as a second office. There was a large cherrywood desk and chair, walls of bookcases, a big grandfather's clock and a ruby leather settee. Gavin gazed at the family pictures on the desk and shelves and at the framed letters of commendation Mommy had received for her performances at Sarah Bernhardt.

"She was so proud of those," I said. He nodded.

"I can't believe it," he said without turning to me. "I keep thinking I'm going to wake up soon."

"Me too."

"She was more than a sister-in-law to me. She was a sister," he said. "And I always wanted to be like Jimmy."

"You will be, Gavin. He was very proud of you and never stopped bragging about you and how well you do in school."

"Why did this happen? Why?" he demanded. Tears flooded my eyes and my lips began to tremble. "Oh, I'm sorry," he said, quickly coming to me. "I should be thinking of what you're going through and not be so concerned about myself." He embraced me and I pressed my face against his chest.

"What are you two doing in here?" Aunt Bet demanded. She was standing in the doorway, her eyes wide with surprise. I lifted my head slowly from Gavin and wiped my eyes.

"Nothing," I said.

"You shouldn't be alone here with everyone gathered in the living room," she said, gazing from Gavin to me and then to Gavin. "It's not . . . proper," she added. "And besides, Jefferson's not behaving. You had better speak to him, Christie," she said.

"What's he doing?"

"He won't sit still."

"He's only nine years old, Aunt Bet, and he's just lost his mother and father. We can't very well expect him to be as perfect as Richard," I retorted. Her face flamed red.

"Well, I . . . I'm just trying to—"

"I'll see to him," I said quickly and took Gavin's hand. "I'm sorry," I said after we had rushed past her. "I shouldn't have been so short with her, but she's been taking over everything and bossing everyone around. I just don't have the patience."

"I understand," Gavin said. "I'll help with Jefferson. Let's find him," he offered. Gavin was wonderful with him, taking him up to his room and occupying him with his games and toys.

Aunt Fern didn't arrive until the morning of the funeral. She appeared with one of her boyfriends from college, a tall, dark-haired young man. She introduced him only as Buzz. I couldn't believe she had decided to bring a boyfriend to the funeral. She behaved as if it were just another family affair. The whole time she was at the house before we left for church, she and Buzz remained aloof from the other mourners. A number of times I caught them giggling in a corner. They both chain-smoked. I reminded her that Mommy hated people smoking in the house.

"Look. Buzz and I are not going to be here that long, princess, so don't lay all the heavy rules on me, okay? The fruit doesn't fall far from the tree," she told Buzz, who smiled and nodded at me.

"Well, where are you going?" I asked.

"Back to school for a while. I don't know. I'm beginning to grow bored with the schedules and the homework," she said. Buzz laughed.

"Daddy wanted you to graduate from college," I said.

"My brother wanted to live my life for me," she said dryly. "Don't remind me. Well, he's gone now and I can't keep worrying about what other people want me to do. I've got to do what I want to do."

"But what will you do?" I asked.

"Don't worry about it," she whined. "I won't be coming around here that often, especially since Philip and his brood have taken over the place," she said.

"They haven't taken over the place," I insisted.

"Oh, no? What do you call it: a temporary situation?" She laughed.

"Yes," I said.

"Face reality, princess. You're too young to be on your own. Philip and Betty will become your guardians. Well, I don't intend for them to be mine. Cheer up," she added. "In a few years, you can leave, too."

"I won't leave my brother, ever."

"Famous last words, right, Buzz?" He nodded and smiled as if she had her fingers on his strings and he was only her puppet.

"I won't," I insisted. Aunt Fern could be so infuriating. Now that Daddy was gone, there wouldn't be anyone to watch over her and rescue her from the pools of trouble she usually fell into, I thought. She doesn't know it now, but she's going to miss him more than she ever dreamed. I left them as soon as I was told Aunt Trisha had arrived.

Aunt Trisha had begun her Broadway show and despite her great sorrow, had to perform. I didn't blame her; I knew the show must go on. Mommy always talked about the sacrifices people made when they became professional entertainers. But Aunt Trisha and I had time to cry together and console each other. Jefferson was happy to see her too, and rushed into her arms. She remained at our side from that moment until the end, when she had to leave to get back to New York.

The limousine led the line of traffic to the church. The thick gray sky was appropriate. I could just hear Daddy saying, "Oh no, the weather's going to make her even sadder still." The hearse had been parked on the side by the time we arrived. The church was overflowing with mourners. Bronson had Grandmother Laura sitting up front. She wore an elegant black dress and a black hat and veil. I saw she had put on pounds of makeup and had especially overdone the thickness of her lipstick. She seemed in a daze, confused, but still smiled at everyone and nodded as we filed in to take our places. Jefferson clung tightly to my hand and sat so close to me that he was practically on my lap.

As soon as the minister came out, the organ master stopped playing. The minister led the mourners in prayer and read from the Bible. Then he spoke lovingly and admiringly of Mommy and Daddy, calling them the two brightest lights in our community, always burning warmly and giving the rest of us reason to be hopeful and happy. He was sure they were doing the same for all the souls in Heaven.

Jefferson listened wide-eyed, but neither of us could shift our eyes off the two coffins for long. It still seemed unreal and impossible to believe that Mommy and Daddy were lying in them. When I turned to leave after the church service, I saw that most people had been crying, some quite hard.

The funeral procession went directly to the cemetery. At the site of their graves, Gavin held my hand and Aunt Trisha held Jefferson. We stood like statues, the cold breeze lifting my hair and making my tears feel like drops of ice on my cheeks. Just before the coffins were to be lowered, I stepped forward to kiss each one.

"Good-bye, Daddy," I whispered. "Thank you for loving me more than my real father could ever dream of loving me. In my heart you will always be my real father." I paused and had to swallow hard before I could continue.

"Good-bye, Mommy. You're gone, but you will never be far away from me."

I gazed up at Uncle Philip who had come up beside me. He was staring down at Mommy's coffin and the tears were streaming freely down his face and dripping off his chin. He touched the coffin softly and closed his eyes and then stepped back with me. The coffins were lowered.

I heard the sobbing. I wanted to comfort Jefferson, but I couldn't stop my own tears. Gavin embraced me. Granddaddy Longchamp had his head bowed and Edwina stood beside him, her arm around his waist. Fern wasn't laughing anymore, but she wasn't crying either. She looked tired and uncomfortable and her boyfriend looked confused, probably wondering what he was doing here. Bronson had managed to get Grandmother Laura back into her wheelchair and down to the gravesite. I could see he was explaining things to her and she was shaking her head, the realization of what had happened maybe just settling in.

"Come, everyone," Aunt Bet said, ushering Richard and Melanie ahead of her. "Let's go home."

Home? I thought. How can it ever be home without Mommy and Daddy there? It's just a shell of itself, a memory, a house full of shadows and old echoes, a place where we hang our clothes and lay down our heads, a place where we will eat a thousand meals more quietly than we had ever eaten them, for gone would be Daddy's laughter after he had just teased Mommy, gone was her singing and her warm smile, gone was her kiss and soft embrace to help keep the goblins and ghosts of our bad dreams from lingering behind.

The sky grew darker, the world was angry, and rightly so, I thought. We stumbled away from the gravesites, past the other deceased family, past the large monument for Grandmother Cutler. I was certain Mommy wouldn't have to face her again, for she could never be in Heaven.

"Remember, children," Aunt Bet said when we got back into the limousine. "Wipe your feet before you go into the house."

I looked up at her sharply and wondered if the nightmares had really only just begun.

Compromising

WITH UNCLE PHILIP SO DISTRAUGHT, AUNT BET HAD taken over the management of the reception at our house after the funeral. Just about everyone at the hotel was eager to do anything Aunt Bet wanted. Mr. Nussbaum and Leon cooked and baked what she thought was appropriate. They worked in the house under her supervision. She asked Buster Morris and other grounds people to bring over tables and benches and set them up on the front lawn. We knew there would be mobs of people coming to pay their last respects and console the family. Neither Jefferson nor I were in any mood to greet people, even people who sincerely wanted to show their love and sympathy; but I knew it was something we had to do, and anyway, Aunt Bet made sure to assign us our roles and position in the house.

"You and Jefferson will sit there, dear," she said, pointing to the sofa in the living room. "Melanie and Richard will sit beside you, of course, and I'll bring people to meet you."

"I don't want to meet people," Jefferson said, a little plaintively.

"Of course you don't, dear," Aunt Bet said,

smiling, "but you have to do it for your mother and father."

"Why?"

"He's always driving people crazy with questions," Richard commented, twisting up the corner of his mouth. His lips were as thin as rubber bands and sometimes, when he did that so severely, I thought they would snap.

"He has every right to ask questions, Richard," I said sharply.

"Of course, he does," Aunt Bet said in an annoying sing-song voice. She reached out to stroke Jefferson's hair, but he tried to move his head out of her reach. "You ask anything you want, dear."

Jefferson tightened his mouth and made his eyes small and hateful, but Aunt Bet just patted his head again and left us. Before we could argue about anything else, the people began arriving. Even Jefferson was impressed and overwhelmed. It seemed everyone who lived anywhere near Cutler's Cove appeared, and even some of our most faithful hotel guests had made the journey once they heard of the tragedy.

Aunt Bet flitted around like a canary, the boundaries of her cage being the living room and entry way. She greeted people and pointed them in our direction. It became exhausting rather quickly, but I couldn't help noticing that the people who embraced and kissed Jefferson and me were truly sorrowful. I'd never fully appreciated how many people Mommy and Daddy had touched.

Aunt Trisha looked after us as best she could, seeing that Jefferson and I had something to eat and drink. She remained as long as she was able to and then pulled us aside to say good-bye.

"I *have* to make this flight to New York," she said. "It breaks my heart to leave you two."

"I understand, Aunt Trisha," I said, recalling the way Daddy used to tease her. "After all, you're in the theater," I added, mimicking him. She smiled briefly.

"I'm going to miss them so much." She looked at Jefferson. He shook his head in bewildered fashion, the tears flowing. "Oh, pumpkin," she said, squeezing him tightly to her. "Be a good boy and listen to your aunt and uncle, okay?" Jefferson nodded reluctantly. "I'll call you soon, Christie, and maybe in a few weeks or so, you will be able to visit me in the city and come to the show every night. Would you like that?"

"Very much, Aunt Trisha."

She stood up, biting down on her lower lip and nodding. Then she spun around as if chased by ghosts and fled from us. Only minutes later, Gavin came to tell me Granddaddy Longchamp was anxious to go, too.

"It's tearing him apart to sit here and see all these people in mourning parade by," Gavin explained. "He's even willing to sit in the airport lobby and wait."

"I understand," I said even though my heart dropped with the news Gavin would be going.

"He said I could come back soon to visit," Gavin said.

"Oh Gavin, you were going to work here this summer. We were going to have so much fun together," I reminded him. His eyes told me I didn't have to.

"Mother wants you two to return to the sofa," Richard said, shoving himself between us. "She says there are still a number of important people to greet."

"Hey," Gavin said, turning sharply on him, "make like the wind and blow."

"Huh?"

"Make like a tree and leave, get it?"

Richard's mouth twisted in confusion for a moment. Then it all registered.

"I'm just doing what Mother said to do," he whined defensively.

"Well, now do what I say to do." Gavin's furious face turned him around quickly and sent him running.

I laughed; it felt so good to do so.

"Do me a favor, Jefferson," Gavin said, "tie his socks together every morning, will you?"

"Yeah," Jefferson said, his eyes brightening.

"Don't you dare, Jefferson. Gavin, he doesn't need new ideas."

"If he bothers you, tell him I'll be back," Gavin told Jefferson.

"Daddy wants to go, honey," Edwina said softly, stepping up beside us. "He's not doing too well," she added apologetically to me. "Philip's having the limo take us."

"I'll walk you out," I said.

"Me too," Jefferson echoed. He wasn't going to leave my side for a second.

When we stepped out front, we saw Aunt Fern and her boyfriend over by one of the tables laughing and joking with some of the waiters and bellhops. She didn't appear to be bereaved; she could have just as well been a stranger who had wandered onto the grounds. Edwina went over to her to tell her they were leaving, but she wasn't very interested.

"Sure, good-bye," she said and waved quickly at Gavin and Granddaddy Longchamp.

"She doesn't act like any child of mine," he muttered, "and certainly no child of Sally Jean's. I guess she must take after some of the bad eggs on my side of the family. We sure had more than our fair share of 'em," he added. I was intrigued and wondered if Gavin knew any of his own dark history.

"Well now, you take care of yourself, Christie," Granddaddy Longchamp said, turning his big, sad eyes on me. "And look after your brother the way your Momma and Papa would have wanted you to. And you call us if there's anything we can do for you children, understand?"

"Yes, Granddaddy. Thank you," I said. He took one last look at the house and then bent over to get into the limousine. Edwina followed.

"I'll call and write as much as I can," Gavin said. "I hate leaving you like this," he added, his eyes soft with sympathy. I nodded, my eyes down. He ran his hand through Jefferson's hair and then, quickly, almost so quickly that I couldn't feel it and no one could have seen it, he leaned forward and kissed me on the cheek. By the time I opened my eyes, he was lunging into the limousine behind his parents.

Jefferson and I stood there holding hands, watching it disappear down the driveway. Suddenly, I was chilled. Twilight had come like a quickly dropped shade and deepened all the shadows around us.

"There you are, children," Aunt Bet cried from the front door. "You two just have to come back inside and man your stations," she declared.

"We're both tired, Aunt Bet," I said, still holding on to Jefferson's hand and walking past her. "We're going upstairs now."

"Oh—but, dear, what about all the new people who have just arrived?" she cried despondently. Shc grimaced as though our absence would be the real tragedy of the day.

"I'm sure they'll understand," I said quietly. "As should you."

"But . . ."

We walked, heads down, and made our way quickly up the stairway as if we really didn't belong, orphans in our own home.

I took Jefferson to my room, knowing he wouldn't want to be alone. The noise and commotion downstairs continued for hours. Not long after we had retired, Bronson Alcott came up to see us. He knocked on the door and poked his head in when I asked who was there. Jefferson had fallen asleep beside me on the bed, but I could only lie there, my eyes open, staring at the ceiling.

"Oh, I didn't want to wake you," he said, retreating.

"It's all right, Bronson. Please, come in," I said, sitting up and running my fingers through my hair. He stepped into the room and smiled at Jefferson.

"Poor little tyke," he said, shaking his head. "It's not easy for anyone, but for him, it's especially hard. I remember how hard it was for me to lose my mother, and I was quite a bit older."

"How did she die?"

"She contracted a blood cancer," he said sadly.

"And left you to look after your crippled sister?" I recalled some of the details Mommy had once told me. He nodded. And now he's looking after poor Grandmother Laura, I thought sadly.

"How's Grandmother?" I asked.

"She's all right. I left her with the nurse," he said, "so I could come up here to see you two."

"Does she understand what's happened?"

He nodded softly.

"She goes in and out, remembering, then forgetting . . . maybe she's better off. Maybe it's the mind's way of protecting itself against so much sorrow."

"You have your hands full," I said.

"That's what your mother used to say," he replied, smiling. "Laura Sue wasn't always like this, you know. She was once a vivacious, energetic, sparkling woman, full of excitement and laughter, tormenting every man in sight."

"Mommy told me. Bronson," I said after a moment, "you know so much about this family, do you think there's truly a curse on it?" I asked.

"A curse? Oh no, not a curse, despite all this. Don't think that way. I'm sure you will live up to your parents' expectations and do wonderful things," he said reassuringly. Numbly, I shook my head.

"I don't want to do wonderful things anymore. Without Mommy . . ."

"Nonsense now, Christie. You must continue your pursuit of music more than ever," he instructed firmly. "You must do it for her, as much as for yourself."

"But I can't help feeling I'm destined to fail, that these dark clouds . . ."

He knitted his eyebrows together.

"Christie, fate can be cruel sometimes, but it is also fate that has given you your talent. Think of that. Fate sends us down a road, sometimes good, sometimes bad, but if it sends us down a good road and we ignore it or reject it, we are bringing our own curses down on ourselves. Be all that you are capable of being. You have an obligation now to do so," he warned.

I nodded. He was so firm, so strong. No wonder Mommy loved and admired him, I thought. And then a new and wonderful idea blossomed.

"I don't want to live with Uncle Philip and Aunt Bet," I said, "and neither does Jefferson."

"I understand, but they have first claims on being your guardians and with them having to move in here and all, it makes the most sense. It won't be easy, not for a while, maybe not ever, but you're at least with people who care about you and love you. I'm sure Philip will be as much of a father to you and Jefferson as he is to his own children," he said. He saw the disappointment in my face.

"I wish . . . I wish I could take you two to live with us, but I'm afraid my home is not the best environment for two young people right now. Laura Sue is an invalid most of the time, and although she loves you, whenever she has clear enough thinking to do so, she would be only a burden to you as well."

"I'd be willing to accept that," I said quickly. He smiled.

"It's going to be all right here. Don't worry," he said reassuringly. "And I'll come around as often as I can to see that you and Jefferson are doing well."

I bowed my head so he wouldn't see the tears flood my eyes.

"There, there now. You'll be fine, Christie," he said, his voice tender with understanding. He leaned over to kiss me on the cheek. Then he looked lovingly at Jefferson. "As soon as I think it's appropriate, I'll have you and Jefferson over for dinner one night," he said. "It will be good for Laura Sue, too." He started toward the door.

"Bronson?"

"Yes, dear?"

"Before this happened, Mommy told me things about the past, things that have always been kept locked in closets, but there was much she never got to tell me, much I still wonder about. Will you tell me these things?"

"As much as I know," he pledged. "When everything's calmed down, you and I will spend an afternoon together just talking about the past and your family, okay?"

I nodded.

"Thank you, Bronson."

"I was very, very fond of your mother, Christie. She developed a certain wisdom beyond her years, maybe because of some of the difficult things you know about and will learn about, but she had unique insight, patience, understanding. I'm sure you've inherited it. You'll see," he said and then he left.

No one looked in on us after that. The funeral reception took on a lighter tone as it dragged into the evening. I heard more laughter, more cars coming and going, doors slamming, people calling to each other. Jefferson woke up and cried for our mother. I comforted him and he fell asleep again. While he slept, I sat on the floor by my closet and thumbed through old photo albums, smiling and crying over pictures of Mommy and Daddy.

She had been so beautiful, I thought, so very, very beautiful.

I embraced my knees and lowered my head to them, trying to restrain the sorrow and tears that threatened to ravage my body. While I was still on the floor by the closet, my door was thrust open.

"Oh, there he is," Richard said.

"What do you want? Don't you knock first?" I demanded. He smirked.

"Mother sent me looking for him. He's got to move some of his things or I'll move them," he added.

"What are you talking about? He doesn't have to move anything," I said standing up. "Especially tonight."

"Mother says it isn't right for Melanie and I to be sleeping in the same room. We're too old for that. She says boys should be with boys. She is going to have some men move my bed into Jefferson's room. I want him to make room for my stuff in the closets and dresser drawers. If he doesn't, I'll do it myself," he threatened.

I shuddered to think of it. Jefferson would hate having Richard hovering over him day and night, and Richard wasn't like any other twelve-year-old-boy I knew. He was so prim and proper with his things. He would surely get into terrible fights with Jefferson over the messy way Jefferson took care of his possessions.

"Don't you dare touch his things," I cried.

"What . . . what's the matter, Christie?" Jefferson said, sitting up quickly and rubbing his eyes.

"Nothing. Go back to sleep. I've got to go downstairs and speak to Aunt Bet," I said and marched out of the room, practically pushing Richard out of my way.

There were still many people in the house having coffee and cake. Some stragglers had come in to feast on what remained of the trays and trays of food Mr. Nussbaum and Leon had prepared. I looked around for Aunt Bet or Uncle Philip. People smiled at me and some stopped me to offer condolences, but I went quickly from room to room until I found Aunt Bet saying good night to some people on the front porch. I didn't know where Uncle Philip was; I hadn't seen him anywhere in the house.

"Oh Christie, dear," she said when I appeared.

"You've come down. How nice. Are you hungry, dear?"

"No, Aunt Bet, I'm not hungry," I snapped. She held her smile. "I'm upset. Why are you having Richard's things moved into Jefferson's room tonight of all nights?"

"Oh, I just thought the faster they started to share things, the better it would be for them. I thought Richard would be good company for him and comfort him. And really, dear," she said, stepping up to me, "you don't want me to keep Richard and Melanie sleeping in the same room any longer than I have to. Melanie's becoming a young lady and all young ladies need their privacy and their space, don't they?" she said. "You do," she added firmly.

"I'm not saying no, Aunt Bet, but Jefferson has just been at his parents' funeral. He doesn't need to be upset any more tonight. We can wait to discuss the sleeping arrangements," I retorted. "I think we should have something to say about it anyway. This is our house," I added, my flag of pride hoisted.

Aunt Bet held her smile.

"Where's Uncle Philip?" I demanded.

"He's in and out, dear, but he's been too upset to really be of any help right now. I'm only trying to do what's best," she said.

"What's best is not to shove Richard into Jefferson's room tonight. It's going to be hard enough for him to go to sleep, and he's much too tired to start rearranging his closets and dressers now."

"Very well, dear," Aunt Bet said. "It will wait until morning, if that makes you happier." She smiled, but something about that smile seemed false. It was a queer, shadowy smile.

"Not having it happen at all would make me happier," I said.

"We've all got to make compromises right now, Christie," she replied somewhat sternly. "Your loss is great, but we've lost much too. We've lost our home and the hotel and . . ."

"All that can be replaced, Aunt Bet," I said, shocked she would even think of making a comparison. A fiery rush of blood heated my face. "Can you bring back my mommy and daddy? Can you?" I cried, the hot tears streaming down my cheeks.

"All right, dear," she said, cowering back. "I'm sorry I upset you." She flicked a smile at some people who were leaving. "We'll discuss it tomorrow. Please tell Richard to come down to see me," she said and left me quickly to say good-bye to some members of the hotel staff.

I pivoted and quickly charged back upstairs. Richard was already in Jefferson's room. When I threw open the door, I found him rearranging Jefferson's closet.

"LEAVE HIS THINGS ALONE!" I screamed. Richard stopped and scowled at me. "Aunt Bet wants to see you immediately. You will not be moving your things in here tonight," I said firmly. "Now get out." I stepped back, standing firmly as a rooted tree, and pointed.

"This room isn't half as nice as the room I had," he muttered.

"Then don't bother coming into it again," I said to his back. He hurried down the corridor and the stairs. Jefferson was standing in my doorway, his face streaked from tears, his eyes drooping with fatigue and confusion.

"Come on, Jefferson," I said. "I'll get you ready for your own bed now."

"Where's Richard going?" he asked.

"To blazes for all I care," I said and helped my little brother wash and dress for another night on this earth without his parents.

When I returned to my room, I was surprised to find Aunt Fern sorting through the clothes in my closet.

"Aunt Fern," I cried. I looked around and didn't see her boyfriend. "What are you doing?"

"Hello, princess." She flashed a silly smile at me. I didn't have to draw too close to smell the odor of whiskey. "I was just looking at some of your sweaters. You've got some nice stuff. I especially like this watch," she said, holding up her left wrist. "Can I borrow it a while?" It was my birthday present from Mommy and Daddy.

"Take that off!" I cried. "That was my last present from Mommy and Daddy."

"Oh." She wobbled.

"You can have anything else," I said. "Please."

"Hold your water," she replied and struggled to get it off her wrist, nearly ripping the band apart. She dropped it harshly on the bed. I scooped it up quickly, vowing to myself never to take it off my wrist again. "You could be a little nicer to me," she moaned. "I'm leaving and who knows when you'll see me again."

"Aren't you going to stay overnight?"

"There were some end-of-the-year parties at some fraternities I wanted to attend," she said. She sauntered over to my vanity table and inspected my perfumes and colognes.

"You really aren't going to attend summer school like you promised Daddy, are you?" I asked.

"No," she said. "I'm going to spend the summer with some of my spoiled, rich friends on Long

Island. I've already told Philip and told him where to send my allowance. But I don't think he heard much of what I said, so I'm sure I'll be calling Dorfman."

"But I thought you had to make up the courses you failed this year," I said.

She spun around.

"You know you're just like an old lady . . . nag, nag, nag. When I was sixteen, I had already lost my virginity." She laughed at the expression on my face. "You read the chapter, didn't you? Didn't you?" she accused. "That's all right, keep your little secrets," she said bitterly, "everyone else in this family does. Your mother certainly did."

"Don't you say anything nasty about my mother," I spat back at her. She wobbled again and shook her head.

"It's time you stopped living like Alice in Wonderland. Your mother and Daddy grew up living in the same room, practically on top of each other until she was sixteen, and after that, she fell in love with Philip without knowing he was her brother. What do you think they did on their dates, play paint-by-numbers? Of course, they would keep all that secret, but I never let any of them tell me what to do. None of them are better than me."

"That's not true; that's not true about my mother and Uncle Philip," I said. She shrugged.

"Ask him one day," she said. "And while you're at it, ask him about all the times he walked in on me while I was dressing and he claimed he was looking for Jimmy or Dawn.

"Take one look at his wife, Christie, and you can understand why he looks elsewhere."

"That's terrible, Aunt Fern. I know you're drunk again and you're saying horrible things because of that, but it's not a good enough excuse anymore. I don't want to hear any more," I said.

She laughed.

"You don't?" She walked toward me, her face twisted in a vicious imitation of a smile. "You don't want to hear how Dawn and Jimmy thought they were brother and sister but still slept in their underwear beside each other on pull-out sofas?"

"Stop it!" I said, putting my hands over my ears.

"You don't want to hear how your mother French-kissed with Uncle Philip, how she swooned when the most handsome boy in her high school kissed her on the neck?"

"STOP!" I ran into the bathroom and slammed the door. Then I embraced myself and crouched down on the floor, sobbing. I heard her laugh and then I heard her come up to the door.

"All right, Princess Christie, I'll leave you in your wonderland. I feel sorry for you. They always pampered you and favored you. It was Christie this and Christie that. You were the most wonderful and talented little girl and I was a load of trouble. Well, you're on your own now, just like I was really. See how you like it," she spat. I heard her footsteps as she pounded her way out of my room.

For a while I just lay there, crying. How ugly and hateful she could be, I thought. Daddy wanted only to make her happy and Mommy tried so hard to love her and treat her fairly. I was glad she was leaving and I hoped she would never come back.

I got up slowly and washed my face. I thought it would take hours and hours for me to fall asleep, but once I lay my head down on my pillow, emotional exhaustion washed over me like an ocean wave, and it wasn't until the dismal, gray light of early morning, a morning with bruised angry clouds traveling across the sky like a caravan of singed camels, seeped in through my curtains that I opened my eyes. I gazed straight ahead. The sight of my black dress draped over a chair reminded me painfully that what had happened and what we had done yesterday were not part of some horrid nightmare, but were events in horrid reality instead.

But before my eyes could even begin to tear again, the small sound of someone sighing spun me around, and I was shocked to discover Uncle Philip. He had pulled a chair up to the other side of my bed and was sitting there gazing at me wistfully. His hair was messed and his shirt was open. He wore no tie or jacket. I thought he looked very pale and very tired.

"Uncle Philip!" I cried, clinging to my blanket. Some of the hateful things Aunt Fern had said lingered like mold on the walls of my memory. "What are you doing here?" I had no idea how long he had been sitting there, staring at me while I slept.

He sighed again, louder and longer.

"I couldn't sleep," he said, "and I was worried about you, so I came by to see how you were doing and I guess I fell asleep in this chair. I haven't been awake much longer than you," he concluded, but I thought he looked like someone who had been awake all night.

"I'm all right, Uncle Philip," I said, still confused by the look on his face and his actions.

"No, no, I know you well. I know how fragile and sensitive you are and what you are suffering," he said and leaned forward. His eyes turned softer, meeting and locking with mine. "You need extra-tender loving care and I mean to give it to you as best as I can." He smiled softly, his eyes two pools of tenderness, and then he kissed my forehead. "Poor, poor Christie," he said, stroking my hair.

I relaxed. "It's all right, Uncle Philip. Go get some sleep yourself. I'm fine," I said. He continued to smile and stroke my hair lovingly.

"Dear, dear Christie. Lovely Christie, Dawn's Christie. I remember the day she brought you back to the hotel. I told her not to worry that your real father had deserted you. I would always be a father to you, too. And I will. I will," he promised.

"All right, Uncle Philip. Thank you," I said. I sat up quickly and leaned away from him. "I'm all right now. I'm going to get up and shower and dress and get Jefferson up. Usually, he's in here by now," I added. Uncle Philip nodded. Then he sat back and took a deep breath with his eyes closed. He pressed on his knees and stood up. With his shoulders slumped, he started to leave. He stopped at the door.

"I'll shower and dress, too," he said. "So we can all have breakfast together . . . like a family."

As soon as he left, I got out of bed and went into the bathroom. I stood under the hot shower for as long as I could. It was as if I were scrubbing the sorrow off my body as well as washing away the fatigue. I dressed as quickly as I could and went in to see if Jefferson was awake. Mrs. Boston had already gotten there and helped him get dressed. He was in the bathroom brushing his hair. He stopped to look at me as soon as he heard me enter.

"Oh, good morning, Mrs. Boston," I said.

"Good morning, honey. I came looking in on Brother," she told me, "but he was already awake and thinking about getting up and getting dressed. He really is a big boy now," she added more for his benefit than mine.

"Yes, he is. You didn't have to do this and get breakfast for everyone, too, Mrs. Boston," I said. She wasn't family, but she couldn't have taken my parents' deaths any harder even if she was.

"That's okay, honey. Your aunt Betty, she was up bright and early this morning laying out the orders for what she wanted served. I got it set up and waiting, so I figured I'd slip up here and look in on Jefferson," she explained.

"What is it she wanted served?" I asked, curious.

"It seems she takes her eggs poached and Master Richard takes his soft-boiled, not longer than one minute precisely, as does Miss Melanie. Mr. Cutler, he just has coffee and toast. She's very particular about her toast. She likes it just lightly cooked, and the children, they want strawberry jam. Luckily, we had some in the pantry," she added. "Otherwise, I would have had to get up even earlier to get some."

"Mommy was never so particular," I commented. Mrs. Boston nodded.

"I'd better get down there. She told me they'd all be sitting down at eight this morning sharp," she said and started out.

Jefferson stepped out of the bathroom and looked at me. Neither of us wanted to go downstairs and face the first morning without our parents, but there was nothing else we could do. I reached out for his hand and he gave it to me slowly, his head down. Then we went downstairs.

Everyone was seated at the table, Uncle Philip sitting where Daddy used to sit and Aunt Bet sat where Mommy would have. Jefferson was annoyed immediately by that, but also by the fact that Richard was sitting in what was usually his place and Melanie was sitting in mine.

"Good morning, children," Aunt Bet said with a syrupy smile. "How nice and clean you both look."

Jefferson glared back at her and then turned toward Richard.

"I sit there," Jefferson said.

"Oh, where we all sit isn't that important," Aunt Bet quickly replied, keeping her smile. "As long as we sit properly and eat our meals politely. We should always remember," she instructed before we had even taken any seats, "that there are other people eating at the table and they might be upset if we don't follow the proper etiquette."

I looked at Uncle Philip. Although he had a small, tight smile on his face, his eyes looked glazed. He looked like a man who was still in a daze. He said nothing; he just waited, his hands tented and under his chin, his elbows on the table. Richard sat back, a self-satisfied smile on his face. Melanie looked bored and annoyed.

"We can't begin until you take your seats, children," Aunt Bet said.

"Maybe Christie should sit here, beside me," Uncle Philip said, indicating where Richard was sitting. "After all, she is the oldest child."

"I'll sit with my brother," I replied quickly. I moved Jefferson and myself to the table, placing myself beside Melanie. I nodded to the seat across from me and Jefferson took it reluctantly.

"Now, then, we're all together," Aunt Bet declared. "Mrs. Boston, you can begin," she commanded.

"Yes, ma'am," Mrs. Boston said from the kitchen and brought out the pitcher of juice. Usually she placed it at the center of the table and we just served ourselves. Mrs. Boston helped Mommy with the preparation of food and looked after the house, but we never made her into a waitress, too. Neither Aunt Bet nor Uncle Philip lifted the pitcher to pour the juice, however. They sat back and waited for

Mrs. Boston to do so. She winked at me and began pouring juice into everyone's glass.

"Now then," Aunt Bet began, her hands clasped on the table before her, "it will be in everyone's interest to set ground rules right away, don't you think?" Her smile became colder, sharper. "Philip will be busy with the reconstruction of the hotel," she began, "which means I will have to bear most of the responsibility for looking after you children this summer. I want everyone to get along, of course. Our lives have been dramatically disrupted and changed. Everyone . . . everyone," she repeated, fixing her eyes on me, "has to make some compromises, but I don't see why," she added, bursting into a brighter smile, "we all can't become one happy family."

She turned to Uncle Philip, who, I thought, was watching intensely for my reactions.

"Philip always wanted us to have a larger family. Now, he's got one. But," she said, sighing, "all this responsibility has fallen on his shoulders like an avalanche. Richard and Melanie understand how important it is to be cooperative." At the mention of their names, the twins widened their eyes simultaneously and turned toward us. "We've got to want to help each other," she concluded.

Mrs. Boston began bringing out the eggs and serving. Richard put his spoon into his soft-boiled egg and smirked.

"It's too hard," he complained immediately.

"I didn't cook it more than a minute," Mrs. Boston said.

"Let me see that," Aunt Bet demanded and Richard handed his dish to her. She poked the egg with her spoon and shook her head. "Maybe the fire was too hot or something, but this is a bit too hard for Richard."

Mrs. Boston became upset.

"I think I've made enough eggs in my time to know if the fire's too hot or not," she said.

"It must have been this time," Aunt Bet insisted. "Or maybe you just misread the clock."

"I thought we were all going to make some compromises," I said quickly. "A few seconds more or less boiling an egg doesn't seem like much of one to me."

Aunt Bet's eyes turned to glass for a moment but just when I thought they would shatter and spray me with the slivers, she smiled.

"Christie's perfectly right, Richard. This isn't so bad and after a while, I'm sure Mrs. Boston will get better at preparing eggs the way you like them," she said, handing the dish back to her son, who grimaced.

"I'll eat as much as I can," he offered.

"That's very nice of you, Richard," she said. I nearly laughed at the way Mrs. Boston raised her eyebrows and shifted her eyes in my direction. She finished serving the eggs. Jefferson just poked at his. He'd only sipped once at his juice.

"Jefferson," Aunt Bet said. "You're going to eat, aren't you? We don't want to waste any food."

Reluctantly, Jefferson put a forkful in his mouth.

"Christie, dear. Wasn't Jefferson ever taught to place his napkin on his lap?" Aunt Bet asked.

"Yes," I said. "But I don't think he's worrying about that right now."

"Neatness and cleanliness are the twin sisters of a healthy, happy life," Aunt Bet recited. "We always have to worry about those things.

"I know," she said, continuing, "that your parents had so much on their minds because of the hotel. That's why this house . . ." She shook her head.

"What about this house?" I asked quickly.

"It was probably too much for them to look after it and the hotel at the same time. But that's not going to be a problem for me," she said, leaning over and smiling.

"I don't understand. What's wrong with our house?"

"It could be a great deal cleaner and neater, dear," she replied nodding.

"This house is always very clean. Mrs. Boston works very hard and Mommy never complained," I cried.

"Precisely my point, dear. Your mother didn't have time to complain or be concerned. She had so much responsibility at the hotel. But don't you let this worry you. I've decided I'll get this house into proper condition, which was another reason why I want to get our sleeping arrangements settled quickly.

"Now after breakfast, Richard and Jefferson will work out the arrangements for their room," she declared firmly.

"It's my room!" Jefferson retorted. "And I don't want him in it!"

First Aunt Bet's face paled and then her cheeks flushed crimson and her eyes tightened at the corners. She flicked a look at Uncle Philip, who had been sipping his coffee and staring ahead like a man under hypnosis. He didn't disagree with anything she said, nor did he seem at all interested in any of it.

"It's not nice to raise our voices at the table, Jefferson," Aunt Bet said slowly. "If you have something to say, say it softly. Now then," she continued, "I know it's your room, but for a while, until we find other solutions, you're going to have to share it with your cousin.

"You're both young boys," she continued, smiling. "You should be happy to have a companion like Richard. Why, it's as if you suddenly had an older brother. Won't that be nice?"

"No," Jefferson replied, threw down his fork, and folded his arms tightly across his chest.

"That's not nice behavior at the table," Aunt Bet said firmly. "After today, if you don't behave properly, you won't be able to sit and eat with the family."

"I don't care," Jefferson said defiantly.

"He's just like that in school, too," Melanie whined. "Always talking back to his teachers."

"I bet you threw away your bad report card, didn't you?" Richard added.

"Stop it!" I screamed and stood up. "All of you, stop picking on him. Don't you have any feelings for him?" I said, going around the table to his side.

"Christie," Aunt Bet said, "there is no need to get so upset and ruin our first breakfast together."

"Yes there is," I said. "There's a need to scream and shout when people are so mean, especially people who are your relatives and are supposed to love and care for you more. Come on, Jefferson." I took his hand and we started away.

"Where are you going?" Aunt Bet cried. "You haven't finished your breakfast. And you should always ask to be excused from the table."

"Christie!" Uncle Philip called as if he just realized something was happening.

I didn't reply, nor did I turn around. I led Jefferson out of the dining room and out of the house. I didn't know where I was going. I just walked. Tears streamed down my face, but I didn't sob. Jefferson was practically running to keep up with me as I charged down the stairs and sidewalk. No one came after us.

Ahead of us was the charred remains of the hotel. The sight of the blackened shell, the broken windows, the dangling sides of the building, wires exposed, furniture tossed and destroyed caused my heart to sink even further.

I took Jefferson to the rear of the hotel and we sat in the gazebo, where we watched the bulldozers and the men tear down the destroyed remains of walls. Neither of us spoke. Jefferson laid his head against me and the two of us tried to keep warm under the heavily overcast and gray sky that made the ocean breeze even more chilling. Could we ever be sadder than we were at this moment? I wondered.

Unclean

WITH OUR PARENTS' DEATHS AND THE SUBSEQUENT UPheaval of our lives, nightmares began to shadow our days and cast a film of gray over everything, even the bluest sea and sky. I could see and feel the pain in my little brother Jefferson's eyes. He often gazed about the world angrily. I understood his wrath. Someone should have warned him that the young and the beautiful and the desperately needed can die and be gone forever.

Aside from me, who would now hear or care about his complaints and sympathize? No one could ever give him the same smiles and love Mommy and Daddy had. Slowly, like a flower without any sunlight, he began to close up. First, he slept longer and later, and when he was awake, he would often lie listlessly, uninterested in his toys and games. He seldom spoke unless he was asked a question.

Two days after our horrid first breakfast with Uncle Philip's family, Aunt Bet was true to her word. She had one of the beds from what used to be Fern's room moved into Jefferson's. Richard wanted to be closer to the window, so Jefferson's bed was shoved all the way to the right and the dressers were rearranged. When Jefferson refused to cooperate and move his things, Aunt Bet assisted Richard in reorganizing the room.

Richard made labels out of adhesive tape and printed his name boldly on the white strips. Then he pasted them over the drawers that were to be his. Because they had lost so much in the fire, Aunt Bet took the twins shopping and returned with bags and boxes of new clothes, underwear and socks. Richard then made an inventory of his things and neatly folded them in his drawers. When he complained he didn't have enough room, Aunt Bet consolidated Jefferson's clothes even more to provide Richard with an additional set of drawers and more closet space. She then ordered Mrs. Boston to go over and over the carpet, insisting it was so dirty, she wouldn't want Richard to take his socks off and put his naked foot down.

"I do that room every day, Miss Betty," Mrs. Boston protested. "That rug don't have a chance to get that dirty."

"Your idea of what clean is and my idea are obviously miles apart," Aunt Bet declared. "Please, just do it again," she said. She then proceeded to go about the house inspecting shelves, checking the corners of rooms, running her fingers over appliances and under tables, finding dust and dirt everywhere. Melanie followed her around with a pen and pad and took notes. At the end of the inspection, Aunt Bet gave the sheets filled with complaints to Mrs. Boston and asked her to attend to these things immediately.

Not having spent much time in their living quarters at the hotel, I never realized how obsessed with cleanliness Aunt Bet was. The sight of a cobweb would throw her into a tirade and when Melanie brought her hand out from under a sofa and demonstrated dust on her palm, Aunt Bet nearly swooned.

"We're shut up in here so much of our time," she explained to Mrs. Boston, "and we're breathing this filth. Dust and grime is going in and out of our lungs, even when we sleep!"

"Ain't never had any complaints about my work before, Miss Betty," Mrs. Boston said indignantly, "and I worked for the toughest woman this side of the Mississippi, Grandmother Cutler."

"She was just as busy and distracted as my poor dead sister-in-law was," Aunt Bet replied. "I'm the first mistress of Cutler's Cove who's not wrapped up in the business so much she can't see the dust in the air in her own home."

Aunt Bet took personal control of the cleaning and reorganizing of my parents' room. She had some men take out all the furniture and then had the rugs steam-cleaned as if my parents had been full of contamination. Jefferson and I stood off to the side and watched her supervise the work. All of Mommy and Daddy's things were piled outside the door. The walls of the closets were papered over, the drawers in the dressers relined, the mirrors and furniture cleaned and polished.

"I'm going to have all this neatly packed and placed in the attic," she told me, indicating Mommy and Daddy's clothes and shoes, "except for anything I can use or anything you need now. Go through it neatly and take what you want," she ordered.

It broke my heart to do it, but there were many of Mommy's things I didn't want to see shut away in the dark, damp corners of the attic. I quickly pulled out the dress she had worn to my Sweet Sixteen party. There were sweaters and skirts and blouses that were dear to me because I could still vividly see

Mommy wearing them. When I held them in my hands and brought them to my face, I could smell the scent of her cologne, and for a moment, it was as if she were still there, still beside me, smiling and stroking my hair lovingly.

Aunt Bet seized all Mommy's jewelry quickly, and when I protested about that, she said she would only be holding these things until I was old enough to appreciate them.

"I'll keep exact account of what was hers and what's mine," she promised and flicked me one of her short, slim smiles.

She had the linens and bedding changed and, literally overnight, redid the curtains and blinds. Then she attacked their bathroom, deciding she wanted to change the wallpaper.

"In fact," she declared at dinner one night after all this had started, "we should reconsider all the walls in this house. I was never crazy about the decor."

"You have no right to make all these changes," I retorted. "This house still belongs to my parents and us."

"Of course it does, dear," she said, her thin lips curled up at the corners, "but while you're underage, your uncle Philip and myself are your guardians and have the awesome responsibility of making important decisions, decisions that will affect your lives."

"Changing wallpaper and repainting the house is not going to affect our lives!" I responded.

"Of course it is," she replied with a small, thin laugh. "Your surroundings, where you live, have a major impact on your psychological well-being."

"We like it the way it is!" I cried.

She shook her head.

"You don't know what you like yet, Christie dear. You're far too young to understand these things, and Jefferson . . ."

She looked at him and he swung his eyes up to glare back at her.

"Poor Jefferson is barely able to care for his basic needs. Trust me, my dear. I was brought up surrounded by the best things. My parents hired the most expensive and renowned decorators and I learned what good taste is and what it isn't. Your parents, although they were delightful people, grew up in the most dire poverty. Wealth and position were thrust upon them and they didn't have the breeding to understand what had to be done and how to spend their money."

"That's not true!" I cried. "Mommy was beautiful. Mommy loved pretty things. Everyone complimented her on the things she did at the hotel. She . . ."

"Just as you say, dear, at the hotel, but not at her own home. This was"—she looked around as if we had lived in a hovel—"merely a retreat, a place to which they could run away for a few hours. They did all their real socializing at the hotel. Rarely did they have important guests to dinner here, right?" she sang. She leaned toward me. "That's why Mrs. Boston, as sweet as she is, is not really schooled in serving properly. She didn't have to do it very much, if at all.

"But all that is going to have to change now, especially in light of the fact that the hotel has been destroyed and is being rebuilt. While that's being done, Philip and I will have to have our important guests over here for dinners and parties, and you can't expect us to invite the leaders of the community to this house as it is.

"But please," she concluded, "don't let all this disturb you. Let me worry about it. I have willingly accepted my responsibility and my burdens. All I ask is that you and the rest of the children cooperate. Okay?"

I choked back my tears and looked to Uncle Philip, but as usual, he was quiet and seemingly distracted. How different our meals were from what they had been. Gone was the humor and the music and the laughter. No wonder Richard and Melanie were the way they were, I thought. All of the discussion at their dinner table was initiated by Aunt Bet, and Uncle Philip rarely had anything to say.

"One of the ways you can cooperate," Aunt Bet continued, "is to be sure you take off your shoes whenever you come into the house. Take them off at the door and carry them upstairs, please."

She paused, her lips tightening, her eyes growing narrow as she looked across the table at Jefferson.

"Jefferson, dear, didn't anyone ever show you how to hold a fork properly?"

"He holds it like a screwdriver," Richard commented and smirked.

"Watch how your cousins use their silverware, Jefferson, and try to copy them," she said.

Jefferson looked at me and then at her and then opened his mouth and dumped all the food he was chewing back onto his plate, the globs falling over his meat and vegetables.

"Ugh!" Melanie cried.

"Disgusting!" Richard screamed.

"Jefferson!" Aunt Bet stood up. "Philip, did you see that?"

Uncle Philip nodded and smirked.

"You get right up, young man," Aunt Bet said, "and march yourself upstairs right now. There'll be no dinner for you until you apologize," she said and pointed at the door. "Go on."

Jefferson looked anxiously at me. Even though I understood why he had done it, the sight of the globs of chewed food was revolting. My stomach churned from that and from all the tension and anger I felt inside.

"I'm not going upstairs," he shot back defiantly. He got up and ran out of the dining room and to the front door.

"Jefferson Longchamp, you don't have permission to go out!" Aunt Bet called, but Jefferson opened the front door and shot out anyway. Aunt Bet sat down, her face and long thin neck beet-red. "Oh dear, that child is so wild. He's gone and ruined another meal," she complained. "Christie . . ."

"I'll go after him," I said. "But you're going to have to stop criticizing him," I added.

"I'm just trying to teach him good things," she claimed. "We've all got to learn to get along now. We've got to adjust."

"When are you going to adjust, too, Aunt Bet?" I asked, rising. "When are you going to show some compromise?"

She sat back, her mouth agape. I thought I detected a slight smile on Uncle Philip's lips.

"Go get your brother and bring him back," he said. "We'll talk about all this later."

"Philip . . ."

"Let it be for a while, Betty Ann," he added forcefully. She flicked an angry glance at me and then pulled herself up to the table. I left them sitting in silence, which was something I felt they did more often than not.

I found Jefferson on the swing in our backyard. He was moving very slowly, his head down, dragging his feet along the ground. I sat next to him.

Above us, long thin wisps of clouds broke here and there to reveal the stars. Since Mommy and Daddy's horrible deaths, nothing seemed as bright and as beautiful as it had been, including the constellations. I recalled a time Mommy and I had sat outside on a summer's night and stared up at the heavens. We talked about the magnificence and wonder and let our imaginations run wild with the possibilities of other worlds, other people. We dreamt of a world without sickness and suffering, a world in which words like *unhappy* and *sad* didn't exist. People lived in perfect harmony and cared about each other as much as they did about themselves.

"Pick a star," Mommy said, "and that will be the world we've described. Then, every time we're out here at night, we'll look for it."

Tonight, I couldn't find that star.

"You shouldn't have done that at the table, Jefferson," I told him and took the swing beside him. He didn't answer. "You should just ignore her," I added.

"I hate her!" he exclaimed. "She's . . . she's an ugly worm," he said, desperate to find a satisfactory comparison.

"Don't insult worms," I said, but he didn't understand.

"I want Mommy," he moaned. "And Daddy."

"I know, Jefferson. So do I."

"I want them to get out of here, and I don't want Richard sleeping in my room," he added to his list of demands. I nodded.

"I don't want them here either, Jefferson, but right now we don't have any other choice. If we didn't live with them, we'd be sent away someplace," I said.

"Where?" The idea both intrigued and frightened him.

"A place for children without parents, and maybe we wouldn't be together," I said. That ended his willingness to risk an alternative.

"Well, I'm not going to say I'm sorry," he declared defiantly. "I don't care."

"If you don't, she won't let you eat with us and you don't want to eat alone, do you?"

"I'll eat in the kitchen with Mrs. Boston," he decided. I couldn't help but smile. Jefferson had Daddy's temper and stubbornness. That was for sure. If Aunt Bet thought she was going to break him with her tactics, she was in for an unpleasant surprise.

"All right, Jefferson. We'll see," I said. "Are you still hungry?"

"I want some apple pie," he admitted.

"Let's go back in through the pantry door. Mrs. Boston will give you some pie," I said, coaxing him. He took my hand and followed me. Mrs. Boston smiled happily when she saw us. I sat Jefferson at the kitchen table and she cut him a piece of the pie she had just served in the dining room. I wasn't hungry; I just watched him eat. Aunt Bet came in when she heard us talking. She stood glaring angrily in the doorway.

"That young man should come in and apologize to everyone at the table," she reiterated.

"Just leave him be, Aunt Bet," I said firmly. When our eyes locked, she saw my determination.

"Well, until he does, this is where he will take his meals," she threatened.

"Then this is where we will both take them," I said defiantly. She pulled her head back as if I had spit in her face.

"You're not being a good big sister by encouraging and excusing his bad behavior, Christie. I'm very disappointed in you."

"Aunt Bet, you can't imagine how disappointed I am in you," I replied.

She pressed her lips together until they were a thin white line, pulled up her shoulders and pivoted to parade back into the dining room to tell Uncle Philip what I had said. I'd been brought up by my parents not to talk back or be rude to adults and it made me feel bad to do so. But Mommy and Daddy had also taught me about honesty and justice and kindness to those I loved. I knew in my deepest heart of hearts that Aunt Bet deserved the things I'd said. She was not treating Jefferson and me lovingly or even fairly, it seemed to my grief-scarred mind. Every day in so many tiny ways Aunt Bet was wiping away with her cleaning rag any proof that our family had ever existed. By covering over the comforting and familiar with wallpaper and paint and, worst of all, the new rules that we were told to live by, she was covering up my memories. And they were all I had left of Mommy and Daddy.

I expected Richard would tease and criticize Jefferson for his behavior at the table that night. He had been complaining about Jefferson's personal habits from the moment he moved into the room with him. As a result, Jefferson had begged me several times to let him sleep with me. All I could think of was Mommy and Daddy forced to sleep in a sofa-bed pull-out when they were children. Why should something like that be happening to Jefferson and me? We had all this room and beautiful furniture. But I couldn't be mean to Jefferson, so I let him crawl in beside me that first night. Now he wanted to do it every night, and especially tonight because of the turmoil at the dinner table.

"You have to stay in your own room, Jefferson," I told him when he asked me later. "Don't let Richard terrorize you and force you out. It's your room, not his."

Reluctantly, he returned and tried to do what I said: ignore Richard. But in the morning, he came to my room howling. At first I thought Richard had hit him, but Richard wasn't a physical boy. I could see that the idea of striking someone and someone striking him back frightened him.

"What's wrong now, Jefferson?" I asked, grinding the sleep out of my eyes and sitting up.

"He's hidden my clothes," he moaned. "And he won't tell me where my shoes are."

"What?" I got out of bed and put on my robe. "Let's see what's going on here," I said, taking his hand. I led him back to his room, but Richard wasn't there.

"See," Jefferson said, "my shoes are gone."

"Did you look in your closet?" I asked. He nodded. I looked anyway and saw his favorite shoes were not there. I looked under the bed, too. "This is ridiculous," I said. "Where is he?"

"He always goes to Melanie's room in the morning," Jefferson revealed.

"He does? Why?" Jefferson shrugged. I stalked out of the room and went to Melanie's door. When I knocked, she said, "Come in." I opened the door to find Melanie seated at the vanity table. She was still in her pajamas. Richard stood behind her, still in his pajamas too. He was brushing her hair. They both turned and gazed at me with expressions so similar, it was frightening at first. Both looked angry about being disturbed—their eyes wide and blazing, their lips curled.

"What are you doing?" I asked, more out of surprise and curiosity than anything else.

"I'm brushing Melanie's hair. I do it every morning," Richard said.

"Why?" I couldn't help smiling in confusion.

"I just do. What do you want?" he demanded, showing his impatience with me.

"Where are Jefferson's things—his shoes, his clothes?"

"I told him if he leaves them lying around sloppily, I would hide them forever and I have," he replied and started to brush Melanie's hair again.

Rage first nailed me to the floor and then exploded in my chest, sending me charging toward him. He looked up with surprise when I grabbed the brush out of his hand and raised it threateningly. He cowered and Melanie screamed.

"Who do you think you are? What right do you have to do these things in our house?" I screamed.

"What's going on in here? What is it?" Aunt Bet cried from the doorway. She had come running from what was now her and Uncle Philip's bedroom. She was still in her nightgown, her hair under a sleeping cap, her face white with cold cream. It made her lips as pale as dead worms and her small eyes like two dull brown marbles.

"Richard has hidden Jefferson's shoes and clothes," I said. "And he won't tell where."

"He left everything lying on the floor again and his shoes in the middle of the floor. Someone could trip over them in the middle of the night," Richard cried in his defense. Aunt Bet nodded.

"You did the right thing, Richard. Jefferson must learn to take care of his things. Richard's not going to be his valet. Jefferson's old enough to know what to do, how to be neat and clean," she told me.

"If he doesn't tell me this moment where

Jefferson's things are hidden, I'll sneak into the room in the middle of the night when he's asleep and set a fire under his bed," I threatened. I don't know from where I got the idea or the strength to say such a thing, but it drove a knife of astonishment and terror into Aunt Bet's heart. She gasped and brought her hands to her throat.

"That's . . . horrible . . . a terrible, terrible thing to say. What's gotten into you, Christie?" she complained.

"I won't permit my brother to be tormented," I said firmly. Then I turned to Richard. "Where are his things?"

"Tell her, Richard," Aunt Bet said. "I want this deplorable incident to come to an end immediately. Your uncle has gone to supervise the work at the hotel," she added, "or I would bring him in here to see and hear this."

"I don't care if you tell him or not," I said. "Well?" I asked Richard.

"I threw them out the window," he confessed.

"What? When?" It had started raining after dinner and then rained all night.

"Last night before I went to sleep," he said.

"Everything's probably ruined. Are you satisfied?" I asked Aunt Bet.

"Richard," she said. "You shouldn't have done that. You should have come to me, first," she chastised gently.

"I'm just tired of living in a pigsty," he replied coldly.

"Well, I can understand that," she said. "Maybe Jefferson will take better care of his things from now on," she added, turning to me.

"If he touches any of my brother's things again, he'll be very sorry," I threatened. I slapped the brush into his hand. He winced and backed away.

Then I took Jefferson's hand and we marched out of the room. After I got dressed, we went out and found his shoes, pants, shirt and underwear under the window. The shoes were soaked and I was sure they were ruined. Mrs. Boston said that when they dried, they would probably be out of shape and rough to wear.

Still enraged, I put them in a paper bag and walked over to the hotel to find Uncle Philip. Most of the hotel's main structure had been demolished. Now the workmen were in the process of removing the debris. Uncle Philip was conferring with the architect and the engineers about the rebuilding of the hotel and the changes they would make. He looked up from the blueprints when I arrived. It was impossible to look at my face and not see the anger. My cheeks were crimson, my eyes bright with heat, my lips trembling with fury.

"Excuse me," Uncle Philip said quickly and stepped away from the others. "What's wrong, Christie?"

"Look," I said, thrusting the bag of soaked shoes at him. He took it and gazed inside. Then he felt them.

"What happened?" he asked, a look of concern in his face.

"Richard threw Jefferson's shoes and his clothes out the window last night because he didn't like the way Jefferson takes care of his things. He didn't care that it was pouring and these would be ruined."

Uncle Philip nodded.

"I'll have a talk with him," he said.

"Aunt Bet thinks he did the right thing," I declared. Again, Uncle Philip nodded.

"I know this has been extra-hard for you, for

everyone. So many different personalities thrown together abruptly. It's overwhelming at times," he said, shaking his head sympathetically.

"Not for Aunt Bet and Richard and Melanie," I replied.

"Sure it has," he said. "But that doesn't excuse something like this. I'll straighten it all out tonight," he promised and smiled. "I want you to be as happy as you can be, Christie," he said, putting his hand on my cheek. "You're too lovely to be made upset and far too fragile, I know."

"I'm not fragile, Uncle Philip. And it's my brother who is being terrorized right now, not me. I can take care of myself, but he's only nine and . . ."

"Of course. Calm down. I promise, I'll straighten everything out. I'll make it up to you," he said. "In the meantime tell Julius to take you and Jefferson into the village to buy him another pair of shoes, okay?"

"It's not just the shoes," I insisted.

"I know, but there's no point in turning this into World War Three now, is there? We're all too fresh with sorrow from the tragedy. Do whatever you can, whatever you want to calm things down, Christie. You're smarter and older than Richard and Melanie," he said. For a minute, I thought he was going to add Aunt Bet, too. "I know I can depend on you."

My anger subsided. The men were waiting for him and there wasn't much else I could have him do anyway. As long as he understood and promised to do something, I thought.

"All right."

"That's a good girl," he said and drew me to him to embrace me and kiss me on the cheek, his lips grazing mine as he pulled back. I stared at him a moment and then turned and ran all the way home to get Jefferson and go shopping for his new shoes.

Despite Uncle Philip's promises, one crisis ended only to be followed by another. There were arguments between Jefferson and Richard over use of the bathroom, over toys and games, and over what television programs to watch. It was easy to see they were like two feuding cats put into the same cage. Peace could be broken at a moment's notice.

Fortunately, most of the time, Richard wanted to be with Melanie. At first I was happy about it, but as I watched them together, I became curious and then revolted by what I saw. They spent nearly all their waking hours side by side. Besides brushing each other's hair, they would cut each other's toenails and check with each other to see what each wanted to wear before either would get dressed. They never seemed to argue like other siblings their age, and I noticed that Richard never teased Melanie. In fact, neither said a negative or critical thing to the other, ever.

Whenever Jefferson and I were in the same room with them, they would inevitably revert to whispering.

"Your mother's so worried about everyone being polite and following the proper etiquette and behavior," I snapped at them, "you should know that whispering is impolite."

They both smirked. Whenever one was chastised or criticized, the other reacted as if it had been done to him or to her.

"You and Jefferson have secrets," Melanie moaned. "Why can't we?"

"We have no secrets."

"Of course you do," Richard said. "Every family

has its secrets. You have another father, your real father, but you keep everything about him secret, don't you?" he accused.

"I do not. I don't know all that much about him," I explained.

"Mother says he raped Dawn and that's how you were born," Melanie revealed.

"That's not true! That's a horrible lie!"

"My mother doesn't lie," Richard said coldly. "She doesn't have to."

"She has nothing to hide," Melanie concluded.

My heart was pounding. I wanted to walk across the room and slap the expressions of self-satisfaction off both their faces.

"My father, my real father, was a famous opera star. He was even in Broadway musicals and he was a teacher at the Sarah Bernhardt school in New York," I said slowly. "That was where my mother met him and fell in love with him. He did not rape her."

"Then why did he run away?" Richard demanded.

"He didn't want to be married and take care of children, but he didn't rape her," I said.

"That's still horrible," Melanie said. Richard nodded and then went back to the game of Chinese checkers, leaving me steaming.

Not having had to spend so much of my day and night with them before, I never realized how infuriating and self-centered the twins were. No wonder neither of them had any friends besides each other, I thought. Who would want to be their friends? They were so close, they wouldn't permit anyone to come between them anyhow.

One morning, when they left the bathroom door open and they were both inside, I nearly got sick. I saw Richard take Melanie's toothbrush just after she had used it and put it directly into his own mouth.

"Ugh," I cried and they spun around. "You have your own toothbrush, Richard. Why would you do that?"

"Stop spying on us!" he cried and closed the door.

But it was Jefferson who came to me one night and told me the most astounding thing of all about them. I was writing pages and pages of a letter to Gavin, describing all of the unpleasantness that was going on in the house now, when Jefferson appeared in my doorway looking confused and troubled.

"What's the matter, Jefferson?" I asked.

"Melanie's old enough to take her own bath," he said, "isn't she?"

"Of course. She's practically thirteen, Jefferson. You take your own bath. Either I or Mrs. Boston help you sometimes and you like me to wash your back the way Mommy always did, but . . . why do you ask?" I suddenly said.

"Richard's helping Melanie," he announced.

"Take a bath?" He nodded. "I don't believe that, Jefferson. How do you know?"

"She asked him to. She came in and said, 'I'm going to take a bath,' and he said, 'I'll be right along.' Then he got undressed, put on his robe and went to the bathroom."

"They're not taking a bath together, not at their age?" I said. Jefferson pressed the corner of his mouth into his cheek and shrugged again. I got up slowly and went to my doorway to peer down the hallway at the bathroom door. It was shut. "You saw them both go in there?" I asked Jefferson. He looked up and nodded.

Intrigued now, I walked quietly down to the

bathroom door and listened. I heard their muffled dialogue and put my ear to the door. There was the distinct sound of water lapping against bodies and the inside of the tub. This is disgusting, I thought. Surely neither Aunt Bet nor Uncle Philip knew about this. I tried the handle. The door was unlocked. Jefferson's eyes widened with surprise and excitement when I opened the door a fraction. I put my finger on my lips to indicate silence and he bit down on his lower lip quickly. Then I inched the door open until I could get my head in enough to peer.

There they were in the tub together, facing each other. Richard was scrubbing Melanie's hair. Her budding breasts, like two puffs of marshmallow, were fully exposed. Suddenly, Richard sensed my presence and turned my way. He stopped scrubbing. Melanie raised her head.

"Close that door and get out of here!" he screamed.

"Get out!" Melanie added.

"What are you doing? That's disgusting," I said. "You're too old to be bathing together."

"What we do is none of your business. Close that door," he demanded again.

I slammed it shut.

"Go back to your room, Jefferson," I said.

"Where are you going?"

"To tell Aunt Bet. She can't know about this. It's obscene," I said.

"What's obscene mean?"

"Just go back to your room and wait for me," I said. I hurried downstairs and found Aunt Bet talking on the telephone. Uncle Philip was out meeting some contractors who were going to work on the rebuilding of the hotel. She saw me standing there and put her hand over the mouthpiece.

"Christie, what is it?" she asked. "I'm on the phone."

"I've got to tell you something immediately. You've got to go upstairs," I said.

"Oh dear, what is it now? Just a minute. Louise, I have a minor crisis here. Yes, another one. I'll phone you back shortly. Thank you." She cradled the receiver and pressed her lips together to show her annoyance. "Yes?"

"It's Melanie and Richard, they're taking a bath."

"So?"

"Together. They're in the bathtub together. Right now," I added for emphasis.

"So. They've always done things together; they're unique; they're twins," she said.

"But they're twelve years old, almost thirteen and . . ."

"Oh, I see. You think there's something perverted and dirty about it." She nodded as if confirming a suspicion. "Well the twins are special. They're very bright and very devoted to each other. Neither would ever do anything to hurt or embarrass the other. It's just natural; they were formed together in my womb and lived side by side for nine months. Why, I even fed them together, one on each breast. I think there's something spiritual about it."

"But you said you wanted to move Richard into Jefferson's room so Melanie could have the privacy she needs," I reminded her. She looked furious that I had pointed up the contradiction.

"I meant so she could have the room she needs, as well as some privacy," she said sternly.

"But . . ."

"But nothing. I don't expect they'll be doing

everything together like this much longer. As they grow older, they'll grow as far apart as is necessary, but until then, there's nothing wrong with their love and devotion toward each other. Actually, they're an inspiration. Yes," she said, liking the words she had found to defend them, "an inspiration." Her smile wilted quickly and she turned witch-like: her eyes small and beady, her lips thin and her cheeks drawn in, which made her nose seem longer and more pointed.

"It doesn't surprise me that you would find their actions depraved with your unfortunate background and with Fern growing up in your house and all," she said.

"What do you mean, my unfortunate background?" I demanded.

"Please, Christie. Let's not get into nasty arguments. Thank you for coming to tell me about the twins. Don't worry about it. Actually, Richard's complained to me on a number of occasions now about your spying on them."

"Spying? That's not true."

"Everyone deserves his or her privacy at times. You like yours, don't you?" she added. "Just keep a closer eye on your little brother, dear. That, it seems to me, is going to be enough for you. For anyone," she added under her breath. "Now, I must call my friend Louise back. We were right in the middle of an important conversation."

She turned back to the phone, leaving me stuttering in shock. I turned and went back upstairs.

"What happened?" Jefferson asked, coming to his doorway.

"Nothing, Jefferson. Forget about it. Forget about them. They're freaks," I said loud enough for them to hear. I went back to my bedroom and continued to write what was becoming a small book instead of a letter to Gavin. He was the only other living person to whom I wanted to confide.

Gavin, living with Aunt Bet and Uncle Philip has caused me to miss my parents even more. Uncle Philip's family is a family without love. The only times Uncle Philip is with his family is at breakfast and dinner. Aunt Bet acts as if her children were created in a laboratory and as a result, they are perfect little creatures, who can't do anything wrong. But I have yet to see her kiss them good night or good morning or Uncle Philip kiss them good-bye whenever he leaves, the way Daddy and Mommy used to kiss Jefferson and me. I never saw four people who behave so formally toward each other.

But no matter what Aunt Bet says about the twins, to me they are nothing more than some two-headed monster. They're so weird. They would be content if there were no other people in the world but themselves, not even their parents. The only time they ever laugh or smile is when they whisper things to each other. I just know they're whispering about me and Jefferson. Truthfully, I think Uncle Philip finds his own children revolting and that's why he hates to spend time with them or have them around him when he's at the hotel.

I wonder why Uncle Philip married Aunt Bet. He is a handsome man, far too handsome for someone as homely-looking as she is. Fern told me some horrible things before she left this time. She wants me to believe that Uncle

Philip and Mommy were once girlfriend and boyfriend before Mommy found out he was her half-brother. But before the fire at the hotel Mommy told me that nothing significant had ever happened between them. Still, it makes me feel funny whenever I look at Uncle Philip now and whenever I catch him staring at me.

I wouldn't tell these things to anyone else but you, Gavin. Girlfriends like Pauline are interested and considerate, but I am too embarrassed to tell them about these family troubles. I can't wait to see you again, and count the days until you are able to return.

Give my love to Granddaddy Longchamp and Edwina.

I debated how to sign off and finally wrote: *All my love, Christie.*

It was very late when I finally completed my letter. I sealed it in an envelope and put it on my night table so I would remember to mail it first thing in the morning. But I didn't prepare for bed and go to sleep. Instead, I put on my jacket, peered out the doorway to be sure all was quiet and then softly went downstairs.

As usual, a light had been left on in the entry way and one lamp was lit in the living room. I didn't hear Mrs. Boston and imagined she had already retired for the evening. Stealthily, I went to the front door and opened it as quietly as I could. Then I stepped outside and closed it softly behind me. The three-quarter moon illuminated the front of the house like a spotlight. The porch floor creaked as I went forward.

Actually, I thought, Richard and Melanie were

correct when they accused me of harboring secrets. I did have one which I kept even from Jefferson. Ever since my parents were buried, I had found a way to sneak off after dark to visit their graves to cry and complain. Tonight, especially, I wanted to go there and feel near them, but I wasn't prepared for the surprise that would follow on my heels.

Secrets

IN THE MOONLIGHT THE TALL MONUMENTS AND mausoleums were as white as bones, and the air was so still that the leaves looked painted on the branches. From behind me I could hear the rhythmic roar of the sea over which the moon had spread a soft yellow glow. The scent of freshly turned earth from a newly dug grave rose to greet me as I walked under the granite stone archway of the cemetery.

Ordinarily, I would have been afraid to go wandering around a graveyard at night, especially the one in which Grandmother Cutler had been buried. As a child I had been brought here on only a few occasions, but each time I was brought, I gazed fearfully at the tombstone that loomed over her grave and spelled her name and listed her birth and death. I remember once having a nightmare about that stone. In it I found myself lost in the graveyard. I made a turn in the darkness and came upon her monument, only instead of the words and the engraved cross, I found her two cold gray eyes glaring out at me, the same cold gray eyes that glared at me from her terrifying portrait in the hotel, only these nightmare eyes were luminous and terrifying.

But just knowing Mommy and Daddy were buried here now made the graveyard less of a place of fear and nightmares and more of a place of warmth and love. They would protect me just as they'd always protected me, and not even Grandmother Cutler's ghost or evil spirit could overpower their goodness. Her stone, although bigger and thicker than most in the graveyard, was just another stone. Nevertheless, I didn't linger near it; I walked past it quickly and approached my parents' twin graves. There I knelt and shed my tears as I spoke to them.

"Mommy, I miss you and Daddy so much," I said. "And Jefferson is so heartbroken and lost. We hate living with Uncle Philip and Aunt Bet. There is no love in their family." I went on to tell them about Richard and Melanie and how weird they were and mean to us.

"But I promise to always look after Jefferson and do whatever I can to help him overcome his grief and confusion," I said. The tears flowed freely down my cheeks and dripped off my chin. I didn't try to stop them; I let them fall on my parents' graves.

"Oh Mommy, it's so hard to live in a world without you," I moaned. "Nothing's the same: no morning is as warm and bright, no night is as safe, nothing that I loved to eat tastes as good, and nothing that was pretty to wear looks pretty to me anymore. I feel empty inside. Surely my fingers will be numb on the piano keys. The melody is gone.

"I know you hate me to say these things. Everyone tells me I must recuperate from my grief and try even harder to become who you dreamt I would be, but the road seems so much longer and harder to travel now without you by my side. And no matter what everyone says, I can't help believing there is a dreadful curse on our heads."

I sighed deeply and nodded as if I had actually heard Mommy reply.

"But I know I must try and I must succeed and my responsibility has grown greater. I must live and work imagining how proud of me you would be. I will try, Mommy. I promise," I said. I stood up slowly. I was so tired, so drained. It was time to go home to sleep.

But just as I was about to leave, I heard footsteps. Someone was coming up the pathway behind me. I turned and peered through the moonlit cemetery to see Uncle Philip. He stopped at Grandmother Cutler's tomb. When he did so, I drew back into the shadows behind another large monument. I didn't want him to know I came here privately at night. I waited, expecting him to leave after he had visited his grandmother's grave, but he surprised me by continuing to my parents' graves after only a few moments. He paused before Mommy's and knelt down to put the palms of his hands on the cold earth. Then, with his palms still flat against the ground, he raised his head and spoke in a voice that was loud enough for me to hear.

"I'm sorry, Dawn. I'm sorry. I know I never told you that enough. A thousand apologies wouldn't suffice, nor ever wipe away what I did to you. Fate had no right to take you from me so soon, especially before I truly won your complete forgiveness."

What had he done? I wondered. What could be so horrible that even a thousand apologies wouldn't be enough?

"I feel half of me has died along with you. You know how I felt about you and how I couldn't help those feelings. Nothing stopped me from loving you. I married Betty Ann, but she was a poor substitute. I dreamt and hoped for the day you and

I would pronounce our true feelings toward each other.

"Oh, I know you refused to acknowledge it, but once we loved each other purely and passionately, and if we could do so then, I hoped we could do so once more. Perhaps I was foolish to have such a dream, but I couldn't help it.

"Now," he said, his head bowed, "every time I look at Christie, I think of you. I think of her as our child, or at least what our child would have been like."

His words fell like cold rain over me. So this was why he gazed at me so intently at times, I thought; but rather than make me happy to hear he had such strong feelings for me, it made me shudder. A trickle of ice slid down my spine.

"Never in my wildest imagination," he continued, raising his head again and speaking in a fiery voice, "did I ever think you would die before I did. Surely, the angels themselves were jealous of my love for you and worked to destroy it. Well, they have taken you from me, taken you from this world, but they can never take you from my heart.

"I pledge to you I will care for Christie lovingly and see to it that she is happy and secure. I will rebuild this hotel as a monument to you, bigger and brighter and more wonderful than it ever was, and as soon as it is completed, I will have a gigantic portrait of you placed on the lobby walls.

"You sing on, my love, on and on in my heart." He lowered his head again. "But forgive me, forgive me," he begged. Then he stood up slowly and walked away, his head down.

I watched him disappear down the cemetery path, my heart pounding. What deep, dark secret did he keep in his heart, a secret so painful he had to beg forgiveness at a grave? Was it just that he loved Mommy more intimately and passionately than he should have loved his half-sister or was it something even more sinful? Aunt Fern's horrid words, spat at me before she left, returned: "What do you think they did on their dates, play paint-by-numbers?" It frightened me to think about it. When I felt confident he was gone, I came out of the shadows and then hurried along the same path to home.

The light above the front door was still burning. I tiptoed over the porch, trying desperately to keep the floor from creaking, and then I opened the door and slipped inside quickly. I waited and listened. All was quiet. Perhaps Uncle Philip had gone up to bed already, I thought, and started down the corridor to the stairway. But when I reached the entrance to the living room, I saw that one small lamp was still lit and Uncle Philip was sitting in an easy chair, his head back, his eyes closed. In his hand he held a glass of whiskey.

I hurried past the entrance to the steps of the stairway, but the first step betrayed me by creaking loudly.

"Who's there?" Uncle Philip called. I stood perfectly still. "Is someone out there?" I decided not to answer, but my heart was pounding so hard, I was sure he could hear the thump, thump, thump against my chest. He didn't call again nor did he come to the doorway. I made my way up the stairs quickly and went directly to my room. I undressed, put on my nightgown, and slipped into bed. As usual I turned off all but my small night light. And then, only moments after I had turned over in bed and closed my eyes, I heard my door creak open.

My heart began to pound when I didn't hear Jefferson's cry and footsteps. I didn't move; I didn't turn to see who it was; I didn't have to. In seconds I could smell the scent of the whiskey. I held my breath. It was Uncle Philip. Was he just checking to see if I was in my bed? Why did he linger so long? Finally, I heard the door close and I released my breath in relief, but before I could turn around, I heard his footsteps and realized he was at the side of my bed.

I kept my eyes closed and didn't move, pretending to be asleep. He stood there staring down at me for the longest time, but I didn't open my eyes or acknowledge his presence. I was too frightened. I heard him release a deep sigh and then finally, I heard him walk away. When I heard the door open and close again, I turned my head and saw he was gone. Then I sighed with relief myself.

What a strange and wondrous night this proved to be, I thought. Mysteries hung in the air around me like pockets of thick sea fog. I lay there wondering for the longest time and then finally drew sleep around me like a cocoon and curled up slowly in its warm, protective walls.

I awoke to the sounds of great commotion and, a moment later, Jefferson came charging into my bedroom. I could hear Aunt Bet in the hallway crying for Uncle Philip to send for the doctor. Even though it was quite bright outside, I gazed at the clock and saw it was not quite five-thirty in the morning. Jefferson looked very frightened.

"What is it?"

"It's Richard," he said, his eyes wide. "He's got a bad tummy ache, so bad he's crying."

"Really?" I said dryly. "Maybe he ate some of his own sour grapes."

"Melanie ate them, too," Jefferson added excitedly.

"Melanie too? What do you mean?"

"She's got a tummy ache also and Aunt Bet is

angry about it. Can I sleep with you? They're making too much noise," he said.
"Get into my bed," I said, but I got up and reached for my robe. "I'll see what's going on."
Uncle Philip, still in his pajamas, was in the hallway, his hair disheveled. He looked confused and sleepy and yawned hard and loud. He scrubbed his face with his palms and went to Melanie's doorway.
"What is it? What's all the noise?" he demanded.
"She's as white as a ghost and so is Richard. Go look at him," Aunt Bet cried from inside. "They've been poisoned!" she added.
"What? That's ridiculous," Uncle Philip said. He turned and saw me standing there. "Oh, Christie." He smiled. "I'm sorry they woke you."
"What's happening, Uncle Philip?" I asked.
"I don't know. It's always like this," he said. "When one of the twins gets sick, the other one inevitably does too. It's as if every germ that attacks them has a twin in waiting," he added, still smiling. Then he went into Jefferson and Richard's room. I went to the doorway of Melanie's room and peered in.
Aunt Bet was sitting on the bed, holding a cold washcloth on Melanie's forehead. Melanie groaned beneath her and clutched her stomach.
"I've got to go again," she cried.
"Oh dear me, dear me," Aunt Bet said, standing to get out of her way. Melanie shot off the bed and, bent over and still clutching her stomach, hurried toward the doorway and the bathroom. I stepped out of her way.
"What is it?" I asked when she rushed past me and lunged into the bathroom, slamming the door behind her.
"What is it? They were poisoned by something

rotten, I'm sure," Aunt Bet said. "That . . . that incompetent cook and maid . . ."

"Mrs. Boston? You can't believe Mrs. Boston did something wrong. Mrs. Boston is a wonderful cook."

"Humph," she said, pulling her narrow, bony shoulders back. She walked past me and went to Richard. I could hear his groans. Uncle Philip emerged, a look of disgust and fatigue on his face.

"We all ate the same things, Uncle Philip," I said. "None of the rest of us are sick. The twins must have eaten something else on their own," I added.

"I don't know. I don't know," he chanted and went to call the doctor. I returned to my bedroom and crawled in beside Jefferson, who had already fallen back to sleep. Less than an hour later, the doctor arrived. After he examined the twins, I heard him step into the hallway with Aunt Bet and prescribe some medicine and bed rest and then leave. Shortly afterward, Aunt Bet came to my bedroom door.

"Christie," she said, "please have Jefferson sleep in Melanie's room for a few days. I don't want him to be contaminated and it will be easier for me if the twins are in the same room."

"What's wrong with them?"

"It could be some kind of a food poisoning or some stomach virus," she explained and twisted her mouth up in disgust.

"It must be a virus. I don't feel bad and neither does Jefferson."

"Even if it was a virus, they contracted it because things aren't kept clean enough around here, especially in the kitchen. You two were just lucky," she replied. "Somehow," she added and left.

Later that morning when Jefferson and I went

down for breakfast, we found only Uncle Philip at the table reading the paper. He smiled and said good morning as if it were just any other morning.

"Where's Aunt Bet?" I asked.

"She brought some tea and toast up to the twins. She will nurse them back to health in no time all by herself. She always does. Anyway, I'm glad you two are fine," he added.

"There's no reason for us not to be," I said sharply. He nodded and went back to his paper.

Mrs. Boston emerged from the kitchen with our hot food. She looked very unhappy and very angry. I never saw her mouth so tight.

"How are your stomachs this morning?" she asked Jefferson and me.

"Fine, Mrs. Boston," I replied.

"Thought so," she said with satisfaction and pulled her shoulders back, but Uncle Philip kept reading as if he hadn't heard a word. Mrs. Boston went back into the kitchen and didn't come out again. I had promised Jefferson I would take him for a walk on the beach to look for seashells after breakfast, so we went upstairs to get him a light jacket. I knocked on his bedroom door and then poked my head in to see if it would be all right for me to go get the jacket from his closet.

Aunt Bet had taken a seat between the two beds. She sat there holding Richard's hand in her right hand and Melanie's in her left. The twins had their blankets up to their chins and their eyes closed.

"Shh," Aunt Bet said. "They're finally asleep."

"I just want to get Jefferson's little jacket," I whispered and tiptoed to the closet. Even though I made less noise than a baby mouse, Richard's eyes popped open.

"What . . . what is it?" he cried.

Melanie's eyes snapped open instantly, too.

"Who is it?" she said.

"Now you see what you've gone and done," Aunt Bet snapped. "And they needed to rest so much."

"A fly couldn't have made less noise, Aunt Bet," I said. "They obviously weren't really asleep." I took Jefferson's jacket off the hanger.

"Where are you going?"

"For a walk on the beach," I replied. "It's a beautiful day. Too bad the twins can't come out," I added and left them quickly. I put my letter to Gavin in the mailbox for the mailman to pick up and then went down to the ocean with Jefferson.

Jefferson enjoyed our hunt for interesting shells, but every once in a while, he would stop and look out at the ocean and ask a question about Mommy and Daddy. Did I think they were together in Heaven? Would they have new children up there? Was there ever a time when they could come back, even for only a moment? None of my answers satisfied him. His dark eyes only widened and took on the shine of forthcoming tears. He wanted only one answer—someday we would all be together again.

As we came up the driveway toward home afterward, we were surprised to see the hotel limousine in front. Suddenly Julius emerged from the house carrying a suitcase in each hand. He put each in the limousine's trunk.

"Who's leaving?" Jefferson asked me. "I hope it's Aunt Bet," he muttered, but it wasn't. It was Mrs. Boston, all dressed up in her Sunday church clothes and carrying a smaller suitcase when she appeared. As soon as we saw her, we broke into a run.

"Mrs. Boston!" I called. "Where are you going?" She looked up and smiled.

"Oh, I'm so glad you two come back before I left," she said. "I wanted to say good-bye."

"But where are you going, Mrs. Boston? I didn't know you were going anywhere."

"Neither did I," she said angrily. "You know that your aunt came down this morning and accused me of serving spoiled food. After breakfast, she returned to tell me I didn't know how to keep a kitchen properly clean and I didn't know how to properly serve people of quality and she didn't have time to teach me. She said it would be better for everyone if I just left. Then she paid me off and asked me to go immediately.

"I told her good riddance," she added.

"Oh no, Mrs. Boston. She can't fire you. You don't work for her; you work for us," I said desperately. What would life in our home be like without Mrs. Boston? I wondered.

"Poor, poor child," she said, putting her gloved hand on my cheek. Then she smiled at Jefferson who was looking up at her sadly. "I did work for you, but you ain't in control of the money strings for a while yet, honey. Miss Bet let me know that for sure.

"It's best this way, I suppose. After a while she and I would only be at each others' throats. That woman . . ." She shook her head. "I'm sorry, babies. I took care of you both, helped raised you and it breaks my heart to have to go, but I can't stay now."

"Where will you go, Mrs. Boston?" I moaned, my tears starting to flow.

"Down to Georgia to my sister Lou Ann for a while. It's time I visited her anyway. We're both along in our years, you know," she added, smiling.

"We'll never see you again," I complained.

"Oh, I'll make my way back in due time. You take care of your little brother," she said. "And Jefferson, you mind your sister now, hear?"

I looked at Jefferson. His sadness had turned to fury quickly. He bit down on his lower lip and then broke from my side to run around the house.

"JEFFERSON!"

"Go look after him," Mrs. Boston said. She kissed me on the cheek and we hugged hard. "I'll miss you, child."

"I'll miss you, Mrs. Boston. Terribly," I added. She wiped a tear from her cheek and nodded.

"Quickly," she told Julius, "before I turn into mush on the spot." She got into the limousine and Julius closed the door and went around to get into the vehicle. The last thing I saw was the feather of Mrs. Boston's Sunday church hat in the rear window before the sunlight washed over the back of the limousine and turned the window into a mirror of light. Shocked, feeling a scream in my throat that just stayed there, I stared even after the car was gone. My legs had turned to lead along with my heart.

Slowly, in small ways, everything that had been a part of our wonderful world was slipping away. I never felt more lonely or more afraid of what was to come.

Jefferson had crawled through an opening in the lattice under the back porch of the house. I suspected he was under there. It was one of his hideaways and places to pretend and play. He sat snuggled in a corner, mindlessly moving a stick over the hard-packed ground.

"Come on out, Jefferson. You're getting yourself filthy under there and there's no point in hiding," I coaxed.

"I don't wanna," he said. "I don't want Mrs. Boston to leave," he added quickly.

"Neither do I, but she has. I'm going in to speak to Aunt Bet about it right now," I added. He looked up hopefully.

"Will Mrs. Boston come back?"

"Maybe," I said. "Come on, Jefferson." I reached in and he took my hand and crawled out, but he had gotten the knees and seat of his pants black with dirt, as well as his elbows. I brushed him off the best I could and then we went inside. Aunt Bet was in the kitchen, banging pots and pans as she took everything out of the closets and cabinets. I went to the doorway and looked in at her. She wore plastic gloves and apron over her dress. She had her hair tied under a thick bandanna.

"Aunt Bet," I said and she stopped to turn around.

"What is it?"

"How could you fire Mrs. Boston?" I demanded. "What right did you have to do that?" My voice took on the steely edge of a razor.

"How could . . . what right did I have?" she stuttered. Her eyes turned crystal-hard and cold. "Are you blind? Look at this place. You wouldn't believe the dirt and grease, the dust and grime I'm discovering in these closets and cabinets. Everything has to be washed down with disinfectant. I don't think it's ever been done. I'm taking charge of this myself before we hire a new servant. I'm going to reline every closet, every shelf and sterilize all the dishes and silverware."

"That's not true! Mrs. Boston was always very clean. We love Mrs. Boston. She's been with us . . . forever. You've got to send for her to return," I insisted.

"Send for her return?" She laughed her thin

laugh as if I had suggested the most ridiculous thing. "Please." Then her eyes fell on Jefferson and her face went into a contortion of disgust. She stood up quickly and came across the room in a rage.

"What has he been doing? How did he get so filthy? Why did you bring him into the house like this? Look at his feet. I told you two to always take off your shoes before you come inside the house. Don't you know that germs stick to the bottoms of our feet? Don't you realize the twins are sick upstairs and their resistance is low? Quickly," she said, seizing Jefferson at the right elbow, "strip off these filthy things and pile them in that corner," she pointed.

Jefferson wailed and struggled to pull out of her grasp, but in her rage and intensity, she had great strength for a woman of her size. Her bony fingers locked around his small arm like an iron vise. Jefferson fell to the floor, kicking and screaming.

"Let him be!" I screamed.

"Then take him into the downstairs bathroom and clean him up," she ordered, her eyes blazing, her mouth twisted. "Don't dare bring him upstairs like this. I don't believe the extra work you've made for me. Now I've got to go back over the entry way and the floors." She bent down and ripped Jefferson's shoes off his feet quickly. "Go on," she commanded.

"Come on, Jefferson," I said. "She's gone mad." I pulled him to me, lifted him into my arms and hurried out of the kitchen.

"Take him directly into the bathroom!" she called behind us, but I didn't listen to her. I went up the stairs quickly and took him into my room, slamming the door behind me. There, I caught my breath. Jefferson was gasping from his deep wails.

"It's all right, Jefferson," I said. "She won't hurt you. I'll give you a warm bath. Afterward, I'll speak to Uncle Philip," I promised.

He ground his small fists into his eyes and dried the last few tears. His face was streaked with dirt and grime, and he didn't put up any resistance to taking the bath. Grief, sadness and fear had combined to overwhelm him and turn him into a clinging baby. How different he was from the little boy who couldn't wait to burst into my room every morning and from the little boy who was rarely depressed and unhappy. Seeing him this way made me even angrier. I didn't have time to feel sorry for myself any longer. I was determined to see to it that he didn't suffer any more pain. I told him to take a nap and I went out to look for Uncle Philip.

Aunt Bet had scrubbed the entry way, just as she promised, and now had sheets of newspaper over it. I walked over them and hurried out. But just as I started down the front steps, Uncle Philip drove up.

"Aunt Bet's fired Mrs. Boston!" I cried when he stepped out of his car. "And she's being terribly mean to Jefferson and me."

"What's this? Mean to you?" he said, coming around the car. "Oh no, Christie. She wouldn't want to be mean to you," he said. He put his arm around my shoulders. "She's just nervous and upset about the twins being sick. She always gets this way when they're ill."

"She's fired Mrs. Boston," I wailed. "And Mrs. Boston's gone."

"Well, maybe it's for the best for now. Aunt Betty is the mistress of the house and the servants have to get along with her. Mrs. Boston was set in her ways after all these years. She should have retired years ago anyway," he replied.

"Mrs. Boston is not old and she's not set in her ways. She was part of my family," I insisted.

"I'm sorry," he said. "But if Aunt Betty isn't happy and Mrs. Boston isn't happy, what good is it to continue this way? It's for the best, believe me," he repeated and smiled.

"No it isn't," I said, pulling away from him. "She's making things even harder than they are!" I cried. "Jefferson and I are not coming out of my room until she apologizes for screaming at him and frightening him to death."

I charged back into the house ahead of him and returned to my bedroom. Jefferson had already drifted into a nap from his emotional exhaustion. I sat staring at him, at his little face shut tight in sleep. Every once in a while, he moaned. Probably from a bad dream about Aunt Bet, I thought angrily. A little over an hour later, there was a small knock on my door.

"Come in," I said and Uncle Philip opened the door. He was carrying a tray with two bowls of soup, two sandwiches and two glasses of milk.

"Betty Ann sent this up to you," he said and nodded toward Jefferson, who was still sleeping. "How is he?"

"He's exhausted from all that's happened," I replied coldly.

"Betty Ann is sorry," he said, putting the tray down on my desk. "She didn't mean to upset everyone. It's what I thought—her nervousness over the twins. Everything will be all right again. You'll see," he promised.

"Hardly," I said dryly. "She had no right to fire Mrs. Boston," I added.

"Let's give it some time," he pleaded. "When things calm down, we'll talk it all over in a sensible way like grown-ups, okay?" He riveted his eyes on me. “I’m sure we’ll be able to work out all our problems once the twins are up and around again. None of this is easy, Christie. We’ve all got to learn to live together peacefully. I know it’s harder for you two,” he added sympathetically.

I fixed my gaze on his soft, blue eyes. Now he sounded more like a concerned uncle should sound. I wanted to tell him yes, it is harder for us. We lost our parents and Aunt Bet is a poor substitute for Mommy. She could never be a mother to us, not in our minds.

“This initial work to reconstruct the hotel has taken up most of my attention and time, but I promise, I will soon devote more of myself to you and not leave Betty Ann with all the responsibility. Just between you and me,” he added in a low voice that was almost a whisper, “I think it’s been a little too much for her. She’s overwhelmed and with the twins getting sick and all . . . well, she’s not as strong a woman as Dawn was. You’re old enough now. I can talk to you and trust that you will understand,” he said.

Since he was being so trusting and revealing and treating me like an adult, I wanted to burst out and ask him for what he had begged forgiveness at my mother’s grave, but I was afraid to reveal I had been there and had overheard his most secret thoughts.

He stepped up to me and knelt down to take my hand. Then he beamed that charming smile on me, his eyes bright and happy.

“Can we make a pact together?”

“What sort of a pact?” I asked suspiciously.

“To promise to trust and depend on each other from this day forward; to tell each other things we wouldn’t tell anyone else; to work hard at making everyone happy and safe. From this day forward,” he vowed, “what makes you sad, will make me sad, and what makes you happy, will make me happy. Can we make that pact?" he repeated.

How strange he sounded, I thought. It was as if he were asking me to marry him. I shrugged. I didn't know how to react, or what to say. He was so intense, his eyes so determined and locked on mine.

"I guess so," I said.

"Good. Let's seal it with a kiss," he said and leaned forward to plant a kiss on my cheek, only his lips touched the corner of my mouth as well. He kept his eyes closed for a moment afterward and then smiled again. "Everything's going to be fine," he said. "Fine."

Fine? How could it ever again be fine? The wonderful world of sunshine and happiness I had known was gone forever. Not the bluest sky, nor the warmest day, nothing would bring back those loving, soft feelings.

He stood up. "Better wake Jefferson and have him eat his soup. I would have told you two to come down to eat, but Betty Ann just scrubbed the kitchen floor on her hands and knees.

"She's always obsessed like this when the twins get sick," he said, widening his smile. "It's the only way she can deal with her nervousness. As long as she keeps busy, she's all right. I have to go back to the hotel, but I will be home early and we'll all have a nice dinner together.

"Oh," he added at the door, "we'll have to pretend that whatever she makes tastes very good. She's not a very good cook, but until Mrs. Boston's replacement arrives . . ." He smiled. "I'm sure you're old enough to understand," he added and left.

I wasn't old enough to understand. Why did he let her fire Mrs. Boston? Why wasn't he in control?

Why did he tolerate all this unpleasantness and why did he permit these things to happen? Daddy wouldn't have, I thought mournfully. Mommy had once told me how weak Uncle Philip's father, Randolph, had been, how he had put up with Grandmother Laura's antics and temperament. Apparently, Uncle Philip wasn't much different when it came to his wife.

How I wished time would move quickly and I would finally be old enough to be in charge of my own life and Jefferson's. No matter how many promises and vows we made, and no matter how hard we all tried, it would always be difficult to live with Uncle Philip and Aunt Bet, I thought.

Jefferson woke up and we ate our lunch together in the room. His tears had stopped, but the anguish in his eyes stayed, so afterward, mostly to keep his mind off things, I played one of his games with him. Richard and Melanie remained bedridden the rest of the day and were unable to go down to supper. In my mind they were the ones who were better off. Aunt Bet had tried making a roast chicken, but she overcooked it and it came out dry and tough. She undercooked the potatoes and they seemed more like apples.

Uncle Philip tried to make the dinner pleasant by talking about the reconstruction of the hotel. He promised Jefferson he would take him over in the morning after breakfast to watch the bulldozers and wrecking machines complete the clearing of the burned-out structure. It was the first time since Mommy and Daddy's deaths that Jefferson showed any interest and excitement in anything.

During most of the meal, Aunt Bet continued to run up and down the stairs to check on how the twins were getting along. They were able to hold down their first solid food, according to her. She rattled on and on about them, how they looked, how they chewed their food, and how they each ate exactly the same amount. Uncle Philip shifted a conspiratorial gaze my way and smiled as if to say, "See what I mean? But we understand."

She never actually came out and said she was sorry for screaming and manhandling Jefferson, but she did say she hoped there would never be any such unpleasantness between us again. To make up for it, she brought out a double chocolate cake she had had Uncle Philip buy in town. She gave Jefferson a piece so large it made his eyes bulge. Even so, he nearly finished all of it.

Afterward, he and I watched some television together until he got sleepy. I took him upstairs and put him to bed in Melanie's room. Then I went into my room to read and write a new letter to Gavin. I told him all about what had occurred at the graveyard the night before and then described the day's events. I asked him not to tell Granddaddy Longchamp any of it because it would only upset him and there was little he could do. I ended by telling Gavin once again how much I looked forward to seeing him. This time, under my name I drew four X's which meant four kisses. Then, seeing his face behind my closed eyelids, I kissed the letter before sealing it.

Exhausted myself now from a most trying and emotional day, I filled my bathtub with hot water and sprinkled in Mommy's scented bubble bath powder. When I slid under the water, put my head back and closed my eyes, I felt myself relax and drift into my memories of Mommy, soft and loving, brushing my hair and telling me about all the wonderful things we were going to do at the hotel the next day. I was so lost in my reverie, I didn't hear the bedroom door open and close, nor did I hear Uncle Philip's footsteps nor realize he was there until I opened my eyes and saw him standing in the bathroom. I had no idea how long he had been there staring down at me.

I gasped and covered my breasts with my arms and slid down as far as I could under the bubbles. He laughed. He was holding a package.

"I'm sorry to disturb you," he said, "but I wanted to give you this before you went to sleep tonight. When I went into town to buy the cake for dessert, I saw it in the department store window and couldn't resist getting it for you."

"What is it?" I asked.

"It's a surprise gift to make up for some of the unpleasantness you've had to endure today," he said and continued to stand there. "Should I open it up and show it to you?"

I nodded. I thought the faster he did so, the faster he would leave.

He put the box on the sink and took the lid off so he could dip his hands in and come up with what was the sheerest white lace nightgown I had ever seen. He held it up.

"Isn't it pretty?" he asked. He put his cheek against it. "It's so soft and feminine, I couldn't help but think of you when I touched it. Wear it tonight, especially after a bath. It will make you feel good," he said.

"Thank you, Uncle Philip."

"Will you wear it tonight?" he asked. I couldn't understand why that would be so important to him, but imagined he just wanted to be sure his gift compensated for the nasty things that had occurred between Aunt Bet and us.

"Yes," I said.

"Good. I'm good at washing backs," he said after he put the nightgown back into the box. How could he suggest such a thing? I wasn't a child anymore. The look in his eyes frightened me. For a moment I couldn't speak.

"That's all right," I said, afraid he would come farther into the bathroom. "I'm almost ready to come out."

"Are you sure?" He took a step toward me.

"Yes," I said quickly, my heart pounding.

"All right," he said, obviously disappointed, "but you're really missing something." He stared at me a moment longer and then left. I listened for the sound of my bedroom door opening and closing and then I got out of the bathtub and dried myself. I looked at the nightgown. It was pretty and very soft. I slipped it over my head and gazed at myself in the mirror. It was so light and transparent, I might as well be naked, I thought. What sort of a gift was this for an uncle to buy his niece? I wondered, but I wore it to sleep.

Some time late at night, I woke abruptly after dreaming that Uncle Philip had come into my bedroom again and quietly come to the side of my bed. He peeled back my blanket softly and gazed down at me for the longest time and then covered me up and left as quietly as he had come in. The dream was so vivid, my eyes snapped open and my heart was racing. I gazed around anxiously, but there was no one there. Even so, I lay awake for a long time before my lids became heavy again and sleep washed over me.

The next morning the twins made a miraculous, complete recovery. Both Richard and Melanie were full of energy and had great appetites at breakfast. Aunt Bet looked very pleased.

"We'll keep the sleeping arrangements the way they are for one more day just to be sure," she declared, "and then everything can return to normal. Our new maid and cook will be arriving later today, too," she announced. "She comes highly recommended. She used to work for friends of my parents, so we can be sure our meals will be made well and served properly and everything will be kept spotless.

"Oh, I feel so good about the future now that Richard and Melanie are healthy again," she cried and clapped her hands together. Although neither Richard nor Melanie smiled or said anything, they both wore expressions of approval.

Uncle Philip nodded and smiled and then announced he was off to the hotel.

"Jefferson's coming with me to inspect the work. Would you like to come too, Christie?"

"No thank you, Uncle Philip. I'm going to visit Grandmother Laura."

"I would like to go along with you, Father," Richard said.

"Me too," Melanie chimed.

"Oh no," Aunt Bet said. "You two need one more day's complete rest. You don't know how sick you were."

Both of them pouted simultaneously.

"Okay, ready, Jefferson?" Uncle Philip asked. Jefferson flicked a glance my way. I knew he wanted me to go along and my refusal to do so made him hesitant, but the promise of seeing all those machines was too great. He nodded and followed Uncle Philip out.

"Christie, would you help me with the dishes?" Aunt Bet asked.

"Yes," I said and began gathering them. I often helped Mrs. Boston and just doing it brought back the memories of our warm and happy talks together in the kitchen.

"I can help too," Melanie said.

"Oh no, Melanie. You go sit in the living room and read," Aunt Bet said. "You're liable to drop something."

"Why is she able to do it?" she whined.

"She wasn't sick, was she?" Aunt Bet said. "Thank you, Christie. Please bring in the glasses," she said and headed for the kitchen with some of the dishes.

"Here," Melanie said, thrusting her glass at me after I had picked up four already. She let it go before I had my fingers on it and it fell over a bowl, shattering both the bowl and the glass.

"What happened?" Aunt Bet cried from the kitchen doorway.

"She's so clumsy," Melanie accused.

"That's not true. You didn't give me a chance to hold the glass," I retorted.

"She tried to take too much," Richard said, pulling the corner of his mouth in. "It wasn't Melanie's fault."

"That's a lie!"

"All right, children. All right." Aunt Bet glared at me. "Just leave everything for me before something else gets broken," she said.

Both Melanie and Richard looked satisfied, both softening their lips identically in the corners. I glanced once more at Aunt Bet and then rushed from the room and the house, frustrated by the irony that I wanted to leave my own home as quickly as I could.

No One Understands

ALL OF THE HOTEL STAFF HAD LEFT, OF COURSE. WITH the hotel burned down, there wasn't anything for them to do. But some of the grounds people had been kept on to help with the removal of debris and the rebuilding. Since the family still needed a chauffeur, Julius remained on salary and continued to live in the staff quarters behind the hotel. I found him outside, washing the limousine.

"When you're finished, Julius, will you please take me to my grandmother's," I asked.

"Sure, Christie. I'm just about done. Get in. I'll do the detail work while you're visiting," he said.

I got into the limousine and stared out the window at the workers buzzing around the debris and machinery. I could see Jefferson standing beside Buster Morris. Jefferson stood with his hands on his hips just like Daddy used to. It made me smile, but it also brought tears to my eyes. How much he missed his father, I thought. How cruel it was to live in a world where a young boy's father could be ripped away from him before they had a chance to really get to know each other.

It made me think of Mommy and how horrible it must have been for her to learn that the man and woman she thought were her parents weren't, and how difficult and frightening it was for her to be returned to her real family after so many years. As the limousine turned down the driveway and headed toward Buella Woods, Bronson Alcott's home, I couldn't help wondering what it must have been like for Mommy the first day she came face to face with her real mother. How I wish my grandmother was clear-minded enough to tell me about those days. However bad things were for her then, they were wonderful for her now. She was married to a man who loved her dearly. She should feel secure and happy.

Buella Woods stood on a high hill looking down on Cutler's Cove. The house was big enough to be a castle. It had been built with gray stone wall cladding and decorative half-timbering. It had a prominent round tower with a high conical roof. The tower housed the main entrance, which was a dark pine door set in a single arched opening. Under the windows on the second floor were small wrought-iron decorative balconies. Jefferson always wanted to crawl out on those balconies and could never understand why anyone would have built them just for show.

Julius opened my door for me and I went up the steps and rang the door chimes. The entry way was so deep, the chimes sounded like chimes in a cathedral. Mrs. Berme, Grandmother's private nurse, surprised me by answering the door. Usually, Bronson's butler, a dark-haired, stout man named Humbrick, did.

"Oh Christie," Mrs. Berme said. "Your grandmother just dozed off in the parlor, but I'm sure she won't be asleep long. Come in," she said. "Mr. Alcott's in his office."

"Thank you, Mrs. Berme," I replied and walked

down the corridor. I looked in on Grandmother and saw she was asleep in her favorite soft chair, a blanket tucked around her and up to her throat. She looked gray and pale, except for where she had dabbed her rouge too hard on her cheeks. I hurried on to Bronson's office. The door was open, but I knocked on the jamb. He was behind his desk reading some papers.

"Christie," he said, standing immediately. "I'm glad you've come."

"Grandmother's asleep," I said.

"I'm sure she won't be for long. Her naps are frequent but short these days. Come in. Sit down. Tell me how you and Jefferson have been getting along," he said, pointing to the burgundy leather settee. I sat down quickly.

"Terribly," I said.

"Oh?" He lifted his eyebrows and tightened his mouth and narrowed his eyes. "What's wrong?"

"Everything, Bronson. Aunt Bet is horrible to us. And she's fired Mrs. Boston!"

"What? Fired Mrs. Boston? I don't believe it," he said, sitting down.

"She did. My cousins got sick with stomach aches and she blamed it on Mrs. Boston's cooking and cleaning," I said.

"Really? How extraordinary."

"She told her to leave and Uncle Philip refused to interfere. He says she's the mistress of the house now and the servants have to get along with her," I cried.

"Well . . . he's right about that, I'm afraid. But I can't imagine anyone not getting along with Mrs. Boston. Why, she was one of the few servants Grandmother Cutler respected." He shook his head and then looked up at me. "I'll ask Philip about it, but if there's a personality clash between

Mrs. Boston and Betty Ann, there's not much that can be done. Why did you say that your Aunt Bet's horrible to you and Jefferson?"

"She is. She's always yelling at Jefferson for being too messy. She wants us to take our shoes off before we come into the house," I said. The moment the words were out of my mouth, I realized how silly and petty I sounded. I could see Bronson thought so, too.

"Well, you know Jefferson can be a little Huckleberry Finn, Christie," he said, smiling. "I remember that time he crawled into the wood pile out back. I'm sure Betty Ann's just trying to get him to be a little more responsible. And now, with Mrs. Boston gone . . ."

"That's her fault," I moaned.

"Maybe. But it's happened and we'll have to live with it," he said.

"She moved Richard into Jefferson's room and they don't get along," I said, moving quickly to a new complaint so Bronson would see my justification for being so upset. He squeezed his chin between his forefinger and thumb and nodded.

"Young boys should share a room. I'm sure after a while they will get along better. Anyway, what choice did Betty Ann have? She would have had to have Richard and Melanie share a room otherwise, right?"

"Yes," I said and blew air out of my lips with frustration.

"It doesn't sound so terrible, Christie."

"She's moved most of my mother's things into the attic," I moaned, "and Daddy's."

"Well, what could they do? They need space," he said.

"She kept some of my mother's jewelry, but I

know each and every piece . . ." Bronson smiled as my words slowly drifted to a stop.

"I doubt that they'll be a problem with jewelry, Christie. Betty Ann comes from a rather wealthy family. She doesn't need to keep someone else's things."

I folded my arms and sat back, my failure to impress him expanding like a balloon about to burst.

"I know this isn't easy for you. On top of losing two wonderful parents, you have to get used to living with another family, and that's difficult even though the family's your uncle and aunt," Bronson said softly. I stared at his kindly face for a moment.

"Bronson, you told me you would tell me everything you knew about my family," I said.

"Whatever I can," he replied, sitting back, his soft smile becoming a serious expression.

"When Mommy went to that fancy public school with Daddy, she met Uncle Philip and they became boyfriend and girlfriend, didn't they?"

"She didn't know Philip was really her half-brother," he said quickly.

"Were they . . . were they in love?" I asked timidly.

"Oh," he said smiling again. "They were young, teenagers, just infatuated. It was nothing," he added, shaking his head.

"Uncle Philip doesn't think so," I blurted without thinking. I didn't want to tell Bronson about my visit to my parents' graves at night and my overhearing Uncle Philip's conversation with my dead mother. He might think I was spying on my uncle.

Bronson's eyes grew small again and he leaned forward. "What makes you say such a thing?"

"Just the way he talks about her and something Mommy said to me not long before . . . before the fire," I replied.

"What did she say?"

"She said Uncle Philip's never gotten over their young romance and the discovery they were brother and sister," I said. He nodded thoughtfully.

"Well, it had to have been quite a shock. I don't know any more about it than I've been told, Christie, by both your mother and Philip. And of course, what your grandmother knew. As far as I've been told, it was a very short, school crush. They had barely gotten to know each other before the police arrived to take her back to Cutler's Cove. What sort of things does Philip say?" he wondered.

I hesitated and then blurted.

"He always talked about how beautiful she was and how much he loved her."

"Well, she was very beautiful," Bronson said. "And a very easy person to love. There's nothing wrong with his saying that, Christie," Bronson added smiling.

"He says I'm getting to look more and more like her."

"You are," Bronson agreed. "I'm sure you're not upset about that, are you?"

"No, but . . ."

"But what, Christie?" We stared at each other. "Well?"

"He's . . . strange. He's always hugging me and kissing me and . . ."

"He's just trying to give you the love he thinks you need. Philip's very devoted to both you and Jefferson," Bronson said. "You're lucky to have him."

"He bought me a nightgown and gave it to me last night," I revealed.

"Oh? Did he say why?"

"He said it was a surprise to cheer me up because of some of the things that happened."

"So? That's very nice of him, isn't it?" Bronson asked.

"But a nightgown?"

Bronson shrugged.

"He probably thought it was something a young girl would want. I can't fault him for that. I'm always confused and stupid when it comes to buying gifts for your grandmother." He paused to study me a moment. "Why does this upset you so?" he asked. "What are you thinking?"

Everything I said sounded so silly. I didn't know how to explain my real feelings. Bronson would just have to see it, witness it, I thought, and even then, he might not feel what I do.

"Aunt Fern told me the romance between Mommy and Uncle Philip was more serious," I said. "She upset me very much."

"Oh," Bronson said sitting back again. "I see. Well, I'm afraid I wouldn't listen to anything your Aunt Fern had to say about anyone." He shook his head. "She's quite a problem for everyone these days."

I dropped my gaze to the floor. I wanted to tell Bronson more—how I had overheard Uncle Philip's plea for forgiveness at the gravesite and how he had come in on me while I was bathing and offered to wash my back, but I was too embarrassed and afraid that I was sounding more and more ridiculous. I sighed deeply.

"Christie, your uncle is just trying to be a father to you now. I'm sure that's it. He feels all the responsibility has fallen on his shoulders. You shouldn't be afraid of him or read anything more into it.

"Matter of fact, I spoke with him just the day before yesterday," Bronson continued. I looked up sharply.

"Oh?"

"And he told me how much your deep sorrow pained him. He pledged to do all he could to make your life as pleasant as possible and help you do the things you want to do. It has become a major goal for him. You'll see," Bronson continued, smiling and coming around his desk to me. "Everything will work itself out eventually . . . Aunt Bet, the twins."

Maybe he was right, I thought. Maybe everything was just a product of my imagination, a result of all these emotional peaks and valleys. Bronson put his arm around me when I stood up.

"I'm sorry, Christie, so sorry this tragedy has befallen you and your little brother, but your uncle and your aunt and I will always be here to do what we can."

"Thank you, Bronson," I said. Then a new thought came. "Bronson, has anyone told my real father about this?"

"Your real father? As far as I know, no. Unfortunately, he is not someone I would care to know. The only time he showed any interest in you, he was really trying to squeeze money out of your mother."

"I know. She told me. I vaguely remember him coming to see me that time."

"If he found out what's happened, he would only try to profit from the situation, I'm sure," Bronson said. "No, dear, you are with the people who love you the most now. Bear with them. Give Philip and Betty Ann a chance. I know they're not what Dawn and Jimmy were to you, but they want to try. They really do," he said.

I nodded. What he was saying was not unreasonable.

We walked out together and went to see if Grandmother Laura had woken up. She had, but she was very confused and in the same breath referred to me as Dawn and then Clara. She babbled about some new skin cream and then suddenly fixed her eyes on me and said, "But you have a long, long time to go before you have to worry about wrinkles.

"Wrinkles!" she cried and lifted her eyes toward the ceiling. "They are a slow death for a beautiful woman."

The thought and the outburst exhausted her again and she closed her eyes and dropped her chin to her chest so quickly, I thought she had snapped her neck. I looked up anxiously at Mrs. Berme, who only shook her head. There was nothing else to do; Grandmother had fallen back into a deep repose once more. Unfortunately, she was no one I could confide in and look to for advice and help. My parents were gone; Mrs. Boston was gone; Aunt Bet was too insensitive; Aunt Trisha was too far away and too involved in her own career; and Bronson, as loving and concerned as he was, was too distant from my immediate world and had his hands full with Grandmother Laura.

When I stepped out to get back in the limousine and return to my house, I felt as alone and as powerless as the small cloud sliding helplessly across the light blue sky, abandoned and left behind by the bigger, thicker clouds that had already arrived at the horizon and were slipping over the world into someone else's tomorrow.

The slow, warm days of early summer that followed seemed gray and gloomy to me no matter what the weather. Gradually, we all fell into a daily routine. Aunt Bet spent a large part of her day breaking in the new cook and housekeeper, Mrs. Stoddard, a short, stout woman in her early sixties who kept her dull pewter gray hair tied in a loose bun behind her head, strands curling every which way like broken wires. She had small brown age spots over her forehead and cheeks which were so pudgy they made her nose look sunken. Her smile was warm enough and she had a pleasant manner when she spoke to us, but for Jefferson and me no one could take the place of Mrs. Boston. During the first few days, Mrs. Stoddard trailed through the house behind Aunt Bet as if Aunt Bet had tied one end of a string around the new servant's waist and the other around her own.

For the most part, the twins kept to themselves. They organized their days rigidly, breaking them up into periods of recreation (mainly thought-provoking parlor games like chess and Scrabble), reading, and their educational tapes. They had tapes to advance them in vocabulary and geography and they were both studying French. Despite the melancholy I continually endured, I couldn't help but laugh to myself whenever I walked past the living room and saw them sitting in a lotus position on the floor, facing each other, and practicing their French pronunciations, each mimicking the way the other's lips formed vowels and consonants.

Although it was summer and most children their age were enjoying the sunshine and the beach, outdoor sports and the company of friends, the twins spent most of their time indoors with each other. Even I, who felt too down most of the time to do more than take walks through the tattered remains of our once-beautiful gardens and an occasional walk on the beach, had more color in my cheeks than they did. But none of that bothered them. What others did was either stupid or wasteful. I had never realized just how arrogant and snobbish they were.

Fortunately, Jefferson was interested in the rebuilding of the hotel. Buster Morris had become his pal. Jefferson would go off with Uncle Philip after breakfast, but he would spend the day beside Buster, sometimes riding along with him on a bulldozer or in a pick-up truck. Often Aunt Bet was at the door waiting for him when he returned after the day's work. She would always make him take off his shoes, but one day, she insisted he strip off his pants and shirt as well because they were so dirty. Jefferson disliked doing it and disliked her even more, but he tolerated her and did what she asked, afraid that she would stop him from being with Buster.

I did a great deal of reading myself and wrote my daily letter to Gavin. We spoke on the telephone a few times, too. He had taken a job as a stockboy in a grocery store to earn enough money for his plane fare to Virginia. He was planning on visiting in late August. I wanted to send him some money, but I knew only the suggestion of doing that would ruffle up his feathers. It was just that I was so anxious to see him again. He had become the only person in whom I could confide.

Aunt Trish phoned as often as she could, but the second time she called, it was bad news. Her show had flopped on Broadway and she had decided to take a position with a traveling show. In a week they were to be off cross-country. She promised to call as often as she could, but I was so disappointed. I had hoped to go visit her in New York City very soon.

Finally, more to fill my days than out of a deep

desire to return to music, I began playing the piano again. Mr. Wittleman had phoned to see how I was doing and when I wanted to resume my lessons. I told him I would let him know. I thought it would be better if I practiced for a while on my own and brought myself at least back to the level I had been at before the tragedy had befallen us.

At first it was very difficult for me to sit down and run my fingers over the piano keys. I couldn't help but see Mommy's proud smile every time I tapped out a page of sheet music. I had never realized just how much of a part she had played in my musical development and just how important it had been for me to please her. Now, with her gone, there was such a great emptiness around me and an even greater emptiness in the pit of my stomach. To me, my music sounded mechanical, lifeless, hollow, but apparently, not so to Uncle Philip.

One afternoon, when I was trying to relearn a Beethoven sonata, I finally felt the notes take over and for a while provide a kind of escape from my unhappy world. I was so involved in it that I didn't hear Uncle Philip come in and sit down, but when I finished the piece, he clapped. I spun around on the stool and saw him sitting there, smiling.

"I'm so happy you've gone back to the piano," he said. "Your mother would be happy too, Christie."

"It's not the same for me," I replied. "Nothing is."

"It will be," he promised. "Give it time and keep practicing."

He was so happy about my playing that he made it the chief topic of conversation at dinner that night. Aunt Bet smiled and said encouraging things, too. Only the twins looked glum. Jefferson, as usual, ate quietly, kept to himself, and left the table as soon as he was permitted. Dinners would never be the same for him, never hold the magic and warmth they had when Mommy and Daddy and the two of us sat around and talked and teased each other lovingly. Mrs. Boston wasn't coming out of the kitchen to chide Daddy for teasing me or Jefferson. She had been as protective of us as Mommy.

Anyway, I continued to practice and two days later took my first lesson with Mr. Wittleman. He said I had remarkably maintained and even improved some of my skills. That night, at dinner, Uncle Philip begged me to play something for the family afterward. I tried to refuse, but he pleaded and pleaded until it became embarrassing. Finally, I agreed. After dessert had been served, everyone, including Jefferson, came into the parlor and sat behind me. I played a nocturne by Chopin I had been practicing with Mr. Wittleman.

When I was finished, Uncle Philip stood up and applauded. Aunt Bet did too. Richard and Melanie clapped quickly, both looking annoyed.

"That was spectacular, absolutely fantastic!" Uncle Philip exclaimed. He turned to the twins. "Your cousin is going to be a very famous pianist some day and you will be proud to be related to her," he told them. Neither seemed impressed.

"I can't wait for the hotel to be rebuilt and a new season to start," Uncle Philip continued, "so that Christie can play for our guests. We'll be the envy of every coast resort from Maine to Florida."

He rushed over to give me a kiss, and out of the corner of my eye, I saw Melanie look down. Uncle Philip's over-exuberant accolades embarrassed me, but there was nothing I could say or do to stop him once he had begun. Finally, Jefferson asked to watch some television and we were able to escape. The twins rarely watched television with us. They usually read and listened to music or played one of their board games.

But late the next afternoon, when I went into the parlor and sat down to prepare for my next lesson with Mr. Wittleman, I touched the piano keys and then screamed in shock. Both Mrs. Stoddard and Aunt Bet came running in from the kitchen. And the twins came flying down the stairs.

"What's wrong?" Aunt Bet asked grimacing. I was holding my hands up, bent at the wrist, my fingers dangling.

"Someone . . ." I couldn't speak for a moment. "Someone poured gobs and gobs of honey over the piano keys!" I cried. "They've ruined my piano."

Richard and Melanie approached and stared down at the keys. Melanie touched one and smelled the tip of her finger.

"Ugh," she said, turning to show Mrs. Stoddard and Aunt Bet.

"Oh dear," Mrs. Stoddard said, shaking her head. "How dreadful."

Aunt Bet's face turned pink with rage.

"That's a horrible, horrible prank," she declared. "I must tell Philip immediately." She marched out of the house. Mrs. Stoddard ran to the kitchen for some washcloths, but it was futile to try to repair the damage, for the honey had dripped down in between the keys and under them, making them stick.

"It's no use, Mrs. Stoddard," I said. "We've got to have someone come to take it all apart."

"I'm so sorry, dear. It's such a cruel and vicious thing for anyone to do."

I nodded and gathered up my sheet music, and

then I went to phone Mr. Wittleman to tell him so he could make other arrangements for me and find someone to repair the piano. He couldn't believe what I told him. He was outraged.

"It's an inexcusable violation," he declared. "Whoever did such a thing is barbaric."

A few minutes after I spoke with Mr. Wittleman, Aunt Bet returned with Uncle Philip and took him into the parlor to show him the piano. He shook his head and grimaced with disgust.

"I'm sorry about this, Christie," he said. "We'll get to the bottom of it fast."

"I just spoke with Mr. Wittleman. He's getting someone to clean the keys."

"Good."

We all turned at the sound of Richard and Melanie pounding down the stairway. They both appeared in the parlor door, out of breath with excitement.

"Father," Richard said, "look what I found."

He held up a small dish towel. Aunt Bet took it from him slowly.

"It's full of honey," she said. "Someone's wiped his hands in it. Where did you find this, Richard?"

"On Jefferson's side of the closet," he said smugly and nodded as if he had always known.

"That can't be," I said. "Jefferson would never do this."

"That's where I found it," Richard insisted.

"You're lying. My brother wouldn't do this."

Aunt Bet turned to Uncle Philip.

"Where is he?" she demanded.

"With Buster," he replied.

"Go get him this instant," she commanded. Uncle Philip glanced at me and then nodded.

"No!" I shouted. "I'll go get him myself." I fixed

a hateful gaze on Richard, who continued to look quite smug and confident.

I turned away and ran out of the house to fetch my little brother. It was true that Jefferson could be mischievous, but his pranks were always pranks of fun and never vicious and mean. He hated to make anyone else cry and I knew he loved me more now than ever and would never do anything to upset me so. I found him by the tool shed. Buster had put him to work shellacking a new door. He was obviously very proud of his assignment and work.

"Jefferson, you've got to come home with me right away," I said. He looked up disappointed.

"Why?"

"Someone poured honey over the piano keys and ruined them," I said. He widened his eyes. "Richard found a dish towel on your side of the closet filled with honey and he's got Aunt Bet and Uncle Philip believing you did it."

"I did not!"

"I know you didn't. I'm sure he did it," I said. "We'll go back there and make them see the truth."

"I don't wanna," Jefferson said. "I gotta finish this door." I could see the fear in his eyes.

"It's all right, Jefferson. She won't hurt you," I promised. "I won't let her."

"If she does," he said. "I'll run away forever."

"She won't. I promise."

Reluctantly, he put down the brush and wiped his hands on a rag.

"Buster's going to be mad," he muttered.

"Uncle Philip will explain what happened. Don't worry." I took his hand and we walked home.

Aunt Bet conducted her mock trial in the living room. We were all commanded to take seats, even Uncle Philip and Mrs. Stoddard. The twins sat on the sofa and glared with simultaneous expressions of indignation and accusation at Jefferson, who sat beside me on the matching settee. If the air wasn't so filled with tension, I might have burst out laughing, for Aunt Bet paced about cross-examining everyone like Perry Mason in a courtroom. Even Uncle Philip sat back and stared up at her in fascination.

"This terribly cruel deed was performed some time between last night and this afternoon," she began and stopped to rest her palm on the piano. "Mrs. Stoddard and I have checked the kitchen cabinet and found a nearly empty jar of honey." She nodded at Mrs. Stoddard, who then unfolded her hands to reveal the jar in her palms. "Mrs. Stoddard and I recall the jar was nearly three-quarters full. Isn't that correct, Mrs. Stoddard?"

"Oh yes, ma'am."

Aunt Bet smiled as if that was enough to solve the case.

"Since Mrs. Stoddard was in the kitchen at six-fifteen this morning, whoever did this, did it before then."

"Unless the jar was taken earlier and replaced afterward," I said. Aunt Bet's self-satisfied smile faded.

"She's right about that, Betty Ann," Uncle Philip said, smiling at me.

"This deed was done last night after we had all retired to our rooms," Aunt Bet insisted. "Now then," she continued, crossing the room first to pick up the dish towel lying on the floor beside the sofa and then to stand in front of Jefferson and me, "how did that dish towel get into your closet, Jefferson?"

"I don't know," Jefferson said, shrugging.

"Didn't you get up last night and come down here to do this to the piano?" she asked outright.

Jefferson shook his head.

"Didn't you go into the kitchen, get the jar of honey, spill it into the piano keys, put the jar back, grab this dish towel to wipe your hands, run back upstairs and throw the dish towel into your closet, hoping that no one would find it?" she followed, stabbing down at him with her questions and her accusing eyes. Jefferson shook his head and began to cry.

"You're crying because you did it, aren't you?" she demanded. Jefferson started to cry harder. "Aren't you!" She seized his little shoulder and started to shake him. *"You did this!"* she screamed.

"Leave him alone," I cried and ripped her hand off his shoulder. Jefferson threw his arms around me immediately and I hugged him and glared back at Aunt Bet. "He didn't do it. He couldn't have done it. He wouldn't do such a thing."

She straightened up and smirked, folding her arms under her small bosom. I turned to Uncle Philip.

"He's never gone wandering through the house alone at night, Uncle Philip. He's afraid to do that. He's just a little boy."

"Not too little to try to destroy a valuable piano," Aunt Bet snapped.

"He didn't. Mrs. Stoddard," I said. "Let me see that honey jar, please." She looked up at Aunt Bet who indicated it would be all right. Mrs. Stoddard handed it to me and I looked at it and then flicked a quick glance at Richard, who sat expressionless. Not even his eyes betrayed any emotion.

"Was the jar this clean or did you wipe it off, Mrs. Stoddard?" I asked.

"It's the way we found it," she replied.

"Even if Jefferson did such a thing, which he didn't," I said firmly, "he would never be this neat about it. There's not a drop outside the jar."

"That's a good point, Betty Ann," Uncle Philip said.

"He wiped it off," she replied quickly. "With that towel he threw in his closet."

"You can't wipe honey off a jar with a dry towel and not have it still be sticky," I insisted. "Whoever put that towel in Jefferson's closet," I said, glaring at Richard, "simply poured some honey into it and rubbed it around."

"That's . . . that's . . . ridiculous," Aunt Bet said, but Uncle Philip didn't think so. His gaze moved swiftly toward Richard.

"Did you do this, Richard?" he demanded.

"Of course not, Father. Would I vandalize something?"

"I hope not. Melanie, did Richard get up during the night and come downstairs?" Uncle Philip asked. She shifted her eyes to Richard and then back to Uncle Philip and shook her head. "Are you sure?" She nodded, but not firmly.

Uncle Philip stared at his twins for a moment and then looked up at Aunt Bet.

"I think we'll have to leave this where it is," he said.

"But Philip, that piano . . ."

"It's going to be repaired. From now on," he said, "I don't want to see anyone but Christie near it. Understand? No one is even to touch it." He glared at the twins and then turned back to Jefferson and me. Jefferson had stopped sobbing and had lifted his head from my shoulder.

"I hafta go back and help Buster," Jefferson said.

"Go on," Uncle Philip replied.

"He should be punished," Aunt Bet insisted. "He should . . ."

"He didn't do it, Aunt Bet," I cried and threw my hateful glare at Richard.

"But he . . ."

"Betty Ann!" Uncle Philip shouted. "Let it be," he said slowly and firmly. She bit down on her lower lip.

"Very well," she said after a moment. "I believe we have established our unhappiness and given fair warning that if anything like this should ever happen again . . ."

Her words were left hanging in the air. Jefferson walked out of the living room slowly, rubbing his eyes. I handed the jar of honey back to Mrs. Stoddard and the twins scurried out of the room and up the stairs like two mice who had miraculously escaped the claws of a cat.

Aunt Bet was terribly frustrated by her failure to prove conclusively that Jefferson had vandalized the piano, and she demonstrated that frustration in many ways, the chief one being her tone of voice whenever she spoke to my little brother. Whereas she would speak softly, kindly, respectfully to the twins, she wouldn't speak to Jefferson without snapping at him and making her eyes like two cold, polished stones. She criticized him every chance she had, still finding fault with the way he ate, with what he wore and how well he washed his face and hands. She even criticized his posture and walk. If there was a smudge on a wall or a spot on the floor, it was always Jefferson's fault. Jefferson tracked in dirt; Jefferson touched things with stained hands. The peace of the day and night was continually shattered by Aunt Bet's shrill voice crying, *"Jeffer-*

son Longchamp!" Her scream was always followed with some accusation.

When I complained to her about the way she was picking on him, she gave me her small, icy smile and replied, "It's only natural for you to defend your brother, Christie, but don't be blind to his faults or he will never improve."

"He won't make any improvements if you continue to shout at him and pick on him," I told her.

"I don't pick on him. I point out his faults so he can concentrate on eliminating them. Just as I do with my own children."

"Hardly," I said. "According to you, your children are perfect."

"Christie!" she said, pulling back her shoulders as if I had slapped her. "That's impudent."

"I don't care," I said. "I don't like being disrespectful, but I won't stand by quietly and watch you tear my little brother into pieces."

"Oh my . . ."

"Just stop it," I said. Even though tears flooded my eyes, my backbone straightened like a flag pole, my pride waving. All Aunt Bet could do was stutter and rush off.

"Well . . . well . . . well," she said.

It wasn't hard to predict that the trouble between us would not end soon. Her ego was bruised and the more Uncle Philip defended me or Jefferson, the angrier and meaner she became. Her smiles were cold and short. Often I would catch her glaring at me when she didn't think I would see. Her thin lips were pursed together to become a fine line or her small nostrils flared. I knew she wasn't thinking nice thoughts about me because blood would flood her face as if she had been caught red-handed doing something cruel.

I put all of this in my letters to Gavin and waited

for him to write back or call. When nearly a week passed and no letters arrived and he didn't phone, I phoned him to see if something was wrong.

"No, nothing's wrong," he said. "I've written back twice."

"I don't know why I didn't get the letters," I said.

"The mail can be slow. Anyway, the good news is I will be coming to see you in three weeks," he said.

"Three weeks! Oh Gavin, that sounds like three years to me," I replied. He laughed.

"It's not. It will pass fast."

"Maybe for you," I said, "but life here is so unpleasant now, every day seems like a week."

"I'm sorry. I'll see what I can do to speed it up," he promised.

Two days later, I inadvertently discovered why I hadn't received a letter from Gavin for over a week. Mrs. Stoddard had made the mistake of putting out our garbage the night before instead of early in the morning of the pick-up, and some stray dog or perhaps a squirrel had torn open a bag and strewn the contents all around the can. I got a rake from behind the house and began gathering up the debris when I happened to notice an envelope addressed to me. I stopped and picked it up.

It was a letter from Gavin and it was dated only last week. Someone had taken it from the mailbox before I had gotten to the mail and had ripped it open to read it and then dropped it in the garbage.

Outraged, I stormed into the house.

The twins were sitting on the floor in the parlor playing Scrabble. Aunt Bet was reading one of her society papers and Mrs. Stoddard was in the kitchen. Uncle Philip and Jefferson were already at the hotel.

"Who did this?" I asked and held up the letter. "Someone took my mail and threw it away."

Aunt Bet shifted her gaze casually from the paper and looked up at me. The twins paused, both nonplussed.

"Whatever are you talking about, Christie?" Aunt Bet asked.

"My mail, my mail," I raged, frustrated. "Someone took it before I could get to it and read it and threw it away."

"I don't think anyone here would be interested in your mail, dear. It must have been thrown out by accident. Perhaps you did so yourself."

"I did not!"

"Christie, I must insist you stop this tantrum immediately. In our house we are not accustomed to such outbursts," she said.

"This isn't your house! It's my house. Which of you did this?" I asked, turning on the twins. Both cowered as I stepped toward them.

"Christie, leave them alone. They're playing so nicely," Aunt Bet warned.

"You did this, didn't you?" I accused Richard.

"I did not. I couldn't care less about your stupid mail."

I shifted my eyes to Melanie and she looked down quickly.

"You did it then," I said. She shook her head.

"If they said they didn't do it, they didn't. Now are you going to stop this, or do I have to send for your uncle?" she threatened.

"Send for the President of the United States, for all I care," I told her. "If you ever touch a piece of my mail or any of my things," I threatened Melanie, "I'll tear out your hair strand by strand."

"Christie!"

With that I rushed from the parlor and hurried upstairs to read the letter I had never received. That night our usually depressed dinner conversation was even more so. Every once in a while I caught Uncle Philip staring at me. Whenever I did, his lips would quiver into a small smile. Afterward, when I retired to my room for the night, he came to my door.

"May I speak with you a moment?" he asked after he knocked softly.

"Yes."

"Betty Ann told me what happened today. I'm sorry someone took your mail, but you shouldn't accuse anyone unless you're sure. It's as bad as what happened to Jefferson," he added quickly.

"Melanie looked very guilty," I said in my defense.

"Maybe, but Jefferson looked very guilty too and had a record of committing pranks and being a nuisance. Oh, nothing as serious as vandalizing the piano, I suppose, but still . . ."

"Someone took my letter," I moaned. "It didn't walk its way into our garbage can."

"No, it didn't. But it might have happened by accident."

"It was opened; it couldn't have been an accident. And there are other letters missing, too," I said. He nodded, his face tightening, his eyes growing smaller.

"All right. I'll see what I can learn about it, but please, let's try to live in peace for a while. Okay?" he asked, smiling. "Everything's going fine with the rebuilding of the hotel. The insurance covered a lot more than I first expected. We're going to do all right and be an important family in Cutler's Cove once again."

I wanted to tell him none of that was important to me. I didn't care if I ever walked back into that hotel. The hotel had betrayed my parents, killed them. It was never a great love of mine, but now it was something evil. But I didn't say any of this. I knew he wouldn't understand or he would stay and try to convince me otherwise.

Instead, I did what he asked. I avoided controversies, practiced the piano and took long walks on the beach. In the evening I read, wrote my letters, spoke to some of my friends and watched some television. I had a calendar on my wall and marked off the days until Gavin's arrival. That and my music were the only reasons I got up in the morning.

Things did quiet down and I became friendlier with Mrs. Stoddard. After all, I thought, it wasn't her fault Aunt Bet had driven Mrs. Boston away and she was asked to replace her. Jefferson got to like her more, too, and I could see she began to favor him. The twins saw it as well and before long, they were complaining about Mrs. Stoddard, and Aunt Bet was finding fault with the way she cleaned and cooked.

No one could work for these people, I thought. They were despicable.

I still made nocturnal gravesite visits and cried and complained to Mommy and Daddy. It usually left me feeling better. I never caught Uncle Philip there again at night, but one evening, after I had returned from the cemetery and quietly entered the house as usual, tiptoeing up the stairway, the interlude of family peace came to an abrupt and explosive end.

Aunt Bet burst out of my room just as I reached the second floor landing.

"Where were you?" she demanded. She had her hands behind her back as if she were holding something she didn't want me to see.

"I went for a walk," I said. "What were you doing in my room?"

"What walk? Where? Who did you meet? You met someone, didn't you?" she fired.

"What?"

"I told you," she said to Uncle Philip, who had come to their bedroom doorway. He stared out at me, not with a look of anger on his face as much as a look of genuine surprise. "You have a secret boyfriend, don't you? You meet him somewhere." She shook her head in disgust. "You're just like Fern."

"Aunt Bet, I don't know what you're talking about, but I'd like to know why you were in my room. What do you have behind your back?" I demanded.

She smiled gleefully and slowly brought her arms around.

"Disgusting," she said and held out my copy of *Lady Chatterley's Lover,* the marker I had left in chapter ten still there.

One Betrayal Too Many

"HOW DARE YOU GO SNOOPING AROUND THROUGH MY closets and drawers!" I cried. "What right do you have going into my room and looking at my things? You're not my mother! You could never be my mother!" I raged.

Aunt Bet straightened up and lifted her head in a haughty manner. The twins came to the doorway of their bedrooms simultaneously and peered out with sleepy but curious eyes. Only Jefferson remained asleep, something for which I was thankful. He had seen and been victim of enough of Aunt Bet's actions.

"I don't intend to be your mother, Christie, but your uncle Philip and I are your guardians now and that brings heavy responsibility with it. We're here to be sure specifically that this sort of thing doesn't happen," she added, waving the book.

"What sort of thing?"

I turned to Uncle Philip, but he continued to stare at me with this amazed look on his face.

"The same sort of improper behavior your aunt Fern is famous for by now," she replied coldly. "I know how you so-called modern teenage girls carry on," she said nodding. "You're far more promiscuous than girls were when I was your age."

"That's not true . . . at least it isn't true for me," I replied.

"Really?" She smiled coldly. "Then why did you mark off these particular passages in this obscene book?" she asked, opening it. I felt my face turn crimson. "Would you like me to read the passages out loud?"

"No! Fern marked those passages. She gave me the book for my birthday as a mean joke. I've never even looked at it again since then."

"Isn't this your primer, your textbook on sexual behavior? Did you get ideas from it and then sneak out at night to practice them with some town boy?" she asked in a tone of accusation.

"I didn't meet anyone!" I said, but she wasn't listening to me any longer. She was off and running on her own train of thought, regardless of what I or anyone else would say.

"I often told Philip that Dawn and Jimmy were losing their grip on Fern. It got so they couldn't control her any longer and she continued and continues to get into serious trouble at school. It's a wonder she isn't pregnant yet," Aunt Bet concluded. "Now you're following in her dirty footsteps."

"I am not!"

"Only I won't stand for it," she said, ignoring my denial. "I won't be as weak and forgiving as Dawn was. After all, your uncle's reputation and mine are now forever tied to yours. What you do with yourself is no longer only your concern. Your actions reflect on us, too."

"I haven't done anything wrong!" I cried, the tears now streaming freely down my cheeks.

"And you won't. I forbid you to read this sort of prurient material in my house," she said.

"Your house?" I muttered. In her mind she had taken over Jefferson's and my lives completely, taken over our home, our possessions, our very thoughts.

And while she ranted and raved at me, waving the book Aunt Fern had given me in my face, Uncle Philip stood by like a statue of himself, the only movement in his face coming from his continually blinking eyelids and the tremble in his lips.

"I will keep this book," she said.

"You're probably going to take it to read it yourself," I muttered hatefully.

"What? What did you say?" she demanded. I embraced myself and stared at the floor, unable to keep my shoulders from shaking with my sobs.

"You had no right to go snooping in my room," I complained mournfully.

"I didn't go snooping in your room. Mrs. Stoddard happened to see this book while she was cleaning and told me about it. I came to your room to ask you about it and discovered you had snuck out for some rendezvous. Then I looked for myself, hoping what Mrs. Stoddard said wasn't true. Unfortunately, it was."

I didn't believe her, but I was too tired to argue any more.

"From now on, I don't want you leaving the house after eight without specific permission from either your uncle or myself. And we have to know where you are going and with whom. Is that clear? Is it?" she demanded, stabbing her words at me like tiny daggers when I wouldn't reply.

"Yes, yes," I said and stormed past her and into my room, slamming the door behind me. I threw myself on the bed and buried my face in the pillow, which soaked up my stream of tears. I cried until my spring of sorrow was empty and then I sighed and sat up slowly. I ran my fingers over the gold watch Mommy and Daddy had given me. My heart ached because I missed them so very much.

Defeated and exhausted, I got up and began to dress for bed. Increasingly sleep had come to resemble a path of escape. It frightened me to realize how much I looked forward to closing my eyes and retreating from what had become this dark and woeful world. I would want to sleep longer and longer until . . . I'd want to sleep forever, I thought.

I washed my face and put on a pair of flannel pajamas, a pair Mommy had bought me. I couldn't get the chill out of my body and even after I had crawled under the blanket, I shuddered and trembled so hard, my teeth clicked. I tried clamping my eyelids shut in hopes of falling into a deep sleep, but moments later, I heard the sound of a gentle rapping at my door. At first, I thought I had imagined it, but it came again.

"Who's there?" I called weakly. The door opened and Uncle Philip entered, closing the door softly behind him. He was in his pajamas. In the tiny glow of my night lamp, I saw his small smile. "What is it now, Uncle Philip?" I asked.

He came directly to my bed and sat down beside me.

"I didn't want you to go to sleep unhappy," he said. He lightly brushed the back of his hand over my cheek. Then he took my hand into his. "Betty Ann can be a bit too harsh at times. She doesn't mean to be; it's part of her nervous condition," he explained.

"She doesn't have a nervous condition," I

snapped, pulling my hand from his. I was tired of hearing excuses for her. "She's just mean."

"No, no, she's simply frightened," he insisted.

"Frightened? Of what? Of me?" I started to laugh. "She does whatever she wants here no matter what I say anyway—torments Jefferson, fires Mrs. Boston, sets down her strict rules and insists we walk a fine line," I rattled.

"She's frightened of caring for and being responsible for a mature young lady," he said.

"Why? She has Melanie, doesn't she?"

"Yes, but Melanie's still a child. You're a blossoming woman who is obviously feeling a woman's needs and desires," he added softly, his eyes smaller. He ran his tongue nervously over his lips. "You can tell me the truth. Did you meet someone tonight?" he asked softly.

"No. I went for a walk. It helps me think," I said. I wouldn't dare tell him I had gone to the cemetery. He might easily guess I had been there the night he was at my mother's grave.

His smile widened.

"I believe you," he said. Then he grew very serious. "But these feelings, these new desires, they can confuse a young person so badly that he or she thinks he's going mad at times." He clutched at his chest and closed his eyes. "These feelings twist and torment you inside, making you feel as if you might explode if you don't find relief. You want to touch something, feel something, press yourself against something that will . . . will calm you down. Am I right? Is that what's been happening to you?"

"No, Uncle Philip," I said. His eyes were wide when he spoke, the glint in them maddening and frightening to me.

"I know," he said smiling again, "that it's a bit embarrassing for you to tell me these things. It's something you would rather discuss with your mother. But alas," he said, wagging his head, "your mother's gone and Betty Ann . . . well, Betty Ann's not the sort who is receptive to these thoughts and discussions. I understand your need to confide in someone who cares a great deal for you. I came here tonight to offer you myself. I want to help you," he said quickly. "Oh, I know, I can't replace your mother and I don't even want to try to do that, but you can trust me, Christie. I will keep your secrets locked tightly in my heart."

"I have no secrets, Uncle Philip," I said.

"I don't mean secrets exactly. I mean feelings," he said. "That's why you were so eager to accept that book from Fern, right? You wanted to know about these things, and it's only natural you do. You're at that age. Why should you flounder about, ignorant of what goes on between a man and a woman, just because your mother's no longer here to explain things to you?

"Well," he continued, smiling again, "I'm here. Can I help you? Can I answer a question, explain a feeling?"

I shook my head. I didn't know what to say. What sort of questions did he expect I would ask? My hesitation didn't discourage him.

"I realize," he said, nodding, "that you can't get yourself to put these feelings into words. It was the same for me as it was for your mother.

"When I first met her, she wasn't much older than you are now, and I was about your age, you know. We confided in each other then," he said in a whisper. "We revealed our innermost thoughts and feelings. We trusted each other. If she trusted me, you certainly can."

He pressed his right palm over the small of my stomach and slid it slowly and smoothly up a few inches. I jumped at his touch, but that didn't dissuade him. He didn't care or seem to notice how I cringed under him.

"You know, I was the first boy, the first man, to touch her here," he said, moving his palm lightly up and over my breast. My heart began to pound so hard, I thought it might beat his hand away. I held my breath, unable to believe what was happening.

"I helped her to explore, to understand," he said. "I can do that for you, too. You don't have to go to books and read them secretly in your room to discover these things. Just ask me anything you want . . . anything," he said quietly.

I couldn't move; I couldn't speak; I couldn't swallow. He closed his eyes and moved his hand from breast to breast slowly over my pajama top, his thumb pressing a bit harder, until he touched my nipple. I jumped and he opened his eyes.

"Uncle Philip!"

"It's all right; it's all right. There, there, don't be frightened. You want to understand everything, don't you?" he asked. "So you don't get yourself into trouble. Sure you do," he added nodding. "Too many young girls your age falter about and fall into the wrong hands. They don't know how far they should go and they get themselves into desperate situations. You don't want that to happen to you, do you?"

"It won't happen to me, Uncle Philip," I managed to say and pulled myself up in the bed so that his hand dropped from my breasts. Quickly, I embraced myself, covering my bosom with my arms protectively.

"Don't be arrogant and overconfident about it," he warned. "You don't understand what goes on in a man and how he can lose control of his own emotions. You should know what not to do," he advised, "what sort of things can drive a man to lose control of himself. Don't you want me to help you understand that?"

I shook my head.

"If Betty Ann is right and you're meeting someone . . ."

"I'm not," I said.

He stared at me a moment and then his smile returned and he reached out to stroke my hair.

"It's just that you're so pretty, and at a desirable age. I'd hate to see anything, anyone ruin you, spoil you, especially some oversexed teenage boy," he added, his expression changing to one of anger and indignation. "I'd feel terrible; I'd feel responsible. I'd feel I hadn't done my duty," he added.

"That won't happen, Uncle Philip."

"But you'll promise me you will come to me if you have any questions, any confusion. Promise me you'll trust me and let me help you," he said.

"I promise." I would promise anything at this moment to get him to leave, I thought.

His smile returned and he took a deep breath.

"I'll calm Betty Ann down and see to it that she lifts her restrictive curfew from you," he promised. "Can we . . . can I . . . have these personal talks with you from time to time? We won't tell Betty Ann," he added quickly. "She wouldn't understand and she's far too nervous to appreciate how important this can be. All right?" he persisted. His hand was on my knee.

"Yes," I said quickly.

"Good. Good." He patted me on the thigh and stood up. "Sleep well and remember I am here for you. I will be a mother and a father to you. You don't even have to call me Uncle Philip, if you don't want to. You can just call me Philip. Okay?"

I nodded.

"Okay. Good night, my sweet one," he said and knelt down to kiss me on the cheek. His lips felt like two tiny flames on my face and I snapped back quickly, but he didn't notice. His eyes were closed and he wore a look of deep satisfaction. He remained beside me a moment and then stood up again. "Good night, princess," he said and finally left me.

Even after he had gone and closed the door behind him, I couldn't move. My body felt frozen in a cake of ice. What had happened seemed more like a nightmare. Had it happened or had I indeed dreamt it? The memory of his fingers on my breasts was too strong and remained too vivid for it to have been anything but real, I thought.

Aunt Bet tormented Jefferson and me with her horrid rules and her insane attention to neatness and cleanliness; the twins were spiteful and jealous and sought only to make our lives more miserable, and Uncle Philip terrified me with his strange sexual advances and weird ideas.

How miserable our lives were now, and for what reason? What had we done to deserve this wretched and contemptible fate? Surely, I was right to believe there was a curse on our family. It wasn't something anyone else could appreciate or understand. I felt the inherited strain of disaster running through our destinies, saw the perennial gray clouds of gloom hovering over our heads, and understood that no matter how hard we tried, how fast we ran, or how much we prayed, the cold rain of anguish and grief would drop torrents of misfortune on our heads.

This spell had begun because of some horrible sin committed by one of our ancestors. Whoever he or she was, he or she had shaken hands with the devil and we were still paying for that evil act.

Somehow, some way, I hoped I could discover what it was and beg God's forgiveness. Perhaps then and only then, we would be free and safe, as much as anyone could be free and safe in this world.

I said a little prayer for myself and Jefferson and then, finally, fell asleep.

The next day Aunt Bet was like a hot and cold faucet. In the morning at breakfast, it was as if nothing terrible had happened between us the night before. I imagined Uncle Philip had done what he had said he would—calm her down. She didn't bring up *Lady Chatterley's Lover* or our confrontation. Instead, she rattled on and on at the breakfast table about all the changes she was planning on making in the house—the curtains she would replace, the carpets she would tear up, the painting she planned to have done. Then she declared she wanted to have Julius take us all shopping in the new mall that had just opened in Virginia Beach.

"We'll go on Saturday," she said. "Christie needs some new things to wear, especially something new for her first recital since . . . since the fire."

All of Mr. Wittleman's students were to participate in a recital the first week of August. I had no enthusiasm for it, but I didn't refuse to participate. Aunt Bet was well aware that the recital was an affair usually attended by the most influential and wealthiest citizenry of Cutler's Cove and its immediate surroundings. I knew she was looking forward to attending and sitting in the front row.

"I don't need anything new," I said.

"Of course you do, dear. You want to bring your wardrobe up to date, don't you?" she asked sweetly.

"It is up to date. Mommy bought me some of the latest fashions before she died," I replied.

"Your mother was never really up on what was fashionable and what wasn't, Christie," she said with that syrupy false smile on her lips. "She was always far too busy at the hotel and she didn't subscribe to the proper magazines or read the fashion columns as religiously as I did and do."

"My mother never looked out of fashion a single day of her life," I said vehemently.

"I never caught Dawn looking unattractive," Uncle Philip agreed. "Not even when she was exhausted at the end of the day."

Aunt Bet snapped herself back in her chair.

"I didn't say she was unattractive. It's one thing to be attractive, but another to be in fashion," she lectured. "You will always be attractive, Christie. You've been blessed with pretty features, but that doesn't mean you shouldn't be in style, does it?"

"I don't care," I said, tired of the argument. She took that as my admitting she was right and she smiled and chattered on like a happy canary once again. Jefferson kept his head down and ate his food. Whenever he looked up, I saw by the darkness in his sapphire eyes that he was listening to his own thoughts. Thankfully, he had gotten so he could turn Aunt Bet off and on at will. The twins, of course, sat perfectly straight and listened to everything she said attentively.

After breakfast I retreated to the parlor and my piano, moving through each part of the day like a somnambulist, vaguely aware of where I was and what I was doing. When I ate lunch, I chewed mechanically and swallowed without really tasting my food. When I read in the early afternoon, my eyes drifted off the page and my gaze seemed to float about the room like an aimless balloon. The only time I came to life was when the mail was delivered and I ran out to see if a letter from Gavin had arrived. Since my mail had been tampered with, I tried to make it my business to be around when the mail was delivered.

There was a letter from him, a short one, but a wonderful one because in it, Gavin told me he had sold his valuable collection of baseball cards and made the equivalent of another week's wages. It meant he could come to see me a whole week earlier than he had originally planned. I hated the idea that he had sold something he had cherished, but he wrote that nothing was more important than his getting back to see me. He had already discussed and confirmed it with Granddaddy Longchamp.

The news washed away my recent unhappiness and depression. When I returned to the piano, I played lighter, happier music, my fingers dancing over the keys. I permitted the sunshine and blue sky to find their way into my heart, and my music was filled with renewed energy. Mrs. Stoddard interrupted her housework to come in to listen.

Afterward, I ran upstairs to write back to Gavin, but I wasn't spread out on my bed and writing for long before I heard the screaming across the hall. I opened my door and listened. It was Aunt Bet. Her faucet had turned cold again. This time she sounded hysterical, her voice so high-pitched, I thought she would break her vocal cords.

"HE'S JUST A LITTLE ANIMAL!" she cried. "HOW COULD HE NOT KNOW WHAT HE STEPPED IN? HOW COULD HE TRACK IT INTO OUR HOME?" She appeared in Jefferson's bedroom doorway, Richard beside her looking very self-satisfied. Her arms were extended so that the shoes she held in her hands were as far away from her as could be. She pulled her head back as well and turned her nose away.

"What is it, Aunt Bet?" I asked in a tired and disgusted voice.

"Your brother, your little beast of a brother . . . look!" she exclaimed, holding the shoes toward me and lifting them so I could see the soles clearly. Gobs of what looked like dog droppings were stuck to the bottoms.

"Richard was complaining about an odor in his room. I sent Mrs. Stoddard up here to redo the rug, but nothing seemed to help. Then I came up and looked in Jefferson's closet and found this on the floor. How could he take off these shoes and carry them up here without noticing the stink? How could he? He must have done it deliberately. It's another one of his horrible pranks," she said, drawing up her puckered little prune mouth like a drawstring purse.

For a moment I wondered if it really could have been one of Jefferson's shenanigans. Jefferson would have loved to have found a way to torment Richard, I thought. I was unaware that the possibility had brought a small smile to my lips.

"Do you think this is funny?" Aunt Bet demanded. "Do you?"

"No, Aunt Bet."

"The moment he comes through that front door, I'm sending him upstairs," she declared. "The very moment." She held the shoe away from her and started away. "I should just throw these in the garbage. That's what I should do instead of giving them to Mrs. Stoddard to clean," she muttered and descended with her eyes closed, Richard trailing behind her and guiding her down.

It was terrible to think it, but I had come to the

point where I hoped Jefferson *did* do it deliberately. I returned to my room and described the whole incident to Gavin in my letter. I was sure it would bring a smile and laughter to his lips. When I was finished writing, I went downstairs and out the back door where I found Mrs. Stoddard cleaning Jefferson's shoes. She worked with a pail of soapy water and a sponge.

"He's a terror, that one," she said shaking her head, but I could see some amusement in her eyes.

"I don't know if he did it deliberately, Mrs. Stoddard, but I'll find out when he comes home."

She nodded and started to dry off the shoes with an old towel. Suddenly though, I took a closer look at the shoes.

"Let me see them please, Mrs. Stoddard," I asked. She handed the right one to me and I turned it over, thinking. "Jefferson doesn't wear these shoes anymore, Mrs. Stoddard. He's outgrown them. My mother was going to give them to the Salvation Army."

"Is that right?" she asked.

"Yes," I said, pressing my lips together and nodding with the realization of what this meant. "Richard's still doing it. He's still trying to get my brother blamed for things," I concluded. Mrs. Stoddard understood and nodded in sympathy. I took the other shoe from her and marched back into the house. I found Aunt Bet in the living room reading one of her magazines and smiling proudly down at Richard and Melanie who were demonstrating their self-taught fluency in basic French.

"You little bastard!" I cried from the doorway.

Aunt Bet's mouth gaped open. Melanie and Richard turned and mimicked her look of shock. I strutted into the room, holding the shoes out, soles up, and approached Richard. He cowered back.

"How dare you use such profanity? What are you doing?" Aunt Bet demanded.

"I'm going to rub these in his face," I said. "He dipped them into the dog dung and put it in Jefferson's closet, just the way he put that towel with honey there," I accused.

"I did not!"

"Yes you did," I said, moving closer. He pulled himself back, leaning behind Melanie for protection.

"Christie!" Aunt Bet cried. "Stop it this instant."

"He made a major mistake this time, Aunt Bet," I said. "This time your precious, perfect little angel messed up. You picked the wrong shoes, Richard," I said, turning back to him. "You should have taken more time and done better planning."

Richard flicked a glance at Aunt Bet and then at me.

"What are you talking about, Christie?" she demanded.

"These shoes, Aunt Bet. Jefferson has long grown out of them. He can't wear them anymore; they pinch his feet. Mommy was going to give them to the Salvation Army along with some other clothing he and I have outgrown, only she never got the chance. Richard didn't know that, though, did you, Richard? You took these shoes and dipped them and then planted them and complained so you could get Jefferson in trouble again."

"I can't believe . . ." Aunt Bet looked at him. "Richard?" He tried to smile and look undaunted, but I could see the fear in his eyes.

"I didn't do that, Mother."

She shook her head at me.

"Richard couldn't . . . he wouldn't be so coarse as to go looking for dog stool and . . . oh no," she said, refusing to believe it. "He couldn't."

"He did," I said. "And this time, he got caught."

"You're a liar!" Richard screamed. He got to his feet, but backed away.

"She's making it up, Mother," Melanie said quickly and stood up to be beside him. "How do we know those shoes don't fit Jefferson?"

"Yes," Aunt Bet said, liking the possibility. "How do we know that?"

"I'm telling you, that's how," I said. "And I wouldn't lie about it."

"We'll have to see. I'm not saying you're lying, Christie, but you might be mistaken. We'll have to wait until Jefferson comes home; we'll have to see," she insisted.

"Fine, and once you see, you will owe him an apology and you will punish Richard. That's only fair. You can't just punish us," I said.

Richard's face turned more frantic—his eyes wide and wild.

"I didn't do anything," he claimed.

"Yes you did, and I think your punishment should be having your face smeared with doggy-do," I threatened.

"Christie!" Aunt Bet gasped. "Remember you're older and you're supposed to be a lady and . . ."

Before she could go on, we all heard the front door thrust open abruptly. It sounded as if someone had smashed it open. No one spoke. All eyes were on the living room doorway to see who it was.

Uncle Philip appeared, his eyes ablaze, his mouth twisted in an ugly grimace of horror and sadness. His hair was wild and he looked as though he had run all the way from the hotel to our house.

"Philip!" Aunt Bet said. "What . . ."

"It's my mother," he said. "My mother . . ."

"Oh dear." Aunt Bet's hands flew to her throat like frightened birds.

"What happened to Grandmother Laura, Uncle Philip?" I asked softly, my heart pausing, my breath still.

"Mrs. Berme . . . found her on the bathroom floor . . . a stroke," he said. "My mother . . . Dawn's mother . . . Clara Sue's mother . . . she's gone," he finished. "Gone, forever."

He turned to the left and stopped. Then he looked back at us as if he didn't know us. In confusion, he walked out the way he had come bearing the burden of new sorrow. Aunt Bet fell back in her seat, overwhelmed for the moment. The twins went quickly to her side, each taking one of her hands. Numbly, I shook my head. I had gone dead inside. My heart felt empty and cold. Poor Grandmother Laura, confused and lost in her maze of thoughts. She had spent her final days grappling with her memories, desperately trying to sort out her life, but moving about in circles like someone who had wandered into a wall of spider webs and struggled to get free. And now she was dead.

I went to the front window and gazed out at Uncle Philip. He was pacing back and forth on the front lawn, talking out loud, gesturing wildly with his hands as if he had come into contact with all his descendants. The family of ghosts had gathered around him to hear about the latest victim to fall under the shadow of the great curse.

Another funeral, and so soon with all my funeral memories still fresh, was upon us. Once more we were all draped in black; once more people only whispered to each other in our presence; once more the sea was gray and cold and the sky was overcast, even if there were no clouds.

Neither Jefferson nor I had really gotten to know Grandmother Laura as well as we should have known a grandparent. For as long as I could remember, she was confused and distracted, sometimes clearly recognizing us and sometimes gazing at us as if we were strangers who had wandered into her life.

After I had learned the truth about my mother's kidnapping and Grandmother Laura's complicity in it, I asked Mommy if she hated her for what she had permitted to be done. Mommy smiled a little, her blue eyes softening, and shook her head.

"I did once, very much, but as time went by, I grew to see that she had suffered deeply for it and there was no need for me to add any punishment to the one her conscience had already inflicted upon her.

"Also, I longed to have a mother and in time, we began to share some precious, lost moments, the kind of moments a mother and daughter should share. She changed when she went to live with Bronson. She mellowed, I should say. He is a strong influence on her, making her aware of the consequences of her actions and words. All it takes is for him to lower those brown eyes in her direction and she quickly becomes less selfish. She becomes . . . a mother," Mommy told me and laughed happily.

Now, as I sat in the church beside my little brother and listened to the minister's sermon, I could only remember Grandmother Laura asleep in her wheelchair. I couldn't envision her when she was still pretty and active. But when I looked at Bronson, I saw a soft smile on his face, the kind that reveals a wonderful memory being replayed inside. Surely he was able to recall her as a beautiful young woman spinning on a ballroom dance floor, her laughter music in itself. I had only to take one look at him to see the deep love he had borne and realize how much he had lost. I cried for him more than I cried for myself or Jefferson or even Grandmother Laura herself.

Uncle Philip was surprisingly devastated. I recalled how much he used to complain about going to dinners at Buella Woods. He was always grateful when Mommy volunteered to do something with Grandmother Laura if it meant that he was relieved of the responsibility. One time, when Mommy had to leave in the middle of a busy afternoon to go to her, I went along. I remember feeling so badly for her because of how nervous she was, thinking about the work she had left behind.

"Why can't Uncle Philip go?" I demanded. I don't think I was more than ten or eleven at the time, but I was capable of great indignation when it came to something hurting or bothering Mommy.

"Philip is incapable of facing reality," she replied. "He always was. He refuses to see Mother the way she really is; he wants only to remember her as she was, even though he used to make fun of her all the time. The truth is he was very attached to her and adored her. He was proud of how beautiful she was and made light of the effects of her self-centeredness, even when it affected him. Now, she's as much of a stranger to him as he often is to her."

She sighed and then added, "I'm afraid there is more of Randolph in Philip than Philip cares to admit to, and," she said, her expression darkening, her eyes small, "maybe more of Grandfather Cutler too."

I remember that frightened me and remained under my skin like a persistent itch.

But today, in the church, Uncle Philip looked more like a lost and frightened little boy himself. His eyes went hopefully to anyone who approached him as if he were expecting one of the mourners to say, "None of this is really happening, Philip. It's just a bad dream. In a moment it will be over and you can wake up in bed." He shook hands vigorously and accepted kiss after kiss on the cheek. When it was time to leave, he looked about in confusion for a moment until Aunt Bet took his arm and started him off behind the casket.

We all got into the limousine and followed the hearse to the cemetery for the final rites at the gravesite. As soon as it ended, I went right to Bronson and hugged him. His eyes shone with unshed tears.

"She's at rest now," he said. "Her ordeal has ended."

"Are you coming to our house?" I asked him. Aunt Bet had made arrangements for another funeral reception. She was becoming an expert. "No, no. I'd rather just be alone for a while. I'll speak to you soon," he promised and walked off, his shoulders slumped with the weight of his deep sorrow.

There were far fewer mourners at our home than there had been for Mommy and Daddy, and the reception was quite subdued. Uncle Philip sat in one chair the whole time gazing out at people and nodding or smiling only when someone came directly to him to shake his hand or kiss him.

Both Jefferson and I were tired and overwhelmed, the impact of this funeral tearing the scabs roughly off our recovering feelings. Early in the evening, I took Jefferson upstairs and helped him go to bed. Then, instead of returning to the wake, I retired myself, anxious to close my eyes and escape the sorrow. I didn't even want my small night light on as usual. I wanted to pull the blanket of darkness over me quickly, and that urge was stronger than my childhood fears. I did drift off quickly and never heard the mourners leave.

But some time in the middle of the night, I woke

to the sound of my door clicking shut. It was as if someone had nudged me with a finger. My eyes snapped open. I didn't move and for a moment, heard nothing and guessed I had only dreamt it. Then I heard the distinct sound of heavy breathing and the shuffle of footsteps. A moment later I felt the weight of someone's body on my bed and turned to see Uncle Philip silhouetted vaguely in the darkness. My heart began to pound. It looked like he wore no clothing, not even his pajamas.

"Shh," he said before I could utter a word. He reached out and put his fingers on my lips. "Don't be frightened."

"Uncle Philip, what do you want?" I asked.

"I feel so alone . . . so lost tonight. I thought . . . we could just lie beside each other for a while and just talk."

Before I could say another word, he lifted my blanket and slipped himself under it, moving in beside me. I shifted away quickly, surprised, shocked and very frightened.

"You're so much older than your age," he whispered. "I know you are. You're certainly older than your mother was when she was your age. You've read more; you've done more; you know more. You're not afraid of me, are you?" he asked.

"Yes," I said. "I am. Please, Uncle Philip. Go away."

"But I can't. Betty Ann . . . Betty Ann's like a stick of ice beside me. I don't even like it when my leg grazes against her bony knee. But you, oh Christie, you're just as beautiful as Dawn was, even more so. Whenever I look at you, I see her the way she once was to me.

"You can be that way to me," he added, reaching to put his hand on my waist, "just tonight, at least tonight, can't you?"

"No, Uncle Philip. Stop," I said, pushing on his wrist.

"But you've been this way with boys. I know you have. Where else would you go at night if not to meet some boyfriend and have a rendezvous? Where do you meet . . . in the back of a car? Dawn and I were once in a car."

"No. Stop it," I said, covering my ears with my hands. "I don't want to hear such things."

"Oh, but why not? We didn't do anything ugly. I'll show you what we did," he said, moving his hand up the side of my body to my breast. I started to push myself away and off the bed, but he seized my wrist with his other hand and pulled me toward him.

"Christie, oh Christie, my Christie," he moaned and smothered my face with wet kisses. I grimaced and struggled. He was stronger and threw his leg over mine to hold me in place. In moments, he had worked his hand into my pajama top and found my breast. When his skin touched me, I started to shout and he clamped his other hand over my mouth.

"Don't," he warned. "Don't wake the others. None of them will understand."

I moaned and shook my head. He took his hand away, but before I could utter a sound, he brought his mouth to mine and pressed his lips so hard against my lips, he lifted them away from my teeth. I felt the tip of his tongue touch mine and I began to gag.

I choked and coughed when he lifted his mouth away, but while I struggled to catch my breath, his hands were pulling down on my pajama pants. The buttons began popping off. When my pajamas were down as far as my knees, he turned so he could put his body over mine and I felt it—I felt his hardness poked between my locked thighs. The realization of what it was and what was happening threw me into a frenzy. I was able to free my right hand and with my fist I pummeled his head, but it was like a fly trying to tip over an elephant. He didn't appear to feel anything. He groaned and pushed.

"Christie, Christie . . . Dawn . . . Christie," he said, mixing my name and my mother's as if he could literally bring her back to him through me.

"UNCLE PHILIP, STOP! STOP!"

He was so strong and heavy, I couldn't do much to resist. Slowly, my legs began to give and make room for his to push against them even harder.

"You don't have to sneak off to learn about these things," he muttered. "I can help you as I promised. We need each other. We should depend on each other, now more than ever. I have no one but you, Christie. No one . . ."

"Uncle Philip," I gasped. His mouth covered mine again. I tried to scream, but the scream was trapped inside me. I felt the tip of his hardness prodding, pressing forward while I was pinned down beneath him.

And then the shock of it, the realization that he was moving inside me. I tried to deny it, to scream NO! But the reality came in an avalanche, burying any denials. He groaned and pressed onward, chanting my mother's name and mine as if that was what gave him the strength. His hot wetness spurted inside me. I lay there limply waiting for it to end and when it did, he slid off me like ice. I didn't move, afraid that if I uttered a sound or nudged him in any way, he would return a second time. His heavy breathing slowed.

"Christie," he said, touching me. I pulled back, gasping. "It's all right," he said. "It's all right. We've done nothing wrong; we've only helped each other, comforted each other. Great sorrow demanded it.

"You're old enough to understand. It's good; it's okay. Everything will be fine," he said. "Are you okay?"

I didn't move.

"Are you?" he asked again, this time turning toward me.

"Yes," I said quickly.

"Good, good. I've got to go back before Betty Ann wakes up and wonders where I've gone. Sleep, my little princess, sleep. I will always be here for you, forever and ever, just like I was for her."

I watched, holding my breath as he sat up and then left my bed. He moved very quietly through the darkness of my room, slipping out and disappearing like a nightmare, gone, but still lingering about me.

For a few moments I lay there trying to deny the reality of what had happened. Then I began to sob, my sobbing growing so hard that it shook my whole body and the bed. The ache in my chest felt hard enough to split me in two. I sat up, terrified, and caught my breath. For some reason, all I could think of was Jefferson. Jefferson . . . Jefferson . . .

I rose quickly. My pajama pants fell to my knees. I kicked them off and went into the bathroom to strip off my pajama top and then I turned on the shower, making it as hot as I could take. It turned my skin red, but I didn't care. I scrubbed and scrubbed, my tears mixing with the water that streaked down my face. Afterward, I dried myself vigorously. Still feeling polluted, I hurried out to my bedroom and dug my smallest suitcase out of the closet. With no organized thought, I scurried about packing away underwear, socks, skirts and blouses. Then I dressed as quickly as I could. I dug out all the money I kept in the drawer of my night table and put it in with the money I had in my pocketbook. I was always saving for something or other and had managed to accumulate a few hundred dollars.

I opened the door and peered out into the dimly lit corridor. Tiptoeing across, I opened the door to Jefferson and Richard's room and slipped in. I knelt beside Jefferson's bed and shook him gently until his eyes opened.

"Shh," I warned. His eyes widened. I looked over at Richard who was turned away and asleep and indicated we should not wake him. Then I went to Jefferson's dresser and took out some of his underwear and socks, scooped up a couple of pairs of his pants and some shirts and threw it all quickly into his smallest suitcase. I brought him something to wear and had him slip quietly into his pants and shirt, shoes and socks. Then I handed him his jacket and indicated he should follow me quietly and quickly.

I had left my own suitcase in the hallway. I picked it up quickly, and moved Jefferson and myself as quietly as I could to the stairway. I looked back once. Confident no one had been woken, I started down the stairs with Jefferson right behind me. We went to the front door.

"Where are we going?" he whispered.

Away," I said. "Far, far away."

I looked back one more time at the house that had been so happy and safe. I closed my eyes and heard Daddy's and Mommy's laughter. I heard the music from my piano and Mommy's beautiful voice. I heard Mrs. Boston calling us to come in for dinner. I heard Daddy coming home from work and crying, "Where's my boy? Where's my birthday boy?"

I saw Jefferson scurrying quickly from the living room to rush into Daddy's arms. He lifted him and kissed him and carried him in to join Mommy and me.

It was a world of smiles and love, of music and laughter. I opened the door and looked out at the darkness that awaited. Then I took Jefferson's hand in mine and stepped forward, closing the door behind me.

The music and the laughter died.

All I heard was the beating of my frightened heart.

We were truly orphans, fugitives fleeing from the great curse. Could we escape its hold or would it trail behind us through each and every shadow that awaited?

A Real Father

WE WALKED ALL THE WAY INTO CUTLER'S COVE. JEFFERSON had never been outside this late. The stillness around us, the gleam of the stars on the inky calm ocean and the depth of the pockets of darkness in every corner kept him clinging to my side, his little hand wrapped tightly around mine. The only sounds we heard were the squeaks and creaks of the docks and boats as the waves lifted and fell, and the click-clack of our own footsteps over the sidewalk and street. It wasn't until the street lights of the seaside village loomed brightly ahead of us that Jefferson relaxed some. His surprise and excitement overtook his fear and fatigue and he began to throw questions at me.

"Where are we going, Christie? Why are we walking so much? Why don't we just ask Julius to drive us?"

"Because I don't want anyone to know we're leaving, Jefferson. I told you—we're running off," I said, my voice low. It just seemed natural to whisper.

"Why?" Jefferson whispered too. "Christie?" He pumped my hand. "Why?"

I spun around on him.

"Do you want to stay and live with Aunt Bet and Uncle Philip, Richard and Melanie for the rest of your life? Do you?"

Frightened by my outburst, he shook his head, his eyes wide.

"Neither do I, so we're running off."

"But where will we go?" he demanded. "Who will we live with?"

I walked on faster, practically dragging him along. Where were we going? It wasn't until this very moment that I actually thought of a destination. We couldn't go to Aunt Trisha. She was on a road trip. Suddenly, I had an idea.

"We're going to New York City," I said finally. "We're going to find my real father and live with him. Nothing can be worse than where we're living now and whom we're living with," I muttered.

I didn't look back to see how Jefferson had reacted to the idea; I just continued along, moving us down the side of the street, clinging to the shadows for protection. I didn't want anyone to see us and report us.

One of the only places open in Cutler's Cove this late at night was the bus depot. It was a small station with a lobby that had just one worn wooden bench, a water fountain and a cigarette machine. Behind the counter was a man who had salt-and-pepper curly hair, the spiraling curls falling over his forehead. He looked at least fifty years old. When we entered, he was reading a paperback novel. For a moment he didn't realize we were there. Then he sat up quickly and gazed at us, his squirrel-like eyes full of curiosity and surprise.

"Well, what are you two doing out so late?" he demanded, his slightly gray eyebrows lifting and turning like two question marks.

"We're here to catch the next bus to New York

City," I said, trying to sound older. "My cousin dropped us off at the wrong place and we walked," I added. He scrutinized us suspiciously.

"How much is it to New York City?" I asked firmly. "And when is the next bus?"

"New York City, huh? Well, round trip fare is . . ."

"No, just one way," I said quickly. He looked up sharply. "We have another way to get back," I added.

"Hmm . . . well, his fare would be half," he said, nodding at Jefferson. He considered me. "You would pay full adult," he said. I didn't want to put out the extra money, since we didn't have all that much, but I was happy he thought I was old enough to travel alone with my brother. "Bus don't run directly to New York from here, you know," he added and began punching up the tickets. "It stops at Virginia Beach and then again in Delaware."

"That's all right," I said, setting down my suitcase and stepping up to the counter.

"Actually, you're in luck because we've got a bus due through here in twenty minutes. But it's only a shuttle that runs through two more stations before it reaches Virginia Beach. You'll have to get off there and take the . . ." he checked his schedule card. "The first one's the eight-forty. Goes to Port Authority station, New York City."

"Port Authority is fine," I said and counted out the money on the counter carefully. He raised his eyebrows again.

"You been to New York before?" he asked skeptically.

"Many times. My father lives there," I said quickly.

"Oh, I see. Onc of them families where the father's one place and the mother's another, huh?"

"Yes," I replied. His eyes softened and he seemed more sympathetic.

"And your mother don't want to take you to see your father, I imagine?"

"No sir." He nodded, smirking.

"Well, I suppose I could squeeze you in for the cheaper fare. It's no skin off my back," he added.

After I got our tickets, I directed Jefferson to the bench. He stared at the ticket seller until the man went back to his paperback book. Then he turned and fixed his eyes on me with that sharply inquisitive gaze.

"Why did you tell all those lies?" he demanded.

"Shh," I said. I pulled him closer. "If I didn't, he wouldn't sell us the tickets. He would call the police and tell them he had a pair of runaways."

"The police would arrest us and put us in handcuffs?" Jefferson asked, incredulous.

"They wouldn't arrest us, but they would take us back to the hotel."

"Mommy said it's wrong to tell lies," he reminded me.

"She didn't mean these kinds of lies; she meant lies that hurt other people, especially people you love and who love you," I explained. Jefferson narrowed his eyes and considered it. I saw him digest the idea and then sit back with approval. Shortly afterward, the shuttle bus arrived. There were a half-dozen other people on the bus, sitting mostly in the center and rear and apparently asleep.

"Up awful early," the driver said.

"Yes sir."

"Well, it's the best time to travel," he said. He took our suitcases to put in the luggage compartment and then he went in to talk to the station attendant. I settled Jefferson and myself in the second seat on the right and looked at the driver and the ticket seller through the window. They both gazed our way. My heart was pounding. Were they discussing us? Would they call the police? After a few more minutes, the two of them laughed about something and the bus driver returned. He closed the door and started the engine. I held my breath and tightened my grip on Jefferson's little hand. A moment later we were pulling away from the station. The bus turned down the main street of Cutler's Cove and the driver accelerated. We drove past the stores and shops I had known all my life. We passed the mayor's office and the police station and then we passed the school. Soon we were on the road to Virginia Beach, and Cutler's Cove fell farther and farther behind us. This was my first time traveling alone, but I closed my eyes and swallowed my fear.

Jefferson fell asleep during the ride to Virginia Beach and was practically walking in his sleep when I led him off the bus to wait at the much bigger and busier Virginia Beach station. But the activity and noise were not enough to keep his eyes open. He drifted off again, falling asleep against my shoulder as we waited for the next bus.

This time, after we boarded and took our seats, I fell asleep too. Hours and hours later, when we stopped again to pick up passengers in Delaware, I awoke and found that it was raining. Jefferson's eyes snapped open a few moments later and he immediately asked to go to the bathroom.

"I hope you're not afraid to go in by yourself, Jefferson," I said. "I can't go in there with you."

"I'm not afraid. It's just a bathroom," he declared bravely, but he looked very worried as he went in. While he was in the bathroom, I went too and then I bought us some things to eat.

"I wanted scrambled eggs," Jefferson complained when I handed him a container of milk and some oatmeal cookies. "And toast with a glass of orange juice."

"We'll get good things to eat when we get to New York," I said.

"Does your real father live in a big house, too?" he asked. "With a maid and a butler?"

"I don't know, Jefferson."

"Does he have a wife who will be our new mother?" he inquired.

"I don't know if he ever got remarried. I don't know much about him at all," I said sadly. "So please don't ask any more questions, Jefferson. Just sit and look at the scenery, okay?"

"It's boring," he complained, folding his arms across his chest and pouting. "I should have brought one of my games. Why didn't I bring any toys?" he whined.

"Jefferson, we didn't have time to pack a lot of things. Please, just be good," I pleaded, practically in tears. What was I doing? Where would I really go?

Jefferson shrugged, drank his milk and ate his cookies. He drifted off and on during the rest of the trip, as did I. The rain slowed down to a slight drizzle. Finally, I saw the New York skyline in the distance. As we drew closer and closer, it seemed to grow higher and higher, the tops of the buildings practically scratching the gray sky. When I saw a sign that said Lincoln Tunnel and I knew we were about to cross into New York City, my heart began to pound. I started to recall all the things Mommy had told me about New York—how it was so big and how there were so many people, it was hard to be a stranger there. But I also remembered how much Aunt Trisha loved New York. If she was so excited by it, it couldn't be all that bad, I hoped.

Jefferson became excited when we entered the Lincoln Tunnel. It seemed to go on and on forever, and then, suddenly we burst out into the light and the streets of New York. The traffic and the noise was just as Mommy had described. No one seemed to mind or care that it was still raining lightly. Jefferson kept his face glued to the window, drinking in everything: the street vendors, the taxicabs, the policemen on horseback, people begging and sleeping in entryways, and many fancily-dressed people hurrying to and fro, some with umbrellas, but most without. Moments later, we pulled into the huge bus station and the driver announced: "New York, Port Authority. Watch your step getting off."

I took Jefferson's hand, holding him so tightly, he grimaced with pain as we stepped down. We waited as the driver pulled our small suitcases out from the luggage compartment. I took them, handing Jefferson his, and then we entered the station. People were rushing about everywhere, everyone else seemingly knowing where to go.

"Where's your real father?" Jefferson asked, looking around.

"He doesn't know we're here yet," I said. "I have to find his phone number and call him." I spotted a wall of pay phones and hurried us to them. The size of the telephone book was overwhelming. Jefferson's eyes bulged with amazement.

"That's a lot of telephones!" he exclaimed.

"Watch our suitcases and my pocketbook while I look up his number, Jefferson," I said. He nodded and I began to turn the pages. When I came to Sutton, however, my heart sank. There were more than two pages of Suttons and more than a dozen had either Michael, Mike or just M. as first names.

"I've got to get more change," I said. "Lots more." I took out my remaining money and looked about for a place to get change. I saw a newspaper stand and hurried over.

"Excuse me," I said when the man turned to us. "Could I get change for the telephone?"

"What do I look like, the Chase Manhattan Bank?" he replied, pulling the corners of his mouth into his cheeks. "Buy something, you get change," he said.

"But . . . all right. Give us a Hershey bar," I said. I handed him five dollars. "All in change, please."

"Who you calling—everyone in Manhattan?" He shook his head but gave us the change. Jefferson was happy with the Hershey bar.

I began to make the phone calls, my fingers trembling as I dialed the numbers. What would I say? How would I begin? What would I call him when he answered—Daddy? Michael? Even Mr. Sutton? No one answered at the first number. An elderly lady answered on the second.

"Is this the home of Michael Sutton, the singer?" I began.

"Singer? No. Michael's a plumber," she said.

"I'm sorry."

Down the list I went, some people politely replying no, some very annoyed with the phone call. One man thought I was making a prank call and started to curse. Finally, I called one of the M. Suttons and after four rings, a woman answered, her voice sounding dry and deep like the voice of someone who had just been woken.

"I'm looking for Michael Sutton, the singer," I began.

"So am I," she interrupted.

"Do I have the right number?" I asked.

"Who are you, one of his students?"

"Students? Yes, ma'am," I said. "And I'm supposed to have a lesson with him today."

"Well, I hope it's not until this afternoon," she said curtly.

"It is."

"Well what do you want?" she demanded.

"Is he there now?" I asked.

"In body but not in spirit," she replied. She followed it with a laugh.

"Can I speak with him, please?"

"He's sort of indisposed at the moment. Call back in about . . . an hour," she said.

"But . . ."

She hung up before I could say another word. At least I had the right Michael Sutton, I thought, and copied the address out of the phone book. Jefferson, who was sitting quietly and observing all the people and noise around him, looked up expectantly.

"All right," I said. "I've found him. Let's go find a taxicab."

"A taxicab? Okay," he replied with excitement. I followed the signs that directed us to the 41st Street entrance. When we stepped out, we saw the line of taxicabs parked along the curb. The rain had stopped, but it was still very gray and dismal. The driver at the first cab moved toward us quickly. He was a tall, thin man with a thick brown mustache.

"You need a cab, miss?" he asked.

"Yes, sir."

"Well you got one," he said, taking our bags and

putting them into the trunk. "Get in," he said, nodding toward the rear seat. Jefferson slipped in quickly and immediately looked out the window on the other side. "Where to, miss?" the driver asked after he got in.

I told him the address.

"Oh, Greenwich Village, huh?" He turned on his meter and pulled out into the thick traffic as if we were the only vehicle on the street. Horns blared, people shouted, but he turned and accelerated with indifference after the light changed. In moments we were flying down the city street, both Jefferson and me holding on to the handles for dear life.

"Your first trip to New York City?" the driver asked us.

"Yes sir."

He laughed.

"Thought so. You looked pretty terrified when you first came out of the building. Don't worry. Just keep your nose out of other people's handkerchiefs," he said, "and you'll be all right."

"Ugh," Jefferson chortled.

The driver made a few turns, took us down a long street and then made another turn around a corner where there was a restaurant and a flower shop. He drove slower and finally stopped. I gazed out the window at a row of old-looking buildings. Most had faded and worn-looking front doors with chipped stoops. The buildings themselves looked gray and dirty; the windows on the lower levels were streaked with dust and grime hardened after the rain.

"This is it," the driver said. "That'll be five forty."

I took out six dollars and handed it to him.

"Thanks," he said and stepped out of the taxicab to get our suitcases.

"Which one is eight eighteen?" I asked, looking at the stoops.

"Numbers are a bit faded, but if you look closely, you'll see eight eighteen right in front of you, sweetheart." He got into his cab and drove off. Jefferson and I stood on the sidewalk and stared up at the front door of the building in which my real father lived.

"Come on, Jefferson," I said, lifting my suitcase.

"I don't like it here," he complained. "It's ugly. And where's the playground?" he asked, looking about.

"Just come along, Jefferson," I ordered and took his hand. Reluctantly, he lifted his little suitcase and followed me up the stoop to the front door. We walked into a small entryway. On the wall were boxes for mail and above each were the names of the tenants. I found the name Michael Sutton next to Apartment 3B. Just seeing the name made me so nervous I could barely move. Slowly, I opened the second door and we entered the first floor. I saw the stairway on the right, but I didn't see an elevator.

"I don't want to walk upstairs. I'm tired," Jefferson moaned when I started us toward the steps.

"We have to," I said. "Soon you will be able to sleep in a bed."

I tugged him along and we began to climb up the stairs. When we reached the third floor, I stopped to look around. It was a dark, dingy corridor with only a small window at the far end. It looked as though no one ever washed the glass.

"It smells funny in here," Jefferson said, grimacing. It did smell musty and stale, but I didn't say anything. Instead, I went down the corridor until we stood before 3B. Then I took a deep breath and pressed the buzzer. I heard nothing, so I pressed it again. Again, there was no sound.

"Maybe it doesn't work," I muttered and knocked gently on the door. We listened for footsteps, but heard none.

"Maybe he's not home," Jefferson suggested.

"No, I just spoke to someone here," I insisted and knocked again, this time a lot harder. Moments later, the door was thrust open and we were facing a woman who had thrown on a man's faded blue robe. Her bleached blond hair, with its thick dark roots showing, was unbrushed. She wore no make-up and had sleepy eyes. A lit cigarette dangled from the corner of her mouth.

"What?" she demanded.

"I'm here . . . we're here to see Michael Sutton," I explained.

"Are you the one who called a while ago?" she asked, stepping back with a look of annoyance.

"Yes ma'am."

"I told you . . ."

"Who the hell is it?" we heard a man call.

"One of your prodigies, so anxious to become a star she has to wake us up," the woman replied. "Come on in," she said. She first seemed to notice Jefferson. "You brought your little brother?"

"Yes ma'am."

"Baby-sitting, huh? What's with the suitcases?"

"Can we see Michael?" I asked. Jefferson was glaring up at her in awe. She gazed down at him, looked at me, shook her head and went into another room. I looked around the living room. Clothes were strewn about the sofa and chairs and there were dirty cups on the coffee table and some dirty dishes on a side table as well. The carpet was a faded brown with many stains and spots in it that looked like holes burned by cigarette ashes. Off to the right was an old piano, the stool so worn that it had lost most of its color. Sheet music was opened on the top of the piano and there was a glass with some liquid still in it on the piano as well. The yellow window shades were drawn almost to the bottom, permitting only a bit of gray light to enter.

Wearing a pair of old jeans and buttoning his shirt as he came out, my real father appeared. He was barefoot and looked like he had just rolled out of bed, too. His graying dark hair was long and wild, the strands pouring over his eyebrows and down his temples. His unshaven face was ashen and thin, almost gaunt, with his blue eyes dull from sleep. He slumped a bit so that his narrow shoulders turned slightly inward. As he stared at us, he tucked in his shirt.

My heart sank. This was far from the way I had imagined the mysterious man of my dreams. This man did not look like a debonair musical star. It was impossible to imagine him ever a celebrity. There was no strength in this face, no confidence and hope. This man looked drained, lost, empty. I couldn't believe those fingers would play piano or that weak mouth with the lips turned down in the corners could make pleasing musical sounds.

Where was the dark, silky hair and the elegant sapphire eyes my mother said would sparkle with an impish glint? Where were those broad shoulders?

He shifted his eyes from Jefferson to me and then put his hands on his hips.

"So?" he said. "What do you want?"

"This is Jefferson," I said, nodding at my little brother, "and my name is Christie." I waited a moment to see his reaction, but there was none.

"Yeah, so?" he said. "Someone sent you here for lessons?"

"No sir. I'm Christie Longchamp."

"Longchamp?" His eyes widened a bit and he scratched the back of his head. "Longchamp?"

"Yes sir. My mother's name was Dawn."

The woman who had greeted us at the door came up behind my father and leaned against the wall. She was still smoking her cigarette.

"Dawn? You're . . ."

"Yes. I'm your daughter," I finally declared. How strange it sounded and how odd it felt to tell this man he was my father. His eyes widened even more.

"Who'd she say she was?" the woman behind him asked with a tone of laughter in her voice.

"Quiet," he replied without looking back. "You're little Christie? Sure, sure," he said, nodding and finally smiling. "One good look at you tells it. You've got her face, all right. Well, well, well . . ." He straightened up a bit and brushed his hair back with the palms of his hands. "And this is your brother, eh?"

"Yes."

"I can't believe it. Wow." He shook his head and smiled. "Wow." He spun around on the woman behind him. "My daughter," he declared. "Not bad, eh?"

"Terrific," she said and flicked her cigarette ash to the floor.

"Well, what are you two doing here? I mean . . . how did you get here?" he asked.

"We took the bus," I said.

"No kidding. All the way all by yourselves, huh? And your mother let you?" he asked.

"My mother . . . and father were killed in a fire," I replied as quickly as I could.

"Fire?" He shook his head. "What fire?"

"The hotel burned down and they were trapped

in the basement," I explained. Even now, talking about it brought heavy tears to my eyes, tears that blurred my vision.

"Well, I'll be. That's terrible," he said. "So there's no more hotel, huh?"

"My uncle is rebuilding it," I said. I couldn't imagine why that would be of any importance to him. Why wasn't he more upset about what had happened to Mommy?

"Oh, sure. There must have been insurance. So . . . your mother's . . . gone." He shook his head and looked at the woman. "Why don't you put up some coffee?" She smirked as if he had asked her to perform a major feat and reluctantly strutted toward the kitchen. "That's er . . . that's er . . . Catherine. She's a singer at one of the studios in town. Here," he said, moving toward the sofa to clear away some of the clothing, "have a seat. Tell me about yourself. How old are you now?" he asked as I moved Jefferson and myself to the sofa.

"I'm sixteen." How could he not remember how old I was? I wondered.

"Oh yeah, sure. And how old's . . ." He nodded toward Jefferson.

"Jefferson's nine," I said.

"Almost ten," he added.

"Well, that's a ripe old age," my father quipped, but Jefferson didn't smile. He simply stared up at him with that characteristic fixed glare of his that unnerved some people. My father laughed. Then he sat on the easy chair, not bothering to remove the skirt that had been draped over the back of it.

"So . . . it must have been horrible for you guys . . . a fire, and they couldn't get out." He shook his head. "She was something else, your mother, quite a beautiful woman and quite talented. I could have made her a singing star, but . . ." He shrugged. "So," he said, "who's in charge of you guys? Your uncle?"

"No," I said quickly. "We don't want to live with him."

"Oh no?" He leaned forward. "Why not?"

"He and our aunt Bet are not very nice to us," I said. Something my real father detected in my expression or tone made his eyes narrow as he weighed my words. He had shrewd, sophisticated eyes that seemed to know all the wicked and tricky ways of the world.

"I see."

"Neither is Richard and Melanie," Jefferson added.

"Who?"

"Their children, twins," I said.

"Uh huh." His eyes shifted to our suitcases. "Now let me understand this. You two left and came here on a bus?" I nodded. "Does your uncle know this?"

"No. We ran away," I said.

"Oh, I get it now. How did you find me?" he asked with interest.

"I just called all the Michael Suttons until I found the right one."

He laughed.

"Well," he said, clapping his hands together, "you guys have got to go back. You can't just run off like this. Everyone back there is probably worried sick about you."

"We're never going back," I said firmly.

"Well honey, you didn't expect . . ." He smiled. "You didn't imagine you could live here with me, did you?" I said nothing; he understood. His smile faded and he sat back, contemplating us a moment. "How much money do you have with you?" he asked.

"Only twenty-three dollars left," I replied.

"Twenty-three . . ." He shook his head again. "Well, what about inheritance? You must have inherited quite a bit."

"I don't know," I said. "I don't care."

"Well you should care. It's yours. You can't let your uncle take it all. I'm sure there are legal documents. Sure. You can go back and in a few years, you'll get your share of the hotel and property and . . ."

"I don't care about the hotel. I can't go back," I said vehemently. I wished I could tell him everything, but it was like talking to a complete stranger and I couldn't get myself to describe what Uncle Philip had done to me.

"Well, you can't live here, honey. I don't have the room for you and besides, I don't have any right to take custody of your little brother there. You could get separated from him," he added.

"Separated?" Jefferson's hand found mine quickly. "No, we'll never be separated," I said firmly.

"And you shouldn't be. That's why you have to go back. After a few years, when you're eighteen, or when you've gotten your inheritance, you'll call me and I'll come out," he said, smiling. "Sure. We'll have a real father-daughter relationship then, okay?"

I said nothing. Disappointment put tears in my eyes.

"Coffee's ready," the woman said, standing in the doorway. "I'm not serving," she added, fixing her eyes on me. "So come get your own cups."

"I don't want any coffee," I said.

"I need a cup," my father announced. "Maybe we got some milk and cookies. I'll look." He stood up. "You sing too?" he asked.

"No. I play the piano," I said.

"Great. Before you go, you can give us a little recital. That would be nice, right, Catherine?"

She smirked.

"We got to go to Mr. Ruderman, don't forget."

"Oh yeah. I got a little problem with the IRS and have to see my accountant today. Nothing serious," he said, then added, "I hope. Let me get some coffee." He went into the kitchen. Jefferson and I could hear him and Catherine whispering.

"I don't like it here," Jefferson said.

"No, neither do I," I replied. My heart felt so heavy I thought it would drop into my stomach. What had I been thinking to come here? I wondered. How desperate I had been. And now all I had left was twenty-three dollars.

"Come on, Jefferson," I said standing.

"Where are we going now?"

"We'll go someplace to get something good to eat and think, okay?"

"Okay," he said and took hold of his suitcase quickly.

"Hey," my father said, coming to the kitchen doorway. "Where are you two going?"

"I think you're right," I said. "We're going back."

"Sure. That's the smartest thing. Put in your time, get your inheritance first. You have your return ticket, right?" he asked hopefully. I nodded even though I didn't.

"Wait a minute," he said, digging into his pocket. "Take this for extra spending money." He handed me a five-dollar bill.

"I thought that's all the cash you had on you," Catherine said, coming up behind him quickly. "How are we supposed to get uptown?"

"Relax. We'll take the subway," he replied.

"Subway!" She grimaced.

"Good-bye," I said quickly and reached for the doorknob. Jefferson shot out as soon as I opened the door. I looked back once. My father stood there, smiling. It wasn't until I had closed the door and had gone down the stairs and back onto the street that I realized he hadn't kissed me hello or good-bye.

It was as if we had never met.

It had begun to rain hard again, the drops splattering over our faces and bouncing up from the sidewalk and street. I pulled Jefferson closer to me and charged up the block to the corner where I had seen that restaurant. The rainy wind hissed around the corner to greet us. Finally, we stepped inside and shook off the water. Both our heads were soaked. When we sat down at a booth, I used some napkins to wipe our faces and hands. I had little appetite, but Jefferson was ravenously hungry and ate everything on his plate and even some of mine. The bill came to a little over ten dollars. After I paid it, I sat there staring out the window, wondering what we should do next.

"Where are we going now?" Jefferson asked. "Can we go to a movie? Or find a playground?"

"Jefferson, please. We have to think of more important things," I said.

"I should brush my teeth. Mrs. Boston told me to brush my teeth after every meal if I could," he explained.

"Mrs. Boston," I said, recalling her and smiling. "I wouldn't mind living with her."

"Let's go," he said. "I wanna."

"We can't, Jefferson. She's not a relative. She would have to send us back, too. I guess we're going to have to go back," I said sadly. I saw that it had stopped raining again and thought we had better move on before it resumed. "Come on."

We went outside and looked for a taxicab. One was parked on the side, but the driver looked asleep. He opened his eyes when he sensed we were standing there staring at him.

"I'm off duty," he said.

"How do we get a taxicab then?" I asked him.

"Just wave at them, honey," he explained. Jefferson liked that. To him it was the first chance to have any fun. He stood just off the sidewalk and waved at the cabs flying to and fro. Finally, one pulled up in front of us.

"Port Authority, please," I said. This time we took our suitcases into the rear with us. The drive back was just as hectic as it had been before and the cost was just as much. With only a little over ten dollars left, we re-entered the big station. I was hoping I could get us bus tickets and have them paid for when we arrived in Cutler's Cove, but when I explained my situation to the ticket seller, he said it couldn't be done.

"Go find a policeman," he said. "Next, please."

We stepped away from the window and walked slowly across the huge lobby to a row of benches.

"What are we going to do now?" Jefferson asked when I sat him and myself down.

"I need to think," I said.

"Me too," he said and closed his eyes.

I didn't want to call Uncle Philip and Aunt Bet. I thought the best thing to do would be to call Bronson. I hated giving him new worries on top of his grief over my grandmother's death, but I didn't know anyone else back home to call.

"You just wait here, Jefferson, while I make a phone call," I said. He nodded, closed his eyes and leaned against his suitcase. As I walked toward the bank of pay phones on the wall, the memory of what Uncle Philip had done to me returned with a vivid intensity. I could hear his voice, feel his fingers crawling over my body and then . . . it made me cringe inside. The idea of returning to Cutler's Cove and living with Uncle Philip and Aunt Bet again terrified me. I couldn't return; I just couldn't. So when I lifted the receiver and started to dial, I changed my mind and called Gavin instead.

"I can't tell you everything over the phone right now, Gavin," I said, "but I had to get away from Uncle Philip."

"Where are you?" he asked after a moment.

"Jefferson and I are in New York City."

"New York City!"

I told him about my real father and how that had been a disaster and then I told him we didn't have much money left.

"If you tell your father, he'll probably call my uncle Philip," I added.

"What did he do that was so terrible you can't tell me over the phone?" Gavin asked.

"It happened at night, Gavin. In my bedroom," I said, choking back the tears. There was a long silence.

"Don't do anything else," Gavin said. "Just wait there for me."

"You're going to come to New York?"

"I'll leave right away. Can you wait there for me?" he asked.

"Oh yes, Gavin. Yes."

"I'll be there, Christie . . . as soon as I can," he promised.

I hung up and returned to Jefferson and told him about Gavin.

"Good," he said. "Maybe he'll take me to do something that's fun."

"I don't know what we'll do yet, Jefferson, but at least . . . at least Gavin will be here," I said, filled with renewed hope. "Until he comes, we'll have to occupy ourselves. It will be hours and hours. Come on," I said, "I'll buy you a coloring book and crayons."

"And clay. I want to make some soldiers."

"We'll see how expensive it all is," I said. "We need some money for dinner, too."

"Won't Gavin be here by then?" he asked.

"No. It's going to be a long time, so don't start whining and complaining like a little baby," I warned.

"I'm not a little baby."

"Good. Come on. We'll buy you the coloring book." One of the shops sold travel toys and games. Everything was more expensive than I had imagined, however, and I was able to buy him only a small package of crayons and a small coloring book. I had just six dollars left and hoped it would be enough to get us something decent for supper. Jefferson and I went off to a corner of the big lobby and sat on a bench. For a while his coloring book and crayons kept him occupied, but he soon grew tired of it and began to complain.

"Can I go walking around?" he asked.

"You can't go far. This is a big place and you could get lost in it," I warned.

"I won't go far," he promised. I was tired and I didn't have the patience to argue with him.

"Just go over there," I pointed, "and stay where I can keep an eye on you."

"Okay." He hopped off the bench and went to look at the posters and watch the people hurrying to and fro. I watched him staring at people and smiled to myself when an elderly woman stopped to talk to him. She patted him on the head and continued on her journey. He glanced back at me and then walked a little farther away.

"Jefferson!" I called, but he didn't hear me. As long as I could see him, I thought it was all right. But my eyes were so tired and my lids so heavy, I had to fight to keep them open. The emotional burdens from the night before, the traveling and the disappointment I received meeting my real father all combined to wear me down. Fatigue crept up my body. It was as if I had stepped into a pool of exhaustion and sunk deeper and deeper into it until it washed over my face. I let my eyes close, telling myself it would be just for a little while, but almost as soon as I did, sleep took a firm hold of me and I slumped to the side, sliding, sliding, sliding until my head rested comfortably on my suitcase.

Sometime later, I woke with a start. A man in a torn and dirty jacket with soiled pants and shoes that had rags tied around them to keep them together and block the holes in the soles stood a few feet away staring at me. He had his hands in his pockets, but I could see his fingers moving against the material. It looked like he had two mice in his pants. I sat up quickly. He smiled, revealing a mouth with many teeth missing. He was unshaven, the dark stubble appearing in patches over his chin and cheeks, and his hair was matted, some strands looking plastered over his forehead and temples. The tempo of movement in his pockets increased and his tongue slid back and forth over his lips as if it were a small animal itself trying to break free and escape.

I gasped and stood up. Where was Jefferson?

There were fewer people moving through the great lobby, so I had no trouble seeing that he was not where he had been and was supposed to stay. My heart began to thump.

"JEFFERSON!" I called. I looked back at the man who had taken a few steps closer. It was then that I saw that the zipper on his pants was open. Panic nailed my feet to the floor for a moment. Then I turned away and moved quickly down the aisle and out to search for Jefferson.

First I went toward the entrance, expecting him to be there watching people come and go, but he wasn't to be found by the doors. I started across the lobby, my heart racing, my face flushed with fear. I charged down to the right and stopped at every booth and store, asking clerks and counter people if any of them had seen a little boy who fit Jefferson's description. No one had.

My panic grew more intense. I thought my heart was pounding so hard and fast, I was sure to fall into a faint at any moment. Finally, I spotted a policeman and rushed to him.

"I've lost my brother," I cried. "I've lost him!"

"Whoa there, easy," he said. He was a tall man with light brown hair and friendly green eyes. "What do you mean, you lost your brother?"

"We sat on the benches back there and he got up to walk around and I fell asleep. When I woke up, he was gone," I cried quickly.

"Easy, easy. How old is he?"

"Nine, almost ten."

"Uh huh. And you?"

"I'm sixteen."

"Have you been here before?" he asked.

"No sir."

"So he doesn't know his way about," he said

more to himself than to me. "All right, show me where you saw him last," he said and I led him back to the benches. That horrible man was gone. "He was standing right there," I said. "And then .. ."

Suddenly, Jefferson appeared around a corner.

"JEFFERSON!" I screamed and ran to him. "Where were you? Why did you walk away from where I told you to stay?"

"I just went to the bathroom," he said, terrified by my outburst. He looked up at the policeman.

"What are you two doing here anyway?" the policeman asked.

"We're waiting for someone," I said.

"Uh huh. All right, young man," the policeman said, shaking his finger at Jefferson. "You make sure you stay where your sister can keep a close eye on you, hear?"

Jefferson nodded, his eyes wide.

"There are bad people here who steal children sometimes," he warned. Jefferson's eyes grew even wider.

"We'll be all right now, thank you," I said, putting my arm around Jefferson. I needed to feel him close to me. "We're just going to go back there and . . . oh no!" I exclaimed. "Oh no!"

"What is it now?" the policeman asked, straightening up and putting his hands on his hips.

"Our suitcases and my pocketbook!"

"You left them there and went off?" the policeman asked me with incredulity.

"I got frightened when I didn't see my brother and I . . ."

"Where you from?"

"Virginia," I said, unable to hold back my tears.

"Man, oh man," the policeman said, pushing his cap back. He dug a notebook out of his back pocket and flicked it open. "Okay, let's have it. Your name and address," he said. I told him. "Who are you waiting for?" he asked. I looked at Jefferson.

"My brother," I said quickly.

"All right. Give me a brief description of your stolen property," he said and I described our suitcases and my pocketbook.

"There was a horrible-looking man watching me before I started to look for Jefferson," I said.

"Uh huh. Well, we've got a few of those around, but give me a description anyway," he said and I did.

"All right, I'll file a report," the policeman said. "My advice to you, young lady, is don't move from where you're supposed to meet your brother."

"We won't," I promised and led Jefferson back to the benches. Even his coloring book and crayons were gone.

"Who took our things?" Jefferson asked.

"I'm not sure," I said softly. I felt drugged, defeated, burdened down with more weight than I could ever carry.

"I'm hungry," Jefferson complained. "When can we eat supper?"

"Eat? All our money's gone, Jefferson. My pocketbook was taken, remember?"

"But I'm hungry," he moaned.

"So am I, but no one will give us anything without money."

"We'll tell them we'll pay them tomorrow," he suggested.

"Not these people, Jefferson. They don't know us; this is New York. Mommy was right," I muttered. "Mommy was right." I put my arm around him and drew him closer. "We'll just sleep and try not to think about food until Gavin comes."

The tears that were burning my eyes broke free and began streaming down my cheeks.

"Don't cry, Christie," Jefferson said. "Gavin's coming soon."

"Yes." I smiled through my tears. "Gavin's coming." I kissed Jefferson and held him close.

And mercifully, we fell asleep in each other's arms.

Someone to Lean On

"THERE YOU ARE!" GAVIN CRIED.

My eyelids fluttered open and I gazed up at him smiling down at me with his hands on his hips, his suitcase at his feet. He wore dark blue dungarees and a white T-shirt under a light black cotton jacket. I was never happier to see him. Even though it hadn't been that long since we had last seen each other, he looked so much older and taller.

Jefferson remained fast asleep with his head on my lap. Exhausted, I had slipped down on the bench and quickly fallen into a deep sleep myself. I had no idea how much time had passed, but it looked so late. Even in this busy place, there were hardly any people going to and fro. With my fingers balled into fists, I ground the sleep out of my eyes.

"Gavin, I'm so glad you're here," I said.

"I've been here awhile looking and looking for you. I almost didn't find you and gave up. I walked past this place once, but you two were down below the back of the benches, so I didn't see you. Just lucky I decided to take one more look," he added.

I nodded and then all of it came rushing back over me—what Uncle Philip had done, our sneaking out and taking the bus all the way to New York, the horribly disappointing meeting with my real father, nearly losing Jefferson in Port Authority, and the robbery of all our things. Without giving Gavin a warning, I simply burst into tears, the floodgates holding them back collapsing completely. My sobs and shudders woke Jefferson.

"Oh Christie," Gavin said, quickly sitting down beside me. "Poor Christie." He put his arm around my shoulders and I buried my face in the nook between his shoulder and neck. My body shook with my sobs. "It's all right now," he said. "Everything will be all right."

"What's the matter?" Jefferson asked, sleepily scrubbing his face with his palms. And then he realized Gavin was with us. "Gavin!"

"Hey, little nephew, how you doing?" Gavin ran his fingers playfully through Jefferson's already quite messy hair.

"I'm hungry," Jefferson declared immediately, "and we don't have any money for food." He scowled.

"No money? What happened?" Gavin asked, looking to me.

Slowly, I lifted my head from his shoulder and began to describe our disastrous experiences in New York, bawling out the ending that related how we had lost all our worldly possessions and all our money. Gavin shook his head sympathetically and then pressed his lips firmly together, assuming a take-charge look.

"Well, the first thing we'll do is get you something hot to eat. There's a small restaurant down that way. I passed it looking for you. Come on," he said, urging me, "some hot food will make you feel better." With the back of his hand, he gently wiped the tears from my cheek and smiled.

"And they took my new toy, too," Jefferson complained. "Can I get another one?"

"We'll see, Jefferson. One thing at a time," Gavin said wisely. How strong and confident he looked to me now, and how happy I was to see him. My heart pitter-pattered and I felt the tension and fear that had nailed me to the bench lift from my body.

I took Jefferson's hand and Gavin took my other hand. He picked up his suitcase and led us to the restaurant. After we ordered our food, Gavin described how he had left home immediately after my desperate phone call.

"I wrote a note and put it on the refrigerator and then snuck off. Daddy's going to be upset, but my mother will calm him down. I promised to call them as soon as I could. I didn't tell them you had run away," he added quickly, "but Philip might call them or they might call him. Do you want to tell me more about what happened now," he asked, "and why you had to run away?"

I shifted my eyes toward Jefferson and then shook my head.

"Later," I said softly. Gavin nodded with understanding.

Now that Jefferson was getting food, he was animated and excited again. He described our trip, going into detail about the people on the bus, the things he saw, our cab rides in New York, and the policeman who chastised him for walking away from me.

Toward the end of our meal, Gavin asked the most obvious and important question.

"What are you planning to do now?"

"I'm not going back to Cutler's Cove, Gavin," I said firmly, my eyes narrow with determination. Gavin studied me for a moment and then sat back.

"Well, I have all the money I had saved for my trip, but it won't last us forever," he said wisely. "Where do you want to go? What do you want to do?"

I thought for a moment. Aunt Trisha was away, my father was a disaster, but there was a place. I had been there only once before with my parents and I had been so small, I barely remembered it, but from time to time, I overheard Mommy talking to Daddy about it, and about sweet Aunt Charlotte.

"I want to go to Lynchburg, Virginia and from there to The Meadows," I announced.

"The Meadows?" Gavin's eyebrows rose with interest.

"It's the old family plantation, remember? I mentioned it in some of the letters I sent you. It's where Grandmother Cutler's dreadful older sister Emily did horrible things to Mommy. It's where I was born. Do you remember it now?" I asked.

Gavin nodded slowly.

"After loathsome old Emily died, my parents went back to visit Aunt Charlotte. I went with them once. I barely remember the visit, but I do recall Aunt Charlotte and her husband, Luther. She gave me something I still have—an embroidered picture of a canary in a cage. She drew it and did all the needlework herself. Oh, it's a perfect place for us to go, Gavin," I said, growing more excited with the idea. "No one will think to look for us there."

"Lynchburg, huh," Gavin said thoughtfully.

"The Meadows is about fifty miles away in a small hamlet called Upland Station, but I remember that no buses go there. It's a very small place. Do you think you have enough money for the bus tickets to get us to Lynchburg?" I asked. "And then maybe a taxi can take us the rest of the way."

"I don't know. I'll find out what the tickets cost, but Christie, you have no clothes, nothing, and neither does Jefferson. Don't you think . . ."

"I won't go back to Cutler's Cove," I repeated, my face screwed firmly into a look of anger as well as determination. "We'll make do; we'll find a way. I'll get a job and earn some money. I'll do anything I have to do not to go back," I added with assurance. "I'll wash dishes, I'll scrub floors, anything." Impressed with my resolve and tenacity, Gavin shrugged.

"Okay, let's go to the ticket booth and see what it would cost," he said.

"Can I get a new toy, too?" Jefferson asked quickly. He had gulped down the last of his milk and cleaned every crumb of the slice of apple pie from his plate.

"We'll see," Gavin replied.

He did have enough money to buy us bus tickets to Lynchburg, but after that, he had only twenty-seven dollars left. Jefferson started to whine when we told him we needed every penny for food and for the taxi ride to The Meadows. Finally, Gavin satisfied him with an inexpensive deck of playing cards. He promised to teach him dozens of games on the trip.

We had to wait another hour before the bus left. After Gavin took Jefferson to the bathroom and I went, we sat on the benches in the lobby again. Jefferson amused himself with his cards and while he was distracted, I told Gavin what Uncle Philip had done to me, skipping over the ugliest details. He listened with his eyes widening more and more every moment. I saw his face change from astonishment to pity and then to anger when my tears burst forth again, hot blinding tears that stung my eyes.

"We should go back and tell the police; that's

what we should do," he said, his dark eyes blazing so brightly they reminded me of polished black marble.

"I don't want to, Gavin. I don't want to have anything more to do with him or my aunt or those horrible cousins of ours," I moaned. "Besides, they always find a way to confuse things and blame Jefferson and me for any of the bad things that happen. I just want to be far away from them. It will be all right, as long as I'm with you," I added.

His cheeks turned crimson for a moment and then he took on a mature and confident look that reminded me of Daddy, especially because of the way he pulled back his shoulders and lifted his chest.

"No one's going to hurt you again, Christie, never again, not as long as you're with me," he promised. I smiled and took hold of his arm. Then I pressed my cheek to his shoulder.

"I'm so happy you've come to help us, Gavin. I'm not afraid anymore." I closed my eyes. I could feel his breath on my hair and then his lips. I smiled and relaxed. Miraculously, I was filled with renewed hope.

Because Gavin was with us and was able to amuse Jefferson, our trip to Lynchburg passed far more quickly than it otherwise would have. He kept Jefferson busy counting cars or telephone poles. We all took a color and then accumulated points every time our color appeared. The rain that had followed us into New York had gone out to sea and for most of our journey, we had blue skies and soft, cotton-candy clouds. However, even though we left early in the morning, the stops and delays meant we wouldn't arrive in Lynchburg until early in the evening. We did with as little as we could for lunch in order to save as much of our remaining money as possible. Gavin claimed he wasn't very hungry and ate only a candy bar, but by the time we arrived in Lynchburg, we had only eighteen dollars and thirty cents left.

Outside of the bus station, we found two taxicab drivers leaning against their cars and talking. One of them was a tall, thin man with a narrow face and sharp nose; the other was shorter, softer and friendlier.

"Upland Station?" the tall driver said. "That's nearly fifty miles. Cost you fifty dollars," he declared.

"Fifty? We don't have that much," I said sorrowfully.

"How much do you have?" he asked.

"Just eighteen," Gavin said.

"Eighteen! Go on, you ain't gonna get no cab to Upland Station for that money." Disappointment almost put tears in my eyes. What would we do now?

"Hold on," the other driver said when we started away sadly. "I live twenty-five miles in that direction and it's about time I started for home. I'll take you the rest of the way to Upland Station for eighteen."

"Desperate Joe will do anything for a buck," the tall driver said sourly.

"Thank you, sir," I said. We all got into the back of his cab. It was an old car with torn seats and dirty windows, but it was a ride.

"Who you kids know in Upland Station? The place is practically a ghost town," the driver asked.

"Charlotte Booth. She's my aunt. She lives in an old plantation called The Meadows."

"The Meadows? Yeah, I know what that is, but that ain't much of a place anymore. I can't take you up that private road either. It would kill my tires and shocks. You'll have to walk from the highway," he said. He went on to talk about the way the small towns had been dying off, the economy in the changing South and why things weren't what they were when he was a young man growing up around Lynchburg.

Although there wasn't a moon, the sky was bright enough with stars for us to see some of the countryside as we rode on, but a little over a half-hour after we left the bus station, dark clouds began to roll in, moving like some curtain shutting away the heavens from us. The farmhouses and tiny villages along the way became few and far between. I felt as if we were leaving the real world and entering a world of dreams as the darkness deepened and spread itself over the road before us. The deserted houses and barns retreated into the pool of blackness and only occasionally could be seen silhouetted against a small group of trees or a lonely, overgrown field, and those houses that had people still living in them looked lost and small. I imagined children no older or bigger than Jefferson too frightened to look out at the shadows that seemed to slide across the ground whenever the wind blew over the roof and through each nook and cranny.

Jefferson curled up closer to me. Not a car passed us going the other way. It was as if we were riding to the edge of the world and could easily fall off. The cab driver's radio cracked with static. He tapped it a few times and complained, but after a while he gave up and we rode in relative silence until finally a road sign announced Upland Station.

"This is it," our driver announced. "Upland Station. Don't blink or you'll miss it," he said and laughed. I hadn't remembered how small it was. Now, with the general store, the post office and the small restaurant closed, it did look like a ghost town. Our driver took us a little farther and stopped at the entrance to the long driveway of The Meadows. There were two stone pillars each crowned with a ball of granite, but the brush and undergrowth had been permitted to grow up alongside the pillars, making it seem as if no one had passed in or out for years and years.

"As far as I can go," the taxi driver said. "The old Meadows plantation is up this driveway about a half a mile."

"Thank you," Gavin said, handing him the rest of our money.

We stepped out and he drove off. Because of an overcast sky, he left us in pitch darkness. Night closed in around us so quickly I couldn't see Gavin's eyes. Jefferson squeezed my hand as if holding on for dear life.

"I wanna go home," he moaned.

"I hope someone's still living up there," Gavin whispered and suddenly I thought, what if they weren't? Something might have happened and they might have moved away. "It could be a long walk in the dark for nothing," Gavin warned.

"It won't be for nothing, Gavin," I promised.

"Uh huh," he said, but not with a great deal of that confidence I had been relying on so heavily before. He took my other hand and the three of us began our journey up the dark, gravel drive that was filled with potholes and bumps.

"I don't blame the driver for not wanting to take his cab up this road," Gavin said. From the deep woods to our right, something made a weird noise. I jumped and spun around to see what it was.

"It's only an owl," Gavin assured me, "telling us we're in his territory. At least that's what my daddy would say."

As my eyes grew more and more accustomed to

the darkness, the tops of trees and small bushes became clearer. They looked like sentinels of the night guarding against unwanted intruders.

"I'm cold," Jefferson complained. I knew he just wanted me to draw him closer. Now that the owl had stopped complaining, the only sounds we heard were our own footsteps over the loose gravel.

"I don't see any lights yet," Gavin said ominously. Then we made a small turn and the tips of the brick chimneys and the long, gabled roof of the plantation house came into view, a dark silhouette against an even darker sky. It loomed ahead and above us like some giant sullen monster who had suddenly risen from the pool of darkness below.

"I don't like it here," Jefferson protested.

"It will all look prettier in the morning," I promised. It was a promise I made to myself as well as to him.

"There's some light," Gavin said with relief. Through the windows on the first floor, we could see the dim, flickering illumination. "Looks like they use candles or oil lamps," he muttered.

"Maybe the electricity is off because of a storm," I suggested.

"Doesn't look like it rained here recently," Gavin replied. Without realizing we were doing it, we were both whispering.

As we drew closer to the front of the house, we could more clearly make out the full-facade porch. Over the great round columns ran thick vines that looked more like the tentacles of some terrifying creature who had the great house in its grip. We found the walkway between full hedges. It was chipped and cracked. We paused a moment and contemplated the murky front porch.

"Have you thought what you're going to tell them?" Gavin asked. But before I could reply, a dark shadow to our right suddenly took the shape of a man and stepped out at us. He was holding a shotgun.

"Stop right there," he commanded, "or I'll scatter you into the wind." Jefferson practically leaped into my arms. I gasped and Gavin drew me closer. "Who are you?" he demanded. "You kids come up here to bother us again?"

"No sir," Gavin said quickly.

"I'm here to see my Aunt Charlotte," I added quickly.

"Aunt Charlotte?" He stepped out farther until the faint light from the windows made his skin shine and his eyes glow. I could see that he was a tall, lean man. "Who are you?"

"My name is Christie. I'm Dawn's daughter," I explained quickly. "And this is my little brother Jefferson and my daddy's brother Gavin."

"Dawn's daughter?" He lowered his shotgun. "You come here all the way from the ocean?" he asked incredulously.

"Yes sir. Are you Luther?"

"Yes I am. Well, I'll be. I'll be. Ain't this something? How'd you git here? Where's your ma and pa?" he asked quickly.

"They're dead," I told him. "Killed in a terrible fire at the hotel."

"What's that? Killed?"

"Can we go inside, Luther?" I asked. "We've been traveling all day and night."

"Oh sure, sure. Go on. Watch yourselves on the steps," he added. "Killed," he muttered behind us.

The three of us hurried up the shattered front steps to the enormous entrance. Our shoes clacked over the loose slats of the porch floor and what looked like bats flew out from under the eaves and roof. Luther moved up ahead of us and opened the door. The additional light illuminated his face and I saw that he had dark brown hair streaked with gray, all the strands going this way and that over his deeply creased forehead. He had a long, drooping nose and deep-set brown eyes with a sharp web of wrinkles at each corner. His rough, gray stubble grew in patches over his dark face. When he drew closer, I caught the aroma of chewing tobacco.

"Go on," he commanded and we entered the old plantation house.

We found a long entry way that led down a corridor lit by candles and kerosene lamps to the circular stairway. The three of us gazed up at the large family portraits lining the walls and Jefferson started to laugh. All the faces of what must once have been dour-looking Southern gentlemen and unhappy women with pinched faces were changed, some would say vandalized. Funny mustaches and beards were drawn over those that had none—even the women! Yellow, pink and red paint had been used to add color to these dark and otherwise depressing old black and whites. Some faces were given dots on the cheeks, making them look like measles victims; some had silly-shaped glasses drawn over their eyes and one woman had a green ring coming out of the nostrils of her thin nose.

"That's Charlotte's work," Luther explained. "She thought they all looked too sad and angry. Emily must've done quite a spin in her grave," he added and smiled, revealing missing teeth.

"I was here once before, but I don't remember this," I said.

"That's fun," Jefferson said. "I want to do a picture too. Can I?"

"Ask Charlotte. She's got dozens in the attic she plans to do over," Luther said and chuckled.

"Where is Aunt Charlotte?" I asked.

"Oh she's around. Either she's doing one of her needlework pieces or rearranging something here or there in the house. Go on into the sitting room on the right. Make yourselves to home and I'll look for Charlotte. That's the only luggage you got?" he asked, nodding toward Gavin.

"Yes sir," Gavin said.

"Our things were stolen in the bus depot in New York City," I quickly explained.

"Is that so? New York City. I heard that's what happens there. You get killed or robbed minutes after you get there," Luther said, nodding.

"It can happen anywhere if you don't watch yourself and your things," I confessed sadly.

We continued down the corridor. The house looked even bigger than I had remembered. Above us hung unlit chandelier after chandelier, their crystal bulbs all looking more like pieces of ice in the dim light of the candles and kerosene lamps. We turned into the first doorway Luther indicated. Two kerosene lamps were lit, one on a round side table and the other on a dark sofa table. Luther went to the right and lit another lamp by a bookcase.

"Rest here a moment," he said and hurried out. The three of us looked around. Over the long semi-circular sofa was draped the oddest patchwork quilt I had ever seen. It looked like dozens of rags, pieces of towel, even washcloths were sewn together regardless of color or material. The same was true for the quilt thrown over the deep easy chair across from it.

On some of the walls, I recognized Aunt Charlotte's needlework. The pictures of trees and children, farm animals and forest animals were hung haphazardly. It was as if Aunt Charlotte had walked into the room and slapped them on wherever she found a space. Here and there, in the midst of this handiwork, were the old portraits and pictures of country scenes, houses and again, ancestors.

"Look at that!" Jefferson cried, pointing to the immediate right corner. In it there was a grandfather's clock, but over the numbers Aunt Charlotte had drawn and pasted pictures of different birds. Twelve o'clock was an owl and six o'clock was a chicken. There were robins and bluebirds, sparrows and cardinals, canaries and even a parrot. They were all drawn in bright colors.

"What the heck's going on here?" Gavin wondered aloud. All I could do was shake my head.

"Hello, everyone. Hello, hello, hello," we heard a jolly voice cry behind us and turned around to greet Aunt Charlotte. She wore what looked like a potato sack covered with strips of multi-colored ribbons. She was as short and plump as I vaguely recalled her and she still wore her gray hair in two thick pigtails, one tied with a yellow ribbon and the other with an orange. Despite her wrinkles, she had a childlike smile with soft, big blue eyes that sparkled with a schoolgirl's excitement. For shoes she wore men's brown slippers, each with a streak of white along the sides and a white dot on top where her big toe was located.

"Hello, Aunt Charlotte," I said. "Do you remember me?"

"Of course," she said. "You're the baby who was born here. And now you've come to visit. I'm so happy. We haven't had visitors for so long. Emily hated visitors. If anyone came to see us, she always said we were too busy or we had no room."

"No room?" Gavin said incredulously. Aunt Charlotte leaned toward him to whisper.

"Emily lied, but she didn't think it was bad to lie. Well now she lies in a cold grave, right Luther?"

"Very cold," he said.

"Now then," Charlotte continued. "We must find you the best rooms to stay in and then we can talk and talk and talk until our throats get dry."

"They probably need something to eat and drink after so long a journey," Luther said. "I'll fix something while you take them upstairs, Charlotte."

"Oh good," she said, clapping her hands together. "Come along then." She started out and Luther stepped toward us. "I didn't tell her what you told me out there about your parents. You can explain it all when you come down to the kitchen. I was very fond of your ma," he added. "She treated us real well."

"Thank you, Luther," I said and we hurried to catch up to Charlotte, who walked and talked as if we were right beside her.

"Luther says we have to do some of the things Emily wanted us to do, like not burn the electric lights much because of the cost. We have so much house to light up," she added laughing. "But I don't mind the candles and the lamps. It's just remembering to fill them with oil all the time. I hate that. Don't you just hate that?" she stopped to ask.

"We don't have lamps like that in Cutler's Cove," I said.

"Oh." She looked down at Jefferson. "Hello. I forgot to learn your name."

"I'm Jefferson," he said.

"Jefferson . . . Jefferson," she repeated and looked up. "Oh there's a man here on the wall named Jefferson," she said.

"A man on the wall?"

"She means a picture, I'm sure," I told him.

"Yes a picture. He was, um . . . a president."

"Jefferson Davis," Gavin offered.

"Yes," she said, clapping her hands. "That's the man. I'll show him to you. Oh, what's your name?"

"I'm Gavin," he said smiling. "Any Gavins on the walls?"

She thought a moment and then shook her head. But then she quickly smiled.

"I know. I'll draw your picture and do it with thread and put it in a silver frame. Just find your spot."

"My spot?"

"Where you want me to put it," she explained.

"Oh." Gavin shifted his gaze to me and smiled.

"I'm changing the house," she continued as we walked on. "Emily made it such a dreary place because she thought it was evil to make it bright and happy. But Emily's gone . . . " She turned to us. "She died and flew out on a broom. That's what Luther says. He saw her fly off."

"He did!" Jefferson said. She nodded and leaned toward him to whisper.

"Sometimes, when it's very dark and cold outside, Emily flies around the house moaning and groaning, but all we do is shut the windows tight and close the drapes," she added and straightened up again. Jefferson looked up at me in astonishment. Even my smile didn't relieve his anxiety.

We walked up the stairs. When we reached the second-story landing, Charlotte stopped and nodded toward the right, now all in darkness.

"That's where your mother was and where you were born. In the morning, I'll show you the room if you like," she said.

"Yes, I would. Thank you, Aunt Charlotte."

"We live this way," she explained, turning to the right where there were kerosene lamps lighting the way. The walls here were peppered with Charlotte's handiwork, too—old pictures marked up and her own needlework pictures framed and hung in between, above and below the others. We passed a small table that was draped in what looked like a bed sheet over the front of which had been painted the face of a clown.

Despite the haphazard manner in which things were hung and placed, Charlotte's artwork was remarkably good. I could see that Jefferson enjoyed all the colors and pictures and I began to wonder myself whether or not Charlotte's childish redecorating wasn't of some value. This dark, cavernous old house was at least made bright and jolly by her work. As we passed other examples—jars and vases painted bright colors with happy designs and shapes, paper lanterns hanging from the ceilings and chandeliers, strips of colored crepe paper strewn over walls and windows—I felt as if we had somehow fallen into the mad but silly world of Alice in Wonderland.

"This used to be my parents' room," Charlotte said, stopping before the door, "and that was them," she said, turning to the portraits hung on the opposite wall. These pictures she hadn't tampered with, even though neither Mr. nor Mrs. Booth smiled. In fact, they both looked angry and unhappy about being painted. Charlotte turned back to the door and opened it. "I always keep a lamp lit in there," she explained. "Just in case their spirits return. Don't want them bumping into things," she added and laughed. Jefferson's eyes went wide again.

It was an enormous room with a great oak bed. It had pillars that went up as high as the ceiling and an enormous half-moon headboard. The bed still had all its pillows and blankets, but the cobwebs were thick. There was an enormous fieldstone fireplace with large windows on either side. Long curtains were drawn tightly closed and looked weighed down with years and years of dust and grime. Above the fireplace was a portrait of a young Father Booth. He stood holding a rifle in one hand and a string of ducks in the other.

There was a lot of dark, beautiful antique furniture in the room and on the night table there was a large Bible and a pair of reading glasses beside it. But the room smelled musty and stale. When Gavin and I saw that the vanity table still had brushes and combs and jars of skin creams on it with some of the jars opened, we looked at each other. It was as if the room were being kept as some sort of shrine, left just the way it had been the day Charlotte's father passed away. I remembered that her mother had died much earlier. Charlotte closed the door and we continued to the next.

"This was where Emily slept," she whispered. "I don't keep any lamps lit in there. I don't want her spirit coming back into the house," she explained. We walked on, passing another closed door and then another. "Luther and I sleep in here," she said, pointing toward one. "Now," she said stopping. "These are two nice guest rooms." She opened the first door and went in to light a lamp.

The room had two single beds separated by a night stand. There were dressers on both sides and two large windows, one to the right of the bed on the right and one to the left of the bed on the left.

"This is a closet," Charlotte explained, opening a door, "and this door," she said, going to another, "is a door adjoining the next room. Isn't that nice?"

We looked into the room. It was nearly identical.

"Is Jefferson going to sleep with Gavin or with you?" Charlotte asked.

"What would you like to do, Jefferson?"

"I'll sleep with Gavin," he said, assuming a male

bravado that made me smile. He wasn't going to admit to the need to sleep with his big sister.

"As long as he doesn't snore," Gavin said jokingly. "We'll take that room," he said, indicating the room through the adjoining door.

"The bathroom is just across the hall," Charlotte said. "There are towels in it; there always are, and there's soap, too, nice soap, not the soap Emily made us use. And we have hot water again, although sometimes it breaks down and Luther has to fix it. Do you have to change your clothes?" she asked.

"We have a small problem, Aunt Charlotte," I said. "When we were waiting in New York City for Gavin to arrive, all of my and Jefferson's clothes and things were stolen."

"Oh dear me," she said, bringing her hands to her throat. "How sad. Well," she said, smiling quickly, "tomorrow we'll go looking for new clothes. We'll go up into the attic where there are trunks and trunks of things to wear, including shoes and hats, gloves and coats, okay?"

"I guess so," I said looking at Gavin. He shrugged.

"Now let's all hurry down to the kitchen to have something to eat and then you can tell me everything from the day you were born until now," Charlotte said.

"That could take quite a long while, Aunt Charlotte," I said smiling.

"Oh," she said, her face turning sad. "Do you have to go home soon?"

"No, Aunt Charlotte. I don't want to ever go home again," I said. Her eyes widened.

"You mean you want to stay here forever and ever?"

"For as long as we can," I replied.

"Well that's forever," she said nonchalantly and clapped her hands together. Then she followed it with a short laugh. "That's forever."

We followed her out. She took Jefferson's hand and started to describe how much fun he was going to have exploring the house and grounds. As she shuffled down the corridor, she told him about the rabbits and the chickens and the sly fox that was always haunting the coops. When we arrived at the kitchen, we found that Luther had prepared cheese sandwiches and tea for us. Charlotte opened a bread box to reveal some jelly rolls she had baked.

"Soon after Emily died," she explained, "we went to town and bought twenty pounds of sugar, didn't we, Luther?" He nodded. "And we buy it all the time now. Emily never permitted us to have sugar, only sour balls occasionally, right Luther?"

"Emily's gone and good riddance to her," he said firmly. The three of us sat around the table and ate our sandwiches while Charlotte went on and on about the things she had done since Emily's death. She had gone into sections of the house Emily had once forbidden her to go into; she had opened trunks and looked into dresser drawers and she wore perfume and even put on lipstick whenever she wanted. Most of all she had gone all out with her artwork and handicraft.

"Do you like to paint pictures, Jefferson?" she asked. He looked up quickly.

"I never did," he said.

"Oh, well you have to try it now that you're here. Tomorrow, I'll show you all my paints and brushes. Luther made me a regular art studio, didn't you, Luther?"

"It used to be Emily's office," he said happily. "I just moved all her things into storage and moved all Charlotte's supplies and materials in."

"Did you ever weave beads, Jefferson?" Charlotte asked him. He shook his head. "Oh, you're going to have so much fun. And I have pounds and pounds of clay, too."

"You do?"

"Yes." She slapped her hands together. "I know what—we'll give you a room to do over. You can paint everything in it anyway you want."

"Wow!" Jefferson said, his eyes bright with excitement. Then Aunt Charlotte sat down and folded her hands. She watched us eat for a moment.

"So," she finally said. "When are your mommy and daddy coming to get you?"

I lowered my sandwich to the plate.

"They're never coming for us, Aunt Charlotte. There was a terrible fire in the hotel and they died in it. We couldn't live there anymore," I added.

"Oh dear. Died, you say?" She looked up at Luther who nodded, his face dark. "Oh, how sad for you, for everyone." She looked sympathetically at Jefferson. "Well, we won't let sadness come into The Meadows. We'll shut the door on sadness. We'll have lots of fun making things and cooking good things to eat like cookies and cakes and we'll think up games to play and listen to music."

"My sister plays the piano," Jefferson bragged.

"Oh, she does." Aunt Charlotte clapped her hands. "We have a piano in the living room, don't we, Luther?"

"Probably badly out of tune and dusty, but it's a nice piano," he said. "Charlotte's mother used to play after dinner," Luther said but then he fixed his gaze on me. "Somebody must be looking after you kids now, though, ain't they? Won't they be coming for you?"

I looked at Gavin and then shook my head.

"They don't know we're here," I said.

"You run away, did you?" I didn't have to answer. He saw it in our faces.

"Please let us stay a while, Luther. We won't be any trouble," I pleaded.

"No sir, we won't," Gavin said. "I'd be glad to help you with your chores around the plantation, too," he added.

"You ever done any farm work?" Luther asked quickly.

"A little," Gavin said.

"Well, we got hay to bale, crops to harvest, pigs and chickens to feed, firewood to cut and split. Let's see your hands," he said and reached out to grab Gavin's wrist and turn his palms up. Then he put his hand alongside Gavin's. "See these, calluses. That's what comes from farm work."

"I'm not afraid of getting calluses," Gavin said sharply. Luther nodded and came close to smiling, his lips twitching in the corners. He stepped back.

"We get by on what we grow here," he said.

"I want to help too," Jefferson said.

Charlotte laughed.

"He can learn to gather the eggs," she said. Jefferson's face lit up.

"And I can help with the house chores," I said. Even with the dull lighting, I could see that the house needed hours and hours of cleaning. "We won't be a burden," I promised.

"Of course you won't, dear," Charlotte said. "They can stay, can't they, Luther?"

"I guess so. For a while anyway," he added.

"I know what," Charlotte said and clapped her hands again, "as soon as you're finished eating, you can try the piano."

"They're tired, Charlotte. They should go to sleep," Luther said.

"Oh just a little," she whined like a child. "You can play just a little, can't you, dear?"

"Yes," I said and when we finished our tea and jelly rolls, which were quite good, Charlotte led the way to the living room, holding Jefferson's hand. I was happy to see how quickly he had taken to her and how he wasn't shy or frightened anymore.

The living room was the most shocking room of all. Charlotte had repainted the walls, making one wall yellow, one blue, one green and one bright pink. Instead of paintings and portraits, she had hung up old clothes with shoes and boots dangling from the bottoms of pants and skirts. In one corner she had a display of costume jewelry. She had painted the legs of chairs and tables, each of them having four different-colored legs to match the walls. Here and there paint was splattered on the hardwood floor and even some paint had dripped over the window panes.

Gavin and I just stood there, our mouths open, gaping.

"Charlotte wanted to make this room her Happy Room," Luther explained.

"Emily never used to let us come in here much," Charlotte said. "She didn't want us messing things up," she added and then followed it with a short laugh that sounded like a hiccup. Jefferson spun around and around, his face broken into a wide, excited smile.

"Can I do this to my room?" he asked.

"You surely can," Charlotte said. "Tomorrow we'll pick out your room and then you'll pick our paints."

"I don't know if he should do that, Aunt Charlotte," I said.

"Of course he should, dear. He's a little boy and

little boys need to do little boy things. Right, Luther?"

"It's all right with me," he said. "If Emily was here, she'd die all over again." How much he had hated her, I thought.

"Now let's all sit and listen to Christie play the piano," Charlotte said. She took Jefferson's hand and led him to the sofa.

Gavin smiled at me.

"Earn your supper," he whispered and sat down beside Jefferson and Charlotte. Luther stood in the doorway.

I went to the grand piano. Charlotte had spared it, leaving the wood the color it was and not touching the piano stool either. It was dusty, but when I tapped on the keys, I was surprised at how in tune it still was.

"Can you play 'Happy Birthday'?" Charlotte asked. "No one's played 'Happy Birthday' for me for a long time."

"Yes," I said and did so. To my surprise, Luther began to sing along and when I reached the place for a name, he bellowed "Dear Charlotte, happy birthday to you." She laughed and clapped her hands and I caught the way Luther gave her a loving glance.

I played some of Brahms' *Lullaby* and as I played, Jefferson's eyes began to close. Charlotte had her arm around him and he had lain his head against her soft shoulder. By the time I finished, he was fast asleep. I nodded at him and Charlotte widened her eyes and said, "Shh."

Gavin scooped Jefferson up in his arms and carried him from the room to the stairway. Charlotte followed us upstairs.

"I'll get one of Luther's clean nightshirts for

him," she said and hurried out. I took off Jefferson's shoes and socks and Gavin helped undress him. He was so tired that his eyelids barely fluttered as we moved him around to get his clothing off. Charlotte returned with a flannel nightshirt. It was way too big for Jefferson, but I thought it would keep him warm and comfortable anyway. We slipped it over his head and then tucked him into bed.

"I can give you one of my nightgowns," Charlotte told me. I told her I would be all right sleeping in my underwear.

"Well then, I'm going to sleep myself. We have a big day tomorrow. So much to do and so little time to do it, as Emily used to say. She was right about that. Sometimes, Emily was right, even though Luther hates to hear me say that," she whispered. "Good night, dears. Sleep tight and don't let the bedbugs bite," she added and laughed. We watched her scurry off.

I went into the bathroom first and then crawled into my bed and turned off the kerosene lamp. The room was pitch dark, but the overcast sky had broken and the light of stars poured a gentle, soft glow through the window. I listened for Gavin and heard him return to his and Jefferson's room. Moments later there was a gentle knock on the adjoining door.

"Yes?"

"You all right?"

"Uh huh."

"Can I come in and say good night?"

"Of course you can, Gavin," I said. He opened the door farther. The lamp was still on in his and Jefferson's room, so I could see him clearly. He was wearing only his underwear. He moved to the side of my bed quickly and knelt down so he was right beside my face.

"It's funny here, isn't it? I mean, Charlotte's sweet and all, but it's like we're in another world."

"Yes, but I'm glad. I hate the world we were in before," I said. Gavin nodded, understanding.

"We can't stay here forever, you know."

"I know, but I'd like to stay here as long as we can. It won't be so bad. We'll help them fix the place up. It will be fun. We can pretend it's our plantation, too."

"You mean like the lord and lady of the manor?" he asked.

"Yes," I said. He laughed.

"Jefferson seems happy. All right," he said. "We'll give it a go. I'd better say good night," he whispered.

"Good night, Gavin. I'm so happy you came to help us and you're with us."

"I couldn't help but come," he said and then he leaned forward and kissed my cheek. "Good night, Christie," he said again, but he didn't move away. I turned my head toward him so he could return with his lips and put them softly on mine. He brushed my hair with his palm and then stood up.

As he turned to go to his and Jefferson's room, I caught the movement of a shadow in the window to my left and spun around.

"Gavin!" I cried and he turned back.

"What?"

"Someone was looking in the window just now," I said, sitting up quickly.

"What?" He moved to the window and looked out. "I don't see anyone." He opened the window more and stuck his head out.

"Gavin?"

"Shh," he said and listened. Then he brought his head back in.

"What?"

"I thought I heard footsteps on the roof, but I guess it was just the wind. I'm sure it was nothing," he said. "Just a shadow."

"There's no moon tonight to make shadows, Gavin."

"Then it must have been your imagination . . . all those stories about Emily on a broom. Are you frightened? Will you be all right?"

I looked at the window. I was sure I had seen something, but I didn't want to ruin our first night here.

"Yes, I'll be okay."

"Good night again." He started away.

"Gavin."

"Yes?"

"Leave the door open just a little," I said.

"Sure."

After he left I lay there with my eyes open, turning every once in a while to look at the window. I didn't see any more shadows or heads and my eyelids grew so heavy, I had to close them and fall asleep.

But sometime during the night, I woke up feeling certain someone had been watching me, that someone had even been in the room!

Through the Looking-Glass

EVEN THOUGH WE WERE ALL SO EXHAUSTED BY THE TIME we went to sleep, we woke up when we heard Aunt Charlotte in the hallway singing, "Get up, get up, you sleepy heads, come on get up, get out of your beds!" Her laughter followed, and moments later when I opened my eyes, I saw Jefferson peering at me through the partially opened adjoining door. The hem of Luther's nightshirt trailed behind and around him as he scampered into my room and hopped onto my bed.

"Wake up, Christie. Wake up," he said, shaking my arm. "Gavin's moaning and groaning. He won't get up," Jefferson complained. I moaned myself. Then I rubbed my eyes and propped myself up on my elbows. Sunlight came streaming through the windows, illuminating the particles of dust that danced in its rays, making them look like tiny floating jewels.

"We had a long day yesterday, Jefferson," I explained in defense. "We're still tired."

"I'm not tired," he declared. "I wanna have breakfast and paint pictures with Aunt Charlotte. She's calling us. Come on," he said, shaking my arm again.

"Okay, okay." I took a deep breath and gazed at the window, recalling my sense of another presence. "Go get washed up and I'll help you put on your clothes," I said. He lifted Luther's nightshirt up over his ankles so he could hurry out to the bathroom, his bare feet dancing over the hardwood floors. Just after I put on my skirt and blouse, I heard a gentle knock and turned to see Gavin, who had risen and gotten dressed.

"You know it's only six-thirty in the morning," he complained, his eyelids drooping. He yawned. "Are you all right? Any more nightmares?"

"They weren't nightmares, Gavin. Someone was looking through that window last night," I said. He smiled. "Someone was here. I think he even came back after we went to sleep!"

"Okay, okay." He rubbed his stomach. "You know, I'm hungry. I wonder what they eat for breakfast."

Jefferson came rushing back in. He was brightly awake and had even tried to brush back his hair neatly. I helped him dress while Gavin washed up and then I washed my face and did what I could with my hair, absent a brush or comb. The scent of bacon drew us all down the corridor and stairway quickly. When we entered the kitchen, we found Luther finishing up a platter of bacon and eggs. Charlotte was wearing another of her personally designed potato sacks, this one covered with different colors and different sized buttons. She had sewn a large pink bow on each shoulder.

"Good morning, everyone. Did everyone have a nice sleep?" she asked. "Mr. Sandman was here last night. I heard him walking through the house, didn't you?"

"Oh, so that's who that was," Gavin said, smiling, his eyes twinkling impishly. He waited to see if I was going to tell them about the face in the window.

"I didn't hear Mr. Sandman," Jefferson said.

"That's because you were already asleep so he didn't have to put sand in your eyes," Charlotte explained. "Now sit down, everyone. We've got to have a good breakfast first and then we can do our chores, right Luther?" Luther grunted and gulped down his coffee as he rose from his seat.

"I'll be out back," he said and then looked at Gavin and added, "in the barn."

"I'll be there right after breakfast," Gavin promised. Luther nodded and left.

"Does everyone want eggs and bacon?" Charlotte asked. "I make them sunny-side-up because they look like little smiling faces that way."

"It smells wonderful, Aunt Charlotte," I said. "Can I help?"

"Everything's done. Just sit down and I'll serve you just the way I used to serve my daddy and Emily years and years ago," she said. She served the food and then sat down and talked as we all ate, describing what life used to be like when she was a young girl.

"After Daddy died and Emily became Miss Bossy Mouth, everything changed," she concluded sadly. "We didn't have breakfasts like this anymore. Emily made us sell most of our eggs to the grocery in Upland Station."

"What about Grandmother Cutler?" I inquired.

"Grandmother Cutler?"

"Your other sister, Lillian?"

"Oh," she said, taking on a strange, pensive look. "She was off and married when I was just a little girl," she said quickly, "and I hardly saw her, but Emily always complained about her." She leaned toward us. "Emily always complained about everyone," she whispered as if Emily were in the other room, listening. Then she clapped her hands together and smiled.

"First, I'll show Jefferson the paints and the brushes and let him play and then later we'll go up to the attic and you can find clothes and shoes to wear, okay? Won't that be nice?"

"Yes, Aunt Charlotte," I said. I looked around the kitchen. There were dishes caked with food from previous meals on the counter and the floor looked as though it hadn't been washed in weeks, if not months. The windows were spotted with dust and grime on both the insides and out. "I'll do what I can to help you clean up the house, too."

"Goody, goody, goody," she said and laughed. "We'll have wonderful times, just like we used to when everyone was little and we had a golden retriever dog named Kasey Lady who poked her nose in my face every morning to wake me."

Gavin looked at me and smiled. Aunt Charlotte was just a little girl at heart, but I didn't mind. I felt safe here, as safe and secure as I would be in a magic bubble. It was as if I finally had been able to escape the curse on the Cutlers.

After breakfast, Gavin went out to help Luther, and Charlotte took Jefferson to her makeshift studio to give him his paints and brushes. I cleaned the kitchen. When I was finished I went exploring through the house. Halfway down the corridor, I stopped because I thought I heard someone behind me. But when I looked, no one was there. Only . . . a curtain swayed.

"Who's there?" I called. No one responded and nothing moved. It gave me goose bumps, so I hurried to find Charlotte and Jefferson. On the way I discovered that Charlotte had painted the stems and blossoms of flowers after they had wilted, making them even brighter shades of pink and white, red and yellow, and then left them in vases everywhere. It was as if she were trying to bring rainbows into what had once been a dull and gray world.

I found Charlotte and Jefferson in a little room off the library. When I peered in, Charlotte looked up from her needlework and smiled. Jefferson was busy painting walls and fixtures. Already, his cheeks were streaked and his arms were full of paint up to his elbows.

"We're having fun," Charlotte said, her face beaming with joy, and then she quickly added, "Little boys are supposed to make messes of themselves."

"You're right about that, Aunt Charlotte. Aunt Charlotte, can you show me the room now where my mother lived and I was born?"

"Oh yes, yes, yes. That's the Bad Room," she said rising. "I was in it once, too."

"The bad room?"

"You'll see," she said and led me upstairs.

When I set eyes on the room, I understood immediately why it would be called "The Bad Room." It looked like a prison cell. It was a small room with a narrow bed against the wall on the left. The bed had no headboard; it was just a mattress on a metal frame. Beside it was a bare nightstand. On the stand was a kerosene lamp, but I could see it had not been used for years. There were spiders living in it. The walls were dark gray and there were no mirrors or windows. To the right was a doorway to the small bathroom. I saw that the fixtures were rusted and rotten. It had been some time since water had run in that sink, I thought.

Looking around this horrid room, I sensed some of the terror and sadness my mother must have felt being locked up in it and forced to give birth in such a hovel. How lonely she must have been, and how frightened all the time. With no sunlight, no fresh air, nothing but dreary colors to gaze at, she surely must have felt like a prisoner or someone evil being punished.

"You're right to call this the Bad Room, Aunt Charlotte," I said. And then I recalled what she had said before. "Why were you put here?"

"I was naughty, too," she said. "And had a baby growing in my stomach."

"A baby? What happened to it? Was it a boy or a girl?" I asked quickly.

"A boy. Emily said the devil took him home. He had the devil's mark on the back of his neck right here," she said, turning around and pointing to the area.

"The devil's mark?"

"Uh huh," she said, nodding emphatically. "It looked like a hoof. And Emily said he was going to grow a tail soon, too."

"That's silly, Aunt Charlotte," I said, smiling. "There really wasn't a baby, was there?"

"Oh yes there was. I'll show you where he lived for a while," she added sadly.

I followed her back down the corridor. As we walked, I couldn't help feeling someone was following us, but every time I turned around, there was no one there. Was it just because the house was so large and full of shadows that I had these feelings? I wondered.

Charlotte stopped and opened the door to what had apparently once been a nursery. There was a crib at the center of the room and in it was a doll with a faded blue blanket drawn up to its chin. It gave me the chills. Had Aunt Charlotte really had a child or was this all some invention of her childlike imagination?

"How old was your baby before . . . before the devil took him, Aunt Charlotte?" I asked.

She shook her head.

"I don't remember. One day he was here and then one day he wasn't. Emily never told me when he was taken off. One day I looked in and found he was gone," she said, looking at the doll.

"And Emily told you the devil took him?"

"Uh huh. One night, she saw the devil enter the nursery and then she heard the baby laugh. By the time she came to the door, the devil had taken my baby and flown out the window in the form of a black bird."

"How could you believe such a silly story, Aunt Charlotte?"

She stared at me a moment.

"My baby was gone," she said conclusively, her eyes beginning to tear. I looked at the crib.

"Who put that doll there?" I asked.

"Emily did because I was so sad and crying so much," she said. "Emily said, make believe that's him and don't complain or the devil might come and take you, too."

"But what about the baby's father, Aunt Charlotte? Wasn't he upset?"

"Emily said the devil was his father. She said the devil came into my room one night while I was sleeping and made the baby grow in me."

How horrid of her, I thought, to frighten simple, sweet Charlotte like that and convince her of so many frightening things.

"Emily must have been the devil herself to do all these horrible things to you and to my mother. I'm glad I never had to meet her," I said.

"Well don't be bad and you'll never meet her," Charlotte said. "If you're bad, you'll go to hell and Emily is the one who greets people at the door. That's what Luther says."

I took another look at the doll in the crib and thought what a strange and evidently horrifying history was locked and hidden in the walls of this old plantation house. Perhaps it was better not to dig so deeply or ask so many questions, I thought and then followed Aunt Charlotte out.

As we went down the stairs, I turned and thought I saw a shadow move across a wall, but I didn't say anything to Charlotte. I was sure if I did, she'd only tell me it was the ghost of her evil sister Emily.

When the grandfather clock bonged twelve, Charlotte put down her needlework and announced it was time to make lunch for the men. I helped her prepare the sandwiches and shortly afterward, Luther and Gavin came in. One look at Gavin told me he had really been doing hard work. His clothing was full of pieces of hay; his hands were streaked with dirt and grease, as were his neck and face, his hair was disheveled, and he looked red with fatigue.

"I'd better wash up first," he told me and then added in a whisper, "He wasn't kidding about the hard work. I'm earning our keep."

"Luther," Charlotte said after we had all sat down to eat our lunch, "can Gavin take time off now to go up into the attic and find things for him and Christie and Jefferson to wear?"

Luther looked up from his plate.

"You be careful up there," he told Gavin. "Some of those floorboards might not be worthy anymore, hear?"

"Yes sir," Gavin said. I could see that anything looked better to him than going out to work with Luther. The idea of exploring an old attic and sifting through ancient things excited Jefferson too, and he was willing to put aside his paint and brushes to go up with us.

Charlotte led the way. She talked an incessant blue streak as she shuffled along with her hands folded over her stomach and her head down like a geisha girl. She described how she would play up in the attic when she was a little girl.

"All by myself and never afraid," she added and paused at the end of the corridor at a narrow door. It opened to a dark stairway lit only by a low-wattage bare bulb dangling from a thick wire. The stairs creaked ominously as we followed Charlotte up.

"No one cared how long I stayed up here," she told us. "Not even Emily," she said and followed that with a little laugh before she added, "because I was out of everyone's hair." She stopped at the top of the stairway and looked back at us. "That's what Momma used to tell me. Charlotte, she would say, stay out of everyone's hair. What a silly thing to say. I never got into anyone's hair. How could I?"

Gavin smiled at me and we waited as Charlotte contemplated the attic.

"There are no lights up here," she said. "Just the light that comes through the windows and the light from lamps you bring. I keep one over here," she said and lit a kerosene lamp that had been left at the top of the stairway. We followed her quickly.

It was apparent that no one had been in the attic for ages. Thick cobwebs crossed the top of the stairway and dangled from every nook and cranny. The dust was so heavy that we could see our footprints on the steps and floor. Gavin, Jefferson and I paused at the top and gazed ahead at the long, wide attic that ran nearly thc full length of the great plantation house. The four sets of dormer windows across the front provided some additional illumination and in the rays of sunlight that filtered through, we could see the thick particles of dust stirred by the breezes that seeped through cracks in the walls and casements. I felt as if we had entered a tomb because the air was so stale and heavy, and everything looked so untouched and buried for years and years.

"Careful," Gavin said as we all stepped forward. The floorboards creaked ominously.

"Look!" Jefferson cried and pointed to the right where a family of squirrels had made themselves a comfortable home. They peered at us, twitched their noses arrogantly, and then scurried into corners and behind trunks and furniture. There were old sofas and chairs, tables and armoires, as well as dressers and headboards from beds. There were more old portraits, too. One in particular caught my eye because it was a picture of a young girl not much older than I was, her face caught in a soft, almost angelic smile. In none of the other portraits did the subjects even crack their lips. Their expressions were usually severe and serious.

"Do you know who this girl was, Aunt Charlotte?" I asked, holding up the silver-framed portrait.

"She was my mother's youngest sister," Charlotte explained. "Emily said she died giving birth when she was only nineteen because her heart was too soft," Charlotte recited.

"How sad. She looks so happy and so beautiful here." Every family has its own hexes, I thought. Some make their own happen, but some just wander into curses like wandering into a storm. The girl in the picture looked like she never even had a nightmare, much less imagined herself dying so tragically. Was it better to live with fear or pretend the world was full of rainbows, like Charlotte was doing? I wondered as I put the portrait back on the dusty shelf.

"I can't believe all this stuff," Gavin said, looking from one side to the other. "There must be years and years and years of things up here."

"My daddy and his daddy and daddy's daddy saved everything," Charlotte revealed. "Whenever something was replaced, it was brought up here and stored just in case. Emily used to call this the household graveyard. Sometimes, she would try to frighten me and look up at the ceiling downstairs and whisper, 'The dead are above us. Be good or they'll come down during the night and peer in at you through windows.'"

"Peer through windows?" I repeated. Gavin raised his eyes, expecting I would talk about what I had thought I saw and felt last night.

"Yes," Charlotte said. "Emily hated coming up here. That's why I played up here all the time. Emily would leave me alone," she said and laughed. "And I didn't have to do all the chores she wanted me to do."

Charlotte may be a child at heart, I thought, but in some ways, she was still very clever.

"Come on," she urged and led us toward the trunks to the right. "The farther in we go, the older everything is," she said.

We walked past rows and rows of cartons, some filled with old papers and old books, some filled with old dishes, cups and antique kitchen implements. We found cartons of old shoes and boots, and cartons just filled with springs and screws and rusted tools. Gavin found a box of old ledgers and took one out to look at it.

"This is amazing," he said. "It's a listing of slaves and how much was paid for each. Look."

I gazed at the open page and read, "Darcy, age 14, weight eight stone and four, twelve dollars."

Gavin continued to sift through the books.

"And there are ledgers describing the crops and what they got for them, things bought and how much they had to pay—it's all very historical and probably very valuable to a museum or something," he said.

Jefferson found an old rusted pistol, the parts locked by age and grime.

"Bang, bang, bang," he cried, waving it.

"Be careful, Jefferson," I warned. "You don't want to cut yourself on anything rusty."

"Christie," Gavin said after opening a small dark cherrywood chest, "look at this." I knelt down beside him. In the chest were all sorts of items from a woman's vanity table: pearl-handled combs and brushes and mirrors, some with cameos on the backs and handles. There was costume jewelry including strings of good imitation pearls and pearl earrings, pins and bracelets and a silver necklace filled with imitation rubies and emeralds. Everything looked handcrafted and in remarkably good shape, despite its age. It was as though this attic were truly a magical place that kept its contents frozen in time.

"It's all so beautiful," I said.

"It will look beautiful on you," Gavin whispered, his face so close to mine. It was as if a warm hand brushed across my breast. I felt myself flush and looked quickly at Aunt Charlotte, who was throwing open trunks and boxes, exclaiming excitedly as she made one discovery after another of things she had known as a child. For her it was like finding old friends.

"Here are some nice clothes, dear," Charlotte

said, opening a large metal trunk. I found dresses with short bodices and gusseted skirts, dresses with bodices high at the neck and sleeves that were close fitting and gathered at puffs at the top. There were colored bodices with white skirts, some with colored waist-belts. Another trunk was filled with thinly padded petticoats.

Additional trunks had more late- and turn-of-the-century fashions. I unearthed cloaks and horseback-riding garments, bonnets and satin shawls, as well as velvet wraps. Jefferson found a trunk filled with parasols and another trunk full of high boots, the leather still in remarkably good condition. Meanwhile, Gavin wandered to the left and found trunks of men's clothing, from knickers to overcoats and army uniforms. He liked the World War One uniforms and tried on one with a jacket that fit him well.

Jefferson and I began trying things on and modeling for each other, laughing as we paraded about in the ancient garments and footwear. Even Charlotte joined in, donning a shawl or a jacket and laughing at her image in one of the old vanity mirrors set back behind the trunks and cartons. Suddenly, we heard an extra laugh. At least, Gavin and I did. Charlotte didn't appear to notice and Jefferson was far too occupied. I grabbed Gavin's arm and whispered.

"What was that?" We looked toward the other side of the attic, but saw no one.

"Just an echo, I suppose," Gavin said, but he didn't look too sure. We listened, but heard nothing more.

Finally, we gathered what we considered sensible garments and filled a trunk with clothing for Gavin, Jefferson and myself.

"We'll take all of it down and wash it," I said.

"Wait," Gavin cried. "I'd like you to wear this one this evening."

He had found a light pink ball gown with what looked like miles of crinoline. The lace-trimmed bodice was designed to be worn off the shoulder.

"And I'll wear this," he declared, holding up a tailcoat and trousers. The tails were narrow and pointed and reached below his knees. The sleeves were wide at the top and very tight at the wrist, but opened out to cover his hands as far as his fingers. Then he reached down and produced a top hat. He dipped into the pocket of the tailcoat and fished out a black satin cravat with a bow in front.

We laughed. Aunt Charlotte clapped her hands and declared that she would find something nice to wear, too.

"We'll have a party. I'll make sweet jelly cookies and ask Luther to take out some of our dandelion wine. Christie will play the piano and we'll all sing. Oh, I'm so happy you're here," she declared, smiling widely and gazing happily at the three of us. "It's like . . . like I was born again with a new family!"

While I worked on our new-found clothing, Gavin took Jefferson out with him to help Luther with the rest of the day's chores. Charlotte helped me with the clothes and I listened to her chatter away about the days of her youth. Every time I asked her about Grandmother Cutler, however, she would grow silent. I had the sense she remembered more than she cared to tell me but whatever she remembered must have been unpleasant. Knowing what I had been told about Grandmother Cutler, it didn't surprise me.

Charlotte decided that it was an important

enough occasion for us to have a chicken for dinner and she went outside to convince Luther. After she had left I heard the distinct sound of footsteps outside the washroom.

"Gavin?" I called. There was no answer. "Jefferson?" Still no reply. Slowly, I put the clothes down and peered out the door. Once again, I saw a shadow move. "Who's there?" Although there was no answer, I had the distinct sense of another's presence. My heart began to pound. "Gavin, if you're playing a joke on me, it's not funny." I waited, but no one spoke. Slowly, quietly, I stepped into the hallway. The floorboards creaked. I stopped and listened keenly. The sound of heavy breathing drew my attention to the right. I took a few steps in that direction and then . . . I saw him!

At first, I was so shocked by the sight of him, I couldn't utter a sound. He was tall and stout with dark curly hair and big dark eyes. He was unshaven and the hair over his lips and along his jaws was as dark as the hair on his head.

Finally, I screamed and my scream sent him scurrying down the hallway and out a side door. After he was gone and I was able to think about him more calmly, I realized he had had a soft, round face filled more with curiosity than threat.

Gavin had heard my screams and came running into the house, Jefferson right behind him, with Luther and Charlotte following.

"What happened? What's wrong?"

I pointed down the corridor.

"I saw him. He was standing right there. It wasn't my imagination this time. He was tall with dark curly hair and a dark face. He had big eyes and wore baggy gray pants with black suspenders."

"Who is that?" Gavin asked and looked at Luther.

"He's harmless," Luther muttered.

"Who's harmless?" Gavin asked quickly.

"It's only Homer," Luther said. "He lives with the Douglases, our closest neighbors. Don't mind him," he added and started away.

"But Luther . . . he just came into the house and last night, I'm sure he was on the roof peering in the windows," I said. "I think he's been spying on us all the time."

"Don't mind him," he repeated and left.

"Who is he, Charlotte? Why does he come here like this?" I asked, turning to her.

She shrugged and smiled.

"He likes us and Luther always gives him things. I leave him cupcakes and cookies. All I do is leave them on the counter on the table and some time during the day, he comes and eats them. Sometimes, he helps Luther with the chores."

"He didn't try to hurt you, did he?" Gavin asked.

"No. I think I frightened him more than he frightened me," I said.

"He just wants to know who you are and why you're here," Charlotte said. "He's shy. Maybe because his mommy and daddy found him in a field."

"They found him?"

"Just outside their house. Like Moses floating in a stream. There he was one day, crying. They had no children so they considered him a gift. But everyone knows that someone left him; someone didn't want him."

She laughed.

"Poor Homer. He thinks he fell out of the sky. Anyway," she said clapping her hands, "Luther said I could make the chicken and we could have a party tonight. Won't that be nice?"

"Will Homer come?" Jefferson asked, wide-eyed.

"Maybe. Maybe he will," Charlotte said and hurried off to start preparing.

"Okay," Gavin said nodding, "I'm sorry for not believing you last night. Homer," he added, shaking his head. "I wonder what other surprises are in store for us here. Come on, Jefferson," he said, putting his arm around his little shoulders, "let's return to our slave labor. The menfolks have to do the real work around here," he added teasingly.

"Is that right? Well, for your information, Gavin Steven Longchamp, household chores are just as hard if not harder than farm chores, especially if the house has been neglected as long as this one has," I fired back, my hands on my hips.

"Uh oh, little nephew. We're in the doghouse. Let's get moving while we still can."

"Huh?" Jefferson said, confused. Gavin leaned toward me to whisper.

"When you get mad, real mad," he said, "you look even more beautiful."

I felt myself flush from head to toe and was speechless as he laughed and hurried off, Jefferson tagging behind.

That evening we did have a wonderful meal. In his quiet way, Luther got into the spirit of things and brought in fresh lettuce, tomatoes and carrots from the garden, as well as one large potato for each of us. Charlotte announced that she wanted us to eat in the formal dining room.

"Just the way we used to when Daddy had important guests," she added and Luther grunted his agreement. I dusted down and polished the long, dark mahogany table and Charlotte produced a beautiful lace tablecloth and then showed me their good china and silverware. She told me Emily used to keep all these things under lock and key in a big chest in the pantry.

"After she died and went to hell, Luther broke the lock and we took everything out and put back where it belonged. We're still finding things where Emily hid them in the house," she added joyfully. "Even money under a rug!"

Luther decided it would be all right to turn on the chandeliers during dinner. With the table set with the fine china and good silverware, the goblets and linen napkins, the dining room did look elegant. Luther produced two silver candelabra and set them on the table, too. Then we all went up to dress. Gavin decided he and I should dress up in the formal clothing we had discovered and Charlotte talked Luther into putting on a clean shirt and pants, as well as brushing his hair.

After Gavin helped Jefferson dress, he knocked on the door of the bathroom, where I had been inside preparing myself. I had used the brushes and combs from the small cherrywood chest to fix my hair so I would look like the young woman in the old silver frame, the sides of my hair brushed back sternly, but the back of it tied and pinned with one of the pearl combs so it flowed down the back of my neck. Then I put on a string of pearls and pearl earrings.

"Is madam ready to be escorted to dinner?" Gavin asked.

"One moment," I called and adjusted my crinoline. How did women wear all this? I wondered. When I opened the door, it was as if Gavin and I had fallen back through time. In his top hat and tails he looked handsome and elegant, and what had been silly and humorous up in the attic now looked proper and fine. I could see the look of surprise and pleasure in his eyes as he gazed at me. For a moment neither of us spoke.

"You both look funny," Jefferson said, laughing.

"On the contrary, little nephew," Gavin replied softly, "I have never seen a more beautiful young woman. Miss Christie," he said, offering his arm.

"Thank you, Mr. Longchamp." Jefferson's mouth dropped open as I slipped my arm through Gavin's and we sauntered down the corridor. Jefferson went running ahead of us to warn Aunt Charlotte we were coming. She stepped out to watch us descend the stairs.

"Oh, how beautiful you two look!" she exclaimed, her hands pressed together just under her chin. Luther came up behind her to look, too. He finally gave us a wide smile.

"Thank you, Aunt Charlotte," I said. Then we laughed and went into the dining room to eat our feast.

Afterward, after Charlotte, Jefferson, Gavin and I cleaned up the dinner dishes and silverware, we did what Charlotte wanted and adjourned to the formal living room so I could play the piano for them. Charlotte brought in her homemade jelly cakes and Luther poured everyone, even Jefferson, a glass of dandelion wine. Then the four of them, Charlotte and Luther, Gavin and Jefferson, sat on the sofa and chairs to listen to me play.

Luther had lit the candles and oil lamps, but the room still had an ethereal, mystical quality because of the dark shadows in the corners and the tired, old, heavy drapes that drooped like ghosts over the windows.

As I played something first by Mozart and then by Liszt, I felt myself drift from this world. I was carried back by the music as if the notes wove a magic carpet. When I looked up at Gavin dressed in his old clothes and caught sight of my own reflection in the glass panes of a bookcase, I felt as if we had made it possible for the spirits of the Booth ancestors to reappear, if only for a few moments. I thought about the young girl in the portrait in the attic and imagined her smile in my smile, her dazzling eyes so full of life and hope now gazing at Gavin through my eyes. I heard a room full of laughter, glasses tinkling, more music, footsteps in the hallways and someone, a hundred years ago, calling my name from the top of the staircase.

I closed my eyes, my fingers gliding over the keys as if they were ghost fingers. Even the music seemed unfamiliar. I played on and on as if I would never stop. Then I opened my eyes and saw a dark shadow toward the rear of the room move. I gasped. Instantly, my hands lifted from the keys.

"What's wrong?" Charlotte asked. I nodded in the shadow's direction. Everyone turned to look. Charlotte smiled.

"Oh, hello, Homer," she said.

"Come over here, boy," Luther called and pointed to a seat. "Stop slinking all about the house. Sit down and behave."

Slowly Homer emerged from the dark corner and made his way timidly across the room. He was wearing the same clothing he had been wearing when I first set eyes on him. He looked timid and shy, just as Aunt Charlotte had said.

"Homer has to be introduced," Charlotte declared firmly. Luther grunted in agreement.

"Homer, this is Charlotte's niece Christie, her brother Jefferson and Gavin Longchamp. They're our guests for a while, so don't go around peering at them and frightening them, hear?"

Homer nodded, his eyes wide with curiosity.

"Have a jelly cake, Homer," Charlotte said and offered him one. He started to gobble it quickly and then saw the way we were staring at him and slowed down.

"Play some more music," he asked me.

"Say please, Homer," Charlotte instructed. "Always say please when you ask someone to do something for you."

"Please," he added.

I thought for a moment and then played "Camp Town Races." It brought a big, beaming smile to Homer's face. Luther enjoyed it too, and got up to pour everyone, except Jefferson, another glass of dandelion wine. I played a few other light pieces and then stopped to rest. We drank some more dandelion wine. Charlotte took out some old records and put them on a wind-up victrola.

"Madam?" Gavin said offering his hand. I got up and we danced, faking a waltz as best we could. By this time we were both feeling our wine so it didn't matter that we looked silly in our clothes pretending to know how to waltz. Charlotte thought it was wonderful and beamed a smile and clapped her hands. Whenever I looked at Homer, I saw him smiling and laughing, too. Charlotte kept the music going and Gavin spun me around and around.

"What a mad, crazy but wonderful evening this has been," Gavin declared. "Are you happy?"

"Yes, yes, yes," I sang, and he turned me this way and that until I protested I was dizzy and we had to stop. Jefferson had fallen asleep anyway. The full day of work and play and the one glass of dandelion wine had done it.

"I guess we should say good night," I said and then laughed as the room took a quick spin. "Oh dear me," I said with my palm against my pounding heart. "None of us are used to working so hard," I added and laughed.

"Good idea," Gavin said and went to pick up Jefferson to carry him upstairs, but Homer jumped up first.

"Let me do it," he said and scooped Jefferson up as if he were made of air. Gavin's eyes widened.

"Careful with him, Homer," Luther warned. "He ain't a bale of hay."

"Good night, Charlotte," I said, standing in the doorway and posturing like Scarlett O'Hara. "Good night, Luther. Thank you both for a lovely evening."

"We haven't had as much fun in years and years and years. Have we, Luther?" Charlotte asked him.

"No," he said, keeping his eyes fixed on Homer. "Come right down after you bring him to his bed, Homer," Luther ordered.

Homer nodded and moved rather softly and gracefully for a man his size as he carried Jefferson up the stairs to his and Gavin's room. He set him down gently in his bed.

"Thank you, Homer," I said. "Come see us tomorrow," I added. He nodded and then quickly left. Gavin pulled Jefferson's shoes off and dressed him for bed while I went to the bathroom. Every time I looked at myself in the mirror, I started to giggle. I couldn't stop and was still giggling when I went to my room. I sat on my bed, laughing. Gavin peeked in on me.

"Hey, what's going on?" Gavin poked his head in and asked. I responded with more laughter. He smiled and approached me. "What's so funny?"

The sight of him in his tailcoat drove me into new hysterics. Soon my stomach began to ache and I groaned, falling back on the bed and clutching myself.

"You're going to pee in your pants if you don't stop laughing," Gavin warned.

I stared up at him and then, as suddenly as I had begun to giggle, I began to cry. I bawled and bawled, the tears streaming down my face, zigzagging over my cheeks, hot, frantic tears that came from the deepest well of sorrow and pain within me. Gavin was frightened by my abrupt change in moods, but quickly knelt down beside me and began stroking my hair.

"Don't cry, don't cry. Everything's going to be all right. I promise. Please, don't cry, Christie. I can't stand it when you cry," he said and started to kiss away my tears. I threw my arms around his neck and buried my face in his shoulder. He continued to stroke my hair and whisper comforting words. My sobbing slowed until I was able to stop altogether. Then, I lifted my face, but held it close to his. Our lips were practically touching.

"Christie," he whispered. We kissed, softly at first and then harder until the tips of our tongues grazed, sending an electric thrill down my body. He kissed my neck and my naked shoulders and I moaned and lay back. I wanted his lips to go lower and lower, but he hesitated at the crest of my bosom.

"Gavin . . ."

"It's the wine," he whispered. "It's made you silly and sad."

"Gavin," I continued, looking deeply into his dark eyes, "have you ever been very close to a girl?"

"Very close?"

"Beside her without clothes?" I asked. Perhaps without the wine in me, I would never have asked such a question. He shook his head and kissed me again.

The horrid memory of Uncle Philip clutching at me, pulling and twisting my body so he would get his pleasure, returned; but I drove it off. That was ugly; this was different. I didn't want to be afraid to touch, to kiss, to want Gavin's body close to mine; I didn't want his lips to remind me of Uncle Philip's.

"Gavin," I whispered, "quickly, touch me, make me forget."

"Christie . . . you're . . . the wine . . ."

"No, it's not the wine. Please," I said. "I don't want to think of anything but you and this moment."

I took his wrist and brought his hand to my breast.

"Christie! No. Not like this," he said. "I'd only feel as if I took advantage of you," he explained, lifting his hand away. I turned my head into the pillow and buried my face so he wouldn't see my embarrassment. "I want to be with you," he said, "but not when you're confused."

I wanted to shout back that I wasn't confused. It wasn't the wine; it was the woman in me demanding to be born in a beautiful and loving way instead of being ripped and torn and dragged into maturity by a sick and twisted man. I wanted to pretend that this was my first time, that I was a girl with a normal life and not one who had been abused. My body ached to be treated tenderly, kindly, softly. I wanted our kisses to be kisses that reached into the farthest corners of my heart to stir my imagination; I wanted Gavin to touch me and set off the fire of passion in a way that made love between a man and a woman something wonderful, not something horrible to haunt me forever.

"Christie." He touched my shoulder. I moaned. "Are you all right?"

"No," I groaned. "I can't keep the horrid memories from bursting out like bubbles of acid burning my heart. I can't stop the nightmares." I spun around angrily. "I've run away from Cutler's Cove, Gavin, but not from the horrible things that were done to me. I feel dirty," I moaned, "and no shower or bath, no matter how hot or how many, can clean me. You think so too, don't you? That's why you won't touch me."

"No, Christie," he protested. "That's not true. I want to touch you. It's taking every bit of strength not to."

"Oh Gavin," I cried. "Stop being so strong. I need you close to me, very close," I said, the words coming from some part of me I didn't know existed. He stared down at me for a long moment and then he began to unbutton his jacket and shirt. I watched him undress himself down to his underwear in the light of the kerosene lamp. Then I sat up and took off my old dress. I kept my bra and panties on. I crawled under the blanket and Gavin, after checking on Jefferson, crawled under beside me. For a moment neither of us did anything. We just lay there letting our bodies touch.

"Christie," he said, "I'm not sure . . . I mean, what do you want me to do?"

Now that he was beside me, I realized how far we had gone and how quickly. Suddenly, it frightened me. Maybe Gavin was right; maybe it was wrong to do this now.

"Just hold me," I whispered, "and let me fall asleep in your arms."

"That's not as easy as you make it sound," he whispered. The hardness growing between his thighs explained why.

"Oh Gavin, I'm so cruel to you, tormenting you, demanding one thing and then another. You should hate me," I said.

"I could never hate you, Christie. It's not possible." His lips found mine again.

"Gavin," I said. "I'm not drunk; I'm not."

"I know," he said.

"Gavin, make me forget," I pleaded. "I need to forget."

His fingers found the clip on my bra and undid it. Then, he moved his fingers up, pushing the bra over my breasts until they were uncovered and his fingers slipped softly over my nipples, stiff and tingling. I slipped the bra off my arms.

"Christie, Christie . . ." His fingers inched my panties down over my hips and thighs. I lifted my leg so he could slip it off completely. Naked beside him, I felt my heart pounding so hard I was sure he felt it too.

He wiggled out of his own underwear and kissed me again as he wedged himself gently between my legs. I felt his throbbing manliness and closed my eyes and then opened them wide so I could look into his eyes and into his face.

"Christie?" he said once more.

"Make me forget, Gavin," I whispered and threw all restraint out the window, telling myself this was love, not mad animal sex. This was the ecstasy I expected. Soon the ugly memory of what had happened to me sunk deeper and deeper, driven down and away by every kiss, every moment of passion until all I saw before me was Gavin's loving face, his eyes so full of love they glowed.

My heart was full of love, too, and hope. Perhaps the love I had for Gavin and the love he had for me could, after all, defeat all the curses befalling our families.

I fell asleep beside him, dreaming of a brighter tomorrow.

A Serpent in the Garden

WHEN I AWOKE IN THE MORNING, I WAS ALONE. SOMEtime during the night, Gavin had returned to his own bed. It was early, just before sunrise, and almost immediately my thoughts went to Mommy. Ever since I had had my first period, she would find an excuse to come into my room to talk about intimate things. Sometimes she would sit beside me at my vanity table and brush her hair; sometimes she would come in to show me something new she had bought to wear, but inevitably, we would have one of our private talks about sex.

I recalled asking her how does a woman know she has made love instead of simply having sex. She put down her hairbrush and gazed at herself in the vanity table mirror for a moment, a small smile forming on her lips.

"There's a sense of fulfillment," she began, speaking in that soft, melodious voice I loved so. "Your heart and soul join in a wonderful and magical way, Christie," she said, turning to me, the light in her eyes revealing her own precious and personal memories.

"Magical, Mommy?"

"Yes, honey." She took my hand and grew as

serious as a Sunday School teacher. "Magical because it makes you aware of things that were so obvious, but things you were blind to or deaf to or simply ignored. Women who are loose with their bodies, who pursue sexual pleasure as an end in itself are only half-alive their whole lives through.

"When I fell in love, really in love, everything was more intense. Suddenly, I noticed things for the first time, even though they had always been around me. I had never realized how beautiful the stars could be, how sweet a bird's song sounded, how wonderful and majestic the ocean was, and how awe-inspiring a simple thing like a sunrise could be. I was never bored. Every moment was as precious as the next.

"Most importantly, Christie," she said, her eyes small but intent, "I respected myself. I wasn't ashamed of my feelings and the pleasure my body gave me. Do you know what I've learned?" she added almost in a whisper. I shall never forget the look in her eyes when she told me. "Girls who give their bodies to men for the pleasure of the moment don't value themselves; they don't even value sex. They've choked and suffocated the best part of themselves; they've closed the doorway to the soul and to love.

"They take the stars for granted; they resent the song of birds waking them in the morning; the ocean is monotonous to them, and they think getting up early enough to see the sunrise is stupid and exhausting. It's as if . . . as if they've missed the ride with the angels and are doomed to drift from one shallow thing to another.

"Do you think you understand what I'm trying to say?" she asked.

"I think so, Mommy," I told her, but it wasn't until now that I did.

Slowly, as the first rays of sunlight lifted the shadows from the trees and the earth absorbed the darkness like a sponge, I felt in tune with everything. I realized that every morning the flowers, the grass, the forest and all the animals were reborn. I opened the window wide and inhaled the warm morning air as if I could also inhale the sunshine. I embraced myself and closed my eyes and remembered that moment when Gavin and I touched each other's souls and with our bodies promised to be true and loving forever and ever. I had not missed the ride with the angels.

"Good morning," Gavin said, coming up behind me. "I went back to my own bed last night because I thought Jefferson would be looking for me otherwise," he added and kissed me on the cheek.

"Where is Jefferson?"

"Would you believe he got himself up, washed and dressed and went downstairs with Luther and Charlotte already. He can't wait to dip his hands into pails of paint. I'd say he and Charlotte are hitting it off real well, wouldn't you?"

"Yes. It's made it all easier and kind of wonderful," I said, sighing. Gavin smiled and then turned serious.

"But you must understand that as happy as we are here, we can't stay here forever and ever like Charlotte thinks. Jefferson needs friends his own age and he has to go back to school and . . ."

"I know," I said, falling back on the pillow. I screwed my face into a sulk and folded my arms under my breasts.

"You must have known this could only be a temporary solution, Christie," Gavin said. "We're going to have to think of something else soon."

"Wise old Gavin," I teased. "I'm the dreamer; you're the sensible one."

"So we're a perfect combination," he said, smiling, undaunted. "Whenever I get too sensible, you hit me over the head with a dream."

"And whenever I've been dreaming too long, you drag me back to reality. Just like you're doing now."

"I'd rather kiss you back," he said and leaned over to plant a soft kiss on my lips. I gazed up into his eyes and felt a tingle start in my breast.

"We'd better get moving before they miss us," I whispered.

"I know," he said, straightening up. "I'm a farmer now," he said, throwing out his chest and jabbing his thumbs against his ribs, "and I have my chores. And so do you. There's butter to churn and bread to bake and floors to wash."

"I'll give you floors to wash, Gavin Steven Longchamp," I said and threw my pillow at him. He caught it and laughed.

"Temper, temper," he said, shaking a finger at me.

We got dressed quickly and went downstairs. Homer had already arrived and was having breakfast with Luther and Jefferson when we entered the kitchen. I was surprised he was here so early. Didn't he eat breakfast with his own family? I wondered. Luther saw the questions in my face.

"Homer's here to help bale the hay in the east field," Luther explained.

"And Jefferson has a good idea," Charlotte declared. "Even Luther thinks so, right Luther?" He grunted and kept eating.

"Oh? And what's the idea?" I asked.

"To paint the barn. We've been thinking about the color. Should it be red like Mr. Douglas's barn or should it be green?"

"I've never seen a green barn," I said.

"I know," Charlotte decided, "we'll paint one side green and one side red, the front red and the back green. Or should we make the front green and the back red?"

"All those colors might confuse the cows," Gavin said. "They'll think it's Christmas in July."

"Oh, you think so?" Charlotte said sadly.

"Cows don't care about colors," Luther muttered. "And they don't know nothing about any Christmas." I could see that he didn't want anything to upset Charlotte and he never wanted to disappoint her.

"Everyone can help," Charlotte said.

"Homer and I will paint the front," Jefferson announced. "Won't we, Homer?"

Homer looked up at us and then at Jefferson before nodding.

"Doesn't Homer have his own chores at his own farm?" I asked.

"The Douglases don't have a working farm no more," Luther said. "They're retired folk."

"Oh. Do you have any brothers or sisters, Homer?" I asked him. He shook his head.

"His ma and pa were quite along in their years by the time he came along," Luther said quickly. He pushed his plate aside. "Well, we'd better get started," he said, looking at Gavin. Gavin gulped down some milk and nodded.

"I'll bake an apple pie today," Charlotte said. "Now that I've got more mouths to feed, I'd better get crackin'."

"Don't you go and overdo it none," Luther warned. "We don't put on airs just because we got some visitors."

"If I want to put on airs, I can," Charlotte shot back. Luther just gave one of his grunts.

"When can we start painting the barn?" Jefferson asked.

"Tomorrow," Luther replied. "If we finish what has to be done today," he added.

"Maybe I should help you then," Jefferson offered. Luther nearly cracked a smile.

"I never turn down a pair of hands, no matter how small they might be," he said. "Let's go."

"Menfolks are off again," Gavin muttered in my ear as he rose to join Luther and Homer. Jefferson pushed his chair in.

"What are you going to do today, Christie?" he asked me.

"I'm going to work on our clothes, do some more cleaning, and then look over the library. Tonight, I'll read to you and you'll practice your reading, too," I said.

"Aw . . ."

"And your multiplication tables. Jefferson didn't do so well in school this year," I explained, my eyes on him firmly. "He needs to work on his math and his reading, especially his spelling, don't you, Jefferson?"

"Homer can't read and spell good and he's okay," Jefferson said in his own defense.

"Really?" I looked at Homer, who looked down quickly. "Well, if Homer wants, I'll help him learn to read and spell, too," I said. His eyes widened.

"Won't that be nice!" Charlotte exclaimed. "We'll have our own one-room schoolhouse, just like the one I went to when I was a little girl. Although I didn't go very long, did I, Luther?"

He shifted his gaze at me quickly.

"No," he said. "Are we all gonna stand around here jabberin' while there's real work to be done?" I sensed that Luther didn't like talking about the past.

"I'm not," Charlotte said. "I've got to cut up apples," she added.

"Good," Luther said and hurried out the door, Gavin, Homer, and Jefferson trailing behind him.

The rest of the morning passed quickly. I went up to our rooms and dusted and polished. I washed the floors and the windows and then sorted out some more of the old clothing for Jefferson and myself. After lunch, I went into the library and perused the shelves. The books were so old and unused, they each had a second jacket of dust, but I found all the classics, collections of Dickens and Guy de Maupassant, Tolstoy and Dostoyevski as well as Mark Twain. Some of them were first editions.

I found one of my favorite stories, *The Secret Garden,* and decided it would be the one I would read to Jefferson and have him practice his reading on, too. Later, after another day's hard farm work and another nice dinner followed by Charlotte's delicious apple pie, I took Jefferson into the library to read to him and have him read to me. Gavin and Homer followed. Homer had been here all day, helping Luther, and had eaten dinner with us. Although he didn't talk very much, I saw he listened and understood everything that went on around him, and I also saw how much he enjoyed Jefferson's company and how quickly Jefferson had taken to him. He was a gentle giant of a man with soft dark eyes.

As I read from *The Secret Garden,* Gavin perused the library and found a book for himself, too. He went off in a corner to read and left me with Homer and Jefferson. First, I let Jefferson do a page. He was anxious to do well in front of Homer and did do better than usual. When he was finished, I handed the book to Homer. He looked up at me, surprised.

"Can you read any of it, Homer?" I asked. He nodded and stared at the page, but he didn't begin. "Go on, read some for us," I said. "Didn't you go to school at all?" I asked him when he continued to hesitate.

"Yes, but I left after the third grade to help with the chores."

"And no one came looking for you?" He shook his head. "That's too bad, Homer. If you learn to read better, you'll learn a lot more." He nodded. I leaned over and pointed to some letters. "What you've got to do is sound them out, Homer. This *A* sounds like the *a* in *hay.* The *b* is like the first sound in *boy* and the *l* is like the *l* in *little.* You don't pronounce the *e* at the end. It's called a silent *e.* Just put the sounds together fast."

"A . . . ba . . . llll," he said.

"Able. That's good. Right, Jefferson?" Jefferson nodded quickly. I smiled and leaned back. When I did so, I gazed at Homer's neck and just under the strands of hair that were usually down the back of his neck but were now off to the sides, I saw the birthmark. There was no question in my mind—it looked like a hoof. I felt a cold chill, recalling Charlotte's tale of her baby.

What did this mean? How could Homer have the same birthmark? Did Charlotte make everything up? I practiced reading with Jefferson and Homer for another half hour and then stopped to let Jefferson show Homer the painting he had done in the room off the library. As soon as they left, I told Gavin what I had seen on Homer's neck.

"So?"

"Don't you remember the story I told you about Charlotte's baby—the doll in the crib, all of it?"

"Yes, but I thought that was just a story like the

stories about spirits flying around and Emily on a broom and . . ."

"Gavin, it's all so strange. The neighbors finding a baby left to die, Homer practically living here most of the time, and now the birthmark. I'm going to ask Luther about it," I decided.

"I don't know. He might not like your poking around. He can get angry pretty quickly. I saw it out there in the fields."

"There's nothing for him to get angry about, but I'd like to know the truth."

"Maybe it's none of our business, Christie. Maybe we shouldn't stir up old memories," Gavin warned.

"It's too late, I'm afraid. I feel something every time I wander through the house. Spirits have already been stirred."

"Oh boy. All right," he said. "When are you going to ask Luther these questions?"

"Right now," I said. Gavin closed his book and sighed.

"Daddy always says curiosity killed the cat."

"I'm not a cat, Gavin. I'm part of the world here at The Meadows. Maybe not through direct bloodline, but still, it's what I've inherited. It's my fate," I said boldly. Gavin nodded, still smiling at me. "Laugh if you want, but I want to know the past that haunts this house and this family."

"Okay, okay," he said and got up. "Let's see what Luther will tell us."

Charlotte told us Luther was out in the barn changing the oil in the pickup truck. It was a very warm night with a sky full of stars. So far away from busy highways and the sounds of traffic and people, we could hear how noisy nature was. Usually, the sounds people made distracted or drowned out the peepers and crickets, the hoot owls and raccoons. To both Gavin and myself, it sounded as if every night creature in the wild had an opinion about something or other. Ahead of us, the glow of Luther's lanterns lit up the barn. We could see him crouched over his truck engine.

"Hello Luther," I called as we approached. I didn't want to startle him, but he looked up surprised. "Can we talk to you?" He wiped his hands and nodded.

"Homer go home?" he asked, looking beyond us.

"No. He's inside with Jefferson. But that's what we wanted to ask you about, Luther," I said quickly.

"Oh? Ask about what?"

"Homer. Who is he really, Luther?" I blurted quickly. Luther's eyes narrowed.

"What'dya mean, who is he? He's Homer Douglas, the neighbor's boy. I told you that before," he said.

"Charlotte took me to the nursery," I began, "and told me the story of her baby."

"Oh that. Charlotte pretends a lot," he said, looking at his engine again. "She always has. It was her way of escaping a hard, cold life."

"She doesn't have a hard, cold life now," I said. "Why is she still pretending?" Luther didn't respond.

"Then she didn't really have a baby?" I pursued. "And the baby didn't have a birthmark that looks like a hoof on the back of his neck?" Luther opened a can of oil and began pouring it into the engine as if we weren't there. "We don't want to make any trouble. I just wanted to know the truth about this family. It's my family, too," I added.

"Your ma, she was a Cutler, but she hadn't no

Booth blood in her from what I understood to be the truth," Luther muttered.

"But we inherited the Booths and their history too. Like it or not," I said.

"It's best you don't know about this family," Luther said, pausing. "They was hard, cruel folk who married some religion with some superstition to come up with their mean ideas and ways. Charlotte, she was blessed with a softness and had sunshine in her face always. Them Booths, especially her father and that Emily, couldn't tolerate it and made her practically a prisoner in her own home. They worked her like a slave and never treated her like kinfolk.

"After Mrs. Booth passed on, there was nothin' left to bring any kindness in that house. Why, they even whipped her from time to time. Emily did it just because she took to thinking there was a devilish spirit in Charlotte making her smile. She tried to whip the smile out of her, but Charlotte . . ." He shook his head. "She didn't understand such cruelty and never gave in to it. You couldn't harden her heart. She forgave everyone everything all the time, even Emily." He spat and fixed his gaze on a memory as he continued.

"She'd come out to me after a beating and I'd comfort her and she would tell me Emily couldn't help it. The devil was in her making her do it . . . stuff like that. I was planning on sending her to the devil myself only . . ."

"Only what?"

"That's how the devil gets you. He makes you commit a sin. Anyways . . . Charlotte and I . . . we got so we comforted each other. After my parents passed on, we was both alone. Especially at night. You understand?"

Gavin and I exchanged knowing glances.

"Yes, we do."

"She got pregnant and as soon as Emily found out, she declared it was the devil's work and the baby would be an evil child. No one outside of the old man and Emily, and me, of course, knew that Charlotte was in a childbearing way. No one in town much saw her.

"I remember the night she gave birth," he said, looking up at the old plantation house. "I remember her screaming. Emily was happy about that. She did everything she could to make things harder."

"They kept her in the Bad Room?"

He nodded, but then looked down.

"Worse. Emily locked her in a closet when the time come," he said. It looked like he had tears in his eyes.

"What? You mean while she was giving birth?" I asked. He nodded.

"Left in there for hours and when she finally opened the door . . . well, instinct takes over, I suppose. Charlotte had bit the umbilical cord in two and tied it herself. She was covered with blood.

"Emily let her put the baby in the nursery, but a few days later, I seen her slip out of the house with the baby in a basket. I followed her and watched her put the baby in a field near the Douglases' house and after she left, I went to Carlton Douglas and his wife and told them someone left a baby on their property.

"They were happy to take him in. They named him Homer and brought him up as best they could. Emily was pretty mean toward him and always chased him off the property."

"But Charlotte must have realized who he was, right?" I asked.

"If she did, she never said nothin'."

"You never told her?" Gavin asked.

Luther stared at us a moment and then shook his head.

"I thought it would have been too cruel, too painful for her. Instead, after Emily finally went to hell, I brought Homer into our lives more and more until you see he's here all the time."

"Charlotte must see the birthmark, if I spotted it," I said.

"Oh, I think she knows who Homer really is. She don't say it outright, but then, she don't have to."

"Does Homer know?" Gavin asked.

"Not in so many words. He's the same as her . . . he feels things, knows things faster through his feelings than he knows them through words. He's part of nature here, as at home in these fields with these animals and with these trees and hills as anything that lives here.

"Well," he said, turning back to his truck engine, "that's the story. You wanted to know it, so you do. I wouldn't be proud of the Booth family history. As far as I can tell, even the ancestors were a hard, mean people. They was the kind of plantation owners who treated their slaves badly, the men raping and beatin' them and the women working the women slaves to death. The west field's full of slave dead. There are no markers, but I know where the graves are. My daddy showed me. If a slave got real sick, he told me, they'd throw him in the grave before he passed on."

"Oh, how horrible," I said, grimacing.

"Still want to own up to the Booth side?" he asked.

"I don't want to disown Charlotte," I said. He nodded.

"Yeah, I guess that's true enough." He wiped his

neck with a rag. "Hotter than a henhouse in heat tonight, ain't it?"

Gavin laughed.

"We got a swimmin' hole over the hill toward Howdy Fred's there," he said, pointing. "You just follow the gravel path and bear left when you reach the big oak tree. It's got a little dock with a rowboat. Water comes from an underground spring so it's refreshing."

He smiled.

"Charlotte and I, we used to sneak off there once in a while."

"Sounds great," Gavin said.

"Yeah, the plantation can't be blamed for the people who owned it, I suppose. Though it must've felt the burden," he added and nodded. "It must have felt the burden."

There was a long silence as the three of us grew deep in thought a moment.

"We better see what Jefferson's up to, Gavin," I said finally.

"Okay."

"Luther?" He looked up. "Thanks for trusting us with the story."

"I figured since you've been through considerable pain yourself, you'd understand," he said.

"I do."

"I gotta grease this truck," he declared. "It's due. In case Charlotte asks after me," he added.

"We'll tell her," I said. Gavin took my hand and we headed back to the house.

Charlotte met us in the entry way and told us Jefferson had been so tired from his hard day's work, he fell asleep on the sofa.

"And Homer carried him up to bed again," she added. No matter how gentle and sweet Homer seemed, I couldn't help being worried and hurried upstairs with Gavin right behind me.

We found Jefferson fast asleep in his bed. He was dressed in his nightshirt and the blanket was tucked in neatly just under his chin. Homer startled us, sitting quietly in the corner of the room in the dark.

"I was just watching him to be sure he was okay," Homer explained. "Until you got here," he added.

"Thank you, Homer. That was very nice of you."

"I best be getting home myself if we're gonna rise early to paint the barn." He started away.

"Good night, Homer," I called.

"Night," he said and slipped away as quickly as a shadow under the moonlight.

"He's all right," Gavin said when I went to Jefferson's side and stared down at his angelic little face. I couldn't help but smile recalling what Daddy used to say: "Jefferson's an angel at least eight hours a day because that's when he's asleep." Gavin came up beside me to whisper in my ear.

"How would you like to try that lake Luther spoke about? It's hot enough tonight, hotter than a henhouse in heat," he added. I felt a hot blush stain my cheeks.

"We'll take some towels, take a lantern to light the way," he continued.

"Jefferson might wake up and be frightened," I said weakly.

"He's not waking up so fast and he knows where he's at by now. Come on," Gavin said. "We earned some fun."

"All right," I said. "I'll get the towels."

Even though we weren't slinking about, I couldn't hclp feeling we were sneaking off in the night. Gavin didn't light the lantern until we were a dozen yards or so from the house. We found the path Luther had described and followed it over a small hill. There below us was the lake, inky and still in the darkness, but the water catching the stars here and there on its surface.

We walked down to the dock and took off our shoes and socks to test the water.

"It's cold," I complained.

"Only until you get in, I bet," Gavin said. "Are we gonna go skinny dippin'?" he asked. "I can put out the lamp, if that will make you feel more comfortable."

"No," I said quickly. "You should leave it on."

"Fine with me," he said and started to undress. My heart was pounding. We had slept side by side naked to the bone the night before, but we had been in the darkness. Now our bodies glistened in the light of the lantern under the stars. Despite how intimate we had been, I couldn't help but be bashful and yet terribly excited. If my heart beat any faster, I would surely faint, I thought. Gavin was naked, his back to me, and I had only slipped out of my skirt.

He turned and looked at me.

"I'll go in first," he said and lowered himself off the edge of the dock. Then he splashed into the water.

"It's great," he called back. He was only a dark, silhouetted head. "Come on, bashful."

"Don't tease me or I'll turn around and run back," I warned.

"My lips are sealed," he said quickly and kicked up his feet, churning water as he swam backwards.

I unbuttoned my blouse and then slipped off my bra. By the time I stepped out of my panties, I was covered with goose bumps. I dipped my feet in the water again and looked for Gavin, but he was gone.

I didn't hear him swimming, nor did I see his head bobbing about.

"Gavin?"

Fireflies danced over the water, their lemon-colored tails flashing on and off. In the branches of trees leaning over the water, birds twittered sleepily in their nests. A soft breeze played in my hair and made some strands tickle my forehead and the tops of my cheeks. All the way across the lake, an owl hooted.

"Gavin, where are you?" I called in a loud whisper. "Gavin, you're scaring me," I said and then he suddenly popped out from under the dock and seized my ankles. I screamed and fell forward into the water, the shock of it making me squeal and scream some more. He laughed and quickly embraced me to keep my head from going under.

"You all right?" he asked, laughing.

"That was cruel, Gavin Longchamp," I cried.

"You were taking so long, I nearly fell asleep waiting," he said. "Besides, now you're in and isn't it wonderful?"

"I'm not speaking to you," I said petulantly.

"All right," he declared, pulling away from me. "I'll go under and stay under until you do." And with that he submerged. I waited. It seemed like minutes.

"Gavin?"

The water was so still, its surface barely lapping against the sides of the dock.

"Gavin?"

"Does this mean you're talking to me again?" he said right behind me.

I spun around on him.

"Gavin. You're terrible. I was so frightened."

"If you refused to speak to me forever and ever,

Christie, I *would* stay under," he said softly and then leaned forward to press his lips to mine. Under the water, I felt his hands find my waist and slowly draw my body closer and closer to his until our thighs grazed. I felt him harden between my legs and pushed myself off, both frightened and shocked by the speed with which his manliness announced itself.

"Hey," he cried, laughing.

"We're here to swim," I declared and stroked away. He laughed again and came after me. Even though he could catch me any time he wanted, he remained half a foot or so away, swimming behind or alongside. I went back toward the dock until I could stand. Then he caught up and took my hands into his.

"It's great, isn't it? Luther was right," he said. "So refreshing."

"Yes, but it's cold enough to wake you up all over."

"All over?" he said and brought his hands to my breasts. Then he drew me to him and we kissed again, only this time when I felt him harden against me, I didn't pull away. We kissed again and again. Naked, under the stars, every part of me felt more alive, more aware than ever. All my senses were sharper, keener. Our kisses were more electric; my breasts tingled and my knees weakened. Suddenly, Gavin lifted me into his arms. I buried my face against his cool, wet chest and let him carry me out of the lake.

"Oh Christie," he whispered after he set me down gently on our towels on the dock, "I can't stop myself from wanting you."

"We can't do it again, Gavin. We've got to be careful. I could get pregnant."

"I know," he said, but he didn't lift himself away from me. He continued to plant kiss after kiss on my face, on my neck, on my shoulders and breasts. When he kissed my nipples, I moaned and closed my eyes.

We're losing control, I thought, but the realization didn't put enough panic in me to push Gavin away. I was hoping he would know when to stop. Just a little more, I thought. We can do just a little more and still rescue ourselves from each other.

"I love you, Christie," he whispered. "I love every part of you: every dimple . . ." He kissed my cheeks. "Every strand of hair." He pressed his lips to my head and then took my hands to his mouth. "The tips of your fingers. Your breasts . . . your stomach . . ."

"Gavin!" I cried. "If we don't stop, we won't stop." I seized hold of his shoulder and kept him from going any lower. He rested his cheek against the small of my stomach.

"I can hear your heart pounding," he said. "Your skin feels so cool."

He moved himself up so he could kiss me on the lips again and then we lay there beside each other, both of us breathing hard and fast. He cradled my head in his arm and we lay on our backs looking up at the stars.

"You're not cold, are you?" he asked.

"No."

"When you look up at the night sky like this, you can feel the earth moving," he said. "Can't you?"

"Yes."

"If you try hard enough, you can imagine yourself falling into the sky, into the stars," he said.

"Gavin," I whispered, turning to him. "I want you to . . . I mean, I love you, I really do, but I keep thinking about Luther and Charlotte and what happened and what could happen to us."

"I know. It's all right," he said. "After all, I'm the one who's supposed to be the realist, right? I'm supposed to be the sensible one who knows we can't live in a dreamworld forever. Only, when I'm with you, Christie," he said, turning to face me, "I want to throw all logic and reality away and live in dreams. I don't care about anything else."

"You'd better care, Gavin Longchamp. I've been depending on you to be the sensible one up until now."

He laughed.

"Okay," he said. "I'll be anything you want me to be." He sat up. "We'd better get dressed and go back," he said, looking out over the water.

Silently, we dried our bodies and put on our clothes. Then Gavin took my hand and we started up the gravel pathway toward the house. At the top of the hill, we turned and looked back at the lake. It seemed unreal, more like a mirror than a body of water. For a while the trees, the stars, every cloud passing lazily above it was captured and locked in its reflection. That was the way the lake held onto its memories, I thought. And now it had the memory of us as well: two young people struggling to understand a world that could be so beautiful and so cruel. Forever and ever the lake would hear our laughter and recall our warm desire in the lap of its waters. Perhaps it heard our heartbeats.

Gavin lifted the lantern so the light would fall ahead of us. We followed the finger of illumination that pointed our way back to the house, both of us still clinging to that cocoon of titillation. The memory of our bodies tingling took its good time to fall back into the vault behind our hearts. Both of us were in such a daze, neither of us noticed the strange vehicle parked in the driveway until we were practically on top of it.

"Whose car is this?" Gavin wondered aloud and lifted the lantern so the light would wash the darkness off all of it. Neither of us recognized the car.

"I don't know, Gavin."

"Whoever it is has come some distance," he said, nodding toward the license plates. "They're from Maryland."

"Jefferson," I said, suddenly afraid for him. "Let's get inside quickly."

We hurried up the walk and the front steps, practically charging into the house. The moment we walked into the entry way, I heard familiar laughter and then the laughter of a stranger, a man. It was coming from the sitting room on the right.

Gavin and I stepped into the doorway and Aunt Fern turned toward us, her hands on her hips, her face molded into her characteristic smirk. Her tall, blond boyfriend sat on the sofa with his legs crossed, smoking coolly, the corners of his mouth lifted so sharply they cut into his cheeks. Charlotte was sitting on a hassock, her hands clasped and pressed against her chest, a look of worry on her face, and Luther stood by the chair behind her looking very unhappy, his face ashen.

"Aunt Fern!" I finally cried.

"Well, well, well, if it isn't the princess and her little prince," she said, stepping toward us. Her eyes drank us in quickly from head to toe and came back to our faces sharply. She saw the towels in my hand. "And where were you two?" she demanded.

"We went for a swim," Gavin said quickly. Her smirk folded into a licentious smile and she turned to her boyfriend.

"Hear that, Morty, they went for a swim." Her

boyfriend's smile duplicated her own. "Skinny dipping is more like it. My, my, my, what have you two been up to?"

"Nothing," Gavin said sharply. "We just went for a swim."

"Sure." Her smile disappeared and was quickly replaced by a sharp, hard glare. "I wasn't born yesterday, you know. You two might fool everyone else, but don't think for a moment you can pull the wool over these eyes. They've seen too much."

"That's for sure," her boyfriend quipped, smiling. He had a very nasal-sounding voice. Now that I took a longer look at him, I saw his eyes were rather close together and his lips were thin and long under a sharp nose. I thought of all the men Aunt Fern had had as boyfriends, this man was the least attractive. He had big ears and a long neck and his cheeks sank in like the cheeks of an old man.

"Shut up, Morty," she replied without taking her eyes off us. Then she smiled again. "Morty and I were on our way to Florida to Morty's beach house when I had an idea you two might have come here, and decided we should take a side trip. Sure enough, I was right.

"You two have got everyone wringing their hands back home, you know. Uncle Philip even made a personal visit to see me because he thought you might have come to me. Fat chance of that, I told him. So," she said, shifting her weight from one foot to the other and bringing her hands to her hips again, "why'd you run away?"

I would never tell her the truth, I thought. If anything, she might just laugh. It was the sort of thing she would be happy to hear.

"Never mind," she said quickly. "You don't have to tell me why. I can see it written on both your faces," she said, looking from Gavin to me and back to Gavin. "You've gone beyond spin the bottle."

"That's not true," Gavin said sharply, his face turning crimson.

"Don't tell me what's true and what's not, Gavin," she snapped, a small, tight and cold smile meeting his challenge. "We're both Longchamps. I know what's in our blood. Anyway," she said, relaxing, "you don't have to worry. I'm not about to tell Philip anything. Unless," she said, nodding, "you make me."

"Then he doesn't know we're here?" I said, breathing relief.

"No. And I don't think he's smart enough to figure it out," she added. "So," she said, looking around. "This is quite a hideaway. Auntie Charlotte has been telling me about her redecorating," she added and laughed. Her boyfriend laughed too. "Who knows, Morty. This might take off and become the rage."

"Yes, art nouveau," he said.

"I want you two to meet Morton Findly Atwood. What do you want them to call you around here, Morty? Mr. Atwood? Or just sir?"

"Mr. Atwood would be fine. Sir's a bit too much," he said, smiling. He flicked his cigarette ash on the floor.

"Mr. Atwood's family is a highly respected one. They're what we call old money . . . dwindling, but old," Fern said and laughed. Morton Atwood laughed too. What kind of respect did he have for his own family, I wondered, if he could let Aunt Fern make fun of them like this?

"Anyway, now we're here," she said, gazing around again, "we've decided to take a mini-vacation on our way to our vacation, right Morty?"

"If you'd like. One thing I have plenty of," he said, "is time."

"What do you mean, Aunt Fern?" I asked. Despair heavied my legs, making them feel nailed to the floor and my heart started to pound in anticipation of her reply.

"What do you mean, Aunt Fern?" she mimicked. "What do you think it means? We're hanging out a while. I'm sure there's plenty of room. Auntie Charlotte was just about to show us the rooms so we could pick out one that suits us, weren't you, Auntie Charlotte?"

"Oh sure, sure," Charlotte said, not really understanding what was happening. Luther glared furiously.

"After all, we're all family," Aunt Fern said. "All except Luther, that is," she added, turning to him. Luther reddened with subdued anger. "Which room have you two taken?" she asked.

"We have two rooms," I said quickly. "One for Jefferson and Gavin and one for me. Next to each other," I added.

"How convenient," she said. "Morton, shall we inspect the facilities?"

"Whatever you say, my dear," he replied, standing. He was a little over six feet tall with narrow shoulders and a very narrow waist for a man.

"Morty happens to be an excellent tennis player," Aunt Fern said. "He might go pro. There aren't any tennis courts on the grounds, are there, Luther?"

Luther's reply resembled one of his grunts more than a no.

"I didn't think there was, but we'll make due. I'm sure there's plenty to occupy us around here. Look at how occupied the princess has been," she said nodding toward me. "Auntie Charlotte, can you show us around now?" she said. Charlotte stood up.

"Oh sure."

"Then do it," Aunt Fern said sharply. Charlotte's eyes flashed toward me as though she were pleading for help. I felt sorry for her, but I didn't know what to do. I couldn't toss them out, although I wouldn't have hesitated to do so if I could.

"And Luther," Aunt Fern said, turning to him, "would you get our suitcases out of the trunk and bring them upstairs."

Luther stared at her for a moment and then turned and left to do her bidding. Aunt Fern laughed.

"I told you this would be interesting and fun, Morty. All my relatives are quite amusing." She scooped her arm under his and they walked after Charlotte.

"Oh," she said, turning back to Gavin and me. "Don't let us interrupt you. Go right on and do what you usually do." She threw her head back and laughed.

Gavin turned to me. He didn't have to say it. We both knew: as quickly as we had found this wonderful and magical world, it was gone.

The Bubble Bursts

OUT OF SPITE, AUNT FERN DECIDED THAT THE ONLY bedroom suite good enough for her and Morton was Charlotte's parents' suite. I thought Aunt Fern was malicious and gleeful about it because she didn't change her mind when she saw how much her decision had disturbed poor Charlotte. The idea of someone else sleeping in that bedroom obviously terrified Charlotte. It was as if her father could still punish her for permitting it. Not that she had much choice. Aunt Fern was adamant, even though the room needed a thorough cleaning.

"No one's slept in here for years and years," Charlotte emphasized. "It ain't been used since . . . since my daddy passed away."

"Well, then it's time it was," Aunt Fern replied undaunted. She found the light switch and turned on the overhead fixture, which revealed even more dust, grime, and cobwebs. "Princess," Aunt Fern said, turning to me, her hands on her hips, "go get some clean rags, a pail of hot soapy water, and wash down all the windows and clean all the furniture."

"That's a lot of work to start doing this late, Aunt Fern," I said. "Why don't you just choose a room that's not so dirty tonight."

"That's a good idea," Gavin added.

Aunt Fern flicked him a scathing glance and then turned to me, smiling scornfully, cruelly.

"First, I doubt that any room is any cleaner anyway, and second, I like this room. Why should it have been so neglected all this time?" she asked as if she really cared. "And why are they using these old oil lamps and candles if the electricity works?"

"They don't mind and it's expensive to run electricity through such a big house," I explained. She smirked.

"They're living rent free," Fern said. "They have no real expenses."

She continued to parade through the suite, deliberately turning on every lamp. She stopped at the vanity table to examine the jars of dried creams and makeup, the old brushes and combs.

"What's all this junk doing here?" she asked. "It should have been thrown out long, long ago. Bring a garbage bag up here," she ordered.

"Oh no," Charlotte said, shaking her head and smiling as if the idea was ridiculous. "That's all my mother's things."

"So?" Fern replied with indifference. "Your mother's dead, isn't she? She isn't going to need makeup and combs anymore." She ran her finger over the mirror, drawing a thick line through the dust. "Don't forget this mirror, Princess. Get it shining."

"Who do you think Christie is . . . your slave?" Gavin demanded. Aunt Fern peered at both of us through her dark, angry slits.

"Oh, I'm sure Christie doesn't mind pleasing her favorite aunt," she replied. "I'm her favorite aunt because I always keep her little secrets," she added, smiling. "Right, princess?"

Gavin and I exchanged looks of frustration while

Aunt Fern continued to examine the suite, her eyes settling on the bathroom. She marched to it and inspected the sink and tub.

"Bring up a pail full of disinfectant, too. I expect these fixtures to shine when you're finished," she told me. "You'll have to get down on your hands and knees and scrub this floor. I won't permit my bare feet on such a dirty surface."

"That'll take hours!" I cried.

"Oh dear, oh dear," Charlotte whimpered.

"I'm really surprised no one's done this room before," Aunt Fern complained and turned back to Charlotte. "Why my sister-in-law and my brother let you run down this place and do all these stupid things to it is beyond me. It's still a piece of property with some value to it, isn't it? Morton?"

"It has a certain residual value," Morton said with disinterest. "Land's always worth something, even though the buildings are in disrepair."

"I just love this bed though," Aunt Fern said, going to it and stroking the post. "It's quite an elegant piece. And look at the work in this dresser and this armoire," she said indicating the carvings.

"Yes, the furniture is worth something," Morton agreed.

"Christie," Aunt Fern said, turning on me. "Why haven't you gone for the pail of soap and water and the rags? We don't have all night, you know."

"I don't think you realize how much work is involved here," Gavin said more calmly.

"Yes I do," Fern replied, smiling. "But if you're so worried about your precious princess doing too much and getting her precious fingers too soiled, why don't you help her?" she said icily. Then she spun on Charlotte. The poor dear gasped and her hands flew up to her throat like two terrified birds seeking the safety of a branch. "Aunt Charlotte, do you want to get us some clean linens, please, and towels, lots of clean towels. Do you own a vacuum cleaner?" she demanded.

Charlotte shook her head, overwhelmed.

"All they have is the old-fashioned push-thing that picks up surface dirt," I said quickly. Aunt Fern smirked.

"Well, I suppose it will have to do. Come on, everyone, get cracking," Fern said, enjoying her role as supervisor.

"You really can't sleep in here," Charlotte said, her eyes wide. "The spirits still come to this room at night, even during the day sometimes."

"Spirits? Oh, you mean like ghosts? Well, that's all right. Morton and I are used to spirits, but spirits of another kind. Which reminds me, what's to drink around here?"

"We have water and milk and juice," Aunt Charlotte listed proudly.

"I'm talking about whiskey," Aunt Fern snapped.

"Whiskey?" Charlotte thought a moment. "In my daddy's office in the cabinet. But it's old," she said, and Aunt Fern and Morton laughed.

"The older it is, the better it is," Aunt Fern said. "Show us the office and we'll have a few drinks and wait for you to get our room ready," she commanded.

"The office is not an office anymore," I said. "It's where Charlotte does her arts and crafts."

"So we'll have our drinks somewhere else. Come on," she said, clapping her hands. "Everyone get moving."

Luther stopped in the doorway with their suitcases and looked in at us.

"You ain't fixin' to stay in this room, are you?" he asked.

"It's all been decided, Luther. Put the bags in here," Aunt Fern said.

Luther looked at Charlotte, saw her pained expression, and shook his head.

"This room's not to be used," he insisted firmly.

"Really? Who are you, the general manager or something?" Aunt Fern said and turned to Morton. They both laughed.

"No one uses this room," Luther simply stated. Fern's eyes grew small and hateful.

"Now look here," she said, stepping boldly up to him. "I happen to know more about you than you think. My brother told me about this place and you," she said sharply. "You're an employee who's been given permission to stay on, but that can change any time." Luther's face grew so hot and red, I thought he might explode.

"Aunt Fern, I'm the one who will change or not change anything," I said. "I'm the one who owns this now."

She smiled coldly at my challenge.

"Doesn't Philip have a part of the estate, too? Not a majority ownership, but still something? Why don't we call him and ask his opinion?" she said, her eyes dancing with glee.

"Don't you threaten her," Gavin said, stepping up beside me. Fern's face flamed red. She whipped her eyes to him and flared them with fury.

"How dare you speak to me like that, Gavin? Does Daddy know where his precious goody-goody son is and what he's been doing? How's your mother going to like all this?" she pursued. Gavin wilted quickly beneath the fire in her voice and eyes. Fern nodded, satisfied with his retreat. "You two have been having a pretty good old time of it around here," she said, looking at us. "My advice to you two is to behave if you want to continue having a good time. Anyway," she said, throwing her head back and sticking her hands to her hips, "you should have more respect for your older sister, Gavin; and Christie, show respect for your aunt.

"You never showed me any real respect, never treated me as an aunt should be treated," she complained.

"That's not so, Aunt Fern. I . . ."

"DON'T CONTRADICT ME!" she screamed, her eyes wide. Then she stepped toward me and spoke softly, in a very controlled but hateful tone of voice, spitting her words in my face. "This isn't Cutler's Cove and you're not the princess. We've always had to cater to you. It was always Christie this and Christie that. Did they ever make me a Sweet Sixteen party like the one for you? Or buy me anything I wanted?"

"Mommy and Daddy loved you and treated you well, Aunt Fern," I said, tears welling up in the corners of my eyes.

"Save it. I've heard it before; it's like a broken record. Luther," she said, turning back to him, "my advice to you is to put our suitcases in here pronto. You know what pronto means?"

Luther hesitated, his pride wounded, his anger still boiling over.

"How do you think Philip Cutler is going to react when he hears you've been hiding out two underage teenagers who ran away from their homes?" she followed when he still hesitated. "There'll be a big investigation of you and Auntie Charlotte. Why, newspaper people might even come around to take pictures of the ridiculous decor and what was done to the paintings and walls. Do you want that?" she threatened. Luther's shoulders slumped in defeat and the defiance went out of his eyes. I felt horrible for him.

"That's not true. Luther didn't hide us out. He

didn't know any of the details. He has no idea why I ran away or that I ran away. He . . ."

"Who's going to believe that?" Aunt Fern said with a mocking smile. Her face turned firm, her lips so taut I thought they might snap like rubber bands. "Now do I have to repeat myself?" She looked at Luther. He lowered his eyes and lifted her and Morton's bags and carried them into the suite. Aunt Fern relaxed her shoulders. "That's better; that's more like it. Christie, dear, the soap and water?" Aunt Fern sang.

What else could I do? I felt trapped. I didn't want poor Luther and Charlotte to endure any more pain because of me. Aunt Fern was just vicious enough to carry out her threats. I dropped my chin to my chest. Aunt Fern's mean words and accusations stung and drove me to carry out her wishes as quickly as I would had she struck me with a whip across the back.

"I'll help you," Gavin said when I turned to start away.

"Oh dear, oh dear," Charlotte said, scurrying off to do Aunt Fern's bidding, "this is not going to be a nice time. No indeed, not a nice time."

"To the whiskey cabinet," Aunt Fern said, laughing.

"That was a rather impressive show of authority," Morton said, complimenting her. Aunt Fern's laughter trailed behind us.

"I've been on the short end of the stick long enough," she told him. "Now it's my turn to be the high and mighty."

They made Charlotte show them the liquor cabinet and then sent her off to change the linens. While we worked on the suite, Aunt Fern and Morton took a bottle of brandy and some glasses and waited in the living room. They played the old records on the victrola and behaved like two children, giggling and knocking things over, ringing the old dinner bells, flicking lights on and off and chasing each other through the rooms. Every once in a while, we heard one of Aunt Fern's shrill laughs carry through the hallways of the plantation house.

I told Charlotte to put the things from the vanity table into a bag, but hide them.

"You can put them back after Fern leaves, if you like," I said. That pleased her, but she was still very troubled about what was happening. Reluctantly, Gavin helped with some of the cleaning. He did the windows. After Luther brought up the broom he left, muttering angrily to himself. I dusted and polished all the furniture and then turned to the bathroom. It took me nearly an hour just to do the sink, tub and commode. Gavin was furious when I did get down on my hands and knees to scrub stains off the floor. I had already dumped three pails of dirty water and my face and hands were streaked with the grime and dust I was removing.

"This is stupid," he said. "Let's just wake up Jefferson and leave. Philip won't find us."

"That won't stop Aunt Fern from doing something to hurt Charlotte and Luther, Gavin. You know how vicious and vindictive she can be when she wants to. Let's just do what she asks. Soon she and her boyfriend will grow bored and leave anyway, and then we can make new plans."

"I don't know how she can be Jimmy's sister and my half-sister and be so mean to people," Gavin said, shaking his head.

"Don't forget she was given to another family when she was only a baby and lived with them until Mommy and Daddy found her," I reminded him. "Her life was quite disrupted."

"Stop making excuses for her, Christie. She's just a cruel, self-centered person who loves only herself and what will make her happy. I don't think she's ever done anything for anyone else her whole life and I doubt she ever will."

"And just who are you talking about, Gavin Longchamp?" Aunt Fern demanded, coming into the room. "Not me, I hope."

"If the shoe fits, wear it," Gavin muttered, but Aunt Fern was too tipsy from her drinking to hear or really care. She and Morton laughed and then the two of them flopped on the bed and groped at each other as if we weren't there. Gavin and I gaped in astonishment. Finally, Aunt Fern looked up, her eyelids drooping.

"Aren't you finished here yet?" she complained.

"This was a lot of work, Aunt Fern. We told you before that . . ."

"Oh, stop lecturing. We're ready for bed. Not for sleep," she added smiling, "for bed. Right, Morton?"

He had his eyes closed, but he formed a silly smile.

"So get your rags together, princess, and shut the door behind you on the way out, comprende?"

"Come on," Gavin said, lifting me to my feet. "Let's go. She's as drunk as a sailor."

"You two should try some of that old, old brandy" she cried, and both she and Morton went into a fit of hysterical laughter again. "Aunt Charlotte thought it was spoiled," she added and then laughed some more.

Gavin guided me to the doorway. When we turned around, Aunt Fern had thrown herself over Morton's prostrate body. He seemed too drunk and too tired to care.

"Oh," Aunt Fern said, turning back to us. "I forgot to ask . . . when do the spirits arrive?"

Her resounding laughter echoed behind us as we closed the door and stepped out of the suite.

"I hope the spirits do come," Gavin said, his dark eyes bright with anger, "and whisk her off to hell where she belongs."

I was exhausted from all the work and too tired to care. We went down the corridor to our bathroom to wash up and go to sleep ourselves. Fatigued and drowning in emotions, I got into bed and fell into dreams.

But maybe the spirits did come. Some time during the night, I awoke to what I thought were the sounds of footsteps in the hallway. I was sure I heard a door slam and the sounds of someone sobbing, but I was too tired to get up and check. The spirits won't harm us, I thought, and if in the morning, we find that Aunt Fern and her boyfriend have mysteriously disappeared, I won't bat an eyelash or shed a tear. In moments, I fell asleep again.

It was the sound of Aunt Fern's shrill scream that woke me in the morning. She hadn't been whisked off to hell, not yet.

"What's going on?" Jefferson asked, rubbing his eyes and standing in the doorway. "Who's screaming?"

"It's Fern," Gavin said, coming in from the hallway. "She's calling for us."

"Fern? Aunt Fern's here?" Jefferson asked.

"Unfortunately, yes," I told him.

"Why is she screaming?"

"I don't know, Jefferson. Maybe she woke up and took a look at herself," I said. Gavin laughed.

I slipped into my dress quickly and Gavin and I, with Jefferson lagging behind, hurried down the corridor. The doors of the master suite had been thrown open. We approached slowly and gazed within.

Morton was apparently still asleep, still in a drunken stupor, but Aunt Fern was sitting up in the bed, the blanket wrapped around her. Her eyes were blazing with excitement. Had she seen a spirit after all? I wondered. She lifted her arm and pointed her shaky finger at the doorway.

"Who was that . . . that . . . creature who was standing there gaping in at us for God knows how long?" she demanded. "I opened my eyes and there he was just a little while ago, spying on us."

"Oh, that was probably Homer," I said. "He's a friend of Aunt Charlotte's and Luther's. He lives nearby."

"Well, how dare he come snooping around here? How dare he! What is he, some kind of pervert?" she demanded.

"Oh no, Aunt Fern. Homer's harmless. He's . . ."

"Don't tell me what he is. I know who's harmless and who isn't," she said icily. "I don't want to set eyes on him again, do you hear me? You march right downstairs and tell that creep to get out of here pronto and not come back until I leave, understand?"

"But Homer won't . . ."

"Don't contradict every thing I say," she moaned. "My head is splitting." She pressed her palms against her temples, dropping her blanket and forgetting she was naked. Gavin was shocked and stepped back.

"Aunt Fern . . . you're still not dressed," I pointed out.

"What? Oh, who cares. Morton, damn it. How can you sleep with all this going on? Morton?" She shook her boyfriend, who then groaned but didn't turn over. Then she fell back against her pillow.

"Get me coffee . . . strong coffee. After I wake up, I want you to draw a warm bath for me. Do you have any bath oils here?"

"No, Aunt Fern. Hardly."

"Well, get the coffee . . . quickly," she ordered. "And get that creature out of the house." She closed her eyes and moaned again.

"How did Aunt Fern get here?" Jefferson whispered.

"She came on Emily's broom," Gavin quipped.

"What?"

"She just drove here last night, Jefferson. Go back and get washed and dressed. Go on."

"What's wrong with her?"

"She drank too much old whiskey," I said. Gavin and I smiled at each other.

"Come on, buddy," Gavin said, putting his arm around Jefferson's shoulders. "I'll help you get organized."

"I'd better see to their coffee," I said and hurried downstairs. Luther was already outside, working. Charlotte was in the kitchen with Homer sitting at the table, looking terrified.

"She scared him near to death," Charlotte complained.

"Because he frightened her, Aunt Charlotte. She's furious about him looking in on her," I explained.

"He didn't mean no harm. He never heard nobody in that room before and had to see," Aunt Charlotte said. I smiled at the motherly way in which she came to his defense.

"I know, but until they leave, Homer should stay away from them. You understand, Homer? That woman upstairs is not very nice. Every time she sees you, she's just going to scream and scream."

Homer nodded.

"I don't want to see her," he said.

"I don't blame you." I poured two cups of coffee, found a tray, and carried them up to Aunt Fern and Morton. Morton was awake and sitting up in bed, rubbing his face and blinking at the sunlight coming through the window. Aunt Fern was still prone, her eyes closed.

"Here's your coffee," I said. Her eyes snapped open.

"Bring it here," she ordered and seized the cup out of my hand when I approached. I went around and handed Morton his cup.

"Thank you," Morton said.

"This isn't strong enough," Fern instantly complained. She spit the coffee back into the cup. "It's more like mud water. Maybe it is," she added, eyes wide. "Did Charlotte make it?"

"Yes, Aunt Fern."

"Don't drink it, Morton. Charlotte's just crazy enough to really have mixed dirt and water." She took the cup out of his hand and thrust both of them back at me so hard, some of the coffee spilled over, spattering my hands and wrists. It burned, but she didn't care. "You make another pot yourself. You know how to make coffee, don't you, princess? Or can't you do anything? She was always waited on hand and foot," she told Morton.

"That's not true, Aunt Fern. I often helped Mrs. Boston in the kitchen," I said.

"She often helped Mrs. Boston," she mimicked in a sing-song voice. "Yeah, I'm sure you did a lot. Well, get us some decent coffee and hurry up about it. I want to take my bath soon and get up to eat a good breakfast. That creature gone?" she asked.

"You frightened him more than he frightened you, Aunt Fern. He doesn't want to be around you, don't worry," I said.

"Good."

"What creature?" Morton asked.

"You'd sleep through an earthquake," Aunt Fern told him. "After you've drunk old whiskey all night, that is," she added and they both laughed and started tickling each other, behaving like two children again. Then Aunt Fern realized I was staring at them. "Why are you still hanging around?" she cried at me. "Get me the coffee," she ordered hotly.

I hurried out and downstairs again. I made her fresh coffee, but I made it so strong that Gavin said it could melt iron. Now that he was fully awake, Jefferson insisted on coming along with me, but when I returned to the master suite, I found the doors closed and thought I had better knock.

"Just a minute," I heard Aunt Fern say in a breathless voice. Then I heard some moans, followed by short cries of pleasure.

"The coffee's getting cold, Aunt Fern," I shouted through the door. I knew what they were doing and was embarrassed for both myself and Jefferson. "Should I come back in a little while?"

Instead of an answer, I heard her cries come faster and louder, followed by one long moan.

"What's happening to Aunt Fern?" Jefferson asked.

"She doesn't feel too well, Jefferson. Why don't you go back downstairs and finish your breakfast and then come up to say hello, okay."

He shrugged and went off. A moment later, Aunt Fern cried, "Enter."

I opened the doors. She had the blanket up to her chin. Her face was flushed, her hair wild. Morton was lying there with his eyes closed, a smirk of satisfaction on his face.

"Here's your fresh coffee," I said. Aunt Fern smiled at me and sat up.

"Good." She took hers and handed Morton his. Then she turned back to me. "Get a little bit of an education out there?" she asked. Had she no dignity? No self-respect? "I bet you had your little ear plastered against the door, didn't you? Or were you watching through the crack in the door?"

"Hardly, Aunt Fern," I said. "I was very uncomfortable."

"Oh come on. You've obviously lost your precious virginity here," she said. I shifted my gaze to Morton who was hovering over his coffee, his eyes on me with interest.

"Aunt Fern!"

She threw her head back and laughed.

"Stop being the little pure princess," she said. "You're no better than I am."

"I never said I was, Aunt Fern, but . . ."

"Actually, I'm glad you're grown up. If I feel like it and I'm in the mood . . . and if you're real nice to me," she added, "maybe I'll give you some hints about men and sex," she said. Morton laughed.

"I want to be around to hear that," he said.

"Like hell you will. This is female talk. You can't let them have their way with you," she told me.

"Aunt Fern, I'd rather not . . ."

"Sure, sure," she said. "I know. You're still too delicate. All right, draw my bath. Make it warm, but not too hot. Well, go on, stop gawking at me," she said, sipping her coffee.

I went in the bathroom and turned on the water. When it was ready, I told her and started away.

"Wait a minute, where are you going?" she demanded.

"Down to have my breakfast," I said.

"Well first, I'd like you to help me take a bath. I'd like my back washed and then my hair. Come on," she ordered. Totally naked, she got out of bed and marched into the bathroom. I looked at Morton, who smiled licentiously at me. "The water's just right," Aunt Fern said and got into the tub. I was afraid that at any moment, Morton might get out of bed naked too, so I returned to the bathroom and closed the door. Aunt Fern handed me the washcloth. "Do my back in small circles. I like my shoulders rubbed, too," she said.

I washed her back and then put the soap in her hair and began to shampoo it.

"Oh, that's good," she said, lying back in the tub. "You make a good servant, princess," she said.

"Aunt Fern, can you please stop calling me princess? I'm not a princess and never was," I said.

"Oh you were all right. You were spoiled rotten."

"That's not true," I insisted. "I worked in the hotel as soon as I was old enough to help out. And I always looked after Jefferson when my parents wanted me to."

"I know you're just perfect," she muttered and then seized my wrist and pulled me down beside her. "Tell me about your love affair with my little brother? Is he . . . was he very experienced? I can't imagine him knowing where to put it."

"Stop it, Aunt Fern," I said and pulled my wrist free. "Gavin is a nice boy, yes, but that doesn't make him a weakling or less of a man."

"Man?" she said, eyes wide. "You have had sex with him then, haven't you?" she asked. I had to shift my eyes and the moment I did so, it confirmed everything for her. "It's all right," she said. "I won't go around telling people. You think I care that much anyway?" She paused and sat back in the water. "I was just curious, that's all. How was your first time?"

"Aunt Fern, I don't like talking about these things," I said.

"Oh come on. Don't tell me you and your little girlfriends didn't talk about these things whenever you could? Did your mother ever talk to you or did she die before she had a chance to do the birds and the bees act?" she asked.

"Mommy and I were very close," I replied. "I didn't have to sneak off to find out things."

"Really? I'm curious. What did she tell you?" She smirked. "Did she tell you what you should and shouldn't do? Did she explain how you keep from getting pregnant or did she tell you to simply say no?"

"We talked about love and about sex, yes," I said.

"Love," she said, smirking again.

"Aren't you in love with Morton?" I asked.

"Are you serious? Morton? He's just a good time." She leaned forward. "And easy to manipulate, you know what I mean?" I didn't. "He does whatever I want him to do. He never argues and if I don't feel like it, he doesn't moan and groan and go off in a huff."

"But . . . you're acting like husband and wife with him," I said.

"Oh princess, you kill me. I've acted like husband and wife many times before," she confessed.

"How many?" I asked.

"Oh, curious now, huh?"

I was curious. I wanted to understand Aunt Fern, to see why she was so loose with her body and if she ever truly enjoyed herself. She acted happy on her own, defiant, wild, but was she happy?

"You want to know about my first time?" she asked. I didn't say yes, but she sat forward and went on. "I was fourteen. There was this boy I liked who was seventeen."

"Seventeen!"

"Yes, and he wouldn't even glance at me. I never did anything before, really, but I read a lot about it and looked at those books with pictures. So one day, I went up to him and whispered in his ear. He turned red as a beet but got very interested in me."

"What did you whisper?"

"I asked him if he wanted to go around the world with me."

"What did that mean?" I asked in a whisper.

"To tell you the truth, princess, I wasn't sure, but it went over big. A few days later, I had an opportunity to be alone with him. He was very upset because it was obvious it was my first time."

"What did he do?"

"Nothing. He never so much as spoke to me after that," she said.

"But didn't you feel terrible?"

She shrugged.

"He wasn't as nice as I thought and I wasn't interested in him anymore."

"But what about what you had done?"

"It had to happen sometime," she said nonchalantly.

"But if you don't really care about the person . . ."

"Don't care about anybody," she said. "You're better off."

"No you're not, Aunt Fern. You're all alone when you care only about yourself," I fired back. She glared at mc.

"I forgot, you're Mrs. Perfect's daughter. Your

mother wasn't so perfect, you know," she said. "That's how you came into the world."

"I know all about it," I replied quickly, before she could add any more cruel things. "I even visited my real father."

"You did? And?"

"He might have been a handsome, charming man once, but to me he was . . . he was a nobody," I said. "Ugly and weak."

"Um. Still, I would like to see what the man who swept Mrs. Perfect off her feet looked like," she said.

"Why did you hate my mother so much?" I asked, shaking my head. "All she wanted were good things for you."

"Don't believe it. She was jealous of every moment Jimmy spent on me," she spat back.

"That's not true. It's a horrible thing to think and say."

"It was true," she insisted. "When it comes to another woman's jealousy, honey, I'm an expert."

She lifted her feet out of the water and set them on the edge of the tub.

"Go to my overnight bag and get my nail polish. I want you to do my toes," she ordered.

I stared down at her defiantly. Right now she looked like a blob of selfishness and cruelty, a heartless creature who lived only for one thing—her own pleasure. I didn't think I was capable of as much hate and anger as I felt at this moment. She must have seen it in my eyes, for her look of self-satisfaction evaporated quickly and her eyes became two luminous hot coals of fury.

"Don't you look down at me like that, Christie Longchamp. You may think you're better than me, but deep inside you're cut from the same cloth. You couldn't wait to call my brother and run off to this out-of-the-way hideout so you could give in to your sexual fantasies. You even were low enough to drag your little brother along," she charged.

"That's not true; that's not why I ran away," I cried, the tears burning behind my eyelids.

"You ran away because you're a spoiled brat who got everything her way, who was the center of attention and who's now just another child in the house. Aunt Bet didn't cater to you like your mother did so . . ."

"Uncle Philip raped me!" I blurted.

For a moment the silence was so heavy, I could hear the pounding of my heart and imagined she could too. She sat up slowly in the tub, never taking her eyes off me. I couldn't stop sobbing.

"Raped you? You mean . . ."

"He came into my room naked," I bawled, "and crawled into my bed."

"No fooling," she said with a sick smile on her face. She wasn't outraged and sympathetic; she was titillated and amused. "Tell me about it," she demanded.

"There's nothing to tell. He came in and forced himself on me. It was horrible."

"What was so horrible about it? Philip's quite a handsome man," she remarked.

"What?" I wiped my eyes.

"Actually, I always hoped he would do it with me," she said. "I certainly gave him enough opportunity and tempted him enough," she added, smiling. "I once arranged it so he came in on me while I was stark naked. He liked what he saw, but he left without laying a hand on me.

"You must have done something to encourage it," she accused.

"I did not."

"Tell me the truth," she said, "you liked it a little, didn't you?"

"No, Aunt Fern. It was horrid from beginning to end and after it was over, I scrubbed myself until my skin burned."

"How ridiculous," she said.

"It wasn't ridiculous. I never felt as soiled, inside and out. I'm shocked that you would want a married man . . . a relative . . ."

"Oh stop. A good-looking man's a good-looking man," she said. "Besides, he's not a blood relative. He's not even a real relative."

"He's a sick man," I said. "He was always in love with my mother and . . ."

"I know," she said dryly. "Everyone was in love with your mother." She looked up at me with distaste and hate written across her lips. "And now they're going to be in love with you. Why you have all the luck . . ." She leaned back in the tub again and again put her feet up. "Get my nail polish," she ordered. When I didn't move, she smiled.

"I should go right to a phone and call Philip and have you delivered back to him. Maybe that's what you need . . . a real education. He'd probably chain you to your bed and come up night after night and do it to you a different way each time until . . ."

"Stop it. You're disgusting."

"My polish," she repeated coolly.

When I opened the bathroom door, I saw her boyfriend was back in bed and under the blanket. His eyes popped open.

"I'm hungry, Fern," he called.

"Just hold your water," she called back. "I'm not finished with my morning rituals."

I went to her bag and found her nail polish.

"Dry my feet first, stupid," she said when I knelt down to do her toes. I got the towel and dried her feet. "Um, that's nice," she said. "It's nice to be treated like royalty. I always envied you, princess."

"I was never treated like royalty." I said.

"Uh huh. Just do a good job on those nails. You never know who might set eyes on them," she commanded. The tears burned behind my eyelids. I fought to keep my vision clear enough to do her toenails. While I worked, she lay back with her eyes closed, soaking in the warm water.

"Morton!" she suddenly screamed. "Morton!"

"What?"

"Get up and go downstairs and tell my aunt I want two scrambled eggs and some bacon for breakfast. See if they have fresh bread, too. If they don't, have Luther go to town and get some."

"Okay," Morton said.

"Luther doesn't have time to run errands like that," I muttered.

"Really. Well, he better find the time," she said.

"Why are you picking on them? They're so defenseless. They've suffered enough. They . . ."

"You didn't have any qualms about taking advantage of them," Aunt Fern charged.

"We didn't take advantage. Gavin's been helping Luther with the chores and I've been cleaning the house and helping Aunt Charlotte with the meals and . . ."

"Oh, you're so wonderful. I keep forgetting. Morton," she cried. "Are you getting up?"

"I'm up, I'm up," he replied. "I need to use a bathroom. I want to wash and shave and . . ."

"Well find another one. We're going to be occupied in here for a while. The princess is going to do my fingernails, too," she said, smiling at me. "Right, princess?"

I didn't reply. I finished her toenails and turned away so she couldn't see my tears and be happy she was making me feel so horrible. I took a deep breath. They'll surely be on their way today, I thought, and then we'll be free of them. As far as I was concerned, I didn't care if I were free of my aunt Fern forever. In fact, that's what I wanted. I was sorry because I knew how much it would hurt Daddy to know that I hated his sister, but I couldn't help it.

Aunt Fern made me give her a manicure. She kept asking me detailed questions about Uncle Philip's sexual attack, but I wouldn't give her the satisfaction of a reply and she finally stopped.

Afterward, I had to lay out her clothes. While she got dressed, she insisted I make the bed and tidy up in the bathroom. She enjoyed watching me work like a maid. Finally, we went down for breakfast. Her boyfriend was sitting at the table studying a road map when we entered the kitchen.

"Did you send Luther for fresh bread?" Aunt Fern demanded.

"I couldn't find him and your aunt's not much help," he replied. "She's out there with Gavin and Jefferson and some other guy painting the barn," Morton said. "Green," he added and laughed.

"Painting the barn green? I think we had better call the nearest insane asylum and ask them to make a pickup," Aunt Fern quipped.

"They're happy here, Aunt Fern, and they're not hurting anyone," I said.

"What do you say we go into town and have some breakfast at a restaurant," Morton said.

"We don't need to go into town. My niece can make eggs. She already proved she can make coffee. I like them a little wet," she ordered. "Not dry like pieces of paper. Well," she said when I didn't move quickly. "Feed us. Poor Morton's starving. What are you doing?" she asked, going to his side.

"Just figuring out the best way to get back on the main highways," he replied.

"We've got time," Aunt Fern said. "Don't you like your little holiday with the folks?" she joked.

"Sure," he said. "But how long do you want to stay?"

I held my breath.

"Until I get bored," she replied. "Besides," she added, smiling up at me, "we don't want to desert my poor niece just when she needs us the most, do we? Oh," she said. "You don't know why she ran away from home. Well, it seems one night . . ."

An egg slipped out of my hand and smashed on the floor.

"Aunt Fern!"

"Now look at what you've done," Aunt Fern said. "Miss Butterfingers. Well scoop it up, Christie. That can be yours," she said and laughed.

I glared at her, finally fed up enough to defy her, but one look at her face told me she was anxious for such a confrontation. She wanted the opportunity to make everyone's lives miserable, as miserable as her own. I bit down on my lower lip and swallowed my pride.

"Why did she run away?" Morton asked.

"Never mind," Aunt Fern said, looking down at me on my hands and knees. "It's private talk between a niece and her loving aunt, right princess?"

I soaked up the broken egg in a rag and tried to ignore her, but she wouldn't relent. She was the kind of person who enjoyed pouring salt into someone else's wounds. I should have realized she wouldn't feel sorry for me. There wasn't an ounce of compassion in her unless it was for herself.

"Right?" she insisted.

"Right, Aunt Fern," I said, swallowing my tears.

I realized I had run from one horrible trap into another. Every time I broke one of the links in the chain that bound me to the family curse, something mended it. I felt just like someone wearing irons around her neck, hands and feet. I rose to my feet slowly and, mechanically, like some galley slave, made Aunt Fern and her boyfriend their scrambled eggs. I did the best I could to keep my tears from dropping into the food.

"Aren't you eating breakfast?" Aunt Fern asked when I served her and Morton their eggs and fresh cups of coffee.

"I don't have any appetite," I said.

"Well, you'd better eat something anyway," she insisted. "You've got to keep up your strength. There's lots more for you to do. Later on in the evening, you can entertain us on the piano."

"I'd rather not," I said.

"Sure you would," she retorted, enjoying every moment of my discomfort. "It will give you an opportunity to show off again and you know how much you like to show off, princess."

"I don't show off, Aunt Fern."

"Of course you do. You're supposed to after all that expense. My brother spent a fortune for her lessons," she told Morton, who nodded with little interest. "A lot more than he wanted to spend on me," she added hatefully.

"I feel sorry for you, Aunt Fern," I said, shaking my head. "You've got a monster inside you, a green monster eating away at your heart. I feel more sorry for you than I do for myself," I added and started out of the kitchen.

"Don't go too far, princess," she called after me

and laughed. "You never know when I might need something done for me," she added and laughed.

Her laughter echoed through the plantation house. It was the kind of laughter that found a welcome home in the dark corners of this old mansion. I was positive it was the sort of evil that had lived so well within its walls.

Bad to the Bone

ALTHOUGH IT WAS A BRIGHT, SUNNY MORNING WITH only puffs of clouds that appeared to be pasted against the deep blue sky here and there, I was so unhappy I might as well have opened the door and stepped into a gray, overcast day. Even the chirping of the sparrows and robins seemed dull, their music sadly off-key to me. A large, black crow, perched on the back of an old wooden lawn chair, stared at me with what looked like morbid curiosity. It barely moved and resembled a stuffed bird more than a live one. Instead of being greeted by the aroma of freshly-cut grass and the blossoms of wild flowers, I inhaled the musty scent of rotting wood beams in the porch floor. Flies danced in the air around the house as if they were celebrating the discovery of a huge carcass on which they could feed forever.

I sighed, realizing I was tuned into only what would make me uncomfortable and sad; I was in the mood to see only what was ugly and bleak, no matter how wonderful the day really was. I used to think it was the weather that would put me into one state of mind or the other, but now I realized it was far more than that. It was Mommy and Daddy who made the world bright and wonderful for me. Their smiles and happy voices created the sunshine. Beauty without people you loved or people who loved you was incomplete, unappreciated, missed.

And just as loving and gentle people could make your world brighter and happier, so could selfish and cruel people, people with hearts made of granite and veins filled with ice water, make your world dismal and gray. Aunt Fern was like a sooty, dark gray cloud hovering over my head now, threatening to drop a hard, cold rain over me and drench me in even more misery. In my flight from the horror my home had become, I had scooped up my little brother and taken Gavin's helping hand, dragging them both along on what seemed now to be a journey into hell. I had taken refuge in the old plantation, but in doing so, I had only permitted the curse to enter the lives of two simple, but gentle, people.

I felt like Typhoid Mary, a Jonah. If I boarded a ship, it would sink; if I got on a train or a plane, it would crash. Maybe, if I ever reached Heaven, the angels would lose their melodious voices. I couldn't recall a time in my life when I felt more sorry for myself and the people who loved me. As I stood there filled with these dark thoughts, I considered running down the driveway and disappearing. Without my being here to torment, Aunt Fern would get bored and leave; Gavin could take Jefferson home with him and have a happy life, and Charlotte, Luther and Homer could return to the idyllic, simple world they once had.

I took a few steps forward, my eyes fixed on the broken and chipped driveway. In the strong breeze, the trees and bushes seemed to be beckoning to me. The voice in the wind whispered "Run, Christie, run . . . run." What differencc did it make where I went, what turns I made, or where I ended up?

People might miss me for awhile. For awhile Gavin's heart would be heavy, but time would embroider me into the fabric of his memory and he would turn to happier and more hopeful things. Living in a world where fires could steal away two people as wonderful as Mommy and Daddy, where people as evil as Charlotte's sister Emily thrived and lived to a ripe old age, where diseases and poverty coexisted alongside the healthy and the fortunate, striking without rhyme or reason to steal away happiness at any moment, was difficult enough. Why add the leaden weight of a curse, too?

My steps grew bolder, longer, faster. Perhaps I would hide in the bushes and watch to be sure Aunt Fern and Morton left and Gavin soon followed afterward with Jefferson. Then I would feel better about my decision. Yes, I could. . . .

"HEY!" I heard. I stopped and turned to see Gavin walking quickly toward me. His dark eyebrows were raised in confusion. "Where do you think you're going?" he demanded.

"I was just . . ."

"Just what, Christie? This driveway takes you back to the road. You were running off, weren't you?" he asked perceptively. "Fern did something else," he followed before I could utter a reply. "What did she do?" he demanded. "I'll go back in there and I'll . . ." He turned toward the house.

"No Gavin, please," I said, seizing his forearm. "Don't do anything. I wasn't running away," I said. He looked at me skeptically. "I was just going to take a walk and I thought this would be the easiest way," I said flatly, hoping that he wouldn't see the pain that was in my eyes. But that was what he saw.

"Christie, I told you I would keep anyone from hurting you, didn't I?" he said.

"I know. I know. Is Jefferson all right?" I asked quickly, hoping to get him off the topic so he would calm down.

"He's in seventh heaven alongside Homer smearing paint over the barn walls. I've been waiting for you all morning. What did she have you do after you brought her coffee?"

"Nothing terrible. I helped her bathe and shampoo her hair and then I made them some breakfast. It will be all right," I promised, even though I wasn't confident. "I'm sure they'll grow bored today and leave."

"Um," he said, nodding, his eyes small. "Maybe."

"Of course, they will, Gavin. What's here for them? You know how Fern's used to a lot of excitement. Why, she always complained about being bored at the hotel with all the activity in full swing."

In trying to convince him, I was helping to convince myself. But it was as if the horrid fates that haunted me had heard my protests of hope and were determined to stifle even the smallest notes of optimism. Aunt Fern and Morton came bursting out of the house, laughing as they pounded over the porch floor and down the steps to their car.

"Could they be leaving?" Gavin muttered.

He and I stepped to the side to watch them back up and then come down the driveway. They stopped alongside us and Aunt Fern rolled down her window.

"Where the hell are you two going . . . back to your love nest at the lake?" she asked and laughed.

"We're just taking a little walk, Aunt Fern," I replied sharply.

"Sure, sure. Anyway, we're going into town to buy some things. Morton wants steak for supper and we want some decent things for our other meals. Also, I don't like the soaps and shampoo you have here."

"Don't forget the fresh whiskey," Morton quipped and they both laughed.

"Yeah, there's no gin and we both like gin. You better go back and clean up the kitchen," she added. "We've got to keep our little hideaway clean. Which reminds me, I want to get some other rooms in shape, make them liveable. We'll do a tour later and I'll show you what I want done."

She rolled up her window and Morton drove on. My heart contracted and my throat closed.

"So much for your belief that they will leave today," Gavin said. "I swear, if she does any more mean things to you, I'll grab her by the scruff of her neck and boot her out the door."

"Let's just humor them a little longer, Gavin. They'll grow bored soon," I promised. "Please," I pleaded. "I don't want to make any more trouble for anyone else."

His eyes grew small.

"All right," he said, "but I don't want to see you walking away from this house ever again without me. Promise? Promise me you won't do anything stupid, Christie," he insisted.

I lowered my eyes and nodded, but he wasn't satisfied. He reached out and lifted my chin so I would have to look into his eyes.

"Christie?"

"All right, Gavin," I said. "I promise."

"Good," he said, satisfied.

"I'll go in and clean up the kitchen. No reason why Charlotte has to have extra work," I told him and started back for the house.

Aunt Fern and Morton returned with bags filled with the things they liked to eat. They had two quart bottles of gin and a dozen small bottles of tonic water. Almost immediately, Morton made them drinks. I was ordered to unpack the bags and organize the dinner. While I did so, Aunt Fern made her promised tour of the plantation house. A short while later, I heard her shouting for me. Charlotte had returned to prepare lunch for Luther and the others.

"Oh dear, why is she screaming so loud? What does she want?" Charlotte wondered behind me. We found her standing at the top of the stairway, her drink in one hand and the doll from the crib in the old nursery in her other. Charlotte froze.

"Be careful, please," she cried up to Aunt Fern.

"Be careful? Be careful of what? What is this? Why is there a doll in a crib?" she demanded.

"Please put it back, Aunt Fern," I said, starting up the stairway toward her. "It's Charlotte's."

"She still plays with dolls?" she asked incredulously.

"No, but it has important memories for her and . . ."

"This is ridiculous. What a ridiculous place," Aunt Fern declared.

"Please," Charlotte said. "Put him back. We don't take him out of the nursery."

"Oh we don't?" Aunt Fern teased. "What do you think will happen? Will he cry?" She held up the doll by its feet and bounced it up and down over the railing, threatening to drop it.

"Stop!" Charlotte cried and started up the stairs behind me.

"Aunt Fern, don't tease her."

Fern took another gulp from her gin and tonic and laughed.

"Morty," she called. "You've got to come out and see this. You won't believe it. Morty!"

"Put him back! Please, put him back," Aunt Charlotte begged, stepping faster.

Morton came out of the sitting room where he had been drinking and relaxing and looked up.

"Let's play monkey-in-the-middle," Aunt Fern declared and held up the doll for Morton to see. Aunt Charlotte reached out for it and Aunt Fern threw the doll down to Morton, who caught it.

"STOP!" Charlotte cried, her palms pressed against her temples.

"Aunt Fern, how could you do that?" I turned and started toward Morton, who was smiling up at Fern. "Give me the doll, please," I pleaded. He laughed and just as I reached him, tossed it back up to Fern. She dropped it, but before Charlotte could get to it, Fern scooped it up and threatened to throw it back to Morton.

Charlotte screamed again. Fern giggled and charged away. I looked at Aunt Charlotte's face and saw the pain and fear in her eyes. In her mind once again someone was taking away her baby, I thought. How dreadful and how cruel of Fern to do something so obviously painful to Aunt Charlotte.

"Aunt Fern," I called and stormed up the stairway. I chased after her with Charlotte right behind me. But when we turned the corner at the end of the corridor, she was nowhere in sight.

"Where is she? Where has she taken the baby?" Aunt Charlotte asked.

"Aunt Fern?"

We heard giggling to the right and started slowly in that direction. But before we reached the doorway of the room Aunt Fern was hiding in, we heard the glass she was carrying shatter on the floor and then we heard her scream. A moment later Homer appeared with the doll cradled in his arms as if he were carrying a real baby. He walked over to

Charlotte and gingerly transferred the doll into her arms. She stroked its head and face gently and then headed for the nursery.

"What's he doing here!" Aunt Fern demanded from the doorway. "He scared the hell out of me."

Homer turned and glared furiously at her.

"I told you to keep him out of the house," Aunt Fern said. "He popped out of nowhere and grabbed that stupid doll out of my hands."

"It's all right, Homer," I said. "Everything's all right. Go on back to the others." He continued to stand there, his eyes fixed hatefully on Fern, his large hands clenched into mallets. "Go on, Homer," I said more firmly. He looked at me and then turned and headed away.

"Where the hell did he come from?" Aunt Fern asked, strutting toward me bravely now that Homer had gone.

"He must have heard Aunt Charlotte's scream and climbed in through a window," I said. "Why did you do that, Aunt Fern? You could see how much it bothered her."

"Well, what is she, nuts? At her age crying over a doll?"

"It's the doll she had when she was a little girl," I said. "It means a lot to her."

"Weird," Aunt Fern declared. "This whole place and everyone in it." Her face was swollen with anger and frustration. She didn't like being forced to stop teasing Charlotte and me. She was indignant and embarrassed.

"Why don't we just leave, Fern," Morton said. He had heard the commotion and had come up the stairs behind us.

"No," Fern replied. She was fuming, her eyes hot, the tips of her ears red. She hated to be thwarted and defeated and she was going to get her revenge somehow. "We bought all that food and all this booze to have a good time here, and we will," she said with determination. She fixed her eyes on me. I had become her whipping boy.

"Let's begin by fixing up that living room downstairs. I want to have a party tonight. Get the floor swept, the windows washed and the furniture polished."

"Fern, let's just leave," Morton implored. Why didn't he just demand? I wondered. What sort of a man was he? How did she get men wrapped up so tightly in her grip? How did she get so firm a hold over them? Was it just the promise of sex? Morton was the one with the car and the money, but Fern decided everything.

"Relax, Morty," she said, calming down and returning that icy smile to her face. "First, we'll have a great dinner and then Christie will give us a concert. After that, we'll play some games . . . one of the games you like," she told him coyly. Whatever she was promising him, pleased him, for he smiled and then laughed.

"Okay," he said.

"Then it's all settled. Get working on the living room, princess. We want to have a good time tonight, don't you?"

"None of us will have a good time as long as you tease and torment people here, Aunt Fern," I told her.

"Oh stop whining. I'm having fun and I like it. Either your mother or my brother were always putting an end to my fun. Well, they're not here now. I'm the adult in charge, understand?"

"Then act like an adult," I said unable to stop myself. Her face flamed red and before I could see it, her hand flew up and slapped me across the cheek, the blow so hard, I stumbled back. My face stung and my eyes burned with tears. She came at me again and I raised my arm instinctively to protect myself.

"You little bitch! Don't you ever talk back to me like that again!" she fumed. "Do you hear me? DO YOU?" She seemed to swell up to tower over me, her black eyes like hot coals, her nostrils wide, resembling those of a mad bull. Every feature in her face became distorted with her rage. I couldn't help but cower. I felt my own blood drain down into my feet; a stinging sensation began behind my ears as my strength grew small, and I stared at the woman who seemed a stranger now.

"I ought to bind you and gag you and just march you down those stairs and throw you into the back of Morton's car and drive you right back to Philip," she spat through her clenched teeth. "Why he could have these people committed to an insane asylum. Yes," she said nodding. "He could.

"And once I testified to finding you living in sin here with Gavin, no one would believe your story about Philip. With Philip as trustee of the estate in control of everything. . . ." She looked around. "He might just give me this place as a reward. Morty and I could tear it all apart and have a hell of a good time here, couldn't we, Morty?"

"It's got potential," he agreed quickly. I had the feeling he was just as afraid of her as I was.

"Yes," she said, nodding, "you see? Morty knows about such things and he says it has potential."

She glared down at me. I shifted my eyes from hers. My heart was pounding so hard, I thought I might faint. The storm of horror she had threatened to burst over me had started. My legs felt as if they were shrinking and I was sinking to the floor.

"I'd like to hear an apology," she said. "I don't know how many times my brother made me apologize to your mother for one thing or another. Well?"

I felt trapped, pinned down by her hate and rage. Who knew what terrible things might be done to Charlotte and Luther and even Homer if she carried out her threats.

"I'm sorry," I muttered.

"What? I didn't hear you," she said, her hands on her hips.

"I'm sorry, Aunt Fern," I said loud enough for Morton to hear as well. I knew that was what she wanted.

"Good," she said, smiling. "Now all can return to normal and we can be friends again. You've been doing so well up to this point, too. Hasn't she, Morty?"

"She's been a fine host," he said, nodding.

"Yes, right, a fine host. All right," she said, turning back to me, "now let's just continue it all. Fix up the living room so we can have our party tonight," she concluded. Then she started away.

"How about another drink?" Morton asked her, holding up his arm for her to put hers through.

"Good idea. I need one after this. Oh, princess," she said, turning. "You'd better go into that room and sweep up the glass that imbecile made me drop. Be careful. Don't cut yourself," she added. "If something bad happened to you, I could never forgive myself." Her peal of laughter trailed after her and Morton as they went down the corridor, both behaving as if nothing horrible had occurred.

I should have run away before, I thought. I shouldn't have been so indecisive about it. I should have flown down the driveway and disappeared. If I had, she wouldn't have tormented Aunt Charlotte.

With my head bowed, my heart feeling as if it

had been turned to stone, and my legs moving as if on their own, I followed in Aunt Fern and Morton's wake to begin my work on the living room so she would be pleased. I still clung to the hope that after a while, she would grow bored with these games and move on into oblivion, for I pledged to myself and took an oath on all that was sacred that once she was out of my life, I would never permit her to enter it again, even if she became destitute and was begging on the streets.

That's how hateful I had become.

That's how hateful she had made me.

At dinner that night, Aunt Fern and Morton were downright disgusting and obnoxious. Without warning, they would break into these silly games. I think she was just trying to demonstrate to us how much control she had over this poor excuse for a man. She would declare something as if she were his master and he would have to obey.

"You're a one-year-old-baby," she decided. "You can't feed yourself. Go 'ga, ga.' Go on."

"Ga, ga," he said and tried to look like an infant: his eyes shifted toward the ceiling, his arms at his side and his mouth agape.

"Hungry, little Morty?" Aunt Fern sang. He nodded quickly. She raised a forkful of mashed potatoes to his lips and when he opened his mouth wide, she pulled the fork away. "No, no, little Morty. Not so fast. Not before you do something nice for Mommy. Here," she said, holding out her other hand. "Lick Mommy's hand. Go on or Mommy won't feed you."

We all watched him do it. Charlotte was fascinated; Luther was disgusted. Jefferson thought it was all very funny and started to act like a baby, too, until I squeezed his arm. Gavin shook his head and closed his eyes to block it out, but it couldn't be ignored. They were there.

"I'm going to put a little of this mashed potato on the tip of Morty's little nose and he's going to try to lick it off." She did it. "Go on, Morty, try. Try for Mommy."

We watched him stick his tongue out and curl it, squinting at the same time to bring his nose closer. He couldn't do it and began to wail like an infant until Fern wiped it off.

"Morty's a good boy; he tried. Okay, Morty, be older and eat by yourself," she commanded. He smiled and dug into his food quickly before she changed her mind.

"What are you gawking at, princess? Don't you and my brother play little games with each other?" she asked.

"Not as stupid as that," Gavin said quickly.

"Oh, don't be an old prude like your brother was," she replied and then turned to me. "You did a good job on this food, princess. You're getting better and better at everything. Who knows? By the time we leave, you might qualify as a household servant. How would you like that, Jefferson?" she asked, leaning over the table toward him. "How would you like your sister to be a household servant?"

Jefferson shrugged.

"Can we stay here if she is?" he asked.

"Of course you can." She fixed her eyes on me. "As long as she's a good servant, you can hide out forever for all I care." She sighed deeply. "But Christie is not really just a household servant. She's very talented. Everyone knows that. We've all been told enough times. Morty's very anxious to hear you play, aren't you, Morty?"

"What?" He looked up quickly from his plate. "Oh yes. Can you do some Chopin?"

"Of course, she can," Aunt Fern replied for me. "She can do anything on the piano. Can't you?"

"I know some Chopin. I did some sonatas for lessons in piano technique."

"Oh, well excuse us. Piano technique. Great," she said, smirking.

"I took some piano lessons when I was younger," Morton volunteered.

"Well isn't that peachy-keen. Everyone's had lessons in this or that but me," Aunt Fern said.

"I know that Daddy wanted you to learn an instrument," I said. "I remember you refusing."

"Well, I wasn't going to do it just because he wanted me to. Anyway, it was probably something Dawn told him to do. We're happy just listening to you, princess," she added, forcing a smile. She wiped her face and dropped her napkin. "Come on, Morty. Let's adjourn to the living room for an after-dinner drink. When you're finished cleaning up, come in and entertain us," she commanded.

"Just a minute," Gavin began. He started to rise in his seat. I grabbed his arm.

"It's all right, Gavin. I don't mind playing the piano, even for Aunt Fern," I said. That brought a smile to both his and Morton's lips.

Aunt Fern pivoted quickly and marched out of the room, Morton following obediently at her heels like a puppy.

While Charlotte and I cleaned off the table and did the dishes, Gavin occupied Jefferson with the deck of playing cards he had bought him during our trip to Lynchburg. Luther, unable to contain himself any longer in front of Aunt Fern and Morton, disappeared to finish up some mysterious work in the barn; and Homer knew enough to stay away, although when I finally did finish the kitchen chores and went into the living room to play the piano, I caught sight of him peering in through a window. Every time Aunt Fern turned in his direction, however, he would disappear.

I played more than a few Chopin preludes. My music was my escape. It resembled a magic carpet, sweeping me off and out of this world of meanness and cruelty. I closed my eyes and visualized Mommy sitting quietly and attentively in our living room back in Cutler's Cove, her smile full of pride. When I played, it was as if all of the terrible things that had happened never happened. The music washed away the sadness and tragedy, making it all seem to be nothing more than a series of bad dreams. We were all alive and well and together.

I really lost myself in the music, for when I stopped and opened my eyes, everyone, even Aunt Fern, was gazing at me with eyes wide and full of amazement. Aunt Charlotte clapped her hands excitedly. Jefferson had fallen asleep with his head resting against Gavin's shoulder.

"That was nothing short of fantastic," Morton said. His expression of appreciation immediately wiped the look of awe off Aunt Fern's face. "You're a very talented young lady," he said, nodding. He was so impressed, I actually blushed with embarrassment.

"She's good, I suppose," Aunt Fern admitted reluctantly. "I told you she had the best piano teachers. No money was spared when it came to the princess."

"It takes more than money to play like that," Morton said.

"Well, I could have done something with my talent too," Aunt Fern whined, "if I had people care about me, really care instead of pretend." She whipped her arms up and folded them under her breasts. Then she sat back, glaring at me in a jealous sulk like a child.

"I'd better take Jefferson upstairs and put him to sleep," I said, going to him. "Come on, Jefferson."

His eyes fluttered open for a moment.

"I'll carry him," Gavin said. He lifted him into his arms. Jefferson's head settled comfortably against Gavin's chest.

"I'm going to sleep, too," Aunt Charlotte announced.

"Good for you," Aunt Fern said. Then she turned to Gavin and me. "Come right back down," she ordered. "We want to play a game."

"Game? What game?" I asked suspiciously.

"You'll see when you return," she replied and smiled at Morton, who smiled back. "Get me another drink, Morty, and make a couple for Romeo and Juliet."

"We don't want any of your drinks," Gavin snapped.

"There you go, being like your prudish brother again," she told him. Gavin ignored her and we left to put Jefferson to bed.

As I undressed him, I came upon an ugly gash on his right thigh. The fresh scab was surrounded by an inflamed mound of flesh, apple-red.

"How did you do this, Jefferson?" I demanded. His eyes fluttered open and closed. "Jefferson?" I turned to Gavin. "Look at this, Gavin."

He studied the wound for a moment.

"I don't know," he said. "He never complained about anything to me. Jefferson, wake up," he said, shaking him. This time Jefferson's eyes remained open.

"How did you do this to yourself?" I asked, pointing to the wound again.

"I got stuck on a nail," he said.

"When? Where?" I asked quickly.

"When we first came here and I was painting the room with Aunt Charlotte," he replied.

"I never saw it," Gavin said.

"Why didn't you tell me, Jefferson?" I asked. He shrugged. "Did Aunt Charlotte wash it? Did you wash it?"

"Uh huh," he said and closed his eyes. I didn't know whether to believe him or not.

"I'll go ask Charlotte and get something to put on it," I said and went to her door. I knocked and when she didn't answer, I peered in and saw her on her knees by her bed saying her prayers like a little girl.

"I pray the Lord my soul to keep . . ."

She saw me and stopped.

"I'm sorry to bother you, Aunt Charlotte, but Jefferson has a nasty cut on his leg. He said he got it when he was painting the room with you a few days ago. Do you remember that?" She shook her head. "Do you have anything for cuts and bruises?"

"Oh yes," she said, getting up and shuffling quickly to her bathroom. She came out with a box of Band-Aids and some antiseptic.

"Good," I said. "You don't remember washing the cut on Jefferson's leg that day?" I asked. She tilted her head and thought a moment.

"Maybe I did," she said. "I get mixed up with the times Luther cut himself. He's always cutting himself on something."

I nodded.

"Thank you, Aunt Charlotte."

By the time I returned, Gavin had Jefferson in

bed. I got a washcloth, cleaned the wound and treated it with the antiseptic. Then I covered it with the Band-Aids. He didn't open his eyes the whole time.

"We'll have to watch this," I told Gavin, "and make sure the infection goes away. I don't think Charlotte washed it when it happened, and he was so excited about painting the room, he didn't tell us he had been cut."

Gavin nodded.

"What should we do now?" he asked.

"We'd better go down and see what stupid game she wants to play," I replied, standing. "If we don't, she'll only come up here screaming and wake Jefferson and Aunt Charlotte."

He nodded.

When we returned to the living room, we found Aunt Fern and Morton sitting on the floor by the center table. On the table was the pack of playing cards and their gin and tonics. At her insistence, Morton had made two drinks for us.

"Come on," Aunt Fern said, beckoning for us to sit on the floor around the table, too. Her eyelids looked half-closed and what I could see of her eyes looked bloodshot. "You're holding up progress. Here are your drinks."

"I told you we don't want any of that," Gavin said.

"What kind of a teenager are you?" she asked him angrily. "You act more like an old man." Then she smiled. "You're certainly not a chip off the old block; that's for sure. Daddy Longchamp," she told Morton, "was a famous drunk." She gulped some of her own drink.

"He was not!" Gavin fumed.

"I know what he was, honey," she said, putting

her glass down and fixing her gaze on him. "There's no sense pretending he didn't drink and he didn't go to prison."

"Well . . . he doesn't . . . doesn't drink now," Gavin stuttered. She had nearly brought him to tears.

"Not in front of you, maybe, but I bet he sneaks it," she said, enjoying Gavin's discomfort. "Once a drunk, always a drunk."

"He doesn't drink like that anymore," Gavin insisted.

"All right, he doesn't. He's pure as the driven snow, perfect, a reformed drunk and kidnapper."

"You don't know what you're talking about," Gavin said. "You shouldn't say those things about Daddy."

"All right, all right," she said, satisfied she had tormented him enough. "Let's have some fun for a change. Sit down."

"I'm not drinking," Gavin insisted.

"Don't drink. Be a minister for all I care," she said irritably. We sat down. "But you gotta play by the rules," Aunt Fern added. I looked at Morton who broke into a wide smile again.

"What rules? What sort of a game is this?" I asked.

"We're playing strip poker," she said. "Cut the cards, Morty."

"What?" Gavin said.

"Don't tell me you two never played strip poker. Do you believe this, Morty?" she asked him. He shrugged and started dealing the cards.

"We're not playing any such thing," Gavin said. He looked down at the cards as if our touching them would contaminate us.

"Oh, you only play with each other, is that it?" Aunt Fern taunted.

"We've never played this," he said.

"So? There's a first time for everything. Right, princess?" she said, turning to me. "You can talk about first times, can't you."

"Stop it, Aunt Fern."

"Then pick up your cards," she ordered hotly. "You know how to play poker."

"Don't do it, Christie," Gavin said. Fern picked up her cards and smiled.

"I bid three pieces of clothing," she said. "Morty?"

"I'll see you and raise you three pieces," he replied.

"Gavin?"

"We're not playing this stupid game, Fern," he said firmly. She lowered her hand.

"I don't like my fun being ruined," she said steely-eyed. "It makes me want to call people, people like Philip."

"Stop threatening us," Gavin snapped.

"And people like Daddy." She turned to me. "And people in authority who come and get old ladies who still play with dolls."

"You dirty . . ."

"Forget it, Gavin," I said quickly. "We'll play her silly game if that makes her happy."

"Fine. Morty has bid six pieces of clothes. Christie?"

I looked at my cards. They were terrible, not even two of a kind.

"I'll pass," I said.

"If you do, you've got to take off six pieces of clothing," she said.

"But that's not the way poker is played," I protested.

"It's our special rules," she said. "Right, Morty?"

"Absolutely," he said.

"This is dumb," Gavin said.

"Everything that's fun is dumb to you," Aunt Fern told him. "Well?" she asked me.

"I might as well stay in if that's your rule," I replied. "Although it doesn't make any sense."

"Good. Gavin?"

He just ignored her.

"I'll take two cards, please," she told Morton. He dealt them and turned to me.

"Four," I said.

"Why are you doing this?" Gavin asked me.

"She wants to have some fun. Loosen up, Mr. Prude," Aunt Fern teased. Reluctantly, he picked up his hand and looked at it.

"Two cards," he muttered at Morton.

I had no better hand than the one with which I had started.

"One for me," Morton said, dealing himself a card. He wore a big smile.

"I raise you two more articles of clothing," Fern said.

"See you and go one more," he replied.

"That's nine if you're in, six if you're out," Aunt Fern explained.

Gavin threw down his hand. I did the same.

"Two pairs, threes and fives," Aunt Fern said, showing her hand.

"A straight, two to six," Morton said, showing his cards. He sat back.

"Lucky you," Fern said. She smiled. "You two take off any six pieces you want. I gotta take off nine. Oh," she said, laughing as she kicked off her shoes, "that will leave me stark naked." She lifted her blouse over her head and then stopped.

"What are your six pieces, princess?" she asked.

I took off my shoes and socks.

"That's two," she said.

"Two? I've taken off two shoes and two socks," I protested.

"Pairs are counted as one," she said. "Our rules, right, Morty?"

"Right," he parroted.

"Keep going," she ordered.

"Don't do it," Gavin told me.

"You don't welsh on a game," Aunt Fern snapped. "It's like breaking a promise to keep a secret," she added, smiling at me.

I unbuttoned my blouse. Morton's smile widened and he licked his lips. Aunt Fern unfastened her bra and without hesitation slipped it down her arms as if she were alone in her bedroom. Her breasts shook as she started on her skirt.

"Fern! You're drunk and you're disgusting!" Gavin screamed, standing. *"I can't believe you're my sister."*

Aunt Fern threw back her head and laughed. With his face red and swollen, Gavin turned and rushed out of the room. That only made her laugh harder.

"GAVIN!" I cried standing. I heard him run down the corridor and out the front door of the plantation house so I started after him.

"Hold it," Fern said, her laughter stopped short. "You haven't taken off your six pieces."

I looked at her and then Morton, who sat back with a licentious smile, gaping at me hungrily.

"The game's over, Aunt Fern," I said, looking down.

"You don't walk out without paying what you owe," she insisted. "Those are the rules."

"Please, Aunt Fern. Can't we stop now?"

"Not until you pay up what you owe," she insisted. "Pay."

I took off my blouse.

"That's three," she said. "Go on."

I unfastened the skirt and it fell to my ankles.

"Four."

All I had left were my bra and panties.

"Do you want help?" she asked. I shook my head. "Aunt Fern . . ."

"It wouldn't be fair," she said. "I didn't hesitate to pay what I owed."

I gazed at Morton. He was staring at me so hard, I felt he could already see through my remaining garments. I reached behind my back and undid my bra, but I hesitated to slide it off my bosom.

"Come on, princess, you did it for your uncle Philip, you can do it for us," she coaxed.

"Aunt Fern! That's horrible, a horrible thing to say," I cried. "I didn't do it for Uncle Philip. I didn't."

I scooped up my shoes and socks and my skirt and holding my bra against my breasts, I shot out of the living room.

"You bitch!" she screamed after me. "You can't welsh on a game of strip poker. You'll be sorry . . . YOU'LL BE SORRY!"

I ran down the corridor and stopped in a room to dress myself. Then I went outside to look for Gavin. He was nowhere in sight, so I went around the house toward the barn. Halfway there, I heard him whisper.

"Christie."

He was standing off in the shadows. I went to him quickly.

"Gavin, you were right. I shouldn't have tried to please her. She's horrid and she'll never stop tormenting us, especially me. I don't care about her threats anymore. I'm not going to do anything else for her."

"Good. Now maybe you'll listen to me and leave."

"Yes, Gavin, I will. I think once we're gone and no longer here to provide her any amusement, she'll leave too. I'll explain it all to Luther and he'll keep Charlotte and Homer away from them until they go," I said. "We'll leave in the morning."

"Good. We'll get up early and ask Luther to drive us into Upland Station."

"But what will we do then, Gavin?" I asked, my excitement waning when I let reality seep into our plans. Gavin thought a moment.

"I guess we're just going to have to call my daddy," he said. "He's not going to be happy we've gone so far away, but he'll help us, especially when he learns what happened to you. And he is Jefferson's grandfather, Christie. Don't forget that."

"I know. I just can't help being scared about it all. But you're right. We should call him," I said.

"He'll help us. You'll see. He's nothing like Fern claims he is," Gavin said, obviously sensitive to her taunts.

"I know that, Gavin. I've always liked Granddaddy Longchamp. Let's go back inside and go to our rooms and go to sleep."

He took my hand and we returned to the house, entering as quietly as we could. We could hear Fern giggling in the living room. As we walked by, we gazed in and saw the two of them naked, embracing on the floor. We hurried up the stairs and stopped at my doorway.

"She makes everything seem dirty," Gavin said, his eyes lowered.

"It's not, if you really care about the person

you're with, Gavin. Then, it's beautiful. We've got nothing to be ashamed of," I told him. He smiled and I kissed him quickly on the lips.

"Sleep tight," he said.

"And don't let the bedbugs bite," I added and went in. Now that we had made our decision, I felt as if a heavy load had been lifted from my shoulders. I went to sleep relieved that we would finally be rid of Fern. I was sorry our time in our special paradise had come to an end, but somehow, things will be all right, I told myself. Just for a while, I permitted myself to crawl out from under that curse that lay over me like a heavy, flat rock.

But I should have known better.

I should have expected that it would find a way to block the sunlight from warming our lives.

Gavin's shout woke me out of my pleasant dreams.

"Christie, come quickly," he cried from the doorway. "It's Jefferson!"

"What, Gavin?"

"Something's terribly wrong with him!" he exclaimed. The terror in his face made my heart stop and I was out of bed in an instant.

The Shadows Deepen

"WHAT'S THE MATTER, JEFFERSON?" I CRIED, UNABLE to keep the alarm out of my voice.

Jefferson was lying rigidly on his back, his arms extended stiffly at his sides. His mouth was open just enough to permit him to voice a low moan. In fact, his jaw looked swollen, the skin around it taut.

"He just started moaning like that," Gavin explained, "and woke me. When I asked him what was wrong, he only moaned again and again. Then he started calling for you."

I put my hand on Jefferson's forehead.

"He feels feverish."

"Christie . . ." Jefferson said when his eyes flicked open and he saw me bending over him. His eyes were so full of pain and sadness, my heart went out to him.

"What's wrong, Jefferson? What hurts?"

"My neck feels like someone's squeezing it," he complained. He closed and opened his eyes with every word as if it was a major effort to utter each syllable. "And my face hurts, too. Make it stop, Christie, make it stop."

"His face hurts? What . . . what could it be?" I asked Gavin. He shrugged.

"A flu, maybe."

"He definitely has a fever," I said. Jefferson's lips were very dry and his tongue looked pale pink.

"Cold," Jefferson said. "Brrrr . . ."

"You're cold?" I asked him and he nodded.

"I'll put my blanket over him," Gavin said and moved quickly to his bed to get the quilt Aunt Charlotte had provided. He and I spread it over Jefferson's little body and tucked it in at his chin. Still, he shuddered.

"Cold," he repeated.

"It's such a warm night," I said, astounded. "How can he be so cold?" I rubbed his arm and shoulder vigorously.

"It's the chills . . . from the fever," Gavin said.

"He looks pretty sick," I said. "His skin is so pale and why is he lying so rigidly? He's as stiff as a board. Just feel his arms, Gavin."

"Maybe because of the fever," Gavin guessed after touching Jefferson.

"I should take his temperature. I wonder if Aunt Charlotte would have a thermometer."

"Somehow, I doubt it," Gavin said.

"We'd better do something quickly. I'll wake Aunt Fern and tell her to look at him."

"I doubt if she knows what to do," Gavin said. "Don't waste your time."

"But her boyfriend might. He looks intelligent," I said.

"He can't be too intelligent if he stuck himself with Fern," Gavin said.

"My eyes hurt, Christie, and my throat, too," Jefferson complained. "It hurts to swallow and it hurts to turn my head."

"It's definitely the flu, I bet," Gavin said, nodding. "I felt the same way when I had it."

"What did your mother do?" I asked, feeling

more frantic with every passing moment. "I had the flu, but I can't ever remember being this sick."

"She called the doctor and he told her to give me aspirin and make me drink a lot of liquids. It took a little more than a day, but I felt better pretty quickly after that. Don't worry," Gavin assured me, "I'm sure it's nothing more."

"Still, I'd better have Aunt Fern or her boyfriend look at him, don't you think?"

Seeing how nervous I was, Gavin reluctantly nodded.

"I hate to ask her for anything," he muttered.

"Stay with him," I said and left to go to Aunt Fern's room.

This late at night, only one lone kerosene lamp remained burning in the corridor. The shadows made the hallway look longer and more lonely. I scurried along as quickly as I could and knocked on Aunt Fern's door. Neither she nor her boyfriend responded. Maybe they're still downstairs, I thought. The flickering light from the small flames in the lamps below made the shadows dance on the walls beside the stairway and above. I decided to knock again, only much louder.

"Aunt Fern? Are you in there? Aunt Fern."

I heard what sounded like a lamp falling over. Something crashed on the floor. The noise was followed by a ripple of curses.

"What the hell is it?" Fern screamed from within and then the door was thrust open. Aunt Fern swayed. She stood there totally nude, her hair wild, her eyes barely open.

"What do you want? It's the middle of the night!" she complained, her eyes opening a little more with each complaint. "Why did you come banging on our door?"

"It's Jefferson, Aunt Fern. He's sick. He definitely has a temperature and he's complaining about pain in his neck and in his face. We don't know what to do," I said.

"What is it? What's the matter?" Morton called from the bed. He put on another lamp and sat up.

"It's my brother," I explained, looking past Aunt Fern. "He's sick."

"So what?" Fern cried, folding her arms over her breasts. "Kids get sick all the time."

"Is he throwing up?" Morton asked.

"No, but his throat hurts and his neck hurts and . . ."

"So, he's got a cold or something," Aunt Fern said. Her mouth twisted into an ugly grimace. "For this, you wake us up in the middle of the night?"

"He's in pain," I emphasized.

"Maybe he's got some kind of flu," Morton said.

"Yes," I said, nodding. "Gavin thought that might be it."

"Get him some aspirin," Morton said. "That's all you can do for now."

"Yeah, get him some aspirin," Aunt Fern agreed and started to close the door.

"But I don't think they have aspirin here," I moaned. "I'm frightened for him, Aunt Fern. Really."

"Damn it," she said.

"You've got some aspirin in your pocketbook, Fern," Morton said. "We bought it a few days ago after we woke up with hangovers in Boston, remember?"

"What? Oh yeah, yeah. Wait a minute," she said and hobbled back to the bed. "I forgot where I put my pocketbook," she groaned. "Did I leave it downstairs?"

"How would I know? I barely remember being downstairs myself," Morton replied and dropped his head back to the pillow as if it had turned to stone.

"What a pain in the rear end you are," Aunt Fern complained. She turned around and around.

"There it is!" I cried, pointing to the vanity table.

"What? Oh. Yeah." She went to it and combed through her things. "I don't see it," she said. My heart felt like a lead brick in my chest. For all I knew, Aunt Fern could have thrown the aspirin away.

"Please look harder, Aunt Fern. He's very sick. We need the aspirin."

Sanguine color flooded her face.

"Either it's you or Jefferson always needing something," she spat. I looked down, afraid she would just throw me out. "Damn, damn, damn," she said and angrily turned the pocketbook upside down and emptied it. "Here it is," she said, finally locating the small tin of aspirin. "Take it," she said, thrusting it at me angrily, "and get the hell out of here so we can have some peace and quiet and get some sleep."

I seized it and turned to the door quickly.

"Don't forget to shut the door. And quit babying him they way they babied you!" she called after me as I started back down the corridor.

"What did they say?" Gavin asked as soon as I returned.

"To give him aspirin."

"The least they could have done was come here and look at him," he muttered.

"Neither of them are in any condition to look at anyone. At least Morton got Aunt Fern to give me some aspirin."

I got Jefferson a glass of water and offered him two tablets, but when I put them into his mouth, he cried that he couldn't swallow.

"It hurts too much, Christie. It hurts!"

"What will we do, Gavin? If he can't swallow . . ."

"Grind the aspirin up and mix it in the water. I remember my mother doing that for me when I was a little boy," he said.

I mixed it as quickly as I could and then held the glass to Jefferson's lips. I started to pour the liquid into his mouth a little at a time, but as soon as it reached his throat, he went into a terrible choking convulsion—his whole body shaking, his eyes bulging.

"GAVIN!" I cried. "He's choking on the water!"

Gavin rushed to take Jefferson into his embrace.

"Easy buddy, easy," he said, holding Jefferson upright. He tapped him on the back lightly.

"What happened? It's just water and ground aspirin!" I said.

"Just went down the wrong pipe," Gavin said calmly. "Let him catch his breath and we'll try again."

My fingers trembled as I brought the glass to Jefferson's lips a second time. He looked like he had passed out; he barely moved.

"Jefferson, open your mouth just a little," I coaxed. His lips remained shut, his eyelids sewn. "Jefferson."

"Maybe we should just let him sleep," Gavin suggested.

I shook my head, frightened. My heart pounded. I had never seen Jefferson this sick, even when he had the measles and chicken pox.

"It doesn't seem right, Gavin. You didn't have trouble swallowing when you had the flu, did you?" I asked. "I know I didn't."

"I had a bad sore throat once . . . even had blisters. He might have that," Gavin said.

"If we don't get the aspirin in him, his fever won't go down," I moaned.

"Let me try," Gavin said. He held Jefferson in a sitting position and brought the glass to his lips. "Come on, buddy. Drink some of this," Gavin coached. Jefferson's eyelids fluttered and he opened his mouth just enough for Gavin to trickle some of the water and aspirin in. Once again, when it reached his throat, he began to cough violently, but Gavin held onto him and Jefferson was able to swallow some of it. Then he went limp in Gavin's hands.

"Asleep again. Let's wait until he wakes up and then try once more," Gavin suggested.

We sat by watching and waiting. Every time Jefferson opened his eyes, we were able to get him to swallow some more of the aspirin, but each swallow caused more choking. Eventually, we got all of it into him. Even so, I decided I would sit up beside him and watch over him until I was sure he was in a deep sleep.

"I'll sit up, too," Gavin said.

Jefferson closed his eyes, but he didn't fall asleep for a long, long time. He moaned and cried most of the remainder of the night. Shortly after he finally did fall asleep, both Gavin and I did, too.

Morning dawned, grim, gray, forbidding. My eyelids fluttered open and I gazed around. For a moment it all seemed like a bad dream; perhaps I had walked in my sleep and sat down here and fallen asleep again, I thought. Then I saw Gavin still sitting on his bed, his head tilted, his eyes closed. He had drifted into a deep sleep watching over Jefferson and me.

I leaned over slowly and looked at Jefferson. Although he was asleep, he looked so strange. It was as if he were having a funny dream. He wore a fixed smile and his eyebrows were elevated. But there was something about that look on his face that told me it wasn't just a smile caused by happy thoughts. No, the turn of his lips and the frozen way his eyebrows remained lifted made my own lips tremble and my hands shake.

"Gavin," I said. "Gavin, wake up." I shook his leg. He opened his eyes and stretched.

"Hi," he said. "How's he doing?"

"Look at him, Gavin," I said. Gavin leaned over and gazed at Jefferson's face.

"That's funny."

"It's weird, not funny. Jefferson?" I put my hand gently on his forehead. He didn't feel any warmer, which I took to be a good sign, but when his eyes opened, he gazed at me with a look of utter terror. "Jefferson?"

He groaned without opening his lips.

And then, without any warning, his whole body began to shake. It was as if he had touched an exposed electric wire. The sight of him in such a convulsion took my breath away. Even Gavin couldn't move or speak for a moment. Then I screamed.

"Jefferson!"

Gavin rushed to him and embraced him quickly. Beads of sweat had broken out on Jefferson's forehead and a small line of perspiration formed down his right temple and cheek. Saliva escaped from the corners of his mouth. He gagged and then his eyes went back in his head and he went limp in Gavin's arms.

"Gavin!"

Gavin, shocked himself, lowered Jefferson to the bed and then put his ear to Jefferson's little chest.

"His heart's beating very fast."

"We've got to get him to a doctor . . . to a hospital!" I cried.

Frantic now, I ran out of the room and screamed as loud and as hard as I could.

"Help! Help! Aunt Fern! Aunt Charlotte! Someone!"

Aunt Charlotte came running out of her bedroom, Luther pulling up his pants as he followed quickly behind.

"What's wrong, dear? What's wrong?"

"It's Jefferson! He's very, very sick. He's passed out," I said and began to cry. Luther went in to see.

"What the hell's all the noise?" Aunt Fern cried, sticking her head out from her doorway.

"It's Jefferson. He's sick," Aunt Charlotte told her.

"Oh no, not that again. So keep giving him aspirin and stop shouting. There are two people who need their beauty sleep down here," she complained and slammed the door.

"Luther wants us to take him to the hospital right away," Gavin said, emerging. "He says he's seen this before."

I looked at Luther who stood behind him, his face full of concern, his eyes dark, the lines in his forehead and temples deep.

"Oh Luther, what is it? What's wrong with my little brother?"

"Can't be certain, of course," he said slowly, "but it looks like what happened to my cousin Frankie thirty-odd years ago after he cut himself on a rusty plow blade."

"What . . ." I asked, my heart hesitating, my breath caught. Gavin and I looked at each other. "That cut on his leg," I said. Gavin nodded. I turned back to Luther. "What happened to your cousin, Luther?"

"He caught tetanus," he said and shook his head. He didn't have to continue. I knew that meant his cousin Frankie had died. Terrified, I hurried into my room and scooped up my clothing. I dressed quickly, my hands shaking the whole time, and then Gavin and I bundled Jefferson in his blanket. Gavin carried him out and we started down the corridor to the stairway. All the while, Jefferson never opened his eyes, never uttered a sound. My heart was pounding as I walked behind them. I kept my head down.

This was all my fault, I realized. If I hadn't run off and dragged my little brother with me . . .

The curse wasn't on him, I thought; it was on me, on my side of the family. I had no right to pull him under the same dark clouds and expose him to the same hard cold rain. Everything and everyone I touch suffers eventually, I concluded sadly.

"Oh dear, oh dear," Aunt Charlotte said, walking beside me and wringing her hands. "The poor little boy."

"What the hell's going on?" Aunt Fern called from behind as we reached the top of the stairway. Luther had already gone down and out to bring the truck around front. I didn't feel like saying anything to Aunt Fern and neither did Gavin. We ignored her and continued down the stairs.

"I'd better get some coffee up here soon!" she screamed.

"Don't you give her anything, Aunt Charlotte," I said when we reached the bottom of the stairs. "Don't even give her a glass of water. She doesn't deserve it."

Aunt Charlotte nodded, her attention and concern more on Jefferson. She followed us out to the truck.

"You sit with him up front," Gavin said, "and I'll sit in the rear of the truck. Get in first and I'll hand him in," he directed. Luther came around to help, but Gavin had firm control of it all. He placed Jefferson gently into my lap. I cradled his head against my bosom and rocked him as Luther got back into the truck.

"Oh dear, oh dear," Aunt Charlotte said, standing aside and wringing her hands. Gavin hopped on and we started down the bumpy driveway.

"Gonna hafta go all the way to Lynchburg," Luther said. "That's the nearest hospital and that little boy needs a hospital now."

I didn't reply. I tried to swallow, but couldn't. All I could do was nod and stare down at my little brother's sickly face. His lips were open very slightly, but his eyes were firmly closed, the eyeballs still.

Oh Mommy, I cried inside, I didn't mean for this to happen. I'm sorry; I'm so sorry.

I didn't realize I was crying until the first tear dripped off my chin and spattered on Jefferson's cheek. Then I sat back, took a deep breath, and prayed. I heard Gavin knock on the rear window and turned.

"Are you all right?" he asked. The wind was blowing through his hair as we traveled down the highway. I saw the deep concern in his eyes. I tried to speak, but couldn't get past the tremble in my lips. I shook my head and looked forward again at the oncoming road. Then I glanced at Luther. He was making the truck go as fast as it could. The engine sputtered and complained, but Luther's eyes were fixed on the highway like a man who had seen death before and was fleeing from the memories this new situation had resurrected.

* * *

It seemed like hours and hours before we saw the road sign that told us we were approaching the hospital. The overcast sky had grown darker and darker during the trip. I saw how the wind swayed the trees. People had begun putting on their headlights because it got so dark. I was sure we would be caught in a terrible downpour before we had reached the hospital, but all we had were a few drops on the windshield. When the buildings finally loomed before us, I let myself take a deep breath. The security man told us where the emergency room entrance was and we drove right to it. As soon as the truck came to a stop, Gavin hopped out and came around to open the door. Jefferson had not awoken, not uttered a sound the whole time. Gavin reached in carefully and gently lifted Jefferson off my lap. He backed away and I got out and followed him to the emergency room door.

"What happened?" a nurse asked the moment we entered.

"We think it might be tetanus," Gavin said. She came around the counter quickly and signaled for another nurse to bring over a gurney. Gavin lowered Jefferson to it and the two nurses quickly took over, one putting a blood pressure cuff on his arm, the other bringing a stethoscope to his chest. They both looked at each other with great concern and then one began pushing the gurney down the corridor toward an examination room, out of which a young doctor had just emerged. I followed behind.

"What do we have here?" he asked them.

"My brother got very sick," I said. "He cut himself a few days ago on a nail and we think he might have tetanus."

"He never had an inoculation?" the doctor asked.

"I don't know," I said. "I don't think so."

"What did he cut himself on?" he asked while he lifted one of Jefferson's eyelids to look at his pupil.

"A rusty nail . . . I'm sure," I said. The doctor looked up sharply.

"Well, where are your parents? Is that your father?" he asked, nodding toward Luther, who waited down the corridor with Gavin.

"No sir."

The first nurse whispered something to him and they pushed Jefferson into the examination room. The doctor followed. I started in, but the second nurse stopped me.

"Just wait out here," she said. "Go to the desk up there and give the receiving nurse the necessary information."

"But . . ."

She closed the door before I could offer any protest. My heart was pounding so fast, I thought I'd be the next one on a gurney. Tears burned my eyes. I backed away.

"What did they say?" Gavin asked.

"They want us to wait out here. I've got to give information to the nurse at the desk," I explained. He took my hand and we approached the counter. Luther had sat down on a chair in the hall and stared at us with that terrible expression of dread written all over his face. I looked back at the closed examination room door.

My little brother is going to die in that room, I thought. I brought him all the way here. He had held my hand and had trusted me from the moment we had left the hotel in Cutler's Cove, and now he's lying in a strange room, unconscious. My shoulders began to shake as my whole body shuddered. Gavin put his arm around me.

"He's going to be all right. Don't worry," he said.

"Is one of you a relative of the patient?" the nurse at the desk asked.

"Yes ma'am," I said, wiping my eyes. "I'm his sister."

"Well, would you please fill out this form. Name and address over here," she said, pointing with a pen. I took it from her hand and looked down at the paper. My eyes were so clouded with tears, everything looked hazy—the words joining together on the sheet.

"This has to be filled out," she said more firmly when I hesitated.

I wiped my eyes again and sucked in my breath. I nodded and began. I filled out as much as I could, but when it called for parent or guardian, I stopped and left it blank. She saw that immediately.

"Why didn't you put your parents' names here?" she asked.

"They're both dead, ma'am."

"Well . . . how old are you?"

"Sixteen."

"Is this your guardian?" she asked, nodding toward Luther, who hadn't moved or uttered a word.

"No, ma'am."

She looked annoyed.

"Who are you and your brother living with, Miss?" she demanded.

"No one," I said.

"No one?" Her confused smile turned quickly to a look of anger. "I don't understand. We need this information," she insisted.

I couldn't help myself. I just started to cry, hard and loud. Even Gavin's embrace didn't calm me. He helped me to a seat beside Luther and kept his arms around me, my face pressed into the nook between his shoulder and his neck. The nurse behind the desk didn't ask any more questions or make any more demands. After a while I stopped crying and sucked in my breath. I sat back, my eyes closed. When I opened them, I felt numb, stunned by the events.

Up until this moment, I wasn't aware of anyone else in the hospital but us, but suddenly, when I turned, I saw other people in the waiting room and other patients in the hallway—one man with a bloody bandage around his forearm, another man in a wheelchair, his head back, his eyes closed. There was a lot more activity around us, too. Nurses were going to and fro, some following doctors, some alone. A nurse's assistant was wheeling patients into the X-ray department. Down the well-lit corridor, I could see people waiting by an elevator, all of them probably coming to visit patients.

Finally, after what was an interminable period of waiting, the young doctor and one of the nurses emerged from the examination room and started down the corridor toward us. They paused at the desk and the nurse handed them the form I had filled out only partially. The doctor's eyebrows rose. The nurse said something to him and then he looked at us and continued to approach us. I held my breath. Gavin squeezed my hand tightly. Luther nodded, his own hands clasped on his lap.

"Christie Longchamp?" he said.

"Yes sir."

"Your brother's name is Jefferson," he said, looking at the chart.

"Yes sir."

"Well then, it does look like he has contracted tetanus. He should have had a shot immediately after that wound on his leg," he said with a note of chastisement in his voice. I tried to swallow, but couldn't. "Didn't your parents know about his injury?"

I shook my head.

"Her parents are both dead," Gavin said. "They were killed in a fire."

The doctor stared at him a moment, his eyes narrow. Then he turned to me.

"First we'll talk about your brother," he said. "He's in a coma, something which usually follows convulsions caused by tetanus."

"Will he be all right?" I asked quickly. I couldn't hold back.

The doctor looked at Luther and then at me again.

"The mortality rate with tetanus is influenced by the patient's age and the length of the incubation period. It's more serious for young children and especially for those not treated soon after the bacteria has been introduced to the body," he said with a cold air. "Don't you have a guardian?"

"Yes sir," I said looking down. "My uncle."

"Well he has to be informed immediately. There are important forms that have to be signed. I'm going ahead with emergency treatment, but I need to speak to your guardian right away," he said. "You people come from . . ." He looked at the chart. "Cutler's Cove, Virginia?"

"Yes sir."

"Are you visiting relatives?"

"Yes sir, my aunt."

"Oh, well can I speak with her?"

"We ain't got a phone at the house," Luther offered.

"Pardon?"

"This is . . . my uncle," I said.

"Your guardian? He's been sitting here all this time?" the doctor asked, his eyes incredulous.

"No sir. That's a different uncle."

"Look, Miss Longchamp," he said, settling back, "this is a grave situation. I want your guardian's name and telephone number immediately." He thrust the paper at me and took the pen out of his top pocket.

"Yes sir," I said and wrote Uncle Philip's name and telephone number.

"Fine," the doctor said, taking it back. He started to turn away.

"What about my brother?" I asked.

"He's being moved to the intensive care unit. We're hooking him up to an I.V. filled with an antitoxin. He's a very, very sick little boy," he said. He looked at Luther as if he instinctively knew Luther was familiar with the seriousness of the illness.

"Can I see him?" I asked.

"Only for a moment," the doctor said. "There's a waiting room up at ICU and a very restrictive period for visitations."

"Thank you," I said and got up. Gavin held my hand as we walked down the corridor to the examination room. When we looked in, we saw a nurse had just completed hooking up the I.V. Jefferson was already in a hospital gown, too.

"Your brother's things," she said, handing me the nightshirt and the blanket.

"Thank you." Gavin and I walked up to the gurney and looked down at Jefferson. I saw his eyeball twitch under the lid, and then his lips tremble and stop.

"Jefferson," I said. My throat ached so from my keeping myself from breaking out into hysterical tears, and my chest felt as if someone weighing three hundred pounds was standing on it. I took Jefferson's little hand into mine and held it for a few moments.

"Will he be all right?" Gavin asked the nurse.

"We'll have to wait and see," she said. "He's in good hands here," she added and offered us the first smile of hope. Gavin nodded.

"He's a strong little boy," he said, mostly for my benefit.

I leaned over and kissed Jefferson's cheek. Then I brought my lips to his ear.

"I'm sorry, Jefferson," I whispered. "I'm sorry I brought you along. Get better, please. Please, please," I chanted, the tears streaming down my cheeks.

"Christie. Come on. They're here to take him upstairs," he said.

He embraced me and we stood back and watched the orderly and the nurse begin to wheel Jefferson out of the room and down the corridor. We followed behind the gurney until they came to the elevator.

"Come up in about an hour or so," the nurse told us just as the doors were closing. We both stood there staring at the closed elevator. Luther came up behind us.

"It's gonna be a while," he said, "'fore we really know somethin' substantial."

"I'm not leaving," I said. He nodded. Then he reached into his pants pocket and produced some money.

"Take this," he said, offering it to Gavin. "You'll want something to eat or drink. I'm going back to see about Charlotte. I'll tell that sister of yours the way things is here," he told Gavin. Gavin nodded. "Maybe she'll have the decency to come this way and look after you."

"Thank you, Luther."

He fixed his eyes on me and I saw the tears locked within.

"I'll be prayin' for him," he said. "He's a fine little boy, one I wished I had myself."

Gavin and I watched him walk toward the exit. After he was gone, we turned and went to keep vigil outside the doors of the intensive care unit.

I fell asleep on and off with my head resting against Gavin's shoulder. We sat on a small imitation leather sofa in the intensive care waiting room. Across from us an elderly woman sat staring out the window. Occasionally, she dabbed her eyes with her lace handkerchief. When she looked at us, she smiled.

"My husband's had surgery," she offered. "He's stable, but with a man his age . . ." Her voice trailed off and she turned to the window again. Outside, the gray skies had begun to lighten here and there and the rain had stopped.

"Has it been an hour yet, Gavin?" I asked.

"A little more than an hour," he said. We got up and went to the ICU door. I took a deep breath and then we entered. The nurse at the desk in the center of the room looked up immediately. We saw patients hooked up to oxygen, one with his legs and arms in casts.

"We're here to see Jefferson Longchamp," Gavin said.

"You can stay only five minutes," she replied curtly.

"How is he?" I asked quickly.

"No change," she said. "He's down at the end on the right." We walked through the intensive care unit. I tried not to look at the other patients, all very seriously ill; but the sound of the heart monitors, the subdued murmur of the nurses' voices, the occasional moan and groan, the sight of bloody bandages and the row of semi-conscious and unconscious people was overwhelming. It made my heart heavy and every breath an effort. I couldn't help feeling we were treading on the boundary line between the land of the living and the land of the dead. My little brother was tottering.

Jefferson was in a separate room in an oxygen tent. The light was off so that the room was darkened. He looked the same, only they had him hooked up to a heart monitor as well as the I.V. now. The wound in his leg had been cleaned and bandaged. Gavin held me close as we both looked at him.

"I never dreamed he was this sick," Gavin said. "We should have done something last night."

"It's my fault; I completely forgot about him cutting himself on that nail."

"Don't you go blaming yourself," Gavin ordered perceptively.

We turned as a nurse entered to check Jefferson's I.V. and take his pulse.

"How is he?" Gavin asked quickly.

"It's a good sign that he hasn't had any more convulsions," she replied.

We remained until the nurse advised us to leave and then we went out and downstairs to the hospital cafeteria. I wasn't very hungry, but Gavin thought we should put something into our stomachs or we would just get weak and sick ourselves. I had some hot oatmeal and ate about half of it with a cup of tea. Afterward, we returned to the intensive care waiting room where we spent most of the day, going into the ICU whenever we could.

Other patients' relatives came and went. Some were talkative, most were not. Gavin and I slept on and off, thumbed through some magazines and simply stared out the window at the ever-clearing sky. The sight of blue patches and more foamy, cotton-like clouds warmed my heart. The next time we went into the intensive care unit, the head nurse told us that with every passing hour, he was improving.

"He's not out of the woods yet by far," she said, "but his condition hasn't worsened."

Cheered by her words, we returned to the hospital cafeteria. With improved appetites, we both ate a good deal more.

"I half-expected Fern might show," Gavin said. "I thought even she isn't that low."

"I hope they're not tormenting Aunt Charlotte and Luther," I said.

"I think Luther's about ready to heave them out," Gavin replied.

When we returned to the intensive care waiting room, we found Luther had returned and he had brought Homer along with him. Homer was dressed in a clean pair of slacks, a white shirt and tie. He had his hair brushed down as neatly as he could. He looked frightened and sad, but his eyes widened with pleasure when he saw us come in.

"Homer drove me near crazy to bring him here," Luther explained.

"That's very nice of you, Luther. Thank you for coming, Homer."

"How's he doin'?" Homer asked.

"He's better, but still very sick."

Homer nodded.

"I brought him something to play with," he said. "For when he gets better," he added and showed us one of those toys that fit in the palm of your hand. It was a little game where you had to jiggle the tiny silver balls and get them all into the holes.

"That thing's so old, it's an antique," Luther said and winked. He leaned forward to whisper. "I gave it to him when he was barely older than Jefferson."

"Thank you, Homer," I said. "I'll see that he gets it."

"What about my sister?" Gavin asked.

"Oh," Luther said. "Once she heard about Jefferson, she and that beanpole she's with high-tailed it."

"You mean they left?" Gavin asked, astounded. "Just left without finding out how Jefferson is?"

"They couldn't have run out of the house faster if it was on fire," Luther said. "I guess we won't miss 'em none," he added.

"I can't believe it," Gavin muttered.

We made our next visit in the intensive care unit. This time the nurses let us stay nearly twenty minutes and they permitted Homer to join us. He stood next to us, his hands crossed at his waist and never took his eyes off Jefferson's face.

When it came time to go, Homer stepped up to the tent.

"You get better, Jefferson. Get better real fast 'cause we still got a barn to paint and lots of other things to do," he said.

I took Homer's hand in mine and the three of us left, our heads bowed, each saying his own private prayer in his own way. When we stepped outside the intensive care unit, however, my heart sank. I should have anticipated it; I should have been prepared and thought what I would do, but my concern for Jefferson overrode every other thought, especially thoughts about myself.

There, standing beside the doctor, was Uncle Philip, a grim expression on his face. My eyes shifted from him to the doctor, who looked very angry, too.

"Everyone's been pretty sick with worry about you, Christie," he said. He turned to Gavin. "And your parents are beside themselves, too."

I lowered my eyes. I couldn't look at him.

"Luther and Charlotte shouldn't have permitted you to stay there," he continued. I lifted my eyes quickly and fixed them with a steel gaze on his.

"Don't you blame them for anything," I said sharply.

"Oh I don't," he said quickly. "I'm sure they didn't understand what was happening, but the point is . . ."

"What is the point?" Gavin snapped.

"The point for you, young man, is your parents are quite upset. They don't have the means to pay for your gallivanting all over the country. I have made arrangements for your instant return home," he said, pulling an airplane ticket out of his breast pocket. "I told them I would take care of this. There's a taxicab waiting outside the front entrance of the hospital to take you to the airport. You've got ten minutes to get down there," Uncle Philip said firmly.

"I'm not leaving Christie," Gavin said, stepping back to stand beside me.

"Christie's leaving too," Uncle Philip said, smiling. "She's going home."

I shook my head.

"No."

"Don't you want to be near your brother?" he asked. I looked at the doctor. "The doctor agrees that in a day or so, Jefferson will be able to be moved by ambulance and plane. We're taking him to Virginia Beach where I have already made arrangements for him to have private care at the hospital. You want your brother to have the best medical attention, don't you?"

"She's not going home with you," Gavin said. Uncle Philip glared at him a moment and then, softening his face, turned to me.

"Christie?"

"I've got to go home with him, Gavin," I said.

"No, you can't. We'll go to the police; we'll tell them everything that's happened. We'll . . ."

"Not now, not with Jefferson so sick," I said. "Don't worry. I'll be all right."

"Of course you will," Uncle Philip said. He looked at the doctor. "There's been some misunderstandings at home. Life has been hard for Christie since her parents' unfortunate deaths, but . . ."

"Misunderstandings!" Gavin cried. "You call what you did to her a misunderstanding!"

"Calm down, young man," the doctor said. "You're not in the street."

"But you don't understand . . ."

"It's not his problem to understand family matters," Uncle Philip said quickly. "You should be worrying about your parents. Your mother is sick because of this and your father . . ."

"Gavin, please," I said, squeezing his arm. "Not now. It's no use now. He's right. Go home first and see your parents. I've caused enough pain and trouble for enough people."

"But Christie, I can't let you go back with him. I can't."

"I'll be all right. I'll call you right away. All I want to do is be with Jefferson. He needs me now, Gavin. Please."

"But . . ."

"The taxi's waiting," Uncle Philip said, thrusting the airplane ticket at Gavin. "You're going to miss your flight and then you'll have to sit in an airport all night."

"Go on, Gavin," I pleaded. "Please." He stood there, his face full of frustration. I mouthed, "I love you."

He nodded and then turned to Uncle Philip and took the ticket.

"If you do one thing to her . . . one thing," he warned. Uncle Philip's face turned crimson.

"Don't you threaten me, young man," he said. He turned to the doctor. "Kids these days."

The doctor nodded.

With his head bowed, Gavin started down the corridor toward the exit.

"GAVIN!" I cried and ran to him. We embraced each other.

"Just call me," he said, "and I'll find a way to come to you. I swear."

He kissed me quickly and hurried away. My eyes went to Luther and Homer who had witnessed the confrontation silently. They were of one face—sad, sympathetic.

"Thank you, Luther. And please, tell Aunt Charlotte thank you for everything, too. Jefferson will write to you, Homer. As soon as he's better, I promise. And someday soon, we'll come back to see you."

He smiled. Slowly, I turned back to Uncle Philip. His face had broken into a grin from ear to ear.

"Christie," he said. "We'll fix everything again. Aunt Bet is anxious to see you and so are the twins. Everything's going to be all right. It'll be just as it was.

"I promise," he said, his eyes twinkling. "It will be just as it was, just like you never left."

The Past Embraces Me

AFTER UNCLE PHILIP COMPLETED ALL THE ARRANGEments for Jefferson's transfer to the hospital in Virginia Beach, we left to return to Cutler's Cove. It was one of the longest trips of my life even though we went by airplane because I was very uncomfortable sitting beside him. Despite his good looks and his immaculate and well-groomed appearance, he would always look ugly and dirty to me. For most of the journey, he behaved as though nothing unpleasant had occurred between us. He rattled on and on about the Cutler's Cove Hotel and how well the restoration was going. Then he talked about the twins, telling me he had convinced them both to take piano lessons.

"I hired your piano teacher," he said. "Now that you're back, maybe you can encourage them and give them some pointers every once in a while. I don't expect either of them to ever be as good as you are, but at least they're doing something worthwhile with their time during the summer."

I sat next to the window in the plane, with my back to him, gazing into the darkness. Occasionally, when we came to a break in the clouds, I could see a star, but it seemed as if it was falling farther and farther away, or I was sinking. I saw another airplane, much higher, going in the opposite direction and wished I was on it.

"I know the twins will be happy to see you," he continued. Both Melanie and Richard were very sad when they learned you had left in the middle of the night with Jefferson."

"I doubt that," I muttered. I don't know if he heard me or not. At this point I thought he was just babbling to keep the silence from penetrating the shield of lies he had forged.

"Of course, your aunt Bet was beside herself with worry. She couldn't eat for days and she's so thin as it is. Both of us feel very responsible for you and Jefferson, as responsible as we feel for our own children. Now that you're back, I can promise you things will be different," he continued.

I gazed at him quickly. He was sitting stiffly in his seat and looking ahead as if I were sitting across from him instead of beside him. But his eyes were glassy and still. He looked like a man asleep, talking in a dream.

"Yes, things will be different. We've learned how to get along with each other. It takes time, takes getting used to, just like anything that important would," he said, nodding. "We've all made mistakes. Fate has thrown us together quickly, abruptly, harshly, but we'll contend with it. It's in our blood to be strong."

He blinked rapidly and then looked at me and smiled.

"We have another new maid, you know. We've replaced Mrs. Stoddard. She didn't work out . . . too much of a personality clash with Betty Ann.

You know how hard it is to get good help these days. Everyone thinks he or she is a manager and a boss instead of an employee. But I leave the running of the house up to Betty Ann. She's more adept at that. I just don't have the patience, not with all I have to do with the hotel now."

Finally, he stopped talking and stared blankly ahead. I sat back in my seat and closed my eyes, but a little while later, I felt his hand cover mine on the arm rest. I opened my eyes and found him staring at me, his face inches from mine.

"Christie, oh Christie, why did you run off like that? I never meant to hurt you or frighten you, and certainly never meant to chase you away," he whispered.

"What did you expect I would do, Uncle Philip?" I asked, shaking my head in disgust.

"We made promises to each other. I thought you would keep them," he said.

"Promises? What promises?"

"Don't you remember? I do," he said, sitting back again, his eyes closed, a smile on his face. "We made a pact. We promised to trust and depend on each other forever and ever, to tell each other things we wouldn't tell anyone else.

"I told you," he continued, turning back to me and putting his hand over mine again, "that whatever made you sad would make me sad, and whatever would make you happy would make me happy. Don't you remember? We sealed it with a kiss," he said, "a wonderful, warm kiss."

I did remember that time in my room, but it had been all his idea. I had said nothing; I was too amazed and confused by his expression of deep affection then.

"If something was bothering you, you should have come to me," he said, nodding. "You should have knocked on my door and told me and I would have done everything I could to fix the problem."

"Fix the problem?" Is that all it was to him—a small problem?

"Yes," he said. "I told you many times—I'm here for you. And for Jefferson, of course. Why, as soon as that doctor called and I had heard what had happened to Jefferson, I rushed out of the house without so much as telling Betty Ann where I was going. I didn't have time for that; I left that for Julius to do. You and Jefferson needed me," he said. "I made all the arrangements quickly and flew out to get you.

"And now we're together again," he concluded, smiling. "You're safe. You'll always be safe with me."

I stared at him. Was he just pretending or had he really forgotten what he had done to me? I was tempted to bring it up, to shout it at him, but instead I turned away, closing my eyes and imagining I was like a clam with its shell shut tight. If I squeezed myself firmly enough and dreamt of other things, I could lock him out of my life, I thought. I would look at him when he spoke and I would nod, but I wouldn't hear him, nor would I really see him. In time he would be as invisible as a ghost. I would even get to the point where if he touched me, I wouldn't feel it.

Julius was waiting for us at the airport, happy to see me.

"How's Jefferson doing?" he asked immediately.

"He's going to be all right," Uncle Philip told him. "With the special and proper care I'm arranging, that is."

"No luggage?" Julius asked surprised.

"No," I said quickly. I didn't want to get into what had happened after I had run away.

"Let's just get home," Uncle Philip said, taking my arm and leading me out of the airport. "Wait until you see the progress with the restoration of the hotel," he said, getting into the rear of the limousine with me. "Even in the short time you've been away, there has been quite a change, right, Julius?"

"Yes sir."

Been away? I thought. He acts as if I had taken a short holiday, gone to visit friends or been to school somewhere. How could he go on pretending like this? How could I? I wondered. Uncle Philip obviously had hopes that this little episode (as he liked to think of it) would simply go away, burst like a soap bubble. However, those hopes were dashed the moment we drove up to the house and opened the front door. Aunt Bet saw to that. She had obviously been waiting by the window in the sitting room and had seen us drive up. Her face was full of fury and anger. Her eyes were so hot I thought they could singe with a glance.

"Well, are you happy now?" she snapped the moment I set foot in the entryway. She stepped forward, her bony hands on her thin hips so firmly that her elbows stuck out sharply. I thought they would cut right through her skin and in moments I would see the ghostly white bone. Her neck muscles strained, causing ripples to appear along the sides of her neck, and her lips stretched thin and taut, revealing her clenched gray teeth beneath.

"Are you happy you caused all this turmoil? Are you happy you had us all frantic and worried and crazy with concern? Are you?" she demanded, her voice as shrill as the screams of frightened terns.

"Betty Ann," Philip began, "let's . . ." She pivoted and threw him a look of rage that made his mouth snap shut.

"Don't you start telling me to calm down, Philip Cutler," she said, wagging her small fist in his face. "Don't you try to defend her. I'm the one sitting here waiting, not knowing everything that's happening. I'm the one left in the dark. I've got to hear it from help, from servants sent to give me messages as if I were some sort of second-class citizen."

"Now Betty Ann, no one meant to leave you out. It was just that I had to act fast with Jefferson very sick and all . . ."

"Look at what you've done!" she screamed at me. "Your brother nearly died!"

My lips began to tremble. I folded my arms under my breasts and stared at the floor while she ranted and raved.

"We have all this grief, all this tragedy, one thing after another. Everyone's trying to deal with it, to make the best of things, to restore a bit of normalcy to our shattered lives and you . . . you rotten and spoiled . . ."

"I am not rotten and spoiled!" I shot back, my spine straightening into a steel rod. "And whose life was shattered? Certainly not yours!"

"Uh huh," she said, shaking her head. "Uh huh." She smiled coldly. It was a sickly, small smile around her lips. "I didn't think I would find you remorseful. I didn't think the pain you put us through would make any difference to you. You think only of yourself." The smile faded quickly. "Well, you're under our supervision. We're responsible for you and for how you behave. You've done a very bad thing and you must be punished."

She straightened up to face me, her eyes fixed on mine.

"You are confined to your room until further notice. You may come down only for meals and then you march right back up there, you hear me.

You will receive no phone calls nor make any, nor will you be permitted any visitors. And let me warn you, young lady," she said, stepping closer and sticking her long, bony forefinger at me, "don't even think of violating any of my rules anymore.

"Go on upstairs. Go on!" she ordered, pointing to the stairway. I looked at Uncle Philip, who seemed subdued by her outburst. Then I charged away from both of them and pounded my way up the stairs. As I hurried to my room, I saw the door to what was Jefferson's and now Richard's room, too, open. He peered out at me, his face full of self-satisfaction.

"What are you looking at?" I snapped.

He kept his smile, but he closed the door.

I burst into my room and stood fuming for a few moments. How dare she talk to me like that? I thought. I should have told her the truth. I should have told her why I ran away. It would have left her so flabbergasted, she wouldn't be able to speak for days. And when she did speak, she would stutter. I felt good knowing I could smash her with the truth any time I saw fit. But once my fury subsided, I realized that announcing what Uncle Philip had done to me was not the easiest thing to do. It would hurt me as well. It was a double-edged sword, just like most tools of revenge.

No, it was better to ignore her, too, I thought, to pretend she didn't exist, to pretend none of them existed. I would tolerate them until Jefferson was well and then, I would think of something else to do. I had no other choice.

In many ways it was good to be home, to be in my own room again and to see the stuffed animals Mommy and Daddy had given me. It was wonderful to smell my own linen and use my brush while sitting at my vanity table. My room was filled with good memories, too, and they were all memories that reminded me of times with Mommy and with Daddy.

I was exhausted. Now that I had stopped moving, now that I was settled in my room again, the events of the past twenty-four hours plowed over me. All the emotions, the tensions, the horror and the hardship came rushing back at me, drowning me in a sea of weariness, draining me of whatever iota of energy remained in my body.

I began to undress for bed, but when I went to my closet to hang up my clothes, I was greeted with another welcome-home surprise. My wonderful Sweet Sixteen dress had been sliced in two. It lay on the floor like a fatally wounded sea gull, the shoulders of the bodice spread like two wings. It had been cut right at the bottom of the neckline and the billowing skirt torn and shredded. It looked like it had been attacked and hacked by a madman.

"Oh no," I cried, kneeling down and embracing the ravaged garment to me. "Oh no!" I screamed. "No!" The door of my room was thrust open.

"What is it? Why are you screaming? Don't you realize how late it is?" Aunt Bet demanded.

"Look," I said, holding my dress out toward her. "Look at what one or both of your precious special twins did."

She gazed at the dress and smirked.

"I'm sure neither of them would have done that. They don't do those kinds of things. Anyway, it's your own fault," she said, folding her arms and straightening as firmly and stiffly as an iron pole. "If you hadn't run away, you would have been here to take care of your things, wouldn't you? Now, stop screaming and go to sleep," she added and closed the door. Then I heard a key turn in the lock and realized she had locked me in my own room.

I sank to the floor, clutching the dress. All I could see was Mommy's radiant smile when she had come in and seen me in it. I felt as if the tears that were streaming down my face were her tears. She was crying through me and with me. My body shook with the sobs until my stomach ached. I sat there bent over with the soft crinoline against my face until finally I could shed no more tears. Then I rose slowly and laid the dress out on the bed and fell asleep beside it, hoping that somehow when I woke up in the morning, I would find that it had all been one long, horrible dream.

I would wake up and it would be the morning of my Sweet Sixteen party. Mommy and Daddy would be alive, Jefferson would be well, Gavin would be coming along with all the wonderful guests and dear friends like Aunt Trisha. The sky would be blue and the ocean would look crystal-clear and fresh.

Was there ever, ever a time like that?

The only thing that got me up in the morning was my desire to find out about Jefferson. Despite the late hour at which I had gone to sleep, Aunt Bet was determined to keep me from sleeping late anyway. She pounded on my door and then opened it abruptly.

"Still in bed?" she asked. I wiped my eyes and sat up slowly. "We have a new maid who follows very specific orders. Breakfast is served only once. If you miss it, you don't eat until lunch and if you miss that, you don't eat until dinner. We're all dressed and ready to go down so I would advise you to get out of bed and get dressed rapidly if you want anything to eat."

"I want to know about my brother," I said. "That's all I want."

"Suit yourself," she said and closed the door.

I fell back against the pillow. My eyes shifted to my torn dress again and my heart ached. Finally, I rose and went to my dresser drawers to get fresh undergarments and then go into the bathroom to shower, but when I pulled open my drawer, I stepped back in horror. Dead worms and clumps of mud had been tossed over my panties.

This was all Richard's work, I thought, but it would be no good to call Aunt Bet in to see it. She didn't care and she would only defend him. I pulled out the drawer and carried it into the bathroom where I emptied the mud and dead worms into the toilet. I took out my panties and put the drawer back. Then I looked around the room. Who knew what else he and his sister had done here? What else would I find broken or spoiled?

I did find more vandalism. Some of my perfumes and colognes had been mixed together and ruined. There were globs of skin cream in my shoes, lipstick smeared on blouses, and water had been poured into one of my jewelry boxes. I repaired as much of the damage as I could and then took my shower, but by the time I was ready to go downstairs, Aunt Bet had declared the breakfast hour over. She did so by appearing at my door before I opened it and turning the key in the lock again.

"Try not to miss lunch," she shouted through the locked door. I pulled on the handle.

"Let me out of here," I demanded. I pounded the door. "Aunt Bet, open this door. I have to find out about Jefferson. Aunt Bet!" I pounded again and again, but she didn't respond. Furious, I kicked at the door, but only hurt my foot. I paused, seething, and then I heard Richard's whisper. He had his lips up against the opening between the jamb and the door.

"Why don't you crawl out your window," he said and laughed.

"You little bastard. When I get out of here . . ." I pulled and pulled on the handle until my arms ached.

"Aunt Bet! Please. Open the door!" I waited, but it was silent. "Uncle Philip!" I cried. "Let me out!" No one came even though I pounded and cried for hours. When Aunt Bet's scheduled lunch hour began, she climbed the stairs and came to my room. She unlocked the door and stood there gazing down at me. I was sprawled on the floor where I had stopped pounding and calling.

"How dare you lock me in like this?" I said, rising slowly.

"Maybe now you'll understand the importance of schedules," she said. "Our lives are very organized now and we don't want anything to disrupt them."

"Don't you ever, ever lock me in here again," I said. She held her cold smile.

"What will you do?" she asked. "Run away again?"

It was as if a cold knife had been dragged down my back along my spine. I suddenly realized she had been happy Jefferson and I had run off. She didn't care; she didn't want us to return. She was hoping we had gone to live with someone else. Revenge, no matter how self-destructive it might be, was suddenly worth it.

"Why do you think I ran away? What do you think was the real reason?"

"I wouldn't know," she said, but she had an anxious look in her eyes. I folded my arms across my chest and stepped toward her, my own eyes firmly fixed on hers.

"You never asked Uncle Philip, did you? You must have been awake that night. You must have known when he left your bed and came into my room," I fired at her with a tone of meanness that amazed even me.

"What?" She stepped back. "What are you saying, you horrible child?"

"He came into my room. He came into my bed," I told her. Her mouth opened and her eyes widened. She shook her head and started to speak, but her lips moved without producing a sound. "He forced himself on me; it was horrible, horrible. He kept telling me he couldn't stand being near you, touching you."

She shook her head vehemently.

"I tried to fight him off, but he was too strong and too determined. In the end . . . he raped me."

She brought her hands to her ears and uttered the ugliest, most twisted scream. Then she reached out to slap me, but I caught her hand in midair.

"Don't touch me!" I told her, "and don't ever lock me in my room again. Don't even think of it!"

She pulled her hand free and fled from me. She retreated to her own bedroom and slammed the door.

"Good riddance," I cried and then I took a deep breath. It felt like a small fire had started in my chest. I hadn't realized how rigidly I had been holding myself. My ribs ached. Although I had driven her off, I didn't feel proud of myself. Even now that it was over and my fury had subsided, I could easily imagine how hateful and ugly I had appeared. It was a side of myself I didn't want to make visible, for I knew it left scars afterward. Maybe no one else could see the scars, but I could. The worst thing vile and repulsive people like Aunt

Bet could do to you was make you like them. That was what she had succeeded in doing right now.

I went downstairs to have some lunch. Melanie and Richard were already seated at the table, he with his napkin tucked in his collar and she with hers on her lap. Both of them sat up perfectly straight, their soup spoons gripped correctly and poised over their steaming bowls of chowder. They looked more like mannequins than real people.

"I found all the terrible things you did in my room while I was away," I told them. "You won't get away with it. Believe me."

My fiery gaze made them both shift their eyes to their soup. Then Richard recuperated and fired back.

"Jefferson's going to die," he said out of the corner of his mouth. "Mother told us so this morning."

"That's a lie. He's getting better. He's being brought to the hospital back here the moment he can travel," I said. He smiled slyly.

"My father just told you that to get you to come home," he said confidently. I looked at Melanie who was staring at me like some coldly analytical scientist anxious to see what my reaction to this news would be.

"You're horrible . . . two monsters!" I cried and in one swift move, I dumped their bowls of soup on their laps. They both screamed and jumped up and away from the table as the liquid quickly went through their clothes and scalded them. Without waiting for Aunt Bet's arrival, I turned and fled.

I ran out of the house, down the steps and toward the hotel. All of the debris had been cleared and the new walls had been started. As I approached, the workers on this side turned and a moment later, Uncle Philip emerged from the group to greet me.

"You have a family of monsters," I began. "I hate them!"

"Now, everyone has to learn how to readjust." He held up his hands. "In time . . ."

"I'll never adjust to them . . . or you!" I said, my chest heaving with each breath. For a moment I simply glared at him. He looked confused, hurt. "The twins told me you lied about Jefferson. They said he's not coming to a hospital here," I said. He smiled.

"That's nonsense. They're just teasing you. Matter of fact, I received the phone call this morning and I was on my way to see you. Jefferson's out of the coma and he will arrive at the hospital at eight tonight. You and I will be there when he comes."

"Really? This isn't another lie?"

"Would I lie about such a thing?" He put his hand on my shoulder and I pulled back as if his hand was on fire. "Christie, please . . ."

"Don't touch me. I don't want you to ever touch me again."

"Christie. We love you. We . . ."

"Love me? Do you know she locked me in my room?"

"She's still a little upset."

"And you let her. You let her do everything she wants," I accused.

"Betty Ann runs the house now and I . . ."

"She runs everything and everyone around her. But not me. I told her what you did. I told her!" I screamed, turned and stormed off. I didn't return to the house until late in the day. In the interim, I went downtown and bought myself some lunch. I walked on the beach for a while and then sat behind the hotel and watched them work on the building. When I did reenter the house, I found it deathly quiet. I marched up to my room. The door to

Melanie's room was open so I looked in as I passed and saw the two of them sitting on the floor, a game of Chinese checkers between them. They glared up at me hatefully. When I paused, they both looked terrified and shifted their eyes to their game.

The door to Aunt Bet and Uncle Philip's bedroom remained closed. I wondered if she had shut herself in there all day. I didn't feel sorry for her; I was just curious. At exactly six-fifteen, however, she came to my doorway and knocked gently. She looked like she had been crying for hours. Now her face had that dry, quiet look, the look of someone moving through the paces without thinking or feeling.

"Dinner is being served," she said and turned away before I could speak. I wasn't very hungry, nor did I look forward to sitting at the table with any of them, but I went downstairs. The twins glanced at me quickly and then looked down at their plates and settings. Uncle Philip was the most animated, but even he looked like a puppet waiting for his strings to be tugged. The new maid served the food without uttering a sound. She was a young girl, but one who had a prematurely aged face. The way she moved about the table indicated she was terrified of Aunt Bet, frightened of making a mistake. I was the only one who thanked her. Her eyes lightened, but she did no more than nod slightly and retreat to the kitchen.

Because they were all so quiet and withdrawn, I was able to pretend and to imagine myself sitting at the table months and months back in time. I listened as my memory replayed some of the funny things Daddy had said. I heard Mommy's laughter and saw Jefferson smile. I imagined Mrs. Boston hovering over us, telling us not to let this or that get cold. I was so lost in my reverie, it took the new maid twice to get my attention. I hadn't even heard the telephone ring.

"She's not to receive any phone calls," I heard Aunt Bet say. "Tell whoever it is . . ."

"The operator says it's long distance," the maid explained.

"Long distance?" I shot up out of my seat.

"No one talks on the phone during dinner," Aunt Bet declared. "It's not polite; it's . . ."

I glared at her. She glanced at Uncle Philip, who looked down at his food, and then she shook herself as if she had just had a terrible chill and went back to her own meal. I went to the phone. It was Gavin.

"I tried to call you all day," he said, "but someone kept telling me you were out or asleep."

"It's horrible here, more horrible than ever," I told him. "As soon as Jefferson is well again, I'm leaving."

"Has Philip . . ."

"He hasn't come near me. Gavin, I told her; I told Aunt Bet. She drove me to it," I said.

"Really? What did she say?"

"She ran away from me, screaming, and now they're all like zombies, but I don't care."

"I've told my mother and she's talking to Daddy. They're going to discuss what to do," he said.

"Tell them not to do anything until Jefferson is well. I don't want any new problems until then," I said.

"I'm worried about you, Christie. All I do is lie around and think about you," he told me.

"I'll be all right, Gavin. I'm not letting them abuse me anymore. Jefferson's being flown in tonight. We're going to the hospital to be with him when he arrives," I said.

"Call me as soon as you know anything, okay? Promise?"

"You don't need me to promise, Gavin. I'll call you. You and Jefferson are the only two people I care about right now."

"I love you, Christie. I loved all of our tender moments at The Meadows," he said softly.

"Me too."

"I'll wait for your phone call," he said. "Bye."

"Bye."

I cradled the phone and returned to the dinner table. They all looked up in anticipation when I arrived.

"I'm not hungry anymore," I announced. "I'll wait upstairs, Uncle Philip. Call me when you're ready."

"Ready for what?" Aunt Bet demanded.

"We're going to the hospital," he said. "Jefferson's on his way."

"You didn't tell me that," she said.

"Didn't I? Oh. Well, it must have just slipped my mind. We had a busy day working on the hotel today," he said quickly and looked down at his food. Aunt Bet scowled at him and then shifted her eyes at me.

"I told you what she did to the twins today. You were going to speak to her about it, Philip. Well?"

He looked up at me.

"Now's not the time," he told her.

"It certainly is the time. Why . . ."

"It's not the time!" he declared with more firmness in his voice than he had shown since I had returned.

Aunt Bet turned crimson and pressed her lips together. She nodded, her head bobbing as if her neck were a spring on which it rested.

"I'll wait upstairs," I repeated and left them sitting and eating in their morgue-like atmosphere.

A little more than a half-hour later, Uncle Philip knocked on my door. He had changed his clothes and wore the strangest things—a pair of jeans, sneakers, a black sweatshirt and a black and gold jacket that had his name embroidered above the breast pocket.

"Ready?" he asked, smiling. He saw how I was staring. "Oh, this is my high school jacket with my varsity letter," he explained and turned around to show me the Emerson Peabody patch sewn on the back of the jacket. "Still fits pretty good, eh?"

I rose slowly and put on my own light cotton jacket. Something frightened me about his wearing his high school clothes. I didn't know why it should, but it did. He stepped back as I walked out of my room.

"You look very nice," he said. "Very nice."

I wondered if Aunt Bet was coming along with us at least to pretend some interest in Jefferson, but she sat downstairs reading and listening to the twins tinker on the piano. None of them even looked our way as we proceeded to the front door. Uncle Philip opened it for me. I was expecting Julius and the limousine, but Uncle Philip had brought his own, rarely used car up front instead.

"Where's Julius?" I asked.

"It's his night off," Uncle Philip said.

"I'm sure he would have wanted to come."

"Oh, Julius has a girlfriend, a widow he sees over in Hadleyville. He even hints about getting married," Uncle Philip said, smiling. He opened the door for me and I got into the car. Then he moved around quickly to get in the front seat and drive us off.

Thc night sky was overcast so that even the sliver of moon was hidden. The darkness seemed thicker to me, especially when we left Cutler's Cove and headed toward Virginia Beach. Uncle Philip was oddly silent. I had been expecting him to babble just the way he had on our plane trip back, but all he did was drive and stare out at the road. When I gazed at him, I saw a strange, soft smile form on his lips.

"What a night, what a night," he finally said. I didn't think anything of it, although I wouldn't have called this night very remarkable. The ocean on our right looked inky. I didn't even see one small boat light. It was as if the stormy sky had joined with the sea and one ran into the other. A night sky without any stars or moon was just a vast empty wasteland of bleak darkness to me.

"You were wonderful," he added a few moments later.

"Pardon me?"

"The faces on the people in the audience . . ." He looked at me. "You couldn't see them like I could, not with the lights in your eyes. I know. I've been on a stage, too."

"Stage? What are you talking about, Uncle Philip?" My heart began to pound.

"You've got the prettiest voice I've ever heard. And I'm not just saying that," he said quickly.

"What?"

"I'm so proud of you, proud you're my girlfriend," he said and suddenly he slowed down and turned the car onto a beach road.

"Uncle Philip!" I sat up. "Where are you going?"

"To the top of the world, remember? I promised I would show it to you. Well, here it is," he said, coming to a stop. He sat back and looked out the window at the pitch-dark night. "Ever see so many lights?"

"What lights? What are you talking about? Uncle Philip, we're on our way to the hospital . . . to Jefferson."

"I told you," he said, not hearing me. "I told you I would teach you things; I would show you things." He slid over to my side and put his arm around my shoulders.

"Stop!" I cried. "Uncle Philip."

He clutched my shoulder firmly and started to bring me toward him, his lips moving toward mine.

"Dawn . . . oh Dawn," he said.

I screamed and pushed my hand into his face, digging my nails into his cheeks to push him back. Then I spun around and grabbed hold of the door handle. He seized the collar of my jacket, but I opened the door and pulled myself forward. My jacket came off in his hands. I felt his fingernails tear down the back of my neck in the process, but I wasn't concerned with the pain; I was only thinking of escape.

As soon as I was out of the car, I ran down the beach.

"DAWN!"

I heard him coming after me. The ocean roared to my right and there seemed to be miles of sand to my left. I charged forward, tripping and falling on the beach and then pulling myself up and running again. Just when I thought I was away from him, however, I felt his arms wrap around my waist and we both went down on the sand.

"I want . . . to show . . . to teach you . . . things," he gasped. His hands were over my breasts and his fingers began to fumble with the buttons on my blouse. I kicked up and twisted myself wildly to get out from under him, but he was too heavy and too strong. His fingernails tore down the side of my neck and onto my chest. I screamed and screamed and then I clutched a handful of sand and turned to him.

Even in the pitch darkness, I could see his eyes gleaming, his skin moist with perspiration.

"Dawn . . ."

"I'm not Dawn! I'm not!" I screamed and tossed the sand into his face.

He cried out and when he brought his hands to his eyes, I spun over, slipped out from under him and scampered to my feet. Then I charged away again, this time running to my left. I ran and ran until I heard the sound of a car and realized I had reached the highway. I broke out onto the road, into the headlights of the oncoming vehicle. I heard the brakes squeal and saw the car veer to the left, but the driver never stopped. He kept going, his tail lights becoming smaller and smaller in the darkness, like the eyes of a retreating wolf.

I walked on and on, afraid now that one of the oncoming cars might be Uncle Philip. Finally, I saw the outskirts of Cutler's Cove. But I didn't go into the village. I turned up the road that led to Bronson Alcott's house instead. It took me nearly an hour more to reach his home on the hill. My clothes torn, my legs aching, dirty and sweaty, I rapped on the door and waited. He opened it himself.

"Christie!" he said in shock, and I fell forward into his arms.

Still in a daze, I lay on the sofa in the living room. Bronson had Mrs. Berme bring a wet cloth to put on my forehead and then went himself to fetch me a glass of water. He returned with it quickly and then he helped me sit up so I could drink.

"Now begin slowly," he said when I lay back

against the pillow on the sofa, "and tell me everything. I didn't even know you had returned. I'm surprised and very upset that no one told me. Your uncle and aunt knew how concerned I've been."

"It doesn't surprise me that he never called you," I said and took a deep breath before starting. Even now, even after this frightening and horrible episode with Uncle Philip, it was difficult for me to seek Bronson's help. It embarrassed me, and even though I was sure everyone would tell me I had no reason to feel guilty and ashamed, I couldn't help but have those feelings.

Bronson listened attentively, his eyebrows lifting when I began to describe my reason for first running away. He gazed at Mrs. Berme and she left the room, assuming he wanted us to be alone to discuss such personal matters.

Afterward, Bronson sat back, stunned. Then he looked at me sympathetically.

"Betty Ann told me you ran away because you were very upset over her household rules. After you and I had had that earlier discussion, I just assumed that was the reason," he said apologetically. "I should have paid more attention to some of the things you were telling me. I'm sorry. I would have never permitted him to fetch you and Jefferson and put you through such a horrible experience. Where did this latest episode occur?" he asked.

"He was taking me to see Jefferson at the hospital," I said and I described the beach road Uncle Philip had taken. Bronson nodded, his face hardening, his eyes growing small and sharp. Then he stood up and went to the telephone. I heard him call the local police.

"This is all very nasty business," he said, returning. "You've been through a terrible time, but it's all going to end now. I promise you that," he said firmly. "You and Jefferson will come to live with me. If you want to, that is."

"Oh yes," I said quickly. "I always did."

He nodded and then smiled.

"It might be nice having a little boy around here. The house could use the pitter-patter of young feet and the sound of a child's laughter again," he said. "And goodness knows, it needs the gentle touch of a young lady once more," he added, looking toward the portrait of his long-dead sister. "I look forward to you and your brother . . ."

"Jefferson!" I said sitting up quickly. "I'm not sure Uncle Philip was telling me the truth now. Maybe he wasn't transferred. Maybe he's still in Lynchburg!"

"I'll find out about him right away," Bronson said. "In the meantime, you go into the bathroom and wash those nasty scratches. I'll have Mrs. Berme bring you some disinfectant. I'm sorry," he said again, "I'm sorry I wasn't more aware of how difficult things were for you and Jefferson."

"Don't blame yourself. You had your hands full with my grandmother, Bronson."

"Yes," he said, finally admitting it. "Yes, I did. But strange as it may seem, I miss her, even in her fragile state of mind. Every once in a while, she would become herself again and we would have some precious moments," he said, smiling at his recollections. "But now I'll have you and your brother to cheer up this big, sad house." He pushed down on his knees and stood up. "Go on," he said. "Take care of your injuries and let me call the hospital."

I went to the bathroom and peeled off my blouse slowly, my shoulders aching and my skin burning in spots. When I looked at myself in the mirror, it seemed I still had the imprint of terror on my face. My eyes remained wild, my hair disheveled. I traced the scratches on my collarbone and chest and then squeezed my eyes shut so I wouldn't start to cry again. Mrs. Berme knocked on the bathroom door and then came in to give me the medicine.

"You poor dear," she said, looking at my back. I hadn't realized how scraped up I was. It must have happened when he threw me to the ground and I struggled to get out from under him, I thought. Mrs. Berme washed and dressed my wounds without asking any embarrassing questions. A little while later, Bronson came to tell us Jefferson was indeed at the hospital in Virginia Beach.

"He's doing fine, too," he added.

"Can we go see him?" I asked.

"Absolutely, my dear. If you're sure you're up to it, that is," he added.

"Oh, I'm up to it. I never thought I would miss him as much as I do."

Bronson laughed. We heard the doorbell ring and Mrs. Berme scurried off to see who it was. It was a tall, dark-haired policeman. I followed Bronson down the corridor slowly to greet him in the entryway.

"Evening, Mr. Alcott," he said. He looked at me. "This is Dawn?"

"Dawn? No, no, this is her daughter, Christie. What made you say Dawn?" Bronson asked. I stepped closer to him and he took my hand quickly. It was eerie to hear a policeman use my mother's name like that.

"Well, we went down to the beach, to where you described, to begin our search and we found the car still there. A short while afterward, Charley Robinson, that's my partner," he explained, gazing down at me, "Charley, he hears someone on the beach. So we walked out aways and sure enough, we heard him screaming for Dawn."

"Oh no," I said, pressing my hand to my heart.

"Mr. Cutler?" Bronson asked.

"Yes sir, himself . . . wandering about screaming. We practically had to carry him off the beach. He insisted Dawn was still out there."

"Where is he?" Bronson asked.

"He's in the back of the patrol car now. He's not in too good a shape, Mr. Alcott. I came up here because I was wondering . . ."

"Yes," Bronson said quickly. "Thank you, Henry. I think Mr. Cutler needs a doctor more than he needs a judge right now . . . a psychiatrist."

"I see."

"You know what to do?"

"Yes sir. We'll take care of it, and you will follow up?" he added, looking at me as well as Bronson. Bronson put his arm around my shoulder.

"Yes, Henry. Thank you," Bronson said and shook the policeman's hand.

The policeman opened the door and went down the steps to the patrol car. I stepped into the doorway with Bronson and we both looked out as the patrol car started away. In the outside lights we could easily see Uncle Philip in the back seat. He turned as the patrol car began its journey down the driveway, and then he pressed his face against the rear window. It looked like he was screaming my mother's name, and although I couldn't really hear it, the echo rippled down my spine and made me shudder.

"It's over, Christie," Bronson whispered, embracing me more tightly. "I promise you . . . it's all over."

Epilogue

INDEED IT WAS OVER, AND INDEED IT HAD JUST BEGUN.

During one of our frequent walks on the beach when I was a little girl, Mommy and I once came upon a dead fish in the sand. It frightened me to see it so still with its eye so glassy. I began to cry. Mommy picked me up and held me as the tide came in and washed around the fish, slowly pulling it back into the sea.

"Will it swim again, Mommy?" I asked her.

"In a way," she said. "It will change into something else, be born again."

"I want to see," I demanded. I was still a child and thought I could command the sun in the morning and the stars at night simply by closing my eyes and wishing hard enough.

"We can't see that," she told me. "Some things are too magical for us to see. Instead, we have to believe in them without seeing. Can you believe in the fish?" she asked me, smiling. "Can you believe in the magic?"

I nodded, even though I wasn't sure what she meant. But I watched the fish float and bob on the waves, and it seemed to me that it did turn and dive and go off. I wanted to believe. I still had a child's faith that anything good and beautiful would never end.

As I grew older, I came to realize that we couldn't command the sun and the stars to appear, but we could feel the sun's warmth and be dazzled by the night sky and that was magic enough. I also understood that each day of our lives, some new part of us was born and some old part of us died.

There was so much I wanted to die, to bury forever in the deepest regions of my memory. How painful those days and weeks after my parents' deaths were. It seemed the agony and the turmoil would never end, but Bronson's promise came true.

Bronson handled the aftermath of my episode with Uncle Philip on the beach as discreetly as possible. Whatever had shattered in Uncle Philip's mind that night, it remained shattered for some time afterward. He couldn't handle his routine responsibilities and had to remain in professional care. Aunt Bet was overwhelmed by the rapid turn of events. In the end she couldn't face people in the community and she decided to move herself and the twins to her parents' estate.

Jefferson made a complete recovery from his illness and when he heard that we were going to move into Buella Woods and live with Bronson, he was full of joy. I'm sure it made him recuperate that much faster. Mrs. Berme quickly became like a grandmother to us and Bronson became a wise and loving grandfather. In his house I began to play the piano as I never had. On summer nights, he would throw open the patio doors so that my music could travel down the hill and "all the people in Cutler's Cove could hear and appreciate it."

I made up my mind that music would be my life and no matter how important the hotel was and how much money the hotel made, it would always take second place. Bronson took over the trusteeship of the hotel. He was always after me to take more interest in the day-to-day management. I tried to be interested, tried for the sake of Mommy and Daddy, but in my secret heart, I hoped it would be Jefferson who developed a love for it and someday would be the real owner of the new Cutler's Cove Hotel.

My dreams led me elsewhere . . . to the school for performing arts, to European tours, to the great concert halls. And of course, there was Gavin.

We spent as much time together as we could and whenever we did, our conversations always wove their way back to our days at The Meadows. One summer we even went back to visit Charlotte and Luther and Homer. We took Jefferson with us and when Homer set eyes on him and he saw Homer, it was as if they had never parted, never missed a beat. Homer took him off to show him where a fox had given birth.

"What ever happened to that Fern?" Luther asked me when we all sat down to dinner.

"She eloped with someone after I put an end to her allowance. But it wasn't the man she was with here," I said. After a pause I added, "I don't miss her."

"Neither do we," Charlotte said and we all had a good laugh. We had a wonderful time. I played the piano for them and when we left, we promised to return as many times as we could.

In the summer of my nineteenth year, I was enrolled in a three-week program that would take me to Paris and then to Vienna. It was a concert tour and I was looking forward to it very much. Gavin came to see me off and we took a walk on the beach.

"I'm going to miss you, Christie," he told me.

"Every time I leave you or you leave me, something in me dies, and every time I see you again, something new in me is reborn."

"It's the same for me, Gavin," I told him.

"I'm jealous of your music," he confessed. "It possesses you the way I wish I could."

"Don't be jealous," I said, smiling. "It does fill me with great joy, but I will share it only with you."

"Promise?"

"For ever and ever," I said, but I stopped walking and stopped smiling.

"What is it, Christie?" Gavin asked. He followed my gaze. There was a fish lying still in the water. My heart felt so heavy and sad, but suddenly . . . its tail fluttered and then it fluttered once more and the fish turned over as if it had been faking death. It dove into the next wave and disappeared.

And as clearly as the day she had stood beside me on the beach, I heard Mommy ask:

"Can you believe in the fish, Christie? Can you believe in the magic?"

I could believe; I could believe for ever and ever. Thank you, Mommy, I thought. Thank you for your gift of faith.

"Are you all right?" Gavin asked with concern.

"Oh yes, Gavin. Oh yes."

Off in the distance, a seagull floated toward the setting sun. I drew closer to Gavin and the two of us walked on ahead of the shadows toward our own special, bright new day.